JUDITH PELLA
TRACIE PETERSON

RIBBONS WEST

SEPARATE ROADS

BETHANY HOUSE PUBLISHERS
MINNEAPOLIS, MINNESOTA 55438

Books by Tracie Peterson

Controlling Interests
Entangled
Framed

WESTWARD CHRONICLES

A Shelter of Hope
Hidden in a Whisper

RIBBONS OF STEEL*

Distant Dreams
A Hope Beyond
A Promise for Tomorrow

RIBBONS WEST*

Westward the Dream
Separate Roads

*with Judith Pella

Books by Judith Pella

Beloved Stranger
Blind Faith
Texas Angel

LONE STAR LEGACY

Frontier Lady   Stoner's Crossing
Warrior's Song

RIBBONS OF STEEL†

Distant Dreams   A Hope Beyond
A Promise for Tomorrow

RIBBONS WEST†

Westward the Dream   Separate Roads

THE RUSSIANS

The Crown and the Crucible*   Heirs of the Motherland
A House Divided*   Dawning of Deliverance
Travail and Triumph*   White Nights, Red Morning
Passage Into Light

THE STONEWYCKE TRILOGY*

The Heather Hills of Stonewycke   Flight From Stonewycke
Lady of Stonewycke

THE JOURNALS OF CORRIE BELLE HOLLISTER

My Father's World*   Daughter of Grace*

*with Michael Phillips   †with Tracie Peterson

Published by Bethany House Publishers
A Ministry of Bethany Fellowship International
11400 Hampshire Avenue South
Minneapolis, Minnesota 55438
www.bethanyhouse.com

Printed in the United States of America by
Bethany Press International, Minneapolis, Minnesota 55438

Library of Congress Cataloging-in-Publication Data

Pella, Judith.
　　Separate roads / by Judith Pella, Tracie Peterson.
　　　　p. cm. — (Ribbons west ; 2)
　　　ISBN 0–7642–2072–1
　　　I. Peterson, Tracie.　II. Title.
　　III. Series: Pella, Judith. Ribbons west ; 2.
　PS3566.E415 S46 1999
　813'.54 — dc21　　　　　　　　　　　　　　　　　99–6609
　　　　　　　　　　　　　　　　　　　　　　　　　　　CIP

To Rich and Dianne

with love and thanks
for all you've done.

Tracie

JUDITH PELLA is the author of several historical fiction series, both on her own and in collaboration with Michael Phillips and Tracie Peterson. The extraordinary seven-book series, THE RUSSIANS, the first three written with Phillips, showcase her creativity and skill as a historian as well as a fiction writer. A Bachelor of Arts degree in social studies, along with a career in nursing and teaching, lend depth to her storytelling abilities, providing readers with memorable novels in a variety of genres. She and her family make their home in northern California.

Visit Judith's Web site at: http://members.aol.com/Pellabooks

TRACIE PETERSON is a full-time writer who has authored over thirty-five books, both historical and contemporary fiction, including *Entangled* and *Framed*, contemporary love stories in the POR-TRAITS series. She spent three years as a columnist for the *Kansas Christian* newspaper and is also a speaker/teacher for writers' conferences. She and her family make their home in Kansas.

Visit Tracie's Web site at: http://members.aol.com/tjpbooks

Contents

PART I

March—May
1864

One

Jordana Baldwin stared at the clock on the wall for the tenth time in as many minutes. Why did Brenton have to choose today of all days to be busy? Normally he would have picked her up from her job at the Omaha Citizen's Bank by four-thirty, but today he had business to attend to and had solicited her employer's help in seeing her home. Unfortunately, her employer was in a meeting himself and was running unusually late.

She tried not to be too upset with her older brother. After all, ever since their arrival in Omaha, Brenton had felt rather displaced. His love of photography and desire to make a career of it was only just now receiving some satisfactory attention—even if his hopes of photographing the Union Pacific Railroad's development had hit a snag. The UP, as folks usually called the eastern extension of the infant transcontinental railroad, was sitting rather idle at the moment.

She sighed and finished checking the final count on her ledger. She had long since completed her regular duties, and while waiting for Mr. Chittenden to conclude his business, she had decided to work ahead on one of her less important projects. But even that was done.

Now what was she going to do to occupy her time? She supposed she could sweep the floor of the lobby. Chittenden had a regular man who came in to polish the wood and clean up the place, but sweeping would at least give her something to do. Stretching, she glanced outside and noticed how quickly the light was fading. Why was the meeting taking so long? Impatient, she began putting her things away and tried not to be frustrated with Mr. Chittenden.

Hezekiah Chittenden was a fair-minded employer, who had taken an uneasy risk in hiring her on as the bank's only female employee. He had been instantly impressed with her uncanny ability to work ledgers and numbers, but was equally unimpressed with the fact that she was a woman. Jordana had managed to convince him to give her a try, and now, after nearly four months of employment, even Mr. Chittenden had to admit to his good fortune in hiring her on.

"Miss Baldwin, I was a-hopin' you'd still be here."

Jordana looked up to see one of the five Wilson brothers standing at her teller's window. His appearance startled her. She'd been so lost in thought that she'd not even heard the front door open.

"The bank's already closed, Mr. Wilson," she stated rather curtly. The Wilsons, along with half the male population of Omaha, made it to her window on a regular basis. They came so often—"Drawn in by her feminine charms and quick wit," Mr. Chittenden had declared—that the banker had posted a sign stating that only customers were welcome inside the hallowed doors of his establishment. New accounts had tripled that day alone, and Jordana couldn't count the number of men, mostly older, who came by simply to "check" on their money.

"I knew the bank would be closed," the man admitted, taking off his dirty felt hat. "But I saw you through the window, and seein's how you're still here and the door's unlocked, I kind of figured on doin' my bankin' business."

She could smell the whiskey on his breath. He wasn't really drunk, just comfortably at ease with himself. "Come back tomorrow," she told him firmly. "The money is already counted for the night."

He looked at her for a moment, disappointment clearly registering on his face. Then just as quickly he perked up. "Say, you wouldn't be wantin' to go with me to the dance next Saturday?" He smiled in a goofy sort of lopsided way, then puffed out his chest and tried to look confident.

"No, thank you, sir," Jordana replied. "I . . . uh . . . shall be otherwise engaged." She hated having to deal with the seemingly endless number of would-be suitors. Apparently just having her in a public position gave every eligible bachelor in the neighborhood license to try his luck with her. She looked at the clock again. Five-fifteen. Mr. Chittenden must truly have an advantageous prospect on the table or he'd have never let banking hours extend past four-thirty.

"I must ask you to leave, Mr. Wilson. I need to lock up and finish putting things in order." She moved out from behind the teller's window, something Mr. Chittenden had told her never to do with customers in the building. "If you come back in the morning, we can take care of your transaction."

"But . . ."

She took him by the arm and pulled him toward the door. "Good day, Mr. Wilson. Thank you for stopping by." She opened the front door and stood waiting.

The dust-laden man was instantly deflated. He scratched his head for a moment, then replaced the felt hat and tipped it at her as he passed by. "Guess I'll see you in the mornin'."

She sighed as he left and quickly locked up. Pulling down the shade, Jordana's gaze fell on the calendar beside the door. March seventh. It was her birthday. Her eighteenth birthday to be exact, and no one had even remembered.

"I have no one to blame but myself," she chided and went quickly to work sweeping the lobby floor. She hadn't reminded any-one that it was her birthday, although Brenton knew full well what day it was. At least she thought he remembered. Surely her own brother would remember. Still, she could hardly expect him to miss an important business meeting just because it was her birthday.

She unlocked the front door only long enough to sweep the dirt into the street, then closed the door once again. She had just put the broom away when Damon Chittenden, Hezekiah's youngest son, bounded into the lobby from his office down the hall.

"I thought you were gone for the day," Jordana stated, feeling just a bit uneasy. Damon had pursued her with more ardent interest than any of the others, and this coupled with the fact that they worked so closely together kept Jordana from finding a way to put distance between them.

At twenty-one, Damon seemed to consider himself the most sought-after man in the Nebraska Territory. Whether by women for love or by men bent on business, he made no distinction and found either to be to his benefit. His blue eyes took in every detail, watch-ing his companions as if they were adversaries in a battle.

He smiled broadly, the wide stretch of his mouth seeming to balance his slightly oversized nose. "I was, but unfortunately—or because you're here, I should say *fortunately*—I promised my father I would attend to some business in Council Bluffs. I forgot the ledger I was to take, however, and had to make my stop here before catching the ferry. I slipped in the back door."

Jordana nodded and turned to go back to her desk. Damon reached out and took hold of her, mindless that his act was a breach of propriety. He was always touching her, and Jordana had tried more than once to put a stop to his familiarity. Now, as at most times, she halted in her tracks and stared at his unwelcomed hand until he released her.

"I wish you'd come to dinner with me. I don't bite, you know. You tell me I mustn't touch you, as we are not well acquainted, yet you won't allow me to get to know you." His expression softened as he continued. "You are such a handsome woman, Miss Baldwin. I only seek to pay you the proper respect and attention you deserve."

Jordana found her aggravation slipping away. It wasn't that she was overly flattered by his pretty words, but he was always kind to her and very gentlemanly for the most part. Still, his constant attention was becoming quite annoying. He thought nothing of bringing her sweets or flowers. He wrote her line after line of sugary poetry, with nearly every poem ending in "and this is the woman I adore." He even suggested that he would gladly pay Brenton to provide him with a photograph of Jordana so that he might have her lovely face gracing his room at home.

Brenton had thought it all rather funny, but Jordana saw it as an annoyance and irritation. She wasn't interested in courtship and marriage. She wanted to explore her freedom by seeing a good portion of the country. She'd even taken to reading books on explorers, poring for hours over the accounts of Lewis and Clark, not to mention others.

"Oh, look at the time!" Damon declared and shook his head. "I'm going to be late."

She watched, relieved, as he hurried past her desk to the black iron safe where all the records were kept. He quickly searched the safe, found what he was looking for, then started to close it again.

"I can take care of that," she told him, going to her desk. "I have to put these away. Please be sure to lock the back door, however."

He nodded. "I will, and I'll speak to you again about dinner."

She said nothing in reply and waited until he'd hurried back down the hall and out the alleyway door before letting out a heavy sigh. She likened him to a case of bedbugs in a store-bought mattress. Either you used the mattress and endured the bedbugs, or you lost out on what comfort could be had. Damon Chittenden was a necessary irritation if she was to maintain her comfortable job at the bank.

She looked at the clock and shook her head. "Five-thirty and it's getting dark. I'd say waiting an extra hour to get home is plenty of time." Having reached the end of her patience, she jotted a quick note to Mr. Chittenden, put the day's records in the safe and locked it, then took up her coat from the broom closet. "I can surely walk a few blocks by myself and not compromise my reputation."

She stepped outside the bank and relocked the front door. The sun had long since set in the west, and now the skies were a darkening lavender blue. Enough light remained to see her home, but with Omaha quickly outgrowing its small-town charm, Jordana knew her impatience could quickly become a liability.

Brenton had warned her, and their sister-in-law Caitlan, that walking about the streets of Omaha unescorted was asking for trouble. With the announcement that the Union Pacific intended to build a railroad west from this town to cross the entire continent came the riffraff and confidence men that every boomtown endured. Not only that, but the population had practically doubled overnight.

"He worries too much," she muttered under her breath, heading down the alley behind the bank, which was a convenient shortcut home. Then as if to prove her wrong, she heard the unmistakable sound of someone else walking directly behind her. Wheeling about, she found Zed Wilson, the man she'd turned out from the bank earlier.

"A lady oughten to walk alone in this town," the man said, coming to take hold of Jordana's arm. "I'll see you home."

"I assure you," she said, jerking away, "that I'm perfectly capable of taking myself home." She hurried on down the alley but found the man to be most intent on his decision.

"You don't need to go gettin' so uppity with me," he said. He grabbed for her arm and this time clamped his fingers tight to maintain his hold. "I'm good enough for the likes of you."

"I never said you weren't," Jordana replied, feeling her breath come in rapid, panting gasps. "Please . . . let me go." She tried to

15

pull away. "My house isn't that far."

"I know where you live," Wilson replied, stepping closer. "I've watched you walkin' home with your brother."

"Then you know he'll be expecting me now," Jordana replied, putting her hands on the man's barrel-like chest to push him away. "I must be going."

"How about a kiss first?" he questioned, licking his lips. "Ain't nothin' wrong with a little kiss between friends, now, is there?"

Jordana began to grow truly afraid. She glanced quickly to the end of the alleyway, wondering how fast she could run—if she could loosen Zed Wilson's hold. "I have no interest in kissing you," she said rather coolly. "Now, if you don't mind—"

"But I do mind. I have this here bet with my brothers. I told them I could get you to kiss me afore you kissed any of them. Now, don't be makin' me out to be a liar." He pressed her back until her foot made contact with a small stack of firewood that edged up against the rear wall of the building.

"Help!" Jordana screamed, seeing some movement in the street at the end of the alleyway. She could only pray that it wasn't another Wilson brother. At the same time she screamed, she kicked Zed hard in the shin, angry that her long skirts kept her from delivering a very heavy blow.

"Ow! Why, you little wildcat. I ought to—"

"Release the lady," a voice sounded.

Jordana breathed a sigh of relief to see the shadowy form of a man running down the alley toward them. She took the opportunity to push hard against Zed's chest. He found her action surprising, but no more so than the sudden appearance of the man who'd interrupted his pleasure.

Jordana turned away quickly as Zed drew up his fist to attack her rescuer. She knew she should run, but her anger got the best of her. How dare Zed Wilson force himself on her—and on her birthday! She bent down to grab a long, thin piece of firewood. She'd give him something to remember her by. Maybe next time he wouldn't be so intent on attacking young women.

It was extremely difficult to see in the growing darkness. She tried to gauge the situation by noting the size of the men, but as they fought and dove at each other, it was increasingly difficult to keep track of who was who. Finally her opportunity came, and Jordana brought the wood down hard against the back of her assailant. Only it wasn't her assailant.

Zed Wilson looked up at her as the other man moaned out in pain and grabbed his lower back. Sinking to his knees, the man continued to moan. Either Zed feared that he was next, or he realized this was his only chance to escape. Whatever the reason, he took off running like someone had lit a fire under his feet.

Jordana tossed the wood aside and began to apologize. "I'm so sorry," she said, taking hold of the man's arm. "Let's get you some help."

"I'm fine," he said, allowing her to pull him to his feet. He kept one hand at his back while she assisted him down the alley to the street.

"I only meant to help," Jordana continued nervously. "I hope I didn't hurt you. Well, I mean, I know I hurt you, but I hope—" She stopped in midsentence as the man lifted his head. "You!" she gasped.

"Miss Baldwin."

She stared up into the face of Captain Richard O'Brian, the same man who had rescued her from bushwhackers in Missouri. She noted the uniform for the first time and realized there was no doubt that this was the same man.

"Captain O'Brian," she murmured. "I had no idea."

"Neither did I, or I might have given it a second thought before rushing to your rescue." He rubbed his back and tried to straighten to his full height. "At least you aren't wielding a knife this time."

She felt her cheeks grow hot at the memory of his rescue in Missouri. He had thrown her to the ground just after the bushwhacker's bullet grazed her arm. She had held tight to the knife she'd taken from her captor and, thinking O'Brian to be yet another of the renegades, had tried to stab at him. Of course her eyes had been closed, luckily for O'Brian, but because of this she had missed seeing that he was a Union soldier—her rescuer.

"I really am sorry," she said, clearing her throat uncomfortably.

"What in the world were you doing in that alley by yourself, and at this hour?" he asked gruffly.

She watched him continue to rub his back and felt a mixture of guilt and anger. Who was he to question her actions? Still, he had helped her in her hour of need. Perhaps she should just overlook his attitude.

"I was walking home," she said, striving hard to keep the emotion from her voice. "I'm sorry, but I thought you were . . ." She saw his smug expression and slightly raised brow and knew then she couldn't talk civilly to the man. "Oh, never mind." She took off down the street, not at all surprised that he quickly matched her pace.

"I believe battling border ruffians is a much simpler task than keeping the company of highbred young ladies," he told her as he gently touched her elbow with his hand.

"I didn't ask for your help," she said.

"Oh, but you did," he reminded her. "You specifically yelled, 'Help!' "

"But I wasn't yelling for *your* help," she countered and stepped out into the middle of the street just as a freight wagon rounded the corner and bore down on her.

O'Brian easily pulled her back to safety. "The East may have its Civil War," he told her quite seriously, "but here in the West we have Jordana Baldwin. And that, to my way of thinking, is twice the work."

Two

*J*ordana stared at O'Brian for a moment. She remembered the handsome face and blue eyes. He seemed genuinely amused with the situation and not at all as angry as his gruff voice might suggest. She jerked away from his hold and squared her shoulders.

"I wouldn't want you to overwork yourself, Captain O'Brian," she said snidely. "Therefore, I am prepared to complete my journey home without your help. My situation came about because of my desire to shorten the distance home. I shouldn't have gone by way of the alley, but what's done is done. Now that the danger is past, there should be no further need for your services."

He smiled. "Pretty speech, but I'm coming with you just the same."

"You are a stubborn man, Captain."

"Yes, ma'am. Most stubborn," he said, not in the leastwise worried that she'd just insulted him.

Jordana considered the situation for a moment. She could either wait for him to give up and go away, an unlikely scenario, or she could just allow him to walk her home. The latter seemed the simpler solution.

"If I allow you to walk me home," she said, eyeing him carefully, "would you promise me something?"

"Depends on what that something is."

"I don't want my brother to know about this little mishap. He would only worry and then blame himself. He has enough on his mind, and it wouldn't be fair."

"Shouldn't you have considered that before taking the alley?"

She clenched her jaw to keep from saying the first thing that came to mind, which was that Captain O'Brian had no right to interfere in her life and that he should leave her alone and mind his own business. However, her mother had always said you could catch more flies with molasses than vinegar.

"I should have," she finally managed to say after calming down. "But I wasn't thinking clearly. It's my birthday, and I think I'm entitled to be a bit in the clouds, if you will." She didn't really feel that way but figured he might be the sentimental kind who would make allowances for her feminine charms.

"Your birthday, eh? What are you now, fifteen—sixteen?"

Jordana gasped. "I'm eighteen, not that it's any of your business! I mean, how ungallant to ask a lady her age."

"How unladylike to require a gentleman to come to your rescue in a darkened alleyway. You know the type of women who usually frequent those locations."

Jordana stamped her foot. "Oh, you infuriate me! All I ask is for you to spare my brother's feelings, but you'd think I'd just asked you to single-handedly put an end to the war."

"That would probably be easier."

She shook her head and sighed. "Will you please not say anything to my brother?"

"Will you promise to never again be so foolish?"

"Deal."

"Done," he said, taking hold of her elbow. "Now, if you would be so kind as to offer up the directions to your home."

Jordana instructed him, then fell silent. She had never known a more irritating man in her life. And this was only their second meeting. What would it be like if she had to see him on a daily basis?

O'Brian whistled a tune as though he hadn't a care in the world— although Jordana guiltily watched him reach behind to rub his back from time to time. She wished most fervently that she hadn't clobbered him with the firewood, but what was done was done.

O'Brian stopped whistling for a moment as they crossed the street and headed up the opposite side. "I see your hair is growing back," he commented out of the silence.

"Yes, I suppose so." Jordana reached up and touched the curls that now fell just below her shoulders. She had been forced to cut her hair in order to escape from the bushwhacker who had been holding it to keep her captive.

She hated pinning her hair up, hated even more allowing Caitlan to fuss over it for lengthy moments in the morning prior to their leaving for work. Caitlan had enough to do working as a house-keeper for the Cavendish family. She didn't need to start her day off by dressing Jordana's hair.

She waited for O'Brian to make some other comment about it looking silly or being completely out of keeping with the styles of the day, but instead he began to whistle again.

She couldn't imagine what Brenton would say when she showed up at the door with Captain O'Brian, and given the lateness of the hour, she supposed she should do the only polite thing and invite him to stay for dinner.

"Captain O'Brian," she said as her little whitewashed house came into view, "I do appreciate your taking time away from your busy schedule to walk me home."

"My schedule isn't all that busy at this point, so it's not a problem."

She swallowed hard as she looked over at him. From the crossed sabers on his black felt hat to the gold trim on his uniform jacket, Captain O'Brian made a striking figure in his Union blue. She instantly thought of her old friend G. W. Vanderbilt. G.W. had cut a dashing presence in his uniform as well. She wondered where G.W. was now and how he was faring. Only last winter they had received news of his family taking him to Europe to recover his health. She tried not to think too often of G.W., but walking here with Captain O'Brian made that rather difficult. G.W. and O'Brian probably had much in common. Both were strong, prideful men, she decided. Both were stubborn, and both liked to boss her around.

But the similarities probably went no further than that. G.W. was born the youngest son of Commodore Vanderbilt, one of the richest men in America, and G.W. had asked her to be his wife. Remembering those painful moments when she had refused him caused Jordana much discomfort. G.W. had refused to speak to her since, and even though his illness was thought to very possibly be terminal, she had no way of knowing if he had forgiven her for breaking his heart.

Men! she thought and sighed heavily. What did they know of women and life? They were so busy being caught up in playing soldier and fighting wars that they seldom took time to understand their feminine counterparts. Why, Captain O'Brian probably knew more about horses than he did about women. This made her smile.

"I don't think you've heard a word I said," O'Brian commented, halting at Jordana's gate.

She shook her head. "No, I don't suppose I have. I've been deep in thought."

"Plotting against me?" His blue eyes glinted wryly.

She looked up and saw the teasing in his eyes. "Yes," she replied, nodding enthusiastically. "That's the way I intend to spend the rest of my days."

"Somehow," he said, rubbing his back, "I wouldn't put that past you."

She smiled. "Well, I'd like to start tormenting you by asking you to stay for dinner. Caitlan is quite the cook, and she will have prepared something hearty and delicious for our meal."

"Harsh treatment indeed," O'Brian replied with a hint of a grin. "But I believe I am up to the challenge. I would be delighted to share company with your brother again. We had no chance to truly acquaint ourselves at our last meeting."

And indeed they had not, for Jordana remembered almost nothing about it, other than O'Brian rescuing her and taking her back to their camp, where Brenton waited nervously for some word on how the women had fared after being stolen away by Missouri border ruffians. O'Brian had done little more than dump her off his horse, introduce himself, and tip his hat before riding off to take the renegades to the nearest fort.

The memory caused Jordana to reach her hand up to the place where the bullet had grazed her arm. O'Brian noted this and gave her the briefest nod.

"I see you recovered from your injuries."

"Yes, but a horrid infection set in," she replied matter-of-factly. "It probably had something to do with that hideous concoction you poured on the wound when you dressed it."

He laughed out loud at this, surprising Jordana. For although he had given her slight smiles while on their walk to her house, Jordana saw him as a stoic, businesslike man. Now he laughed at her comment as though they were the best of old friends.

"Well, you'd better come and let me reacquaint you with the family," Jordana said, reaching to open the little white picket gate. "I'm sure my brother will be happy for the company after living so long without regular male companionship."

"Then by all means, lead the way."

Jordana nodded and walked up the path without any assistance from Captain O'Brian. She was surprised to find the house so quiet. Usually she could hear Caitlan singing even as she stepped onto the tiny porch.

Opening the door, Jordana nearly jumped off the porch, and might have had Captain O'Brian not been directly behind her.

"Happy birthday!" came the shouts of at least a dozen people.

"Surprise!" said Brenton, coming forward to welcome her.

Jordana looked at them in stunned silence for several moments. "A party?" she murmured, catching sight of a cake on the table.

"You did say it was your birthday," O'Brian whispered in her ear.

She startled even more at his warm breath against her neck and quickly moved into her brother's embrace. "I can't believe you planned a party for me."

"Well, it was Caitlan's idea. She wanted to do something special for you, and I thought, 'Why not?' So here we are."

Caitlan squeezed past a couple of the neighbors to give Jordana a hug. "Happy birthday."

"Oh, thank you so much," Jordana replied, hugging Caitlan tightly. "You are so good to me."

"No, 'tis good ya are to meself," Caitlan replied, her Irish brogue thick with her emotion. She stepped back and her green eyes caught sight of the cavalryman behind Jordana. "And ya've brought the good captain who saved our lives."

"Yes," Jordana said, noting Brenton's immediate interest. "Captain O'Brian and I chanced to meet." She looked quickly back at the man as if daring him to say otherwise.

Instead, Captain O'Brian merely nodded, took the hat from his head, and gave a short bow. "Miss Baldwin was good enough to invite me to supper."

"But of course," Brenton replied before anyone else could speak. "You must come in and stay for the party. Caitlan has fixed a fine supper, and there's to be much revelry. We can talk of the news and of how you came to be in Omaha."

Jordana frowned. She hadn't really given his appearance in Omaha much consideration. But now that she did, it was rather strange that he should be here instead of securely stationed at his Kansas fort.

"I was given a special assignment," he told them, eyeing the group quickly. "I'm here with a small company to lend support and security to the Union Pacific surveying team."

"Wonderful!" Brenton declared. "Then I know we must talk."

O'Brian rubbed his back and grimaced as he sat in the parlor, but nevertheless he nodded amicably to Brenton's suggestion.

"Are you injured, Captain?" Brenton asked, not missing the cavalryman's action.

O'Brian looked at Jordana and smiled ever so slightly.

"It's just something that pains me from time to time," he replied.

Jordana arched her dark brow and smiled sweetly. "Well, hopefully, it will never trouble you again, Captain O'Brian. In the meantime, why don't you wish me a happy day and come share in the fun." It was more a statement than a question.

"I believe I would like that very much, Miss Baldwin, and may I indeed wish you the happiest of days."

"Thank you, Captain," Jordana said, turning to see Brenton eyeing her suspiciously. "Now, brother dear, why don't we get on with the party? I seem to have worked up quite an appetite."

After a few minutes of visiting in the front room, Caitlan went to call the guests to supper. Jordana started to follow after her, but O'Brian had leaned down to whisper in her ear once again. "Alley fights do make a person hungry, don't they?"

She elbowed him hard, hearing his breath leave him in a whooshing sound. Stepping forward, she said to Brenton, "I believe Captain O'Brian is feeling a bit taxed. Perhaps you should seat him right away."

"Certainly," Brenton replied. "O'Brian, I will put you across from me, and that way you might give me information on all that has been happening in the war. I've tried to keep up, but it's sometimes difficult. Of course, perhaps you've not had time to keep apprised of it yourself, since you've been recently assigned to help with the railroad."

The next-door neighbor and his wife and two young daughters came forward to introduce themselves at this point. "I'm Matt Zerick, and this is my wife, Ann, and our daughters, Liddy and Belle."

"I'm Captain O'Brian."

"So is it the Injun wars what brung you up to Omaha?" Matt questioned. "I understand there's been nothin' but trouble since the Sioux fightin' in Minnesota."

O'Brian took his place behind the chair offered him, then nodded. "That's part of the problem. The Union Pacific would like to see the line go through without interference from the Indians. However, that doesn't seem likely."

"Everyone, please take up your glasses," Brenton announced, placing Jordana at the head of the table. "Jordana, I would like to make a toast."

She looked up at her brother and found her heart filled with an overwhelming love for him. How could she have doubted that he would remember her birthday?

"We have endured many hardships and adventures together," Brenton said, holding his glass high, "and in all that time, I cannot imagine having better company or companionship." He smiled quickly at Caitlan before returning his gaze to Jordana.

Jordana watched as Caitlan's cheeks flushed red and smiled to herself at the silliness of Brenton and Caitlan's unspoken love for each other.

"You have been all that a man could want in a sister," Brenton continued, "and I thank you for your support and care. But today, I honor you, for you are truly a gem among women. Happy birthday, Jordana."

"Happy birthday!" everyone said, lifting their glasses to her.

Jordana felt her eyes mist. I will not cry, she told herself sternly. I will simply enjoy this wonderful moment and bask in the love given me, but I will not cry. And she might have actually kept to her resolve, but Brenton produced a large gift and placed it before her. A small card on top read, "To our lovely daughter on her eighteenth birthday. Wish we were with you on this day. Love, Mother and Father."

Wiping her eyes with her napkin, Jordana smiled at her collection of well-wishers. "I will open this later. It seems the onions in Caitlan's supper are getting the best of me."

"I'm thinkin' that 'twould be quite reasonable," Caitlan replied, "if I'd been usin' onion in our supper."

Everyone laughed at this, including Jordana. It was the best possible ending for her day, and even the appearance of Captain O'Brian had done nothing to dampen her spirits. She was loved and her life was good. If her mother had been there, she would have said, "God's blessings are on you!" And Jordana knew she would have been right, for never before had she felt so blessed.

Three

O'Brian listened to the conversations around him, surprised that he'd allowed himself to accept the invitation to Jordana Baldwin's birthday party. Never in his wildest imagination had he figured to set eyes again on this spitfire of a young woman, but now that he had, he couldn't help but admit he was enjoying himself.

Jordana Baldwin had a fire about her that he admired. She wasn't like the fretful, mealymouthed creatures that often crossed his path, and neither was she a society belle intent on her looks and possessions. Instead, she seemed quite happy to enjoy the company of these common folk and to celebrate her birthday with nothing more than a supper in her honor and a small cake.

He watched in silence as she opened the gift from her parents and frowned over the two gold pieces and the note to buy herself something pretty to wear and use the rest for fun. Besides this, her folks had included a collection of books. One in particular, entitled *Adventures on the Northern Plains Territories*, looked like something O'Brian himself might have enjoyed reading. Jordana looked at each in great excitement and anticipation, completely taking Rich off guard. She seemed more elated at the prospect of something different to read than the idea of a new wardrobe.

"Jordana is rapidly exhausting the Omaha Library Association's supply of reading materials," Brenton said. "It's always good when Mother and Father send books from home."

"The library is just as happy when I receive books because I usually donate them to the society as soon as I study them through," Jordana added.

27

The party continued with several other small articles offered to Jordana to honor her birthday. Rich felt uncomfortable to be the only one without some such gift, but he knew also that his intrusion had been a last-minute act of graciousness on Jordana's part.

"It's probably a little less noisy by the fireplace," Brenton suggested. "Why don't we go over there, and you can tell me what plans the UP has devised for the future."

Glad for the excuse to draw away from the others, Rich and Brenton walked to the fireplace and sat down on small wooden chairs. "I can't say that I know a great deal about it, Mr. Baldwin. My men and I were singled out for this special assignment after someone wrote to my superior praising our company for our performance in Missouri."

Brenton's face reddened. "I have to admit, I did send a letter. My father also wrote, and he probably offered even more praise. I can't thank you enough for what you did for us. I hope this assignment is one of honor for you."

Rich frowned. How could he admit that he was miserable over the entire matter? The war had caused enough problems for him, sending most of the regular army off to fight the battle back east. Fort Larned in Kansas had become a home to him after a round of tragedies had left him overwhelmed with life, and he liked it there. He longed only to be back at the fort, drilling his cavalry on the open plains, making the land safe for new settlers.

It was bad enough that he'd been transferred to Fort Leavenworth to fight border wars between Kansas and Missouri, but now he found himself playing nursemaid to a bunch of city folk who were trying to map out a route for a railroad. How could he possibly hope that Brenton Baldwin, a man several years his junior and no doubt comfortable in his own existence, would understand that this wasn't the life he envisioned for himself? Or, that while he found it honorable, it was far from desirable?

Brenton seemed not to have noticed Rich's discomfort, for he was moving right along and making comments about things his father had spoken of in his letters from New York. "Father believes the war has to end soon. He sees the problem of too few industries in the South and feels confident that they will yield for lack of goods, if nothing else. I believe they will soon reason this thing out for themselves and realize that this nation should no longer be divided. Causes and standards are all well and fine, but I suppose they should mean very little in light of starving families and dying wounded. The Confederates must sooner or later realize the need to put aside their differences and see this nation healed."

Rich listened to Brenton's idealistic notions before asking, "And how is it that you aren't in the service of your country?"

"I had thought to be," Brenton replied, growing surprisingly sullen. "I labored over the decision because, you see, I have family on both sides of this war."

"Many do," Rich replied.

"I suppose that's true enough, but I grew up in the middle of it all. Our family's ancestral home is just outside of Washington. Our people dabbled in the political fanfare of that city and set up businesses accordingly. Our grandfather owned a plantation and held slaves but desired to free them long before it became an issue of war."

"I see."

Brenton stared into the flames of the fire. "I did go to enlist, but since my parents were abroad, I desired to seek my uncle's counsel on what I was about to do. He had, however, taken up arms with the South, and I never made it to his home. Instead, I was picked up by Confederate troops and would have been hanged for being a spy, but my cousin, a captain like yourself, saved my life."

"I take it he was the commander of the soldiers who would have put you to death?"

"Yes. We discussed the situation, and because he knew me to be answering truthfully, he took my plight seriously. I explained the dilemma. How could I fight on the side of the South, even though most of my family were doing just that, when I agreed with the policies of the Union? He took me to his commanding officer, and after we discussed the matter, I was given a letter to sign. It stated simply that I would be pardoned and released. However, I had to pledge to never bear arms against the South."

"And you signed this letter?"

"I did," Brenton said, looking from the fire to Rich. "I suppose you think that cowardly of me?"

"Not at all," Rich replied. "We all have to do what we think is right. I don't have to live with your conscience, just as you don't have to live with mine."

Brenton nodded. "Well, that's why I am here, instead of there."

"And it's probably to your benefit. The war has taken many a life on both sides. Families have lost sons, husbands, and fathers, and our country has lost a unity that will be many years mending. Things will never be the same."

Brenton nodded. "I suppose not."

"Still, there is the West to settle. That will help some. Folks will come here to put the war behind them. They're already doing that. Some of the Confederates are even signing agreements such as yours and coming west to help fight the Indian Wars rather than go to the overcrowded prisons."

"I heard that southern prisons were certain death. That the conditions are less than humane."

"There isn't enough food to feed southerners, much less northern prisoners. Given the choice between caring for their own and caring for their enemy, I guess we can both figure who they'll see to first."

Brenton's brow furrowed. "I'm sure you're right."

"I wish I weren't," O'Brian said rather harshly. "I also have friends in that war. Family, too. It can't end soon enough for me."

"How is it that you're not there?"

"Someone had to stay behind and train volunteers and raise up support in the forts. The Indians hardly are going to cease to cause problems just because the East is at war."

"I've had nothing but pleasant encounters with the Indians around here. Why, some of the Omaha tribeswomen have been helping with the grading work for the railroad. It seems unchivalrous, but their menfolk stand about watching while their women work. Then come payday, they are there to take the earnings and spend it as they please."

"It's their way," Rich replied. "Men are warriors and hunters, not laborers. Indian men protect their families and hunt. Women do the menial tasks and see to the common work. The Omaha are at peace. There are Indian agents to provide government food and supplies. They have few choices that have not already been made for them, and because of this, they are left rather idle. We aren't always very wise as educated men."

"How so, Captain?"

"What did we expect them to do with their lives once we civilized them?" he asked ironically. He didn't mean to take up a cause for the Indian and, in fact, knew that he would probably fight and kill many an Indian warrior before the wars were behind them and true peace came to the country. But still, he didn't know why the white settlers and government officials were so surprised that the Indians would rise up against the onslaught of people coming into the territory. The coming of the settlers forced changes in the Indian's way of life—a way of life that had existed far longer than the white way of life in this country.

The clock on the mantel chimed eight. Rich looked at his own pocket watch as if to confirm the time, then apologized. "I'm afraid I need to be on my way. It was nice of you to invite me to share in your party."

"I'm sure Jordana was pleased to be able to offer this more formal thanks for what you did for her in Missouri."

Rich nodded as he caught sight of Jordana in an animated conversation with her sister-in-law Caitlan O'Connor. Her cheeks were rosy, and her eyes were sparkling from the merriment of the evening. He touched the place on his back where she had struck him. It didn't hurt much anymore, and in truth, it more amused than encumbered him.

She was some woman. His mother would say she was just the right kind of woman for a man like Rich. Then he frowned and turned to go. No woman was right for him. He wouldn't saddle any woman with the miseries of his past.

"Jordana!" Brenton called as O'Brian crossed the room toward the door.

He saw her look up to catch sight of him taking his leave. She said something to her sister-in-law, then made her way to the door. "Are you leaving us already, Captain?"

"'Fraid so, Miss Baldwin. Duty calls. I do want to thank you for an interesting evening." He knew she'd understand his meaning.

Jordana nodded. "I hope you didn't find it overly stimulating."

She was teasing him. He could hear it in her voice and see it in her eyes. Were he not a confirmed bachelor with so many other issues to deal with, he might well have considered giving her more attention.

"No, it wasn't too stimulating. Perhaps a little out of the ordinary for me, but not to my detriment."

"Good," Jordana said with a smile.

"I do hope yar back gets to feelin' better," Caitlan said as she joined the others at the door.

"I'm sure it will," Rich replied as Brenton opened the door for

31

him. He stepped out into the night air and secured his hat. "Good night, and thank you again."

He heard them close the door as he reached the gate. A part of him wished he could go back inside and spend the evening in companionable conversation, while another part of him was restless from the time away from his men. They had a job to do, and that should be enough to hold his focus.

Jordana's face came to mind, and Rich smiled. "Then again," he muttered out loud, "there's always something to draw you off course."

He remembered her look of surprise when she'd realized who he was and what she had done to him. He remembered too his own surprise to find that the fair lady in distress was none other than the wildcat he'd rescued in Missouri the year before.

Laughing out loud, Rich slapped his leg. "What a woman!"

Four

Jordana yawned as she and Caitlan stepped from the house the next morning. "It was a fine party, Caitlan. I can't thank you enough."

"Oh, go on with ya. 'Twas clear and simple that we needed some fun, and yar birthday was the perfect excuse." Caitlan pulled her brown crocheted shawl around her shoulders and stifled her own yawn. "I'm supposin' we shouldn't have stayed up quite so long."

Jordana nodded. "I wanted only to crawl back into bed this morning. But instead, I have to go to the bank and explain to Mr. Chittenden why I refused to wait for him to escort me last night."

"He won't be givin' ya grief for it, will he?" Caitlan asked as they crossed the street cautiously. The city was only now starting to wake up to a new day, but freight traffic had seemed to double in the last months. And while Brenton deemed the rowdies were sleeping off the night before, giving Jordana and Caitlan safety in walking to work without his escort, there were other circumstances that often put their lives in peril.

"Mr. Chittenden won't say a word. After all, he *was* late. Nonetheless, he'll give me that reproving look, staring down the end of his nose as though a bee had landed there. He'll 'tsk-tsk' the matter, then go about his business," Jordana replied.

"Ya looked to be havin' a good time with that Captain O'Brian," Caitlan said, suddenly changing the subject. "He's a right handsome man. Irish, too."

"Now, Caitlan O'Connor. I thought you were sweet on my brother. How dare you go looking at another?"

"I didn't say I was sizin' the man up for a weddin', just that he

33

was handsome. Ya know ya think the same."

"I said nothing of the sort. Besides, what I happened to notice was that you and Brenton spent most of the evening looking at each other all moon-eyed. When are you two going to stop being so silly and talk to each other sensibly about your feelings?"

Caitlan's teasing tone instantly faded. "There'd be no sense to talkin'. Nothin' can come of my havin' feelin's for yar brother."

"And why not? I happen to be quite confident that he shares those same feelings."

"We're too different. I don't feel about God the way he does, and by yar own admission he'd not go takin' a wife for hisself that didn't share his faith in the Almighty."

"But, Caitlan, I know you believe in God. I know you were brought up to have a strong faith. You can't just throw that away because the Irish have had a hard time of it."

Caitlan looked at her friend indignantly. "It'd be for more than that. My people have had a bad time of it, 'tis true. But religion has played a big part in that sorry part of the world. The Protestants hate the Catholics, the Catholics hate the Protestants. The landowners hate the workers, and the workers spend so much time drinkin' that they hate everyone."

"Not all of Ireland spends its time in hate, does it?" Jordana asked. "You simply found yourself in the midst of more problems than most."

"And what would yarself be knowin' about Ireland? Ya never lived there," Caitlan said in an accusing tone. "Ya've only known a good life, Jordana. Yar folks are good, upstandin' people, and they've always had plenty. Ya don't know what it's like to do without. Not truly. Oh, we've done without some here in Omaha, but even this would be a king's share compared to what my family has known."

"And that's justification for hating God?"

"Now, don't go puttin' words in me mouth or feelin's in me heart. I just know that my thoughts on the matter are far from yar brother's, and we both know that he'd not want a woman for a wife who refused to go to church."

Jordana stopped and looked at her sister-in-law. Since Caitlan had first arrived in America, determined to make her way to California where her brother Kiernan had moved with his wife, Victoria, Jordana had felt a special kinship with her. It was more than the fact that Caitlan's brother was married to Jordana's oldest sibling; it was a true meeting of hearts.

"One of these days, God will make himself real to you."

"Oh, He's real enough now," Caitlan replied. "He just doesn't seem to be carin' about the needs of the folks down here."

"But of course He cares."

"If He cares so much," Caitlan replied, a strand of cinnamon hair catching the breeze, "then why do so many Irish go hungry? Why do they go a-killin' and hatin' until no one is left untouched? You tell me why God hisself allows such doin's."

Jordana shrugged. She couldn't very well tell Caitlan what God's reasonings were for allowing heartache and misunderstanding to abound. "I guess He allows it because we do. I mean, the war back East is pitting brother against brother and tearing a nation apart. I don't suppose I understand why God allows it either, but then I go to wondering why we have allowed it. I have absolutely no say whatsoever in that outcome, but I won't go distrusting God just because it happens to be ripping my country in two. We make our own choices. God doesn't force them upon us."

Caitlan's expression softened. She reached out and touched Jordana in an almost motherly fashion. "I admire yar faith. I do. I just don't happen to have it in me to believe the same. And we both know I can't very well go acceptin' it just for the sake of yar brother's love."

Jordana knew she spoke the truth, but it bothered her deeply that Caitlan wouldn't simply listen to reason and invite Jesus into her heart. It seemed so simple. Just a little matter of acceptance. Why should that be so hard? She could simply let go of her anger and let God guide her life. Why was that so difficult to understand?

They moved up the street, and Caitlan waved to a portly, darkheaded woman who was carrying a basket of laundry on her head. "I see Sadie is near done with her deliveries."

Jordana nodded. "Either she's early or we're late. I'm guessing we're running a bit behind the clock."

Caitlan agreed. "I'm not supposin' Mrs. Cavendish will be likin' it one bit. I'll be leavin' ya here and headin' on up." She paused at the street corner where they usually parted company. "Don't take my attitude to heart, Jordana. It has nothin' to do with yarself."

Jordana nodded and watched as Caitlan hurried up the street. Her goal was the big brick mansion at the end of the next street. It was here that she'd recently taken the position of housekeeper to the Cavendish family. Mr. Cavendish would drive Caitlan home every day at the conclusion of afternoon tea, unless, of course, they were giving a party or having some other event that required Caitlan to stay on. Mrs. Cavendish had a personal maid who attended to all of her needs and lived on the premises, so Caitlan was free to return home in the evenings and tend to Brenton and Jordana—although Jordana strived to do more of the tending on her own account. She hated that Caitlan always saw herself as a servant to the family. She hated, too, that Caitlan allowed this anger toward God to ruin her life.

Crossing the street, Jordana marched into the Omaha Citizen's Bank as though she might well find an answer to her dilemma inside. She was determined to find a way to get through to Caitlan. It was just a matter of time.

"Good morning!" Damon said as Jordana swept past him.

"Good morning," she replied, unfastening the buttons of her coat. The weather was still quite chilly these mornings, and while Jordana had hated the harshness of the Omaha winter, she was told that the spring storms could be even more fierce. She supposed it was all something to be endured and taken in stride. Much like Damon Chittenden.

"You look quite beautiful today," he said, coming up behind her.

Jordana continued to the broom closet. "Thank you, Mr. Chittenden."

"I thought you were going to call me Damon."

"That would hardly be proper, *Mr. Chittenden*," she said, reemphasizing his name.

"I thought you might like to see some information on the sale of land in the Omaha area. It's quite fascinating," Damon said, holding out a sheaf of papers.

Jordana glanced over her shoulder for a moment, then ignored the man. Instead, she put her coat in the broom closet, prayed for patience, and straightened her dark blue serge jacket. She wore the same basic outfit to the bank every day—blue serge jacket and skirt and white blouse with dark blue ribbon at the throat. She thought it allowed her to look businesslike without compromising her femininity. Not that she worried overmuch about such things, but Brenton would be mortified if he thought she'd conducted herself in less than a ladylike manner. It was already scandalous enough that she was holding a man's job.

Turning, she found that Damon continued to stare at her with a sickening look of devotion, the papers still extended toward her like some sort of peace offering.

Eyeing Damon with a sense of caution, Jordana replied, "Land sales aren't usually all that interesting."

"They are when the land is being developed for a university."

"A university? Here?"

Damon grinned triumphantly at her sudden interest and waved the papers. "It's all in here."

She knew he was appealing to her love of intellectual discussions. Frankly, it was the one thing she enjoyed about the younger Chittenden. From time to time, Damon had talked to her about plans he'd been in on for city development or social reform. She had listened to him speak about territorial affairs and the financial benefits of the railroad. And always she learned new tidbits about the city and in turn was able to take them home to Brenton.

"Who's behind this plan?" She moved to her desk in the teller's area.

"Oh, several important men are behind it." Damon followed her. "We could discuss it over dinner tonight."

"Dinner?"

"Yes," he said with a grin. "Remember? I told you I would ask again. I shall keep on asking, over and over, minute by minute, until you agree."

She rolled her eyes and shook her head. "Why would you torment yourself in such a manner?"

"I suppose because I'm used to getting what I want, and you refuse to give in. You have become a challenge to me, Miss Baldwin."

"A challenge," she repeated, considering his declaration. She really did want to know more about the university, and maybe it wasn't so bad to let Damon escort her to dinner. After all, he was highly respected, even at twenty-one. There was nothing wrong with being friends. But would he see her acceptance as a gesture of friendship or a promise of things to come? It was such a dilemma. Why did men have to be so strange?

"If I agree to go with you to dinner," she began slowly, "would you please promise to stop with the poems and gifts? I simply cannot go on in such a manner. I don't mind the friendship you've extended, but I have no desire to be so lavished upon. The gifts must stop."

"No gifts?" Damon questioned in disbelief. "But I thought young women loved to be courted with gifts."

"But we are not courting, Mr. Chittenden, and even if we were, this constant deluge of presents and mementos would hardly be acceptable. My brother would surely have spoken to you by now if I had told him what was happening."

"But I'm sure he would allow me to court you if I sought him out on the matter."

"Nevertheless, I do not wish you to court me. I will, however, consider accompanying you to a dinner *between friends*. I do desire to know more about this planned university, but I will not accompany you unless you agree to stop bringing me gifts."

"Very well," Damon sighed, nodding somberly. He looked as if he had just been stabbed through the heart. "I shall give you my word on it. I shall cease bringing you gifts."

Jordana smiled. "Then you may come around to my house this evening, shall we say, seven o'clock?"

Damon grinned. "I shall be there with the biggest bouquet of—"

"Ah, remember your promise?" she interrupted.

His countenance was crestfallen for only a moment. "Very well. No bouquet."

"Thank you, Mr. Chittenden. Now, might I suggest you allow me to get to work. Your father will be unlocking the doors to business within a matter of moments."

Damon snapped his heels together and gave her a deep bow. "Until this evening, then."

Jordana nodded, hoping he would be true to his word. She glanced at her teller's window, where a dark red rosebud had been left for her. Damon's gaze seemed to follow hers.

"I left that before our agreement, so it doesn't count," he said quickly before she could protest.

With a sigh she nodded. "I suppose not. Thank you."

He grinned again. "My pleasure."

Five

$\mathcal{I}$n spite of a dwindling supply of money and a constant lack of workers, the Central Pacific inched its way out of Sacramento in the early part of 1864. By March the railroad found itself some eighteen miles long, with a rise of only one hundred twenty-nine feet between Sacramento's riverfront and the newly renamed town of Roseville. Such a slight grade increase made the line relatively easy to build. It boosted the excitement of those living around the project. The general population of the area lauded the line and had high hopes for the future of rail travel. And even though a war still clouded their existence from some several thousand miles away, folks were normally given over to a positive nature about their future.

But while the common man knew only that the railroad was finally taking shape, those in charge of the Central Pacific knew better than to overreact to their meager gaining of ground. The CP had enjoyed its honeymoon period and was soon to battle against the full brute strength of the Sierra Nevada, something no one looked forward to.

Kiernan O'Connor, now thirty years old and happily assigned to assist the Central Pacific's General Superintendent Charles Crocker, was among those who dreaded the assault that would take place on the mountains. He knew what it was to labor through mountainous terrain to build a railroad. He'd exhausted his youth working to help build the Baltimore and Ohio through the Alleghenies. Still, Charlie Crocker had latched on to him because of this experience, and Kiernan found it important to honor Charlie's faith by sticking to the job at hand.

Charlie had taken an instant liking to Kiernan, and Kiernan returned the feeling. He liked Crocker's no-nonsense manner in dealing with the young upstarts who thought to run the line in their own manner, and he appreciated Charlie's drive and motivation.

But with the growing success of the Central Pacific's line came a growing attention from the outside world. Charlie had shared not more than two days earlier an article in the *Sacramento Union* in which editor Lauren Upson praised the railroad's efforts. Two members of the CP's "Big Four," as the railroad's founding fathers were called, had taken a party of some thirty visitors from Sacramento to the end of the line, which fell just short of Newcastle, California. The party had included Upson, and he had been most enthusiastic about the line. Charlie had been glad for this bit of news, telling Kiernan that a bad report might well have found them washed up without hope of continuing—at least not until the problems of bond issues and government monies could be sorted through. With a good report, however, folks might be given over to purchasing stock with the railroad, bolstering support for their sagging coffers.

Upson had been generous with his praise, citing proposed plans as though the details were already well in place. He even predicted that once the official passenger cars were in use, the smoothness of the line would allow a man to read as comfortably as if seated in a rocking chair in his own home.

Kiernan would like to believe it might be true. He wanted also to believe that the war back East would be resolved and focus might be given to the building of this transcontinental railroad, but no one thought that likely. He knew full well that the lack of money was only one issue slowing the progress of the line. A lack of men and supplies was equally to blame for the delay. It was now believed that the railroad might take upward of twenty years to complete. By then Kiernan would be fifty and doubted he'd still have it in him to swing a hammer.

Straightening and stretching, Kiernan pulled his cap from his head and mopped his forehead with a handkerchief. His assignment at Newcastle Gap had presented an ever escalating problem. The Gap would mark the end of the first division for the Central Pacific. Newcastle, a small town some thirty miles from Sacramento, was a challenge to reach merely for the altitude of some additional one thousand feet. But an even bigger challenge lay just beyond Newcastle and had taken the name of Bloomer Cut.

Kiernan had never known a more obstinate piece of land in all the world. The Cut itself was to be a deep trough, wide enough for at least one line of track to pass through. Cut through a compressed gravel of natural glacial drift, it had been as hard as granite and nearly impossible to blast through. The laborers were growing deaf from the constant blasting of black powder charges, and still the land would barely yield to them.

Charlie had determined early on that the trough was to be some sixty-three feet deep and eight hundred feet long, and the very thought of such an undertaking exhausted Kiernan. We can scarcely keep men on to do the job, Kiernan thought, slapping the cap back on top of his auburn hair.

"O'Connor!" a voice called out, and Kiernan caught sight of Charlie as he plodded up the trail atop his heavily burdened sorrel horse.

It was payday, and as usual Charlie himself was paymaster. He had loaded his saddlebags with gold coins, at least with what little gold the railroad could spare, and had come to pay his meager troops. Kiernan waved and leaned against the wooden handle of the shovel he'd been using all morning.

The robust man brought his mount to a stop and tossed the reins down to Kiernan. "You look fit to be tied. Tell me it ain't that bad."

Kiernan raised his brows and looked heavenward. "If I were to go tellin' ya a lie, then I'd have to be answerin' to the good Lord."

"Better Him than me," Charlie declared with a laugh. He climbed out of the saddle and groaned as his boots hit the ground. "Ain't harder earth in all the world."

"Well, I can be agreein' with ya on that matter," Kiernan assured his employer.

"So what is it that has you lookin' all hang-dogged?"

"Look around ya," Kiernan replied. "We're gettin' nowhere. I can't keep men on the line when gold fever calls them to the hills. This trough won't go blastin' and clearin' itself. We need workers."

"I know we do." Charlie looked up and down the line at the dwindling crew. "I've been trying to come up with a solution for the situation. I've checked into everything from prisoners of war to allowing Chinese to work the line."

"Chinese? Prisoners?" Kiernan questioned. "Why not just ask the government to go load up me kinsmen in Ireland and ship them directly to California?"

41

Charlie laughed heartily at this idea. "If it weren't so costly to transport them, I would. And why not, if they can swing a hammer and carry a load? We need men, as you so clearly pointed out. Does it really matter who we bring on, so long as they do the work? Would it be so bad to have the Celestials workin' the line?"

Kiernan had heard the almond-eyed Chinese called by this name on many an occasion, but it was the first time he'd heard Charlie use it. It surprised him, because it seemed more a term given over to the ladies, but it surprised him even more that Charlie was serious about bringing the Chinese on as laborers for the railroad. "I can't say that I'd be carin' as for meself, but there are those who would," Kiernan began. "Ya know most of the men don't take to workin' with the Chinamen. Why, they're scarcely civil to them when they're doing little more than offering their laundry or food services. I've seen men take to beating a man nigh to death just for bein' Chinese."

"I've seen the same thing, but with the proper incentive I believe it might be possible to keep both parties at their appointed task. Maybe issue a 'no pay' rule. If they fight, they get no pay. If they attack a Chinaman—no pay."

"Oh, and for sure that would be settin' them against each other if nothin' else did the trick. Besides, thar not much on size. Could ya really be expectin' a small Chinaman to do the work of a brawny ol' Irishman?"

"I think they've answered that question for themselves. Have you ever heard of the Great Wall of China?"

Kiernan shook his head. "Can't say as I have."

"It's like nothing you can imagine. I'm told it's thousands of miles long and all built by the Chinese centuries ago. If they can accomplish a feat like that, surely they would have the stamina to build a railroad."

"But centuries ago, my people weren't the defeated rabble ya see them as now," Kiernan offered. "Who can be sayin' that it's any different for the Chinese?"

"Well, it's just a thought, Kiernan. I have to look at all the possibilities, no matter how farfetched. Understand, we've enough troubles without a lack of laborers on our minds. There are still issues to be dealt with in the financial world—issues that refuse to be resolved and thus keep our funds ever dwindling without hope of renewal." The big man looked past Kiernan to where men were shoveling out the latest blasting debris. Horse-drawn carts and weary laborers seemed to be an inadequate way to haul it all off, but there was no other recourse at this point.

"So are we to be havin' a payday or not?" Kiernan asked, wondering with some concern just how serious the financial problems were.

"Oh, we'll be having a payday," Charlie assured. "At least this week. Who's to say what'll happen later down the road."

Kiernan shook his head and walked Charlie's horse over to the back of his debris cart. Tying the horse off, Kiernan could see that his dusty, rather discouraged friend was still contemplating the cut. "God hisself put that wall o' rock in place," Kiernan said, leaning back against the cart. "I'm supposin' hisself would have the best chance of bringin' it down."

Charlie laughed at this and joined Kiernan. "God's had to deal with old Charlie Crocker on more than one occasion. We've done our share of hagglin' and wrestlin', and God knows I'm a temperamental old cuss."

Kiernan grinned. "Do say?"

"It's true enough, and you well know it. But when I see a thing worth doing, I give it my best. The CP is worth doing. You believe that, don't you, Kiernan?"

Kiernan remembered his now dead friend Ted Judah. It was Ted who had completely enticed Kiernan with the idea of a transcontinental railroad. Ted had died after leaving the Central Pacific over a disagreement of terms and conditions. En route to his home in the East, he had contracted yellow fever, leaving only his widow, Anna, to tell the sad tale. Ted had given his life to the idea of a transcontinental railroad, and Kiernan would have fought to see the thing built if only for the sake of Ted's memory.

"Aye," he finally answered. "I believe it's worth doin'."

"We need to be men of vision," Crocker told him, with a heavy hand upon Kiernan's shoulder. "The others may never see the dream or understand its importance, but we do, and we must fuel the fire that keeps the dream alive. We're building from two separate directions—two separate roads, but the dream is the same from either end."

"Yar soundin' more and more like Ted," Kiernan said, looking up at Crocker.

Charlie smiled and rubbed his whiskered chin. "We need more

men like Ted Judah. He was full of fire and brimstone, and had he not been set on building a railroad, he would have made a good preacher."

Kiernan laughed. "I suppose he would at that."

"Do you still hear from his widow?"

Kiernan nodded. "The missus gets a letter now and then." Even the thought of Victoria, now so far away in Sacramento, made Kiernan long to be back home.

"There you go with that look again," Charlie said, dropping his hold. "I'm thinkin' this has to do with more than just the railroad."

"I've been thinkin'," Kiernan said, although this was the first real thought he'd given the matter, "to bringin' Victoria along with me on the line. I don't like her bein' alone in Sacramento."

"She has friends there. Good women of the community who keep their homes open to her and make themselves available should she need someone," Crocker countered. "You know full well this is no place to bring a lady."

Kiernan knew what Charlie said was true, but he also knew the aching inside to see his wife—to hold her and keep her close and know she was safe from harm. It was a trial by sheer torture. He knew this was a difficult life. She had it much easier in Sacramento, but he knew she was lonely too. "Maybe I could just be movin' her up to Roseville or Newcastle."

"And keep movin' her along from town to town?"

Kiernan nodded. "Maybe so."

"What kind of life would that be?"

"And what kind of life would she be havin' now? She works occasionally in the dry-goods store but otherwise has to get by on what I send home to her. She's not as accepted in the homes of those quality women as ya might be likin' to think. After all, many of their husbands are a-sittin' on the board of directors for the Central Pacific. They're not out here blastin' and pickin' at the earth to build the thing."

"Perhaps they should be," Charlie replied seriously. "Maybe if all of them, the troublemakers in San Francisco included, came out here to see what we were up against, they'd put a stop to arguing about bonds and stocks."

"Mebbe," Kiernan replied, looking overhead to the sun. "It's time for lunch. "Do ya want to join me? I have some roasted pork that I bought off a vendor this morning."

"Sounds good, and to that I'll add the fresh biscuits, wedge of cheese, baked apples, and fried chicken that I brought with me from Roseville."

Kiernan shook his head and grinned. "I suppose if ya insist."

Charlie nodded. "Bring the saddlebags and come to the tent. We'll discuss the problems of the CP over lunch. And maybe even the problems of the O'Connor family and their lengthy separation."

Six

$\mathcal{V}$ictoria O'Connor came awake in a slow, leisurely manner. She heard the melodic sounds of birds on the branches just outside her bedroom window and for a few glorious moments was taken back to her childhood home in Baltimore. Snuggling her chin to the top of her covers, she refused to open her eyes and pretended for a few moments that she was a child again.

Soon her mother would call her to get up and dress and help with her siblings. They would have a lavish breakfast of eggs and ham, sausages and apple fritters. She could smell the rich blend of Cook's coffee and hear the chatter of her brothers and sisters. She had been so blessed as a child. Funny how she couldn't appreciate it then. Now it seemed so very obvious. She had been loved and well cared for, never lacking for any good thing.

Bells chimed in the distance, and Victoria sighed. It was Sunday morning, and she knew there was precious little time to waste if she was to make it to church on time. Yawning, she pushed the covers back and opened her eyes. Gone were the visions of Baltimore. Gone were the sounds of laughter and love.

Staring up at the bare ceiling, Victoria faced her lot in life with a quiet indifference. She had made choices, be they bad or good, and now she was living the life provided by them. Without bothering to pull on her robe, she quickly made the bed, then hurried to the kitchen to light the stove. She wouldn't bother to make a fire in the hearth until evening, and only then if the weather turned truly chilly. She had to conserve their fuel and use only what was necessary to get by.

The stove would warm her soon enough and would double also to heat her bath water and cook her small breakfast. Once she had the fire going, Victoria waited while the kettle of water she'd filled the night before began to heat up. There wouldn't be time or water for a proper bath, but she was used to that as well. Going back to her bedroom, Victoria carefully surveyed her meager wardrobe and finally settled on a reserved brown calico dress. There was no sense in pretending to be something she wasn't. She would show up at church and take her place with those of poorer means, while the women she had once shared company with in the presence of Anna Judah would take their places among those more lavishly adorned.

She tried not to let it bother her. After all, she knew that the women had only accepted her in their circle because of Anna. She had told no one, except for Anna, of her family's wealth and strong ties to eastern railroads. She had wanted to exist on her own merits rather than those of the prestigious Baldwin family. She reminded herself that she was an O'Connor now, and that as such, she had her place, and it wasn't among those who graced the lovely mansions of Sacramento's finer neighborhoods.

Laying out the dress, she double-checked to make sure there were no new holes or worn seams. Satisfied that the gown was in proper order, Victoria hurriedly brushed out her waist-length ebony hair and braided it into a tight single braid. Winding this into a neat coil, she quickly pinned the mass in place and went back to check on the water.

Finding the chill barely off the kettle, she sighed and settled for a bit of breakfast. She toasted a piece of bread, then slathered it with fresh butter, compliments of Kong Li, Anna's former maid. The young Chinese woman had become one of Victoria's only friends, and because her husband had managed to afford a milk cow, Li was often sharing milk and butter with Victoria. Of course, more often than not, it was butter rather than milk, as Li had nine-month-old Jia, her son, to consider.

Victoria finished her toast and washed it down with a cup of cold water before checking the kettle again. This time the water felt more tepid, edging close to lukewarm. It would suffice, she decided, and quickly ladled out a portion into her washbasin. Taking the basin back to her bedroom, Victoria slipped out of her flannel nightgown and hurried to wash. The spring morning appeared bright and sunny outside, but here in her room, the temperature was less than agreeable. Shivering, she completed her task with only one longing look at the now empty bed.

Within minutes she was hastily donning her clothes, pulling on black wool stockings and worn-out brown shoes to complete her ensemble. Not wishing to waste any of the water she'd had to carry upstairs from the community pump on the first floor, Victoria set the basin aside for washing out clothes the following morning. It was a hard, depressing life at times, but the worst of it was facing her days alone.

Kiernan was the first and only man she had ever loved. She had defied her parents' dreams for her to receive an education and had desired nothing more than marriage to this poor Irishman. She couldn't resist a slight smile when she remembered their wedding. Kiernan had cut a dashingly handsome figure in his new suit, but he'd been so uncomfortably out of place. Her parents had lavished upon them such gifts of clothes and parties and revelry that they had scarcely had a single evening to themselves. But this wasn't a world in which Kiernan felt at ease. Victoria might have been born to wealth, but Kiernan had been born into poverty and had grown up in such. He knew how to work with his hands and how to force a living from the land, but he knew very little of dancing and parlor games.

She smiled again, however, remembering how hard he had tried on her account. He couldn't have been nicer about the fanfare and attention given them both. And he had made very few mistakes, easily winning people over with his Irish charm and quick wit. If he stepped on toes either literally or figuratively, he was quick with an apology or easy explanation to point out his own error on such occasions.

Pulling her shawl from the back of a rocker Kiernan had made her as a birthday gift just a few weeks earlier, Victoria felt as though she might burst into tears. Her heart longed for his company; her arms ached to hold him close. The separations were impossible. Sometimes when the railroad work was halted for one reason or another, he was home for weeks. And other times, he was gone for just as long or longer. She had once broached the subject of accompanying him on the line, but nothing much was said about it. After that, Victoria had determined to remain silent and be good-natured, no matter where that left her.

"Oh, Lord," she prayed. "I want to be a good wife and not give my husband anything further to grieve himself with. But I miss him, and I need to be with him."

She remembered her mother saying similar things when she uprooted Victoria and her younger siblings and took them away from the comfort of Baltimore to a wilderness home near the tunnel construction her father was supervising. Victoria had nearly hated her mother for her decision. She had missed her father, too, and could understand her mother's desire to have him at home again, but it certainly didn't merit moving to that horrible little town so far away from the comfortable home Victoria had always known. But moving there had allowed her to find Kiernan, and the years they shared while Victoria finished growing up were precious and dear to them both. Ironically, returning to Baltimore, once her father's job had been completed, had given Victoria pains of misery until Kiernan had announced his intent to join them.

"We vowed never to be separated again," Victoria murmured, running her hand along the back of the rocker. "Yet here we are, so very far apart."

A light knock sounded from the front door, startling Victoria for a moment. She glanced at the clock on the living room wall as she made her way through the small apartment. Who would be coming to call on Sunday morning?

She opened the door to find Kong Li and baby Jia on the other side. The woman's dark eyes seemed to plead with Victoria before her mouth ever uttered a single word.

"You would please to help me with baby?" she asked in a soft, nondemanding voice.

"But of course, Li, what's wrong?" Victoria ushered the younger woman into her home and closed the door.

"Baby sick," Li said, holding Jia up as if for proof. The lethargic infant barely resembled the normally happy baby Victoria had enjoyed during Li's brief visits.

"Oh my!" Victoria reached to take hold of the baby. She instantly felt the heat of the child's fever through his wrapping. "How long has he had a fever?"

"Two day, maybe three. He not eat good for three day now."

Victoria gently placed the infant on her tiny sofa and unwrapped him in order to better ascertain what might be making him ill. She pulled away his tiny gown and noted reddish spots on his chest and belly.

Hiding a frown, Victoria swallowed hard. "I think it's the measles, Li."

"Mee-sil?"

Victoria nodded, and Jia began to fuss very softly. "He's very sick," Victoria told her gently. "We should get the doctor."

"No doctor. No money," Li replied, her voice edged with fear.

Victoria knew Li and her husband were very poor. Probably worse off than the O'Connor family. Struggling to remember the time when her youngest brother Nicholas had suffered a bout of measles, Victoria tried to figure out what they could do.

"We need to bring the fever down," she said authoritatively. "We'll bathe him with cool water." Li only nodded and looked to Victoria as though she held all the answers to their problems. "You can stay here with me," Victoria told her. Li didn't seem to understand, and Victoria didn't wish to insult her by suggesting that the Kong home was less than satisfactory. But given that Li and her husband Kong Xiang lived in a tent not far from the river, Victoria felt certain she could offer Jia a better environment in which to recuperate.

"It's warmer here," Victoria tried to explain. "While we want to bring the fever down, we don't want the baby to get chilled."

Li nodded. "I go get our things and tell husband."

Victoria was surprised that she would just leave Jia behind, but then quickly realized the woman could move much more easily without the sick infant and was probably thinking more of the baby's needs than of her own. With a quick nod, Li headed for the door.

"I be back plenty fast," she told Victoria confidently.

Victoria watched her go, then picked up the fussy baby and held him close. How she longed for a child of her own. She felt goose bumps form on her skin at the very touch of this child against her breast. Would she ever know what it was to hold her own baby? To nurse him? To love him?

Jia protested weakly at her tight grip. Victoria loosened her hold and smoothed his silky black hair. He wanted no part of her comfort. He was miserable with the fever but too weak to really fight her. Quickly Victoria went to work, holding him in the crook of her left arm, while she gathered up rags and a pitcher of water with her free hand. She forced herself to remember the remedies her mother had taught her. A little whiskey and honey were often used for sore throats and coughs. Plasters were made for chest ailments, but what would work best in this situation?

Victoria felt inadequate to the task as she settled down to the kitchen table and began to undress little Jia. That Li would break with her own culture's traditions spoke to the influence of the missionaries who had helped bring her into a better life. Her husband, Xiang, was also a Christian and had faced a great deal of ridicule from his fellow Chinese. Their refusal to follow the old ways was perhaps their greatest testimony to having accepted the Christian God and the white man's religion. And even now, with Jia's very life on the line, Victoria thought it most admirable of Li that she had not sought out some Chinese herbalist or remedy maker. Overwhelmed with the weight of her new responsibility, Victoria began to pray, even as she wiped the baby with cool water.

"Dear Father, please teach me what to do. Let me remember what I've been taught or at least figure out the particular thing that might help Jia. Please don't let him grow even sicker or die." She shuddered at the very thought, thinking how very hard it was to be without a child, but how much worse it would be to have one and watch him die.

She continued to pray as she tended to the baby. There had to be someone with the knowledge they needed. Perhaps one of Anna's old friends might share their wisdom. Then Victoria remembered that most of them would quickly call upon the skills of a doctor whenever the need arose. Perhaps she could go speak to that nice doctor who had cared for her when she'd first arrived in Sacramento. She'd been quite ill with pneumonia, and Dr. Benson had been the man Anna Judah had brought to see to Victoria's needs. Maybe she could at least ask him what might be done, even if he wouldn't see the child because of Li's lack of money or even the color of her skin. It seemed so unfair that there were such prejudices against the Chinese people. Victoria easily remembered such attitudes toward the slaves of the South. Often, even when northerners spoke of freeing their oppressed black brothers, they still held them in contempt, believing them to be somehow less than human. Victoria saw the Chinese treated in the same manner. Especially when their religious views came to light. They held ceremonies that non-Chinese found difficult to understand. They had ancestral worship and honored the dead in ways that Christians found offensive. It only added to the separation of their worlds and caused great strife among the population.

Looking at Jia, once again lethargic, Victoria couldn't understand how anyone could allow their opinions, founded or unfounded, to endanger the life of a child. Couldn't they understand what they were doing to one another? Couldn't they see the hatred they were sowing by refusing to care for even the least of these—a tiny, helpless babe?

"Please, God," Victoria whispered. "Please help this child." It seemed so inadequate to be able to do little but pray, yet Victoria knew that it offered the very best she had. Faith. Faith that God would hear her prayer and heal little Jia. Faith that God was bigger than all the prejudice and hatred in the world.

Seven

$\mathcal{V}$ictoria and Li continued to work at bringing Jia's fever down. Victoria admired the petite Chinese woman. Her patience seemed endless and her love for Jia quite evident. She rocked the baby and hummed songs unfamiliar to Victoria, but all the while she endured this hardship as Victoria had seen her endure others—with a quiet, gentle regard that appeared to need no words.

Victoria stoked the fire in the hearth, knowing she was burning precious fuel that she could hardly afford to spare. Still, she couldn't let the room grow chilly. She had closed down all the windows and built fires in both the fireplace and the stove, and while the room had taken on a warm, stuffy feeling, Victoria worried incessantly that it would not be enough to keep the baby from further harm.

As the days passed and Jia continued to fight his illness, Victoria fretted over one thing and another, but nothing worried her quite so much as the fever's continued hold. It was this concern that drove her to seek out medical advice, but it was clearly God who caused the good doctor to cross Victoria's path. She had barely walked a block from her home when she found Dr. Benson preparing to mount his carriage. Apparently he'd just come from visiting a patient, because he still held his black bag in his hand.

"Dr. Benson," she called, hoping he would hear her and pause long enough for her to question him.

"Mrs. O'Connor, isn't it?" the small man asked. He lowered his spectacles a bit in order to assess her more clearly.

"Yes," she said enthusiastically. She quickened her step. "I apologize if I'm delaying you, but I have something I need to ask you."

"I see," the man replied, putting his black bag into the carriage. "And what would that be?"

"There's a small Celestial baby in my care. Actually, both he and his mother are staying with me temporarily. He has the measles and a high fever. I'm hard pressed to know what to do. We've been trying to bring the fever down by swabbing him with soda water, but it doesn't seem to be helping. Also he refuses to take any milk."

"No, milk would just curdle in his stomach. I suggest a bit of ginseng tea. The mother will know how to make it. Their constitution is different from ours, don't you know? He'll respond better if given something his own kind is familiar with. Maybe have the mother boil in a little wild lettuce to ease the child's pain. Keep the room dark; the light can cause blindness in measles victims. Especially in the weaker Chinese."

Victoria bristled at his suggestion that the Chinese were somehow inferior to their race. Still, she recalled that her mother's freed slave Miriam had many remedies that her own people had used for generations. Remedies that the doctors scoffed at and chided as being "black medicine." Were they really so different in their body's construction that they required two different kinds of medicine? Had she caused baby Jia more harm than good?

But as if receiving affirmation that her choices had been wise, she found Jia feeling a little better when she returned to the apartment. He actually smiled at her for just a moment before snuggling back to sleep in his mother's arms.

"He not so hot now. I think fever not so high," Li told Victoria.

Victoria reached out to touch the child and smiled. Jia's skin felt cooler to the touch. "Yes, I think you're right."

"You talk to doctor?" Li asked, knowing that this had been Victoria's plan.

"Yes. He said not to give the baby milk. But instead to make tea. Ginseng tea, with a little wild lettuce boiled in."

Li nodded. "I can make this." She got up and put the now sleeping infant in the padded dresser drawer Victoria had arranged for him. "I go home and make tea."

"You can make it here, but you'll have to bring the ingredients," Victoria said apologetically. "I'm afraid I have neither ginseng nor wild lettuce."

Li nodded and bowed slightly. "I have both." She pulled on her straw hat and headed to the door without any further explanation.

Victoria smiled and watched the woman hurry away, her linen sahm fluttering gracefully. Unlike many Chinese women, Li's feet had never been bound, thus she had no difficulty running or walking great distances. Her parents had been poor farmers in China— at least this was what Victoria understood from Li. They needed Li's help in the fields, and bound feet were of no use to them. However, Li had explained, without bound feet she could never hope to be given in marriage to a wealthy man of influence.

Li had known a very hard life in China. Her family barely kept food in the mouths of their five children. Victoria frowned as she remembered Li speaking of being sold to a Chinese merchant in order to save the family after a particularly bad harvest. He was supposed to take her to work for his family; instead, he sold her again to a grizzled old sea captain who was headed to America with a cargo of Chinese and a variety of antiquities. The life Victoria had known in California had been hard, but it was nothing compared to the horror stories told to her by Li. She was still lost in such thoughts when Li returned with the needed ginseng root and dried lettuce.

"Husband back from railroad," Li told her. "He say they will let him come to do laundry. We will go soon."

Victoria had known that Xiang was absent from Sacramento. Men from the board of directors had sent him up the line to visit with construction supervisors to inquire about the need or interest in setting up his business along the railroad. Li had proudly told Victoria of Xiang's desires to make a business for their family by taking in laundry and mending. Now it appeared Xiang had received the approval he needed in order to feel confident of taking his family from their meager comforts in Sacramento.

"I wish you didn't have to go," Victoria replied. "Or better yet, if it would take me closer to Kiernan, I wish I were going along."

"You come with us. I think husband not mind. I will ask."

Victoria smiled and shook her head. "I don't think that would work. At least not right now. Kiernan would have to be consulted."

"Con-so-ted?" Li questioned.

"Consulted. It means 'asked.' I would have to ask Kiernan."

Li nodded.

"So how do we make this tea?" Victoria asked as Li began grating a piece of ginseng.

"We make like any tea," Li replied, pushing her dark black braid over her shoulder.

Victoria watched as Li put a kettle of water on to boil. "Did your husband say anything about the progress on the railroad?"

Li shook her head. "He only say he get job washing clothes." She waited for the water to heat, then added the ingredients. Lovingly, she checked her son and nodded. "I think he better now."

Victoria agreed. "He'll be weak for a while, and we have to be careful that he doesn't get pneumonia. Measles weakens the lungs." She remembered her mother saying this. "If he appears to have trouble breathing, we'll make him a mustard plaster."

Li settled down to some mending she'd been working on, and Victoria picked up her Bible and began to read. The twelfth chapter of Mark caught her attention at the thirtieth verse.

> And thou shalt love the Lord thy God with all thy heart, and with all thy soul, and with all thy mind, and with all thy strength: this is the first commandment. And the second is like, namely this, Thou shalt love thy neighbor as thyself. There is none other commandment greater than these.

Her mother had always taught her to live by these two commandments, assuring her that if these were observed, all previous commandments would also be obeyed. Victoria stole a glance at Li. The other woman's attention was riveted on her tiny stitching. She gave completely of herself, no matter the task. And it was always evident in her work. Victoria supposed her attitude was one grounded in her cultural upbringing, for she seldom ever saw Li sit idle. Not that there was much time for anyone of poor means to sit idly by, but Li and the other Celestials Victoria had chanced to know were hard workers who eagerly focused on their task and appeared to never lose sight of the goal. They were good people, when you took time to know them. Many folks considered the Chinese rather queer with their mannerisms and dress, their food choices and different-sounding language, but Victoria had known only goodness from Li and Xiang.

Sometimes it was exceedingly difficult for them to communicate. Li had learned English quickly—first from missionaries in San Francisco and then from Anna Judah, who had labored meticulously with the girl to teach her proper English. Victoria had picked up the task in Anna's absence and, in doing so, had also learned a fair amount of Chinese. But in spite of this, it was still difficult for Victoria to understand the Chinese philosophies of life and religion.

On more than one occasion she had questioned Li about her up-bringing, wanting only to better understand the Chinese people. Li's family had followed the teachings of Confucius or K'ung-fu-tzu, as did most Chinese. It wasn't taken on as a religion, according to Li, but rather as a manner of living one's life.

"Master K'ung did not talk of God," Li had explained. "He taught of goodness. He say, 'Respect the gods, but have little to do with them.'"

But Victoria knew that while goodness was something she had been taught since childhood to strive for, Christianity focused on being saved by grace rather than by works. Of course, it didn't appear to Victoria that Confucius was worried about saving anyone from anything in particular. His teachings were more a litany of conduct—a standard to live by in order to get along with others.

She thought of the verse she'd just read. "Thou shalt love thy neighbor as thyself." The Golden Rule said to do unto others as you would have them do unto you. Confucius, Li had told her, agreed with this philosophy in total. He was quoted as saying, "What you do not want done to you, do not do to others." Li said his words were dated to a time well before the birth of Christ. When Victoria had mentioned this to Kiernan, he had commented that God had a way of getting His message out, no matter the barrier of time or language.

"Li," Victoria said, putting the Bible aside on the table. "Was it hard to give up the training of Confucius in order to become a Christian?"

"Not so hard for me. Hard for others," Li replied, not even looking up from her sewing.

"Why is that?"

Li continued working. "I close door to my people at home. My family sell me and know they will never see me again. I very angry. I no want to live for their ways. The missionaries tell me Jesus good and loves me. So I forget my life there and live new life here. Xiang feel same way. He sold, too. His parents dead, and his brothers no want to share their gold. They sell my husband, and he very . . . how you say . . . bicker?"

"Bitter," Victoria corrected. "He's bitter."

Li nodded and tried the word again. "He bitter. Say Buddha and Master K'ung no help him, so he no care for their ways. Sometime it hard. I raised to remember ancestors, make sacrifices to honor them. I think about my people still—I wonder how my little sisters are and if they get sold too."

Victoria couldn't imagine anything so heartless and horrible. She tried to envision her parents selling her to strangers. The fact that she was adopted served even further to remind her how fortunate she had been to be raised in a loving home with plenty of money and material items.

Li surprised her by continuing on a slightly different line. "The Bible say to live a good life and be good to people. Master K'ung say much the same. It hard to understand eternal life. It hard to understand God."

Victoria smiled. "I agree. Sometimes it's very hard to understand what God has in mind." She paused and studied the petite woman. Li wasn't very old, not even twenty. Yet here she was thousands of miles away from her loved ones and the home she had known. She was married and had a child, and her entire way of thinking had been challenged by foreigners. Not merely challenged but forcefully altered.

Li had told her how the American missionaries had taken away her few possessions, encouraging her to leave behind all of her Chinese influences and to take on only those of American teaching. Of course, now Victoria could better understand why Li didn't put up more of a protest and hide some of her things as many of the Chinese immigrants did.

She had cast off her old life, taking the long skirt and blouse the missionaries offered her—following their encouragement to pin her hair into a tight bun on top of her head. But after marrying Xiang and moving to Sacramento, Li had returned to the more comfortable styles of her people. She might be embracing America as her new home, but some familiarity was still required for happiness.

The long, flowing tunic of linen, sometimes silk for very special occasions, complemented by wide-legged pants of the same material, made up the costume most commonly worn by the Chinese women of the area. And while some pinned their hair up in circular braids around their ears, Li usually preferred to have her ebony tresses braided down her back, in nearly the same queue fashion of her husband. Her high cheekbones and almond-shaped eyes gave her an exotic look that Victoria thought quite beautiful. Her spirit and gentle heart only served to accentuate her appearance. Li was beautiful inside and out.

"Do you miss your homeland?" Victoria asked, only realizing after she'd spoken that the words had been said aloud.

"I miss my sisters," Li admitted. "I not miss the fear and ugly ways of the dowager empress and her soldiers. Many talked of coming to *Gam Saan*, Gold Mountain. But many died for such talk. Dowager empress say she cut off heads of every man who try to leave for Gam Saan." She paused for a moment and looked at Jia, who had begun to fuss. "Tea ready now. I give some to Jia."

Victoria watched her go to work and tried to imagine what it would be like to risk your life in order to seek a dream in a new country. Not only the risk of striking out for an unfamiliar land, braving storms at sea to cross the vast ocean between China and America, but then living with the threat of decapitation if your plans were found out before you could escape. Not only that, but Victoria knew from things Li had said on previous occasions that most of the Chinese who left their homeland had full intentions of returning. They would go to Gam Saan and pick up their basketful of gold and return as wealthy men to their families and native land.

But Victoria knew that was seldom, if ever, the case. She had seen the poverty-ridden Chinese as they struggled to coexist in a world that didn't want them. She had known from Anna Judah of the hideous treatment these people had suffered and of the life of prostitution many of the young women had found themselves forced to endure. Li had been one of those women, and the very idea caused Victoria to thank God for the protected life she had known. It also made her most intent on continuing to help the Chinese in any way she could. The O'Connors might be poor and needy in the sense of possessions, but they were not so poor that they couldn't offer a helping hand to their neighbors.

Eight

$\mathscr{I}$t wasn't long before Jia was back to his laughing, roly-poly self. Li felt confident that he had suffered no long-term effects from his illness, and when Xiang came for them, she heartily thanked Victoria for her generosity.

"You good friend, Victoria. I sorry to go so far away from you."

"Not half as sorry as I am to see you go," Victoria admitted, barely holding back her tears. It was only because of Li and Jia that Victoria had forgotten her loneliness in Kiernan's absence. What would she do to feel better once Li was gone?

Jia laughed and pulled Victoria's dark hair. She reached out and took the baby from Li. "I shall miss you both, so very much. Please come back and visit me."

Victoria touched the downy black softness of Jia's hair and kissed him lightly on the head. He was so very precious. Such a sweet and gentle soul. If she had a son of her own, Victoria knew she'd want him to have just such a disposition.

Her eyes filled with tears, and she quickly handed Jia back to Li. "I'm sorry. I wasn't going to cry."

Li nodded. "We share our tears with our smiles."

Victoria wiped her cheek. "I suppose that's what good friends do."

The house was uncommonly quiet after Li and Jia had gone. Victoria had tried to question Xiang about the railroad, but he wasn't given to conversing much with women, and she could easily see how uncomfortable he was. He did mention the possibility that the Chinese would be hired on as actual workers for the Central Pacific because white workers were often called to the hills by their desire for gold. Victoria could well understand that problem. She'd seen gold fever at its worst. Men fighting, even killing, for the elusive little mineral. It was a powerful motivator.

Realizing she'd not kept up her correspondence during Jia's sickness, Victoria sat down to pen a letter to her sister Jordana. Finally, the two could communicate because their mother had managed to tie up the loose ends of their family and locate her missing children. A strange turn of events had sent her brother Brenton and sister Jordana from their established locations in New York City to Omaha in the Nebraska Territory. The biggest reason for this had come in the arrival from Ireland of Caitlan O'Connor, Kiernan's baby sister. Only to hear her mother tell it, Caitlan was far from a baby. She was a progressively minded young woman with a will of her own and an internal driving force that apparently gave her all the motivation she needed for life. Victoria thought she sounded very much like Kiernan.

Taking up her last letter from Jordana, Victoria scanned it for anything pertinent to the letter she was about to write. Brenton and Caitlan had thrown Jordana a surprise birthday party. Victoria mentally calculated that her little sister was now eighteen years old. That would make her youngest brother, Nicholas, almost thirteen and the baby of the family, Amelia, nearly eleven. How could this possibly be? Time had flown and Victoria had scarcely known its passing. Why, she herself had just turned twenty-seven.

A sigh escaped her lips. Twenty-seven. Could she really be that old? In a few short years she would be thirty, and what did she have to show for it?

She looked at the dingy little apartment. The front room consisted of a living room and kitchen combined together, with a single fireplace and kitchen stove to provide heat for their comfort. There was a small bedroom, but nothing more. Nothing of beauty or elegance. Nothing of her life from so long ago.

Oh, there were a few pieces, packed in a trunk at the end of her bed. Little things, mementos really, that she had brought with her to the West. She had always thought that she and Kiernan would set up a grand house and then send for their things. Or that they would make so much money in the goldfields, they would return to Maryland as wealthy as any two people could be. But neither outcome seemed possible now.

She returned her attention to the letter and dipped her pen.

April 1864

Dearest Jordana, Brenton, and Caitlan,
No doubt by now you are enjoying a pleasant spring. California has turned lovely with flowers of every imaginable kind growing in pots and boxes along the way. The trees are flowering and green, and occasional rains keep everything washed clean. I've not heard from Kiernan in several weeks, but I feel confident of his health and well-being. Charlie Crocker, his supervisor, is good to see to his care, and I know Mr. Crocker would keep me informed should something happen to bring Kiernan harm.

She continued to write about the weather, the rapid growth of the city, and of her longing that they come to California at the first possible moment.

I know that the way is long, but Kiernan is anxious that Caitlan join us, and I am anxious to see all of you. You could stay with us for as long as you pleased.

She glanced up again to observe her tiny home. Maybe she could talk Kiernan into moving them elsewhere before the traveling trio arrived.

A knock sounded on the door, followed by the announcement of a telegram for Mrs. O'Connor. Victoria startled and jumped up, nearly spilling her ink bottle. She steadied it, then went to the door, trying as hard as she could to look calm. Had something happened to Kiernan? Or her parents?

"I'm Mrs. O'Connor," she told the young man.

He shoved the telegram forward, and Victoria frowned. "I have no penny to give you." He shrugged, tipped his hat, and took off down the stairs that stood just diagonally to her apartment.

Victoria quickly scanned the telegram and breathed a sigh of relief. It wasn't bad news. In fact, it was wonderful news.

See Mrs. Hopkins for ticket to join us in Roseville. STOP. Celebration on 25 April. STOP. Will surprise Kiernan. STOP. Charles Crocker

Good old Charlie, she thought, closing the door and smiling. Then glancing upward, her smile broadened. "Thank you, Lord."

This was just the answer to her prayers. She would see Kiernan in a matter of a few weeks.

———

The twenty-fifth of April dawned cool and lovely. Kiernan was in no mood to deal with Charlie's demand that he accompany him to Roseville for the celebration of the opening of the first regular passenger train. The celebration simply held no interest for him. He was happy that the line was finally in place and productive. The promise of generated revenues could only be a bonus for the struggling line. But he had no interest in a party. He was tired and restless. He longed for his wife and for a good hot meal, not for a railroad soirée.

"You've already decided that nothing good can come of this, haven't you?" Charlie questioned as they stood in anticipation of the train's arrival.

"I've seen a dozen or more of these celebrations," Kiernan replied. "I'm not supposin' this one to be much different from the rest."

"Well, you just never know." Charlie gave him a sound slap on the back and a mysterious wink.

They heard the whistle in the distance and knew the first train of the day was running well ahead of schedule.

"Look at that," Charlie said, holding up his watch. "They've made it in just under thirty-nine minutes. Sacramento to Roseville."

Kiernan nodded. It was excellent time. The townsfolk had gathered at the makeshift platform in order to cheer the first regular service train into town. There was great hope for the railroad, and this was just the first of many small towns to benefit from a connection to the bigger cities of California.

A surge of people caused Kiernan to grimace. "I'll just be waitin' by the trees," he told Crocker and took himself away from the crowd and toward a stand of oaks and buckeyes.

He didn't blame Charlie for not understanding his feelings. He'd asked for time to go home—to see Victoria and make certain she was all right. Instead, Charlie requested—no, he demanded Kiernan's presence at this grand opening of locomotive service to Roseville.

Normally, Kiernan wouldn't have minded Charlie's insistence. The man was good to him. But Victoria had been alone in Sacramento for over two months now, and he'd scarcely had a word from her. California's population was nearly seventy percent men, or so Kiernan had heard. And from what few women he'd seen, either reputable or otherwise, he figured this was true. Knowing it only worried him more. Victoria had already experienced the pestering of lonely, eager men in Sacramento. What was he thinking leaving her there to fend for herself?

Of course, he'd had very little choice. First, Charlie had taken him along to Dutch Flat, where they spent several weeks discussing strategies for moving ahead with the Dutch Flat wagon road. This road would open an easier route between Sacramento and Virginia City, saving teamsters over three days of eating dirt on the less congenial, but long established, Placerville stage road. It was hoped this toll road would generate funds for the Central Pacific while laying the railroad through nearby.

After Dutch Flat, Charlie had left Kiernan off at Newcastle to help with the strenuous work at Bloomer Cut. Kiernan thought it was what he wanted. The pay appeared very good, and Charlie had boasted more than once that if he could afford to pay only one man, that man would be Kiernan O'Connor. But some things were more important than money.

He looked off past the trees to a green meadow. Tiny yellow and white flowers waved in the breeze. Victoria would like them, he thought. Tempted to pick a few and press them between sheets of paper, Kiernan smiled. Although it might be silly and sentimental, he could always mail them in his letter home.

Cheers from the crowd rose up, bringing Kiernan's attention back to the arriving train. He'd done everything Charlie had asked of him. He'd cleaned up, even allowed Charlie to pay for him to get a haircut and shave after the man had insisted the CP had an image to uphold. He'd worn his best navy blue wool trousers and the newest bleached linen shirt he owned. Handmade by Victoria shortly before he'd gone away with Charlie, the shirt reminded him of her. He could see her sitting in their tiny apartment, rocking and stitching.

Misery saturated him like a heavy summer rain. He had to stop thinking about Victoria and home. He had a job to do, and like many other men, he had to do it separated from those he loved. He chided himself for being so ridiculous.

He turned back to the fields and gazed on the beauty of the landscape. The trees across the valley were dressed in various shades of green. Klamath Plum trees were flowering white to pink in delicate petals that snowed down on the ground in artistic patterns. Not to be outdone, a few flowering dogwood and Judas trees were doing their best to offer their own colorful show.

"And what would a fine Irishman such as yourself be doin' out here all alone?" came a soft, feminine voice.

He spun around to find his wife, resplendent in a calico gown of green and gold. "Victoria!" He felt frozen in place, mesmerized by the way her dark eyes branded him. She smiled, her face lighting up in amusement.

"Is that all you have to say?" With a coquettish grin she stepped toward him, her arms reaching out to touch him.

His legs worked quickly then, and rushing to her, he pulled her tightly against him and held her for several moments without saying anything at all. He'd lived this scene so many times in his dreams that for a very few minutes, he couldn't be certain he wasn't still dreaming.

"Is it really yarself?" he murmured.

She giggled and pulled away. "And who else would it be hugging my husband?"

He shook his head. "But how?"

"Charlie," she whispered, then standing on tiptoe, offered him her lips. "Charlie thought you could use some company."

Kiernan gave her a lopsided grin. "Oh, he did now, did he? Good ol' Charlie. Always one for figurin' out what a man needs." He wrapped her more tightly in his arms and pressed his lips against hers. He felt her tremble and knew the depth of their love had not changed in his absence. "'Tis good to be seein' ya again," he whispered against her ear, then nipped playfully at her earlobe.

"Kiernan O'Connor!" she declared, pushing him away. "There are people just over across the way. Behave yourself."

He grinned. "I don't suppose ya'd like to be taking a walk with me?" He reached out to take hold of her arm and added, "Away from the crowd. I wouldn't want to be damagin' yar reputation by kissin' ya soundly a second time."

Victoria blushed lightly. "I might be persuaded." She looped her arm with his. "The company seems agreeable, and the day looks promising."

Kiernan laughed low and husky. "I couldn't be agreein' with ya more, dear wife."

They walked companionably to the edge of the meadow. Victoria clung to his arm in a possessive way but uttered not a single word. They were complete now that they were together. Nothing more needed to be said. Kiernan could smell the lavender soap she'd bathed in. She only used that soap on special occasions, and he always loved the way it smelled on her skin. He vowed if he were ever a rich man she would have lavender soap for every bath. Pulling her close, he heard her sigh.

"I've been missin' ya somethin' fierce, Mrs. O'Connor."

"Oh, Kiernan, I thought I'd die of loneliness," she said, keeping her arms around him. "I love you so much, I just wish we could be together always."

"I know, darlin'," he said, kissing the top of her head. "I've been wishin' it meself." He thought of his conversation with Charlie. It was an awfully hard life on the rail line. Too rough for Victoria—especially after having forced her to live in mining camps for the first half dozen years of their marriage. He liked to think that he'd pay most any price to be with her, but he knew it wasn't true. Some prices were too high, and risking her health and well-being was one of them.

That night Charlie Crocker gave a dinner to honor and congratulate the important men of the Central Pacific. Kiernan and Victoria had been given a special place of honor, not far from Charlie himself. After dinner the newly reunited couple took a walk among the trees outdoors under the moonlight.

"I'm glad for ya comin' to Roseville," Kiernan told her as they paused under the canopy of a newly leafed oak.

"Me too," Victoria sighed. "I only wish I didn't have to go back to Sacramento. These separations are so hard. I try not to complain, but I have to admit to pleading with God for a solution."

Kiernan nodded. "Aye. The same goes for me."

"Li and Xiang are coming up the line to wash clothes for the railroad workers. I thought maybe I could join them—if they were to be near to where you were working."

Kiernan would have loved nothing more than to encourage her to do this, but instead he shook his head. "'Tis no place for yarself. The men are coarse and ugly. They give little thought to their manners."

"I've lived in such places before," Victoria said, turning a pleading expression on her husband.

"Aye, and ya never should have had to."

"But love endureth all things," she protested softly.

Kiernan felt his resolve giving way, but then he remembered how sickly Victoria had become living in a tent, constantly exposed to the elements of nature. He shook his head. "Ya cannot do it, Victoria. I want ya near to me, but this isn't the way."

She bit her lip but nodded. He knew she wouldn't argue with him over the matter. He felt somewhat certain that she'd already known well in advance what his answer would be. She turned away from him and gazed up through the trees at the full moon.

"We'll be findin' a way," he sighed and pulled her back against him. Wrapping his arms around her and touching his lips to her ear, he whispered, "Yar right in sayin' love endureth all things. Even this." She nodded again. It was Kiernan's turn to look heavenward. *Please find us a way to be together*, he prayed.

Nine

*M*ay had barely been ushered in, and already Jordana was tired of the spring storms that frequented the area. Night after night, thunder and lightning had awakened her, and this, coupled with the pounding of hail and howling of the wind, left no one with much chance of sleep. Thick black storm clouds would rise up in the west like some form of unofficial announcement of the evening's events. Often the storms blew over by morning, as was the case today, but other times they lingered, dumping rain and discouragement on everyone in the small town.

"Did you hear that wind a-blowin' last night, Miss Baldwin?" Gus Wilson asked as Jordana oversaw his banking transaction.

"I did indeed." She tallied his small deposit and wrote it into her ledger. "That brings your total to four dollars and fifty-two cents."

"Do tell," the man said, scratching his bearded chin. "Don't recollect ever havin' that much money at one time."

"It pays to save." Jordana snapped the book closed and looked at the man in anticipation of his departure from the bank. Just having a Wilson in the bank made her nervous after Zed's little annoyance.

"Well, guess I'll be moseyin' on," Gus said, seeing that Jordana was clearly not interested in small talk.

"Good day, Mr. Wilson," Jordana replied, quickly turning her back to the man.

She pretended to be busy at some task until she heard the door open behind her. Glancing over her shoulder, she watched Gus grab for his hat just before the wind attempted to snatch it from his head.

It was remarkable how very much he resembled his younger brother Zed.

The Wilson brothers had taken Zed in hand after his drunken incident with Jordana, but in spite of their apologies and best wishes, they made Jordana nervous. She hated to be judgmental and write the entire lot off as bad just because of Zed's stupidity. Still, rumor had it that they were notorious outlaws, performing all manner of robbery and misdeed across the Missouri River. Supposedly, they would sneak across the river and ride as far as St. Louis in the hopes of making a big heist that would set them all to living pretty for the rest of their days.

Jordana couldn't vouch for the truth of the statement, but no one ever really saw the Wilsons doing much of anything around their farm. Yet they still managed to amble into the bank on occasion, make their deposit, visit with Jordana, and then take their leave. It was all quite mysterious, but nothing that really held Jordana's attention.

What did hold her attention was the strange bookkeeping she'd discovered in the back of one of the special ledgers. Special ledgers were set up for projects or business ventures that involved extensive dealings with one group or another. This particular ledger had to do with the Union Pacific Railroad.

The entries were clearly made by Damon Chittenden, but understanding those marks were an entirely different story. Words like "Pennsylvania Fiscal Agency" and "Credit Mobilier of America" gave Jordana a horrible case of curiosity. Not only that, but the entries were set in the last pages of the ledger rather than up at the front where all the other information was given. She supposed she could just come right out and ask Damon. She'd found the pages totally by accident. Surely he couldn't fault her for that. If anything, she could defend herself by simply saying it was her job to be thorough.

The sound of Damon whistling in his office down the hall drew her attention. He had been as good as gold on his promise to stop sending her gifts. He'd never so much as uttered another single word of poetry to her, and, quite frankly, since then she'd come to rather enjoy his company. They'd gone to dinner twice, both times with Brenton as their chaperone, and both times he had been downright pleasant. Brenton had even given his permission for Jordana and Damon to attend a local dance, unescorted.

Jordana found Damon to be a pleasant enough companion in a town where there were so few of her own age. She had but to overlook his pushy nature and occasional possessiveness. Nevertheless, she found him to be a tremendous source of information. He was extremely intelligent and quite knowledgeable about many fascinating things. She told herself that it wasn't really taking advantage of him to endure his companionship for information, especially since he was getting what he wanted in return—time with her.

Returning her attention to the ledger, she noted an entry that definitely required some kind of explanation. The perfect opportunity came as the elder Mr. Chittenden came out of his office in a hurry.

"I've promised to help Mrs. Chittenden with an errand. Tell Damon to lock up at exactly four-thirty."

"Yes, Mr. Chittenden," Jordana replied, watching the man hurry to the door.

Nearly fifteen minutes later, Damon himself came to seek out Jordana with a question on some papers he'd had her copy for him.

"Are you certain that these are the figures?" he asked her without explaining anything further.

"I beg your pardon?"

"The papers on the Morris and Briggs transaction. The ones you copied over from the Chicago report."

"I double-checked them," Jordana replied. "And then I checked them again." She looked at his worried expression and tried to figure out what the problem might be. "Is something wrong?"

"No, not really," he said, continuing to worry over the figures for a few more minutes. Finally, he shook his head and gave her a big smile. "No, there's nothing wrong. I simply thought the company assets quoted by Mr. Morris might be higher. That's all."

Jordana nodded. "Well, if that's truly all, then I have a question of my own."

Damon leaned across the desk. "Does it have to do with dinner tonight?"

Jordana shook her head. "No, silly. It has to do with the entries in the back of this ledger." She held up the special book and raised a brow. "The ones marked Pennsylvania Fiscal Agency and Credit Mobilier of America."

Damon cleared his throat. "Those are merely dealings related to the Union Pacific Railroad. They aren't for public consideration. I'll have them moved out of there by tomorrow."

"But if they pertain to the Union Pacific, why would you want to move them out? Shouldn't they be listed up front with the other items?"

"Always the little worrier, aren't you?" He cocked an eyebrow with a hint of amusement in his expression. "It's really nothing you need to bother with, so just stop worrying about it."

"I wasn't worried about them," Jordana countered. "I was simply curious."

Damon gave her a charming look. "You're curious about the wrong thing. Why not be more curious about taking an afternoon ride with me? The weather is glorious!"

Jordana, still not satisfied with his answer, replied, "I might consider it, if I better understood what these entries had to do with the bank. After all, I'm the one who will catch it if the books don't add up."

"Promise you'll ride out with me?"

She nodded. "I promise."

"Very well," Damon said with a sigh. "You see, there are many projects and dealings that accompany any major undertaking in a city with the growth potential of Omaha. The Union Pacific is simply one of those dealings, and the projects are many and varied in connection with it. There are land issues that have yet to be resolved in total, but among those issues are the sales of property, which will be most beneficial to businesses once the rail line is secured."

She listened to his explanation, still perplexed. If she didn't know better, she would have thought he was making use of what she'd heard called "double talk." "So these are land sales records?" she asked pointedly. "The Pennsylvania Fiscal Agency and Credit Mobilier of America are buying property in Omaha?"

"You could say that," Damon replied, seeming to consider his words very carefully. "They don't want anyone to know of their dealings here, however, and I would hate to lose good business. You do understand that discretion is vital?"

"Discretion is one thing, but hiding transactions is another. Is it your intention to keep two sets of books to record Union Pacific activities?"

"Miss Baldwin, you positively amaze me with your imagination. Why not leave it to those in charge? Remember how I told you there are dealings that require the utmost care?" She nodded, and he continued. "Business transactions are often handled in this manner to avoid competition sneaking in to ruin plans. Remember the town of Valley?"

"Yes. It's the one the UP is putting together just west of Elkhorn. I believe you said it would become a supply center as the railroad builds west."

"That's right. There are great plans for Valley. But there are equally great plans for other areas of the territory. You can't let such details get out, or business competitors, or even common everyday folk who own property, will decide to make it impossible for the UP."

"But the UP promises revenue and prosperity to the entire territory. It also ensures statehood for Nebraska, as you told me."

"Yes, but I also told you that bringing Nebraska in as a state has only proven to be a difficult task. The officials are all for it, but the people are less inclined. They don't understand the bigger scheme of things. That's why these entries must remain completely privileged information."

"But these are public transactions. You can't hope to keep the building of an entire town confidential, if indeed that's what these transactions represent. It simply doesn't add up, Mr. Chittenden. Why such secrecy?"

Damon came around the desk and leaned close. His face became solemn, his dark eyes flashed. "You worry too much. Men of power often operate in secrecy." His voice lowered with intensity, almost resembling a growl. The sound of it gave Jordana a chill.

"Is that why you're doing this, then?" she asked softly.

A sudden grin flashed as he leaned closer and whispered, "I'm not the kind to kiss and tell."

"What?"

The word was hardly out of her mouth when Damon closed the space between them and kissed her lightly. It wasn't an unpleasant experience. In fact, Jordana might have thought it rather nice had his previous intensity not been so fresh in her mind. But the idea of Damon taking such a liberty caused Jordana to jump back in surprise.

"Mr. Chittenden! You have no right to kiss me!"

He looked quite crestfallen. "I'm sorry. It's just that you got the best of me. Your lips are so red, your smile so sweet. Your mind blazes with intelligent thought and reasoning, and I felt completely possessed. I do apologize."

Jordana could easily see the sincerity in his expression. "Well, just don't do it again." She tried to sound stiff and unyielding on the matter, but Damon would have none of that.

"I truly am sorry. Not sorry for the kiss itself, but sorry for taking untoward liberties." He smiled and gave her a bold wink. "The kiss itself was actually quite nice."

Jordana felt her cheeks flame and quickly turned away. "I won't speak to you if it happens again."

"Oh, don't be that way," Damon said softly. "Come, let's take our carriage ride and enjoy the beauty of the afternoon."

Jordana glanced up at the clock. "But it's only now three. Your father would—"

"My father has obviously seen the opportunity afforded in such a beautiful day. He's off helping Mother. Why not come and enjoy yourself?"

"But what about the bank? If we close early, word is bound to get back to your father. I wouldn't want either one of us to get in trouble."

"My dear Miss Baldwin, I am your employer in my father's absence. Is that not true?"

"I suppose it is," she replied, turning slowly to see him collect his papers from where he'd placed them on the counter.

"Then it is an official order. We shall close the bank immediately, and I shall take the opportunity to drive you home. If we should, well . . . let's just say . . . take a longer route to get to your place, then that's just the way it will be."

Something inside her set off a very quiet warning, but Jordana ignored it. She could handle Damon Chittenden. After all, he knew better than to take advantage of her. Brenton had made it quite clear that he'd brook no nonsense from Damon in regard to his sister. And she had threatened him as to what might happen if he tried to kiss her again. Oh, I'm just being silly, she thought, giving Damon a slight smile.

"Very well, Mr. Chittenden," Jordana said, eyeing the ledger in her hand. She still wanted more answers, but for now she would simply enjoy the day.

Ten

By the time Brenton saw Damon Chittenden's carriage stop outside the house, he was beyond worried. He was furious. He'd gone to pick up Jordana from the bank, only to learn that the bank had closed early and that his sister was nowhere to be found. For hours now, he'd worried over her whereabouts, and with the sun fading fast on the western horizon, he had begun to fear for her life. Rumors ran rampant in the small town. Indian wars were threatening, Confederate guerrillas were known to be roaming up and down the Missouri River, and not only that, but Jordana's position at the bank seemed to make her very vulnerable to robberies and ruffians.

Hearing her laughter as Chittenden helped her down from the carriage only irritated him more. She hadn't even considered his feelings in the matter. She had apparently given him no thought whatsoever. How could she be so inconsiderate? Without caring how it might appear to the neighbors, Brenton threw open the front door and stormed out onto the walk.

"Chittenden, I want a word with you," he demanded.

Jordana turned quickly, an expression of worry marring her otherwise beautiful features. Seeing her looking so fetching only made Brenton angrier. She had grown up so fast, and now that he was totally responsible for her, he found the job exhausting. What was he thinking in bringing her here?

"Go inside, Jordana. I wish to speak to Mr. Chittenden alone."

"What for?" she demanded.

"Go inside."

Jordana opened her mouth to protest, but Brenton narrowed his gaze and pointed to the house. "Now!" he said firmly.

She gave him a look that suggested she'd see to him later, and no doubt she would, then bid her companion good-evening and did as her brother had asked her. Then, standing there face-to-face with Chittenden and realizing Jordana was safe from harm, Brenton began to calm a bit. It wasn't at all like him to grow so angry, but of late everything seemed to irritate him. It was impossible to explain it or hope that anyone else might understand, especially when he himself didn't.

"Where have you been?" Brenton asked Damon in a tone of forced calm.

"We closed the bank early and went for a carriage ride," Damon replied. "I'm sorry we didn't consult you first, but Jordana indicated that you would be hard to find. We figured we could easily make it back before you missed her." He gave Brenton an uneasy smile and added, "Jordana said you were occupied with some business transaction. I hope it worked out well for you."

Brenton recognized that Chittenden was a master at changing the subject. If he hadn't known it for himself, he would have known it from Jordana. Refusing to be caught up in explaining his own situation, Brenton frowned.

"Chittenden, I'm not at all pleased you would risk my sister's life and reputation by taking her out unchaperoned and without my permission. As you are no doubt aware, there are constant concerns with the Indians, conflict with the riffraff who are pouring into town in great numbers, and conflict with a looser standard of ethics, which suggests that because we live far from the civilization that birthed such rules of conduct, they are no longer necessary to live by."

"I assure you, Mr. Baldwin, risking your sister's life or reputation was the furthest thing from my mind. We only sought to enjoy the day. And I should point out that we only traveled in areas under the observation and protection of the army."

"It's not good enough, Chittenden. She's only eighteen and under my guardianship." He adjusted his wire-rimmed glasses and took a deep breath. "I've not given you any reason to believe that I would disapprove of her accompanying you, if she so desired. I simply ask that you would come to me first. I was very worried." He took another deep breath and forced himself to relax.

Chittenden nodded. "I am sorry, Mr. Baldwin. It was not my intention to worry you. In fact, when calmer times prevail, I would very much like to discuss the possibility of taking my acquaintance with your sister to a higher level."

Brenton felt his calm returning. Jordana was safe. Nothing else mattered. "Are you speaking of courtship?"

Chittenden nodded. "That I am. But we can leave this for another time." He tipped his hat and smiled. "Once again, please accept my apologies."

Brenton nodded. "Good evening, Mr. Chittenden."

With Chittenden regaining his seat in the carriage, Brenton turned back to face the small white clapboard house. Now he would have to deal with Jordana, and he already knew that would be no easy task. She was rapidly becoming harder and harder to handle. He supposed most of it was his own fault. After all, he'd given in to her whims so often, she'd come to believe it an acceptable practice. How could he explain that she needed to conduct herself more properly? It was bad enough for her reputation that she worked in a bank. She knew as well as he did that the other women talked about her behind her back. She knew herself to be snubbed on occasion at church or social events by the ladies of society. But while the women kept their distance, the men did no such thing. And it was this more than anything that worried Brenton. Jordana was naïve. She couldn't see the problems that lay in store for her future.

She spoke openly and commonly with men as though it were the most natural thing in the world. And if truth be told, Brenton figured her to prefer their company over that of her own gender. He'd tried to talk to her about the impropriety of it, but Jordana had defended herself, saying that here in the West there was no time or place for eastern etiquette. He knew that was true to a degree. Women had to work hard to exist in this harsh land. There were few comforts and often the necessities were just as absent, but he hated seeing Jordana lose the gentility that their parents had worked so hard to instill in her.

He sighed heavily and moved toward the house. Life in Omaha was rapidly losing its charm. He had given great consideration to returning to New York, but with the war continuing to drag on, he feared someone might try to force him into service for the Union, and then he'd be left having to explain not only to them but to his parents how he had been forced to sign a letter of agreement refusing to bear arms against the South. No, the smarter thing would be to get Caitlan on to California.

He reached the tiny porch and stopped. Caitlan was a whole different issue, and one that was also getting completely out of hand. Brenton could hardly bear to live under the same roof with her anymore. Not because it brought him any displeasure, but because he felt the situation was becoming quite inappropriate. When they had first begun their travels, they had merely been brother- and sister-in-law. It was innocent, and no one thought anything improper about their keeping company. But that was before Brenton realized he'd fallen in love with the woman. Now, seeing her late into the evening, then upon rising first thing in the morning, as well as any other time that they were all gathered in the house together, Brenton had begun to think of her not as a sister but as a desirable woman. The stress of it all was beginning to severely alter his personality, and often Jordana chided him for being moody or out of sorts.

And he was.

Shaking his head, he knew the matter wasn't going to resolve itself while he stood there reviewing the past. Reaching for the door, he braced himself for the angry woman, possibly *women*, he would find inside.

Sure enough, Jordana paced in front of the fireplace like a lioness about to pounce on her prey. "How dare you embarrass me like that!"

Caitlan stepped between Jordana and Brenton. "Ya'd do better to calm down before takin' up this fight."

Brenton held up his hand as if to silence them both. "I was worried about you."

"It doesn't matter. You treat me like I'm a child," Jordana declared, coming across the small room. "I don't care what you think. You are not my boss. I will make my own choices, in my own time, and it doesn't mean I have to consult you just because you're older." She pushed past the now silent Caitlan and came to stand directly in front of Brenton. "I don't need a guardian."

"Mother and Father put you in my care," he said simply. Brief and to the point was the best way to argue matters with Jordana. Her mind usually worked logically, but this time her emotions were overwhelming her senses.

"I've told you before, just as I told them, I don't desire to be under anyone's care. I'm fully capable of caring for myself. I think I've proven that by taking on a job that pays better than anything you've been able to earn." She instantly clamped her hands over her mouth.

Brenton knew she regretted her words, but they hurt just the same. She was right. He'd been unable to supply them with any form of steady income. His dreams of photographing the country had been put aside in order to find a way to earn them money to move further west, and every time they began to see the possibility of continuing their trip, something came up to put a halt to their plans. The latest problem came in the form of Indian uprisings and threats to the safety of travelers moving west. But those were issues for another day. Right now he had to put his pride aside and deal with Jordana's wayward spirit.

"You are under my care," he stated, working hard to keep his own temper in check. "You'll abide by my wishes, or I'll pack you on the first means of transportation and send you back to our parents."

"You'll do no such thing!" Jordana countered. "You have no right to treat me this way. You know full well that I know how to take care of myself. Damon Chittenden was only being nice. He simply offered me a carriage ride on a pretty day. That's all!"

"That's not all," Brenton said, irritation edging his tone. "He intends to court you. He'd like to marry you."

"Oh, what nonsense. I've no intention of marrying anyone!" she declared loudly.

"Well, maybe you should tell Mr. Chittenden," Brenton suggested, his tone just as loud.

"Maybe I will!"

They were nearly nose to nose when Caitlan interceded. "Look at ya two. Ya need to calm down and leave off with the screamin'. Ya'll have the neighbors over to be seein' to the trouble."

"Stay out of this, Caitlan," Brenton said angrily. "This is between Jordana and me."

"And for sure I'm seein' that. But ya'll not be solvin' anything out of anger."

He turned and looked at her. That was his first mistake. Her spirited expression made her most desirable. How was a man supposed to think rationally when she had eyes that green—no, they were almost turquoise—staring him down. He felt his resolve crumbling, and the only way he found to deal with his helplessness was to lash out.

"Caitlan, this doesn't have anything to do with you! I'm not going to ask again for you to stay out of it. Just because your brother doesn't have the decency to concern himself with your gallivanting doesn't mean I'll follow suit with Jordana." Realizing too late what he'd just said, Brenton was instantly regretful. He hadn't meant to take his frustration out on Caitlan. In fact, she was the last one he had wanted to strike out at.

He refused to look Caitlan in the eye. He focused instead on his sister. Jordana's expression changed instantly, but not in the manner he'd expected. The anger dissolved to a stunned look, and she reached out, not for Brenton, but for Caitlan.

"He's just mad at me, Caitlan. Pay him no mind," she said in a comforting tone to her friend.

Brenton knew he was rapidly losing control of the situation. "This has gone on long enough. Jordana, I think the best thing for you to do would be to go back to Mother and Father. I'll wire Father for the money to send you to them, and for money to send Caitlan to Kiernan."

"No! I won't be goin'," Caitlan declared. "Ya'll not be orderin' me around, and I'll not be takin' yar charity. Go where ya will, do what ya like, but I'll be seein' to meself. Ya may be thinkin' me nothin' but a no-account Irish, but I have me standards and morals. And if me brother keeps hisself from worryin' on my account, mebbe it's because he trusted yarself to take care of matters." Her voice sounded unsteady as she finished.

Brenton had no other choice but to face them both. Jordana had her arm around Caitlan's waist, and there were tears in Caitlan's eyes—as well as fire. He'd seldom seen her so worked up, at least not when he was the focus of her attention. Raising his arms in defeat, he went to the door and took his black felt hat from the wall. He couldn't talk to them about his feelings. He couldn't make them understand that he feared for their safety—that he feared he wouldn't be man enough to keep them from harm.

Slamming the door behind him, Brenton headed in the direction of the small photography studio he'd set up. There was seldom enough business to keep him occupied and certainly not enough business to merit paying rent on the place. He only had the place because Hezekiah Chittenden saw a potential in his work with the

Union Pacific, and because the place was really too small for much of anything else. The elder Chittenden had taken pity on Brenton, willingly loaning him the use of the building until a paying businessman showed up. So far there had been no takers. Not for the small two-room shop, nor for the photographer's talents.

Feeling very sorry for himself, Brenton gave serious thought to giving up on everything. Maybe he should just wire his father and request money enough to bring them all back to New York. He grimaced and muttered an apology as he nearly collided with several uniformed soldiers.

"Is that you, Baldwin?"

Brenton looked up to find Rich O'Brian trailing behind the soldiers. "Hello, Captain. I guess I wasn't being very observant."

"You had me wondering what was so fascinating about the ground." He grinned at Brenton, causing his thick mustache to twitch a bit.

"I just had something on my mind."

"Let me guess. Is that something about five foot two, one hundred pounds, and packs a fine wallop?"

Brenton couldn't help but smile. "If you mean my sister Jordana, then yes. It has a great deal to do with her."

O'Brian sobered instantly. "Is she well?"

"Oh yes, she is well, but she can be a handful. I pity the man whom she finally lets marry her."

With a look that wavered between sympathy and pity, O'Brian said, "I'll be praying for you."

Brenton shook his head and glanced heavenward. "I need all the help I can get." Then curiosity got the better of him. "What do you mean 'packs a wallop'?"

O'Brian laughed. "Don't fret about it. I'll tell you another time. Right now I need to catch up to my men. We've been summoned to a meeting."

"Have a good evening, Captain, and if time permits, you must stop by and see us again soon."

Although he had already turned to leave, O'Brian stopped and turned to offer Brenton a grin. "Maybe after you get your female problems under control."

Brenton nearly moaned out loud. "I could die an old man before then."

He heard O'Brian laughing all the way down the street. For not knowing his sister that well, O'Brian certainly seemed to have a fixed opinion of her.

Passing by the telegraph office, Brenton paused and looked at the sign for several moments. He could go inside and put an end to their misery right now. His father would no doubt have the money wired to the bank in record time, and they could easily purchase tickets on a steamer or cross the river by ferry and take the stage or train. They could be home in New York in ten days, maybe even a week, if the war didn't cause them any interference.

Of course, Jordana would hate him forever, and Caitlan . . . Oh, Caitlan, what have I done to you? He wanted to crawl under a rock when he remembered the way he'd acted and the things he'd said. He'd hurt her, and there was no way he could take back his harsh, unfeeling words.

Again Brenton looked to the skies, but this time there was a prayer on his heart. "Help me to make things right again. I never meant to hurt either one of them. Not by my words or actions. Or for that matter, my lack of action."

Eleven

*W*hen Brenton received a summons the following morning to meet with Peter Dey, chief engineer for the Union Pacific, he felt a tremendous exuberance. He'd been trying for days, even weeks, to get an appointment with this man, and finally his moment had come.

Striding into the Union Pacific's plain office, Brenton found himself one of several men on hand to meet with Dey. So much for his thought of a quick meeting.

The men nodded in greeting, and Brenton did likewise as he slowly scanned the room. The furnishings were nothing to brag about. Wooden floors and simple, unadorned furniture made up the lobby. A large oak door, void of any placard to announce its occupant, was closed to them. With a sigh, Brenton slipped into a polished wooden chair and waited for his turn.

"This isn't anything like the offices old Durant has for himself back in New York," one man was saying to another. "I was there a couple of weeks ago. You should have seen it. Marble fireplaces and black walnut paneling on the walls. The carpets on the floor were probably worth a hundred dollars each."

"Do tell," the man replied. "Well, maybe that's where all the building of the Union Pacific is taking place." The men laughed heartily while Brenton fidgeted with the buttons on his coat.

"They can pretend all they like," another man said, leaning forward from the wooden chair he'd chosen for himself, "grading here and there, ordering up supplies, and opening workshops. But until they get some fixed surveys for this line, they aren't likely to be going anywhere."

"You talk like one who knows," one of the first men replied.

The man nodded. "I'm Samuel Reed, one of the engineers hired on by Dey. I was to be bound for Salt Lake City last month, but it's been impossible to get transportation west. I was about to sign on and head there with the Mormons when Dey summoned me."

His mention of finding transportation west impossible immediately caught Brenton's attention. Maybe his concerns over getting Caitlan to California would be for naught. He could hardly be blamed for the delay if transportation wasn't to be had.

"You're surveying for the Union Pacific?" asked the youngest of the other two men.

"That's the plan," Reed admitted. "We're going to figure out a way to lay track out of Nebraska and the high plains across to the Salt Lake Valley. There's another party exploring through the Medicine Bow Mountains, and they're supposed to hook up with my group near Utah. But we've got to get there first."

"What's the holdup with transportation?" the older man questioned.

Brenton listened with great interest, trying hard to look preoccupied with the simple, yet official-looking, railroad clock hanging on the wall opposite them.

"It's a combination of problems," Reed replied. "There's too many people trying to get west, for one thing, and not enough stagecoaches for another. I've been working to get passage on the stage for me and my men, but it's nigh impossible. The last I heard, the fare's been raised to $200 a person, and any baggage over twenty-five pounds is charged at a dollar a pound. At that rate I'll be paying over $150 just to ship my instruments to Salt Lake."

"Two hundred! Land sakes," the young man declared. "That's outright robbery."

Reed nodded. "Dey says it's due to the Indian scare as well as the big number of gold prospectors heading to the mountains. The stages are running a risk even venturing west, and they intend to be well compensated for their trouble. I told Dey, with that kind of expense we ought to just buy our own wagon and team and head there on our own."

Just then the door opened and a dour-faced man appeared. "Gentlemen, my apologies. I fear I'm running behind. Reed, we have passage for you and your men, but you'll have to take a steamer to Atchison and catch the westbound stage from that point." The man, obviously Peter Dey himself, then turned to the other two men in the waiting room. "Mr. McKeever, Mr. Daniels, I have that information your boss, Mr. Snyder, needs." He handed them a long rolled-up document. "Also there are supplies at the river that need to be freighted to where Snyder is working west of town."

"We'll see to it, boss," the younger man replied.

The two men grabbed up their hats and hurried out of the office, leaving only Reed and Brenton to occupy Peter Dey's time.

"Reed, you'll have a bad time of it, as I hear. The stage is at least ten days and nights with nothing but bacon and hard bread for food. There's a risk of Indian attack, and the driver suggests that no man travel without a weapon. Preferably something that shoots long-range."

"When does the steamer leave?" Reed stroked his long, thick beard.

"In three hours. Can you be ready?"

"I'll be there," Reed announced, getting to his feet. "I'll arrange for mail pickup and deliveries in Salt Lake. Send everything to me there."

"God's speed and care," Dey replied as Reed took up his hat.

"I'm sure we'll need it." Reed turned, leaving Brenton behind as he exited the office.

"Mr. Baldwin, is it not?" Dey then focused on Brenton, now the lone inhabitant of the waiting room.

"Yes, sir." Brenton quickly rose to his feet. "Thank you for seeing me, sir."

"Well, come on inside and tell me what I can do for you," Dey commanded.

Brenton felt his mouth grow cottony. He had practiced what he would say all morning, but now the words fled from his mind. Why am I here? What was it I came to say?

Feeling somewhat panicked, Brenton went into the inner office and took the offered chair, once again a simple, coarse structure, and cleared his throat nervously.

But Dey spoke first. "You mentioned in your note to me that you'd like to photograph the Union Pacific's progress. Perhaps even join up with one of our survey teams and photograph the landscape."

"Yes, that's right," Brenton said, breathing out a sigh of relief.

"I'm a photographer, and I have my own equipment. I'm set up over on Fourteenth Street."

"I see. I suppose what I fail to understand is why you would desire to devote your time to the railroad?" Dey took his seat and narrowed his eyes. His expression looked dauntingly harsh.

Brenton licked his dry lips. "Well, I come from a family of railroad men. My father was involved with the Baltimore and Ohio Railroad, and he shares a great interest in the Union Pacific as well. He has often said that he believes there might be more support for the line if people had a chance to see the course it planned to take and maybe even to see the workers in progress."

"Interesting concept, Mr. Baldwin. I must say, it's one that I'd not considered before this moment. What would you require of the Union Pacific?"

Brenton took a deep breath. "It would be my ultimate desire to be brought on as a salaried employee of the railroad. However, I realize that may well not be in the plans or budget of the line."

"It certainly hasn't been up to this point," Dey concurred dryly.

Brenton nodded. "I can understand. The point is, I have my own equipment, as I stated, and if the railroad were willing to furnish the supplies necessary—my chemicals and photography materials, as well as feed for my horses—I would be happy to work on a room-and-board basis while traveling the line with the crews."

"Room and board generally consists of a tent, if you're lucky, and a bowl of beans and salt pork."

"It would be enough, provided I would be allowed some measure of leniency to take my own photographs, as well."

"Your own photographs? Might I ask to what purpose?"

"I would like to compile photographs of our nation both before and after the effects of the railroad." Brenton began to relax as he focused on his dream. "I would like to use them for my own purposes as well as enticements to others to support the railroad and settle in the West. The Union Pacific could benefit likewise, as well as have a visual account of their development."

"The idea sounds challenging, to say the least," Dey replied thoughtfully. "How about if you put together a list of supplies, their costs, and your fees? I will be happy then to submit the idea to Mr. Durant in New York."

Brenton tried not to look disappointed. He had been hoping Dey would tell him he could start immediately. Of course, had he given

Brenton the word to join the survey teams immediately, Brenton might have had to decline. He first had to see to Jordana and Caitlan. Getting to his feet, Brenton extended his hand.

"I have those figures with me." Brenton withdrew a folded sheet of paper from his coat pocket and laid it on the desk.

"Good enough." The rather impressed look on Dey's sour face lifted his spirits considerably. The engineer shook Brenton's hand with enthusiasm.

Brenton left the office feeling something between elation and frustration. Dey hadn't said no to his proposal and, in fact, seemed quite interested. But Brenton found himself once again faced with another obstacle that demanded he wait. Waiting wasn't his forte, Brenton knew.

I used to be a patient person, he thought. Remembering his days as a boy, he knew many an occasion when his patience to see a project through had left everyone else long exhausted. Maybe it was because he worried over Jordana and Caitlan. He still had no idea what to do with them. His honest desire was to help Caitlan be reunited with her brother, but after listening to Reed, it didn't seem a likely prospect. At least not at the moment.

"Still," Brenton muttered, looking at the progressiveness of the city around him, "everyone has their price. Besides, the stage isn't the only way to move folks west." He thought of this as his gaze fell to a row of covered wagons lining Douglas Street. Maybe he could get Caitlan passage on a wagon train in trade for helping out one of the families. That way she'd be escorted properly and not have to take charity.

The thought of sending Caitlan away with strangers caused Brenton no small amount of displeasure. He didn't want to send her away. But what he really wanted was irrational and unsettling all on its own. He wanted to make her his wife.

He shook his head. It was completely out of the question. He had nothing to offer her. Nothing of value, except his name and the promise of an inheritance when he turned twenty-one in November. Twenty-one would signal his passage into the full rites of manhood, but Brenton didn't feel much like he deserved the honor. He hadn't learned how to care for those in his charge. He couldn't support them financially, not without completely giving up his photography. And while he had taken on part-time duties as a desk clerk at one of the new hotels in town, it wasn't to his liking, and neither did it pay all that well. Jordana was quite right in throwing her success in his face. He was a failure at business, and now he was failing as a brother and brother-in-law as well.

Deciding to head on home, Brenton came to realize that being in charge required more of him than he knew how to give. He'd allowed Jordana to talk him into this great adventure, and while he couldn't actually say he regretted it, he was quickly coming to see that responsibility required a person to sometimes refuse an opportunity. Especially when it had the potential of bringing harm to others.

Kicking at the dusty road, Brenton chided himself for not taking a firmer stand with Jordana prior to now. How was it that she had so easily talked him into risking their lives to go west? He smiled as he thought of her skillful manipulation of him when they were children. He was always the serious one, the one who had to weigh out each consequence and possible solution. Jordana was the one who bid him to throw caution to the wind and have a go at life.

Well, here he was. Having his go at life. He glanced up the street to where another new building was being constructed. The pounding of hammers against nails and boards competed with the shouts of the workers as they offered directions and instructions. To the north of this, two teamsters worked to unload a wagon of new stoves for the hardware store. Beyond them, three men were standing at the edge of the street, gesturing at an empty lot and glancing down at the paper in one man's hand. No doubt another building and business was about to be born. The city had nearly changed overnight. So, too, had Brenton.

He felt an ever growing burden where Jordana and Caitlan were concerned, but more so, he felt a considerable responsibility to become the man his father and mother had raised him to be. Seeking out dreams was one thing, but working to make them a reality often took time and effort. And often the price was much too high to pay.

The little white house came into view, and Brenton decided it wasn't such a bad home. The little yard was sparse, barely capable of growing a few weeds and small patches of grass. The picket fence that surrounded the property needed a coat of whitewash in the worst way. They'd barely been able to afford paint for the outside of the house, and even then, they'd fallen into possession of the paint quite by mistake. Chittenden had received a shipment of paint for his own home and had offered them the excess at half the original cost. Of course, given the fact that the house was technically his bank's property anyway, Chittenden should have probably just given them the paint at no charge, but Brenton wasn't arguing. The white coating had done wonders to cheer up the little house, and the ladies had been quite pleased with the effect.

Brenton stood at the gate for a moment and studied the little box house. Only a tiny porch at the front door kept it from being a complete square. There were four rooms inside and an outhouse not far from the back door, along with a small lean-to-style shed that sheltered Brenton's wagon. If he were here alone, without anyone else to concern himself with, it might be the perfect arrangement. He could turn one of the bedrooms into a darkroom, and then he'd not even need to use the tiny office space on Fourteenth Street.

He saw movement at the window and realized that sooner or later he would have to go inside and face the music. Somehow the only logical conclusion was the one he didn't want to accept—that of wiring his father for help.

Opening the gate, he decided he would simply explain the situation to Jordana and Caitlan. He would tell them of his chance to go out with the surveyors if, in fact, Mr. Durant liked the idea. But in the meantime, he needed to see to Jordana's and Caitlan's welfare. Maybe he should suggest that Jordana and Caitlan both go to California. He smiled. Yes, maybe that would keep Jordana from growing angry with him for threatening to send her home to their parents.

Inside, the aroma of meat cooking on the stove caught his attention first. That meant Caitlan was already busy with supper. He glanced at his pocket watch and saw the hour was still fairly early. Closing the door quietly, he looked up to find Caitlan silently observing him.

"Supper's not yet ready," she said, turning back quickly to the stove.

Brenton glanced around the large room. Jordana was not there. He let his gaze linger on Caitlan at the stove. Her long curly hair had been tied back with a piece of black ribbon, the edges of her curls touching just at the point where her apron was tied to her waist. He tried not to imagine what it would be like to run his hands through that mane—to feel her hair wrap gently around his fingers. He tried not to imagine what it would be like to put his hand on her waist— to kiss her lips. He tried, but he wasn't succeeding.

"Well, you're back early," Jordana said, coming from the bedroom. Dressed in her simplest short-sleeve calico gown, her hair hung in wet ringlets around her shoulders. She ignored Brenton after her initial statement and moved toward Caitlan. "I'm finished with the bath. I can tend to supper if you want to go ahead and bathe."

"I suppose I could be doin' that," Caitlan admitted shyly, with a darting side glance at Brenton. "Won't take me but a moment."

Brenton shuddered and turned away. Why did they talk about such things in front of him? They treated him as though he weren't a man. Such matters shouldn't be shared in mixed company and yet . . . He pushed aside the thought of Caitlan and the bath and turned instead to let his anger still the images in his mind.

"I've made up my mind," he announced. "I'm going to wire Father and ask for the money to send you both to California."

"What?" Jordana and Caitlan both exclaimed.

"You heard me."

"I heard you," Jordana admitted, "but I can't believe you'd suggest such a thing."

"I'll do what is necessary to keep you both safe and well cared for." Brenton drew a deep breath and avoided looking at Caitlan altogether. "I have the chance to travel with the Union Pacific survey team. Nothing definite has been decided as of yet, but I certainly can't even consider taking the position so long as I have you two to worry about."

"Nobody's asking you to worry about either one of us," Jordana replied hotly. "I've just about had enough of you acting like the lord of the manor. I liked you better when you were all soft and sweet."

"You mean mousy and manageable, don't you?" Brenton sneered, eyeing Jordana sternly. "You think that just because I have become more attentive to my responsibility of caring for you, that somehow means I no longer love you or respect you? That simply isn't true. Can't you see, Jordana, I do these things because of my love for you?"

Jordana shook her head. "I don't know what's gotten into you. You used to understand me better than anyone. Now you sound just like every other man I've ever known, with the exception of Father. Would you put me away in some little cottage with a husband and family of my own, never to live my life in the manner I choose? Do you deny me my dream in order to have your own?"

"That's not fair," Brenton replied. "I've denied you nothing. I'm simply suggesting that you go home or at least go to Victoria and give yourself a few more years to mature."

"So now I'm immature. Did you hear that, Caitlan?"

"Ya'd best be leavin' me out of this," Caitlan replied, focusing her attention on peeling potatoes.

"Well, he's certainly not leaving you out of this," Jordana declared, hands on hips. "He's making plans for both our lives without once consulting us as to our desires or needs. I would think that would make you very concerned for your future."

Caitlan put the peeler down and came to where Jordana stood. "I'll not be a burden to either of ya. I made that clear in the beginnin'. Do what you must, Brenton."

He met her gaze but found no joy in her words. Her tone was completely resigned.

"Caitlan, you can't just let him dictate to you!" Jordana swung around and gave her friend a challenging stare. Then, leaning toward her sister-in-law in a conspiratorial manner, Jordana added, "I don't know why he's acting this way, but you shouldn't be made to feel bad. I suppose it would be acceptable to accompany you to California, however. So, if you are of a mind to allow my father to pay our way there, then I will give in to Brenton's demands and go with you."

Caitlan shook her head. "I'll not be takin' charity."

"It wouldn't be charity," Brenton insisted. "You're family, Caitlan."

"Yar sister may be married to me brother, but that hardly joins our blood. It would be yar father's money, and I can't be owing still another person. I'll be makin' my own way, and I'll not be burdenin' yarself with the responsibility."

Brenton wondered at her statement. What exactly was she saying?

"You don't need to worry about me, either," Jordana said. She marched across the room and took up her straw bonnet. "I'll not be dictated to, Brenton Baldwin. I'll wire father myself, if need be, and explain my position, but I'll not be ordered about." She paused at the door, her expression clearly one of anger. "You used to be someone I admired."

"Don't you mean, someone you could control?" Brenton breathed tensely. He hated fighting with Jordana. Hated that she looked at him with such contempt. Why couldn't she understand that he was only looking out for her best interests? "You're not yet twenty-one, Jordana. You're still our father's responsibility, and in his absence you are mine."

She jammed the hat on her head, not bothering to tie the ribbons, and opened the front door with such force that it slammed back against the wall with a dull thud. "I'll join the army before I let you bully me into doing things your way," she declared before she stormed from the house, leaving Brenton to stare after her. Behind him he heard Caitlan sniffing and knew that he'd reduced her to tears.

Dreading his own emotions, Brenton turned. Caitlan dabbed at her eyes with her apron but refused to give in to her tears.

"I never meant to make you cry," he said.

"I never meant to make you fight with yar sister," she answered.

"You didn't." He shook his head. "Jordana and I are just growing up. We're finding our own way and reaching that point where we don't always agree." He smiled. "Not that I always agreed with her in the past, but she was very persuasive and I was very pliable."

Caitlan sniffed and blotted her eyes again. "I meant what I said. Ya don't need to be worryin' that I'll keep ya from yar dreams."

He looked at her quizzically for a moment, puzzled by her words. "I never thought that, Caitlan. I only know that we set out to get you to Kiernan, and so far we've only come halfway. You know for yourself that Kiernan desires you to come straightway to California, and technically he is responsible for you."

She shook her head. "I'm responsible for meself, and I'm sorry for what I've caused here."

Brenton took two quick strides to where she stood. Taking hold of her arms, he fought for control of his feelings. "You aren't to blame for this, Caitlan."

"Then why be so all-fired worried about gettin' me to California? Jordana and I would be fine carin' for each other, even if you went off with the railroad. If it weren't a matter of me bein' in the way, leavin' ya with a burden, ya'd not be worried in the least. Why, Jordana herself would probably go with ya. Ya know her heart for explorin' and such. But then ya'd be worried about me. It's all my fault."

"It's not your fault, Caitlan," he insisted. "It's mine. My feelings for you are making it almost impossible to go on like this."

"I don't understand."

Brenton wanted to shake her and force her to listen to his words. To hear of how much he cared for her—that living in the same house had become painful for him. He wanted to say how hard it was to see her but not be able to touch her. To love her but feel that the issues between them could only cause that love to be harmed in the long run.

Seeing a tear run down her cheek was his undoing. Without thinking, Brenton pulled her close. He'd meant only to offer a comforting embrace, but before he realized what he was doing, his lips had found hers, and he kissed her long and passionately. For a brief moment he felt her yield to his touch, yet she refused to touch him back. She allowed his kiss but didn't return it. His heart nearly tore in two. She doesn't love me—she doesn't want me like I want her.

Pulling away, he shook his head. "That should speak for itself," he said, then hurried to leave the house before she could reply and tell him what a fool he was for thinking that she returned his love.

Twelve

iss Baldwin," Damon called from his carriage. "Might I drive you to your destination?"

Jordana looked up, barely able to contain her anger. "No, I'm not going anywhere in particular."

"You seem upset. Perhaps I can at least take you for a drive. A little scenery would help to soothe your nerves."

Jordana thought of Brenton's admonition not to go unchaperoned without his permission. She thought it the perfect opportunity to exercise control over her own life. "Yes, that sounds quite perfect, Mr. Chittenden." She allowed him to help her into the carriage, then settled into the leather upholstery for a pleasant ride.

"What has you so vexed?" he asked, taking up the reins in his gloved hands.

Jordana shrugged, knowing it wasn't the ladylike thing to do but having no desire to explain herself. "I'm just out of sorts."

"Your hair is wet," he said, eyeing her with considerable interest.

Jordana put a hand to her head. "Yes, well, I suppose it is." She sighed. Her mother would have given her a harsh scolding for appearing in public in such an unkempt fashion.

"It's still quite beautiful," Damon replied softly. "I like it looking all wild and free like that."

Jordana tried not to be upset by what he said or by the way he was looking at her. He was just wanting to comfort her, she told herself. "I'm really not good company," she apologized, folding her hands primly in her lap.

"Well, then, what I have to show you should encourage you considerably," he said rather mysteriously.

Jordana frowned. What did he mean by that? Trying not to dwell on what Damon Chittenden was thinking, she instead began plotting how she might change Brenton's mind. If only there was a way to prove her capability to Brenton. If he could be persuaded that she was able to fend for herself, then maybe he would stop worrying about his all-important responsibility and allow her to stay in Omaha without a fight.

The sun was just beginning to set in the west, and the sky was glorious in tones of gold and orange. Jordana liked this time of day. It gave her a nice settled feeling, and in spite of her anger at Brenton, the moment took hold of her and offered her comfort.

I know I shouldn't be so angry, she silently prayed, *but, Lord, it's so hard. I know I'm supposed to honor my authority, but why must my authority always desire to keep me from what I want the most?*

But what was it that she wanted? Brenton hadn't demanded she return to New York. He was at least willing to send her on to California with Caitlan. That in and of itself surprised her.

I feel so bad for the way I've acted, Father, but my whole world seems turned upside down. I don't know who I am anymore. I don't know what I want out of life. Why must growing up be so hard?

She hadn't realized that Damon had brought the carriage to a stop. Looking up, she noticed they were near the river. The beauty of the area was quite enchanting.

"This is very lovely," she murmured.

"Thank you. I own it," Damon replied. "I brought you here for an important reason."

She sighed warily. "What reason?"

"I wanted to show you this land. I intend to build here. I want to create a masterpiece of architectural styling. And," he said, pausing to take hold of her hands, "I want to build it for you."

She jerked her hands away. "What! Whatever gave you the idea that I would be interested in such a thing?" Her previous irritation with Brenton quickly reorganized to become displeasure with Damon.

"Jordana," he whispered her name and leaned closer. "I've wanted to call you by your given name since the first time I heard it. It's a lovely name, befitting a beautiful woman. Oh, Jordana, I'm in love with you, in case you've somehow failed to notice. I adore you, and I want you to be my wife."

Jordana rolled her eyes heavenward and shook her head. "Don't speak to me of love and marriage, Mr. Chittenden. I have no tolerance nor interest in such matters."

"Perhaps I could change your mind," he said, maneuvering his arm around her shoulders. He pressed her close, then encircled her with his arms and held her tight. "I'm very persuasive."

Jordana pushed against him, but Damon was much stronger than she'd given him credit for. He was also less of a gentleman. "Let me go," she demanded.

"Not until you stop fighting your feelings for me." A harshness crept into his voice, like the time he had spoken about the ledger in the bank. She did not much like it, but it passed so quickly and his voice turned to such gentle entreaty, she quickly forgot the former tone. "I know you care about me," he whispered, leaning down to press a kiss on her cheek.

"Stop it!" She pushed against him and tried to raise her hand to his face, but he pinned her arms neatly to her side.

"I want you, Jordana. I want you to be my wife. I love you." He forced his lips on hers and kissed her hungrily.

Jordana's mind raced with the realization that maybe Brenton hadn't been quite as stupid and overprotective as she'd thought. She was clearly no match for Damon's strength, and being out here in the middle of nowhere, she could hardly expect to call on the assistance of a passerby. As his lips became more demanding and his hands more searching, Jordana brought her foot down hard on his shin. It was just enough of a shock to cause Damon to release her.

Leaving him howling his displeasure, Jordana jumped from the carriage, landing at the very edge of a thorny bush. She grimaced as a long thorn tore at her bare forearm, but she refused to cry out against the pain.

"Jordana, come back! You're acting like a child. There's no reason to be afraid of your feelings."

"The only thing I'm afraid of, Mr. Chittenden, is that I might well lose my patience with you and crown you with the first object I can lay my hands on."

He grinned at her. "You don't mean that. You're just scared. It's normal."

Jordana balled her fists at her side. "Leave me alone, Mr. Chittenden. I find your company to be an abomination."

"You don't mean that," he said, moving as if to step down from the carriage.

Jordana picked up a fist-sized rock and held it aloft. "If you climb down from that seat, I shall knock you in the head with this rock. And, I might add, I'm quite good with my aim."

He frowned and plunked back down. "You're being unreasonable," he said sternly. "Just climb back up here, and I shall take you home. We can talk about this more sensibly after you've calmed down."

"I'm not riding back to town with you," Jordana declared, realizing even as she spoke that she had no other means of getting back home.

"Your brother will have my hide if I leave you here. Now, come on," Damon replied, his tone taking on clear sounds of irritation.

"No," she stated firmly. "I will make my own way back."

"Fine!" he exploded. "Have it your way now, but you won't always get it your way." He grabbed the reins and gave the backs of the horses a harsh flick of his whip. Turning them in a large circle, he gave her one last chance. "Come along now, and we'll forget this ever happened."

"Go home, Mr. Chittenden," Jordana said, moving away from the carriage, her back pointedly to him.

She heard him drive off, then turned to watch him go. The audacity of the man to try to force his affections on her! The very thought made her blood boil. She wanted to throw the rock after him anyway, and very nearly did, but the burning sensation where the thorn had cut her arm was beginning to intensify.

"Oh bother," she said, tossing the rock aside. She inspected the cut and found it little more than a scratch. A minor irritation, much like Hezekiah Chittenden's foolish son.

She decided to wait for a few minutes before trying to walk home. She would have to go in the same direction as Damon, and she had no desire to find him waiting for her around the next bend. Her thin-soled slippers were hardly suited for walking down stony dirt paths, but she had no choice. Her bruised feet would heal, but if she showed up at home after dark, Brenton would probably load her onto the next steamer out of Omaha and never give her another consideration.

"And he'd probably be right to do so," she muttered aloud. "What a fool I've been." It frustrated her to no end that Brenton should be so right about her susceptibility to danger.

A noise from behind caused the hair on her neck to prickle. There was a thick stand of cottonwoods and willows along the nearby riverbank, and these now left her unable to see what or who was making the approaching sounds.

She glanced around for some sort of cover but found nowhere to take refuge. The trees were down a steep bank, and aside from them, only open prairie surrounded her. She could see the outskirts of Omaha in the distance, but it was about a mile away. She would simply have to face whatever danger might now beset her and deal with it as best she could. Picking up the rock again, she clutched it in her hand and waited.

Thoughts of Indians, those fearsome marauders of newspaper legend and church social conversations, caused a tingle of fear to run up Jordana's spine. Worse yet, what if the Wilson brothers had seen her leave town with Damon and had somehow followed them? Jordana hadn't realized she was holding her breath until the sight of uniformed cavalrymen rounded the bend and came into sight. Letting her breath out in one loud exhale, she felt nearly faint from the fear she'd held inside.

Six men, all mounted on a variety of horses, were apparently coming back from their patrol along the riverbanks. As they drew closer, she couldn't help but frown when her gaze met the amused expression of Captain O'Brian. Now she would never hear the end of it.

Ordering his men to continue on to Omaha, Rich stopped his horse and looked down at Jordana. "I must say, I was prepared for Indians or bushwhackers, but certainly not for unescorted young women." There was a galling smirk on his face.

Jordana crossed her arms and glared at him. "I wasn't expecting you either."

"You gonna throw that at me?" he asked.

Jordana couldn't imagine what he was talking about until she looked down at her hand and saw the rock. She gave it a toss, not at the captain but down the bank instead. "I thought you were Indians."

"And you were going to take them on with that rock?"

She shrugged. "I hadn't really thought it through."

He chuckled, then caught sight of the scratch on her arm. "Are you hurt?" His voice held seemingly sincere concern. "What happened?" He climbed down from his horse and took hold of her arm.

"Don't touch me!" She pulled away sharply. "I'm sick and tired of being manhandled."

"Did someone accost you? Is that why you're out here alone?" He refused to let go of her and instead waited for an answer.

"Oh, if you must know, I took a carriage ride with Damon Chittenden. He tried to take liberties with me, and I sent him away."

O'Brian grinned. "You didn't hit him over the back, did you?"

"No, but I wish I had," Jordana declared.

"How'd you get this?" he nodded toward her wounded arm, raising it slightly.

"I jumped out of the carriage and nearly landed in a thornbush." She tried again to jerk her arm away, but he held her fast.

"Tsk, tsk," he said, waggling his gloved finger at her. "This needs to be cleaned."

"I'll take care of it at home."

"I can take care of it right now." He nudged her back with him to where his horse stood contentedly munching grass.

"I was tended by you once before and my wound only festered," Jordana replied curtly. She stood still as he reached into his saddlebag and produced the dreaded blue bottle. "And that's just the stuff that probably did it!" She grimaced, remembering the last time he'd cared for her.

He laughed. "No chance of that. This is a remedy that's helped to keep the army in the field through thick and thin. There's more alcohol in here than anything, so I know it couldn't have caused your infection. Those thornbushes can cause blood poisoning if you don't treat the cut immediately. Now, hold still so I can see if there are any pieces of thorn left in the cut."

"I only scratched the skin," she protested but did as he told her. "Honestly, I've just about had it with men. You're all so bossy and difficult to live with."

"Us?" O'Brian arched an eyebrow in disbelief as he finished inspecting her arm. "I'd say the shoe is clearly on the other foot. You women cause us no end of misery. Why, your brother is probably half-sick with worry."

"He doesn't even know I'm out here. And he doesn't need to know I'm out here either," she added quickly.

"I don't see how I'd be doing you any favors to keep this from him. He should know that your Mr. Chittenden needs to be dealt with."

"He's not *my* Mr. Chittenden. Nevertheless, I'll take care of dealing with him."

Captain O'Brian poured liquid from the bottle over her scratch, and Jordana bit her lip to keep from crying out at the intense burning. "You need to soak this in hot vinegar water. Watch it for a couple of days, and if you see any red streaks coming up your arm, get to a doctor right away."

"Yes, sir," she said, giving him a mocking salute with her free hand. "You surely do enjoy ordering folks around."

"Yup, that's why I'm a captain instead of a private."

She rolled her eyes as he let go of her arm and put the bottle back in his saddlebag. "I do appreciate your concern, Captain, but I'd better get back to town. My brother will have the rest of the army out here looking for me if I don't get going."

"I can't let you go alone, and I suppose it would hardly be appropriate to have you ride double with me. You're hardly dressed for riding," he said, letting his gaze travel the full length of her.

"I can walk," she declared, feeling uncomfortable under his scrutiny. She turned and continued down the path, mindless of the fact that he now followed, leading his mount along behind.

"So why are you so all-fired mad at men?" he asked. "Seems like just one man deserves your anger."

"Mr. Chittenden is only part of the problem, I assure you. My brother started this whole thing by making unreasonable demands on me."

"What'd he do? Ask you to fix supper?"

She stopped and looked up to give him what she hoped was a fierce expression of complete disgust. "No, he did not ask me to fix supper. He wants to send me away. He wants to go gallivanting off with the railroad and send me back to some prim-and-proper setting where I can't get hurt."

"What an irrational and unfeeling monster," O'Brian declared in mock sympathy.

Jordana narrowed her eyes. "Yes, he is."

She began walking again, angry at O'Brian's inability to understand, angry at the throbbing of her arm, and angry that no one seemed interested in what she wanted. "I'm sick and tired of being controlled."

At this, O'Brian laughed. It was not the reaction Jordana had hoped for. She again halted to glare at him. "And what is that all about?"

"As far as I can tell, Miss Baldwin, no man has been able to control you," he said, refusing to be intimidated by her anger.

Jordana had had more than she could take. Surprising herself and O'Brian, she began to rant and rave. She accused him of insensitivity and lacking any ability to communicate with the female gender. She declared Damon Chittenden the biggest bore in the country, lacking social graces and any idea of what women were about. By the time she moved on to Brenton, Jordana suddenly realized she was yelling at the top of her lungs. It shocked her so much she fell silent and stared at Rich with a feeling of sheepish embarrassment.

"Feel better?" he asked softly.

She grinned in spite of herself. "As a matter of fact, I do."

"Sometimes it helps to just get it all out by talking to a friend."

"Men and women can't be friends," Jordana countered and once again began walking in the direction of the setting sun.

"I believe you are wrong on that account, Miss Baldwin," Captain O'Brian said, following close beside her.

"I had a friendship with a man once before," she said, thinking of G. W. Vanderbilt. "He would talk to me like I was an equal. Like I had a brain in my head. Then I thought I could be friends with Mr. Chittenden, and in both cases they ended up asking me to marry them, then getting mad when I refused. Women just can't be friends with men. They always think our friendliness means something else."

"I think it probably depends on the man, Miss Baldwin."

She gave a bemused shake of her head. "Next thing, you'll be telling me that we could be friends."

"If you agree to stop knifing me and clubbing me, we probably could. I have no intentions of getting married or of making myself an unwelcome nuisance, so we could probably share an amicable friendship. Maybe even have an intelligent conversation, when time permitted."

Jordana glanced up at him but kept walking. He wasn't teasing her or putting her on. His expression was completely serious, and his eyes, blue as the summer sky, suggested an unspoken commitment to the words he'd just issued. She wanted to believe him.

Surely a woman could be friends with a man and not cause him to go all crazy with passion and desire to marry. Then again, maybe this was just Captain O'Brian's way of gaining her trust. Maybe he would turn out to be like all the rest. Sighing, she refused to answer or even comment. Instead, she just kept walking, her gaze fixed on town.

Thirteen

*C*hurch did little for Jordana's attitude or spirit. She maintained a heavy heart, resenting her position in life, fearful that nothing could ever work to benefit her desires. She told herself she wasn't mad at God. What sense would there be in that? God was clearly in control of all situations, she reminded herself, but He also expected her to be strong and obedient. That word—obedient—stuck in her throat like a piece of dry toast.

Obedience meant that she might have to yield her will to someone else—in this case, Brenton.

Monday morning dawned with the threat of rain and Caitlan's breakfast-time announcement that she was moving into the Cavendish mansion. Brenton said nothing, and Caitlan gave Jordana a look that made it clear the matter was not up for discussion. But, Jordana being Jordana, she wasn't phased by a mere stern gaze.

"You can't go moving off like this," she protested. "We're a team. We must stick together and work together."

"It's for the best," Caitlan insisted. "I can be savin' me money, and when I've earned enough, I'll make me own way to California."

"This is all your fault!" Jordana accused Brenton. "If you men would stop thinking you had the right to order us women around, we wouldn't have to suffer so."

"Now, Jordana, please don't be blamin' yar brother," Caitlan said, putting her hand out to touch Jordana's shoulder. "'Tis not his fault. I've been thinkin' on this for a long time. Ya know full well that Mrs. Cavendish preferred me to move in when I took on the job working for her. It'll be better this way. I'll not be causin' anyone further worry."

"Oh bother!" Jordana said, slamming down her fork. "If that's the way you want things to be, fine." She got up from the table and went to the door. "I'm going to the bank."

The morning had progressed downhill from that point. First Damon had come to her desk with the biggest bouquet of roses Jordana had ever seen. Why, there had to be at least three dozen.

"I don't want your peace offerings, Mr. Chittenden."

"Please forgive me, Jordana. Being a good Christian woman, you can't very well hold this against me. Not when I'm begging your forgiveness."

Jordana looked him square in the eye. "And being a good Christian man, you should haven't acted the way you did."

He looked down at the floor most mournfully. "I know. I was just overcome. You are so beautiful, and your dress was so fetching, and your smile so warming." He looked up at her with a sheepish grin. "And your hair was all wet."

Jordana shook her head. "It's a good thing that doesn't happen to be a public fashion, or all the women of Omaha might well find themselves victims of your ardor."

"Not all the women, Jordana, just you."

"Stop calling me by my name. We aren't engaged or even courting. I refuse to be *handled* by you or anyone else."

She turned to busy herself at her desk but quickly found that Damon was not put off. Coming up from behind her, he took hold of her shoulders and pulled her back against him. "I love you, Jordana. I won't be put off."

Jordana felt once again an air of something threatening in his tone. She stood stiff and still, not wishing to do anything that might encourage his behavior, but also doing nothing to anger him.

"You must know that I'm a wealthy man," he continued. "I can give you anything your heart desires. I'll build you a wonderful home, take you to Europe every year, and provide you the most marvelous gowns money can buy. Can't you see I adore you?"

Jordana bit her lip and wondered what she could say. Her mind flooded with angry retorts, but something warned her that this was not the smart way to handle this particular situation.

"Mr. Chittenden, I'm flattered," she began slowly. She stepped forward slowly, hoping he wouldn't restrain her. He didn't. She walked around the desk to put the length of it between them, then turned to face him. "I'm sorry if you see me as being unreasonable, but I'm not of a mind to settle down with anyone. I wish I could make you understand."

Damon leaned back against the teller counter and crossed his arms. Jordana had to admit he looked very nice in his navy blue suit and silk waistcoat. If she were just a different kind of woman, she might have truly been honored to be so ardently sought after.

"I never meant to upset you," he said softly.

She watched him study her for a moment, as if trying to make up his mind what to do next. He seemed quite perplexed at one point, and so she offered him a weak smile. "I know you didn't mean to take liberties. I do forgive you, but in return I would very much appreciate it if you would just allow us both to put the matter aside."

The clock bonged out the hour, causing Damon to take his eyes from Jordana. He grabbed for his pocket watch to confirm the time. "I have a meeting in my office in just a few moments." He glanced out the front window. "Yes, there are my colleagues even now." He quickly pocketed his watch and smiled. "I suppose I shall just have to be patient and wait for you to change your mind."

Jordana didn't know what to say and so said nothing. Damon didn't even seem to notice—not her silence, nor her rejection. She had simply never met a man so persistent, so impervious to rebuffs. It was almost as if he truly had not heard her. What could one do with a man like that?

Damon quickly became preoccupied with the situation at hand. "We're having an important meeting, and I'm not to be disturbed."

"But I didn't see your father come in," Jordana commented, knowing that all of the meetings in the past had included Hezekiah as well as his son. "Should I send him to you when he arrives?"

"Father won't be in attendance. He's taking care of some long-standing business at the capitol."

Jordana nodded as three well-dressed men filed into the bank. One of the men Jordana recognized as a Union Pacific official. She had seen him with Brenton once but could not recall his name. The other was Terrance Clayton, a local financier like the Chittendens. The third man was unfamiliar but, though well dressed, had the look of a man more accustomed to dark alleys than respectable banks.

Damon, quickly forgetting his and Jordana's recent conversation and his romantic intentions, turned his attention to the men at hand and all but ignored Jordana.

"Ah, gentlemen, welcome."

An hour later, the men were still working behind closed doors in Damon's office. Jordana's curiosity was aroused when Damon's voice bellowed out in anger, "I don't care what the old man says, we can make this work!"

Glad that no one else happened to be in the bank at that precise moment, Jordana moved from behind her desk and tiptoed down the hall to Damon's office. The door was firmly shut, but the voices carried through the thin wood.

"Old Homer Stanley has had that land for some time, Chittenden. It's going to be difficult to persuade him to just sell out."

"But without it, we can't proceed with Mr. Florence's hotel, now can we?" The voice belonged to Damon, but the ominous tone was like nothing Jordana had ever heard from him.

"If you can assure us of getting that property, Chittenden, I will do what I can to guarantee the railroad's position. It might seem a bit farther south than the original surveys had planned for, but you leave that to me."

"It would mean a great deal of money," Damon announced, "for all of us. The hotel and the railroad would make a fortune. Look at the number of people passing through this town already. And they only have a steamer or ferry to bring them across the Missouri. Once the Union Pacific is in place, complete with bridges across the river, we'll be a prosperous city to rival the likes of St. Louis and Chicago."

The front door of the bank opened, and Jordana hurried back to her teller window. She smiled at the widowed Mrs. Shoemaker.

"Come to make a deposit?" Jordana asked, knowing full well that this was exactly why the woman had come. She could have planned a calendar by the old woman.

Having set up one of the nicer boardinghouses in town, Mrs. Shoemaker collected her rents on Monday morning at precisely seven o'clock. By nine-fifteen she was standing before Jordana's window, money in hand.

The old woman handed the cash to Jordana. "I'm full up again," she announced. "Had a couple of men take my last room just this morning."

Jordana smiled and recorded the money in her ledger. "I would imagine they heard about your wonderful pies. Next thing we know, they'll be coming to church to enjoy the socials."

Mrs. Shoemaker laughed. "You do go on, deary. But because

you're so sweet, I brought you a treat."

This, too, was the routine. Jordana beamed her a smile and sniffed the air. "Fresh muffins? Cookies?"

The old woman brought up a basket and plopped it down on the counter. "Raisin bread."

"Oh, that's my brother's favorite," she declared, then added, "and I'm pretty partial to it as well."

"I knew you were. I saw both of you gobbling it up at the dinner last week."

Jordana nodded. "Nobody can come close to outdoing your cooking, Mrs. Shoemaker."

"I'm planning on you and your brother to sit with me at the church dinner. Bring that sister-in-law of yours, too."

"I don't even know if Brenton and I will be there," Jordana replied, remembering Brenton's anger.

"Why is that? Are you fretting over what old Mrs. Phipps said about seeing you riding without your sidesaddle?"

Jordana blushed but shook her head. "I know I'm always scandalizing the citizens of Omaha for one reason or another. I don't know why some of those ladies get so riled. I had two pairs of woolen bloomers under that dress and enough skirt to cover it all good and proper."

Mrs. Shoemaker laughed. "I imagine they're just jealous."

"Maybe so, but they give my brother cause to complain."

"Oh, there's always someone complaining about something. I wouldn't worry over it for long."

After the old woman chatted about the affairs of her boarding-house, she departed just as the clock struck nine-thirty. Jordana busied herself with paper work at her teller window and nearly forgot about Damon and his meeting until she heard Damon's voice again. This time she knew the door must be open because the sound of his voice was sharp and clear—and rather chilling, too.

"I'll take care of it!" he growled.

"Just remember that we—" began one of the other men.

"Quiet, you fool! We need not speak on the matter again. I have it in hand," Damon said. Then in another moment, he appeared in the main part of the bank with his three companions in tow.

"Until next week, then," Damon told them as he opened the front door.

When the men had gone, he closed the door and headed back as if to go to his office. His face was a taut mask, or perhaps she was glimpsing him before he'd had a chance to don his usual mask. The thought sent a chill down Jordana's spine. The contrast between the man she'd just heard in his office and now saw and the one she had known previously was quite pronounced.

"Is everything all right, Mr. Chittenden?" she asked. "Was there a problem with your meeting?"

The mask now jerked quickly into place. A smile slipped across his face. "Just banking business. Nothing to worry your pretty little head about."

"But I'm in the banking business. In fact, you told me I was a very important part of this bank's business."

"That you are," Damon replied. "We've had a great deal more business these last months, thanks to your wit and charm with the men of Omaha. At first I thought Father had gone positively daft hiring you, but you have proved to be a most valuable asset to this organization."

Jordana rankled at the tone he took with her. He sounded like a father figure soothing and reassuring his child. "So if that's the case," she pressed, "why can't you tell me about the meeting?"

He grinned. "Why can't you say yes to marriage?"

She crossed her arms and stood her ground. "Because I'm not ready to marry just yet."

"And I, my sweet Jordana, am not ready to divulge the purpose of my meeting." He turned to go, then called back over his shoulder, "Just yet."

There had been a glint in his eyes that made Jordana shudder. "I'm being silly," she convinced herself. "Some men, perhaps most men, deal with business matters far differently than they deal with women."

If Damon was upset about something and he didn't want to talk about it, then it wasn't her place to pry. She certainly wanted no more involvement with the man than necessary. And after today's display, she wasn't sure she even wanted that much. She didn't care if men generally behaved that way. It seemed rather two-faced to her.

Fourteen

Caitlan finished dusting the front parlor, mindful to ensure that not a single speck of dirt remained to mar the beauty of Hazel Cavendish's collections. The woman had traveled extensively in her youth, and now as she neared sixty, the collections were prominently displayed as constant reminders of her glorious days abroad.

Caitlan found herself fascinated by the pieces. Sometimes they were not at all the expensive pieces of crystal or porcelain that she had seen in other homes of wealth, but instead were strange pieces of bric-a-brac crudely fashioned from wood or stone. Mrs. Cavendish had grown up the daughter of missionaries—a hearty stock who took it upon themselves to visit the darkest reaches of Africa and beyond. Why, they'd even gone to Australia.

Caitlan had heard a few of the stories. Near-death experiences from snakebites or native uprisings. Strange new tastes and smells originating in native cooking so very foreign to Hazel and her parents.

Caitlan stopped and reached up to wipe a bit of dust away from an oil painting of Mrs. Cavendish as a teenager. The woman had been quite striking—her skin beautifully smooth and clear, her cheeks rosy with color, and her eyes bright, almost mischievous in their glint.

"I was only fifteen when that painting was commissioned," the woman said, coming into the parlor. "We were living in India at the time. It was completed just before I came down sick. Eventually, Mama sent me to Aunt Louise in Liverpool. It was there I made a rather poor recovery from the aftereffects of malaria and smallpox."

Caitlan looked at the short, softly rounded woman. Her face still showed the scars of smallpox. Her once beautiful skin was pitted and shallow, never again recapturing its youthful glow—or so Caitlan deduced.

"And were ya very sick, ma'am?" Caitlan asked lamely.

Mrs. Cavendish smiled and took her ease on a lovely oak and brocade settee near the front window. "I thought I would die. My folks thought so too. I still have times when the malaria hits me, and all I can do is take to my bed."

Caitlan nodded and went back to ensuring that the painting stood free of dirt. She felt a bit uneasy with her new arrangement, and Hazel Cavendish seemed to sense the same.

"Come sit with me a moment, Caitlan. I'd like to talk to you." Caitlan turned and bit her lip, causing Mrs. Cavendish to smile. "Come now, I won't bite."

Caitlan slipped the dusting cloth back into her apron pocket, then took a seat on the edge of a chair opposite her employer.

"I know this arrangement is strange and new to you," Mrs. Cavendish began. "I hope your quarters are acceptable."

"Indeed they are, ma'am," Caitlan replied.

"I am rather surprised that you changed your mind about living here. Especially after so many months. Would you like to tell me about it?"

Caitlan felt a sense of embarrassment creep over her. Her cheeks grew hot, and she knew she could never hope to explain her situation to Mrs. Cavendish. After all, what could she say? I've fallen in love with me brother-in-law, but he's obviously disgusted by the attraction and wishes me gone from his sight? For by now that was what Caitlan had convinced herself had happened. She knew Brenton had a certain desire for her—as evidenced by his kiss—but it was painfully clear in her mind that his feelings were not such that he would ever consider marriage. He probably saw her as a simple Irish peasant, not at all a fitting wife for a Baltimore Baldwin.

"Come now, child, I have a good ear for listening," Hazel encouraged.

"It seemed the right time to go," Caitlan replied. "For more reasons than I can tell." She tried hard to think of what else she could say. "Me brother-in-law is of a mind to take work with the railroad, and he may well be sendin' his sister home to New York. I surely couldn't have supported meself, what with the bank ownin' the house and all."

Mrs. Cavendish nodded thoughtfully. "Well, I am happy for the extra help, but I don't like seeing you so unhappy. I'm sure you miss your family. While they're still here in Omaha, you be sure to see them on your days off, and maybe it won't be so hard. Independence is a fine thing, but family is finer."

Caitlan nodded. Family was everything. This adage rang in her brain from morning to night. Her kin in Ireland had always taught her the importance of family loyalty. She thought again of Kiernan in California. Maybe that was where she belonged. After all, he was all that she could truly call family—at least on this side of the ocean.

Caitlan looked nervously at the hardwood floor. The shine was brilliant, and why not? She'd put it there herself only the day before yesterday. At least she had a talent for cleaning and making things look new again. Mrs. Cavendish had given her high praise indeed for bringing the heavily trafficked floor back to a vibrant glow.

"Happiness often seems so elusive," Hazel said, interrupting Caitlan's thoughts. "But God has a way of reaching inside, deep down in our hearts, to show us that we can have something far better than human emotions."

"I can't be sayin' that these are happy days for me," Caitlan finally replied. She was uneasy with the talk of God and sought only to send Mrs. Cavendish down another path of thought. "But neither will I say they are bad ones."

"Merely different?" Mrs. Cavendish suggested. "A change of course?"

Caitlan met her kind expression. "Aye. A change for sure."

"Your family seems quite nice. I met your sister-in-law at the bank several weeks ago. She's quite capable."

"Aye, that she is. I wish I had half her confidence."

"And your brother-in-law has been commissioned by my husband to take our photograph on the Friday after next. He seems very nice also."

Caitlan bristled and looked away again. She'd not known of the plan for Brenton to photograph Mr. and Mrs. Cavendish. Would he come to the house? She pushed the matter away and replied, "Aye. He's a good man."

Silence flooded the room for several moments, holding Caitlan captive in the closest scrutiny she'd known by this gentle-natured woman since first coming to work for her. She wanted to assure Mrs. Cavendish that her moodiness had nothing to do with her or the job she'd hired Caitlan to do. By her keeping silent, Mrs. Cavendish would merely pry to know the origin of Caitlan's obvious discomfort. Why couldn't the woman be like other employers and not care about her employee's problems? Why couldn't she simply let Caitlan do her job and leave her personal problems alone?

But that wasn't Hazel Cavendish's nature. Every time Caitlan had come in so much as a minute late for work, Hazel had been standing by wanting reassurance that nothing was wrong. Caitlan supposed it was because her nature was so giving. She had spent a lifetime nurturing and caring for people regardless of their station in life or the color of their skin.

"My dear, I know you are my housekeeper, and perhaps in the past, in other more formal settings, you were not allowed to be well acquainted with your employers. But here in Omaha, I can hardly see that such proprieties will work. I might live in this beautiful house with my husband, but my heart is no different than yours. It still suffers hurts and disappointment, and it's still capable of loving."

Caitlan's head snapped up at this. The idea that Mrs. Cavendish should use the word "love" so startled Caitlan that she nearly gasped out loud. Swallowing hard, she struggled to look completely controlled in her manner, but the older woman merely smiled.

"Love is a glorious thing, my dear. You mustn't fight against it, but rather embrace it. If the good Lord has two people in mind for a union, He will have His way. The longer we fight against what must be, the longer we suffer."

Caitlan shook her head and got to her feet. "I'm fearin' me own problem isn't one of wills but rather of station."

Hazel shook her head. "I'm not sure I understand."

Caitlan smiled. "Yar a good woman, Mrs. Cavendish. I appreciate yar letting me take a room here in yar home. Ya won't be sorry. I'll give ya me best work."

She then hurried from the room before the woman could reply. She knew full well it wasn't what Mrs. Cavendish expected her to say, but Caitlan couldn't very well go giving her the real explanation. Especially when the situation had so many complicated issues.

Climbing up two flights of stairs, Caitlan took herself to her small attic room and closed the door. She longed only for a moment to compose herself before going back to the tasks at hand. She knew that Mrs. Cavendish was only seeking to be friendly, but Caitlan felt ill at ease with her lot in life. Americans were a funny sort. She had known the Vanderbilts in New York, as well as Brenton and Jordana, and the contrast had been severe. Brenton and Jordana had a lackadaisical attitude about life and stations, whereas the Vanderbilts were exactly the sort of folk she had been used to in Ireland. People who placed other people in neat, confined little boxes, on precise, exacting levels. They would never allow for camaraderie between the common workers and themselves. Slavery, as most saw it, might well be breathing its final breath in America, but it would hardly account at all for those of poorer class who were forced to sell their souls in nearly the same manner, all for enough money to keep food on the table and a fire in the hearth.

She knew Brenton and Jordana came from great wealth. Knew, too, that they saw themselves as somewhat adventurous and ever so brave to have left the comfort and wealth of their parents for life on the road. But they didn't know what true suffering was like. No matter where they went, help was as close as a telegram. They lived meagerly out of choice, but to Caitlan their sparse, frugal lifestyle was far better than anything she'd known in Ireland.

She still shuddered at the memory of stories told by her older sisters. Stories of the first famines when the potatoes had all turned black. Stories of folks lying dead, their mouths green from eating the grass—their only food. Then there were her own memories of people being burned out of their homes because the landlord had found a better purpose for the property. Memories of landlords taking liberties with her as she struggled to work as a scullery maid. Threats to her and her family if she didn't give in and do what was expected of her.

She tried to push the thoughts from her mind, but they were so much a part of who she was that putting them from her was like expecting her to become someone else. She felt an aching in her throat, a sure sign that her emotions were getting the best of her. She'd done nothing but cry the first nights here at the Cavendish mansion, and she had no desire to waste any more time with tears.

"I need to be strong," she told herself aloud. "I will be strong."

But the words rang hollow as she sank to the small iron bed. On the nightstand beside the bed lay Jordana's Bible. Her sister-in-law had apparently tucked it into Caitlan's bags before allowing her to leave. Jordana and Brenton were the first and only true friends she'd ever had, and now they were in the little house on Marcy Street, while she was here, blocks away on Seventeenth Street.

The Bible lay there as a firm reminder of one of the biggest obstacles between her and Brenton. Jordana had often told her of Brenton's firm faith in God, of his desire to one day find a wife who felt just as strongly as he did about matters of faith.

"I'd like to be believin' they know the truth," Caitlan whispered, reaching out to run her fingertips over the leather cover.

There was so much pain associated with matters of religious indoctrination. People were cruel and mean-spirited, using religion and Scripture to serve their own purposes, rather than God's. She'd grown up hearing whispers about her oldest brother, Red. People believed him to have committed murder, but within their own family they would never consider it as truth. Still, she knew the harshness of the older women, murmuring that God had put a curse upon the O'Connor family. And maybe that much was true, for they certainly seemed to have more than their share of bad luck.

Jordana didn't believe in luck, either bad or good, and she'd made as much clear to Caitlan. Smiling to herself, Caitlan could hear the younger woman reasoning with her now.

"Luck is a part of superstition," she would say. "Superstition is illogically based in a belief that one thing, completely unrelated to that thing, nevertheless has the power to influence or change that thing."

Caitlan could very nearly hear her speaking the words, and the thought warmed her lonely heart. Jordana would handle matters so concisely and logically that often Caitlan could find no easy way to protest what she said. But Jordana broke with this tradition when it came to religion. At least, that was how Caitlan saw it. Jordana said that having a relationship with God required faith. Caitlan saw faith as being illogical, but Jordana protested that faith was perfectly logical—for what other choice did they have?

Caitlan felt she had many other choices. The first and foremost was to recognize that religion was just a system designed to keep folks either in line or at each other's throats. It was as much a matter of culture and tradition for a particular group of folks as was the wearing of multiple layers of colored petticoats for Irish women. As far as Caitlan was concerned, it kept people separated and created an "us against them" mentality that destroyed and wounded everyone in its wake.

But Jordana talked of God in a way that made Caitlan wish that what she said could be true. Jordana spoke of God as a friend and a comforter. Someone who was with her at all times, never leaving her to face the world alone. It always seemed clear that Jordana had something special in her relationship with God. Something quite impossible for Caitlan to grasp.

Caitlan wished she could believe as Jordana did. She wanted to believe that God was more than a harsh and cruel judge. She wanted to believe that there really was something wonderful about yielding your life to Jesus.

"If it is true," she said, picking up the Bible, "I wish ya'd be showin' me for meself. And not just in these words. I've had words aplenty thrown at me. All me life someone has been threatenin' or condemin', and always they use these words. I find no comfort here," she said honestly.

Startled at the tears that suddenly filled her eyes, Caitlan quickly dropped the Bible back on the nightstand. She had no time for such miseries, and if soul-searching caused her to feel so empty and lost, then why should she continue?

Getting up, she dabbed her eyes with her apron and fought to regain control. She must go forward with her day and leave off with these wrenching thoughts of Jordana and Brenton. She couldn't have any peace at all if she considered God's and Jordana's statement that He loved her with an everlasting love.

"What kind of love allows a person such sufferin'?" she questioned aloud, knowing that there was no one there to give her an answer. It was the question that had followed her from Ireland. It was the question that haunted her wherever she went. If God were truly the loving and merciful Father that Jordana and Brenton believed Him to be, why did He allow such suffering?

Fifteen

*K*iernan heard the final explosion fire off, then picked up his shovel and moved into the deep trough of Bloomer Cut. His mind traveled back to his time with Victoria and the sweet reunion they had shared. The time had passed much too quickly, and Kiernan had given strong consideration to petitioning Charlie Crocker to allow him to go back to Sacramento—permanently. There was always work to be done on the established line. He could work in the rail shop there, if nothing else. It wasn't as much money, but they would manage somehow.

He heard someone call out from behind him, but he was too lost in thought to hear the words. The men were probably complaining again. They'd set ten charges with fifteen minutes to spare before the lunch break. No doubt someone figured Kiernan should let them start lunch early.

He glanced at the mess of rock, seeing where the blasts had eaten away at the horseshoe-shaped cut. Slowly but surely they were staking their claim to the land—but just as surely, the land was not giving in without a fight.

"Kiernan!" a man called from the opening of the cut. "I only counted nine explosions."

For the first time, Kiernan realized he'd failed to count off the blasts. He tried to remember how many he'd heard, but of course, it was impossible. He looked down the cut to where the man stood.

"Are ya sure it was just nine?" he questioned, then turned back to eye the mess of rock and debris at his feet. His gaze quickly traveled the areas where they had set the charges, and he had just turned

121

to his right preparing to make a hasty retreat when the final charge, somehow delayed from the others, blasted out the rock wall in front of him. The noise was deafening—the impact debilitating.

———

Victoria was enjoying the warmth of the spring days as much as anything else in her life. She loved being able to open the windows of her apartment and usher in the scented breezes. Life in Sacramento wasn't the best she had known, but in many ways she had come to love California more than either Virginia or Maryland. With two weeks behind her since she'd returned from seeing Kiernan in Roseville, Victoria was already fighting her loneliness. She had worked with Li on several occasions, helping her with her English, even teaching her to recognize written letters and to read. Victoria seemed to have a flair for such things, remembering how easy it had been to teach Kiernan to read.

Li had returned to Sacramento with her husband and son. Apparently, because of a general slowing of construction, the laundry business on the line was not enough to support the family. Victoria felt bad for their disappointment but for herself was thrilled to have this friend return. Hoping to find other work, perhaps as a maid, Li had asked Victoria for more English lessons. Before long Li, who had been so excited with her own progress, invited a couple of her neighbors to join in on the lessons. Victoria had known a great sense of pride and accomplishment when each woman could write her name by the end of the day. They thought it very strange that Americans should have only twenty-six letters in their alphabet, when Chinese had some three thousand characters in theirs. Victoria had teased the shy women, telling them that learning English should be a cinch, given the difference.

But now, back at her apartment with the evening light fading, Victoria could only think of Kiernan. How happy they had been for their two days in Roseville. They'd acted like young lovers again. Holding hands and taking walks. Whispering secret thoughts and dreams. Kiernan was so hopeful for their future. He saw good things coming and had even suggested the possibility of bringing Victoria to Dutch Flat to live. She didn't mind that idea at all. She loved Sacramento with its civilized stores and entertainments, but she knew Dutch Flat from their time spent there before coming to the city. She could manage well enough in that tiny town. Especially if it meant being with Kiernan.

Going to light a fire in the stove, Victoria was startled when she heard knocking on her front door. It was nearly dark outside. Thoughts of Christopher Thorndike entered her mind. He had taken advantage of her loneliness once before. Perhaps this Sacramento entrepreneur had learned of Kiernan's absence and had once again come to press his luck with her. She bit her lower lip and waited. Maybe the person would just go away.

The knock came louder this time, and with it came a voice as well. "Mrs. O'Connor, are you in?"

"Who is it?" she asked, knowing now that it wasn't Thorndike.

"Mr. Hopkins."

She opened the door to find one of Sacramento's most prestigious citizens. Mark Hopkins and his wife had become acquaintances through the Central Pacific, where Hopkins was lauded as one of the original "Big Four." But she'd also shared his company through social gatherings with Ted and Anna Judah.

"Mr. Hopkins, this is a surprise."

"Not a pleasant one, I'm afraid," the bearded man replied.

Victoria stiffened. "What's happened? Is it Kiernan?"

"I'm afraid so. He was caught up in an explosion."

All Victoria could think about was how Kiernan's brother Red had died in a tunneling explosion. Stumbling back against the door, panic rose up in her. She gasped for breath. "Is he . . . is he . . ." The room began to swim before her eyes.

"He's not dead," Hopkins assured her quickly, "but he's been severely injured. It doesn't look good at this point."

"No!" She twisted her hands together. "I don't believe you." Her knees weakened and she suddenly felt as if she'd doubled in weight. A tight band spread across her chest, making it impossible to breathe. "This can't be true."

He nodded sympathetically, his usual sad-faced expression made even more evident by the news he had been given to bear. "I'm sorry, Mrs. O'Connor. Mr. Crocker sent the message straightway to me. I tried to contact you this morning, but you were already out for the day."

Victoria wanted to scream. Kiernan had been lying near death all day, probably longer, and she had been off teaching English to Li and her friends! She could scarcely bear the thought.

"I want to go to him," she declared, reaching for the table in order to steady herself. "Can you make this happen?"

Hopkins nodded quickly. "But of course. It seems to be the very least the CP could do to ease your mind. Come morning, I'll have you on the first train out."

"Morning? Isn't there anything leaving yet tonight?"

He shook his head. "I'm sorry. The train left nearly half an hour ago."

"If I'd only stayed home," she murmured. Moving to the rocker Kiernan had made for her, she slumped into the seat and stared forlornly across the room. "He might already be dead." She instantly envisioned Kiernan laid out for a funeral. She could see his pale skin, closed eyes, and expressionless face. No! She screamed in her mind and pushed the images away. I can't think this way!

Hopkins came to stand uncomfortably beside her. "You mustn't fret so, Mrs. O'Connor. You must have faith to believe he's still with us."

Faith, she thought. Faith was the only thing she had. Faith that God would be merciful and sustain her husband's life. Faith that He would somehow give her the strength to endure yet another problem in their marriage of nine years. Oh, God, where are you now? Why has this happened? What am I to do? The thought of facing the night alone terrified her.

"Why don't you prepare your things and come stay with us for the night? I couldn't rest knowing you were here alone with no one to offer you comfort," the man told her softly.

Victoria shook her head. She barely knew the Hopkinses, and she certainly couldn't go taking advantage of them. On the other hand, she didn't want to be alone. Her imagination could well drive her mad before dawn ever managed to grace the skies of Sacramento. "Thank you, Mr. Hopkins. You are most kind, but I couldn't intrude. If you'll come for me in the morning, it will be enough."

For once she was quite glad she and Kiernan were without children. Children would have caused yet another problem for her in getting to Kiernan, for surely it would have been impossible to take a baby along with her to the railroad campsite. She put her face in her hands and began to weep softly. Oh, Mama, I need you so. How I wish you were here to stand beside me. But there was no one. No one who cared about her the way her family had. No close friend, with exception to Li, who was busy with Jia, and her only other close friend, Anna, who now lived on the East Coast.

Mark Hopkins put his hand on her shoulder. "Mrs. O'Connor, I cannot begin to tell you how sorry I am for all of this. Your husband is a great asset to the line, and I will not even consider the thought of losing him."

Victoria looked up and caught his sober expression. There was something so genuine and gentle in his face. She couldn't help but nod. "You were very kind to come to me." She sniffed back tears and forced her mind to focus. "Your strength inspires me." In fact, his encouragement was all she had. God had evidently known exactly the right person to send to her to inform her of this tragedy. She would simply have to trust that God had also told the man how best to help her. "If you don't mind, I'll take you up on your offer for the night," she decided suddenly.

―――――

They arrived in Newcastle the following morning. Charlie was there to meet her in Roseville, then accompanied her to where Kiernan was still very much alive, but not doing as well as the doctor would like.

"He's taken most of the damage to his face and head," Charlie told her softly as they made their way to the house of Newcastle's only doctor. "You mustn't get too alarmed when you see him."

"Is he completely disfigured?" she asked, trying to imagine the extent of his injuries.

"He took a great deal of rock full in the face," Charlie told her. "The worst of it blasted the left side. He must have turned to the right to shield himself, but it was too late. He has a great many cuts, and the entire face is swollen and discolored. I'm telling you this," Charlie said, pausing outside the doctor's simple one-story house, "because I don't want you fainting dead away from the sight. It won't be easy."

"He's my husband and I love him, Mr. Crocker. It might not be easy, but I'll endure it." She remembered the exchange she and Kiernan had shared not so long ago in Roseville. Love endures all things, she reminded herself. It would endure even this.

Charlie led her inside, and the doctor, a tall, willowy man with huge sad eyes and a neatly trimmed beard, greeted her. His large hands covered her smaller ones. "You must be Mrs. O'Connor."

"Yes," she managed to say. "How is my husband?"

"I'm afraid he's quite damaged. He's not regained consciousness, and that gives me great cause for worry."

"I understand," she said, swallowing hard. "May I see him?"

"Are you certain that you're up to it?"

"I must be," she replied with simple determination.

He nodded understandingly. "Then come with me."

He took her down a short, narrow hall and opened the door to Kiernan's room. "Has Mr. Crocker told you of his condition?"

"Yes. He said that Kiernan's face is cut and swollen and discolored."

"That's the worst of it. The left side of his body and leg were embedded with much debris, and his left arm is broken in two places. He was trying to protect his face, but it did no good. He may lose his left eye—"

"What!" Victoria exclaimed, shaking her head. "Charlie said nothing about that."

"Mr. Crocker most likely didn't know. I've cleaned out the eye, but I have no way of knowing the extent of the damage until the swelling goes down. Right now, his face is bandaged, but if you are to care for him, you will have to see the full extent of his injuries."

Victoria nodded. *Dear God*, she prayed silently, *give me the strength to do what I must. Kiernan needs me now. Please don't let me fail him.*

"Lead me on, Doctor," she said. "I need to be with my husband."

Kiernan lay in a small wood-frame bed. The white sheet was drawn up to just under his chin, leaving Victoria unable to see his wounded arm. His face was swathed in bandages, just as the doctor had told her, and his right eye, the only one visible to her, was closed in sleep.

She went to the bed and reached out to touch Kiernan's right cheek. It was mottled with bruising and cuts, but it wasn't so bad as to require bandaging. "Oh, my sweet Kiernan," she whispered, "what have you done to yourself?"

Two days later, Kiernan regained consciousness. The doctor declared this the best possible sign but still refused to assure Victoria of a full recovery. Kiernan thrashed and moaned. The pain he felt was so severe that the doctor prescribed heavy doses of laudanum. After that, Kiernan drifted in and out of unnatural sleep—sometimes calling out for help—sometimes whispering Victoria's name.

A full two weeks after his accident, the doctor agreed to let Charlie move Kiernan to Sacramento. Victoria felt this would be the best they could do for her husband, knowing that the medical facilities there would surely be better than what Newcastle could offer. Of course, the doctor didn't believe there was much else to be done. Nothing but wait.

Victoria didn't like waiting. Especially when it meant watching her husband waste away. He could barely take anything but soup as nourishment, and the laudanum left him so lost in his own world that Victoria couldn't tell if he was getting any better or not.

Charlie sat beside her on the train. Without a private car for their trip, Charlie quartered off the back portion of the passenger car and arranged a makeshift bed for Kiernan. From time to time Charlie tried to say something reassuring, but Victoria found herself overwhelmed with the sudden worry that now they would have no money coming in. They had very little in savings, for what they could afford to give to his family in Ireland, Kiernan had faithfully instructed her to send.

She couldn't very well share her worries with Charlie. She didn't want him to think she was begging for charity or help that went above and beyond the call of duty. She would simply have to find a way to support them while Kiernan recovered.

Ignoring the passing scenery, Victoria bit at her lower lip as a new thought came to mind. *I could write to Mother. I could just explain the situation and beg them to send me the funds.* But even this thought came with its own problems. They had lied to her parents long ago when the financial crisis of 1857 had stripped her of her fortune. Just prior to that Kiernan had convinced her father to let him control Victoria's money as they moved west to seek additional fortune in California. Her father had agreed, but Kiernan didn't have James Baldwin's knack for investments. And he couldn't have seen the crisis coming that would rob them of most everything they had in the bank.

If I write to them, they'll know we've been lying all these years. They might worry, or even come here, Victoria thought. And while she wouldn't have minded her mother's company, she knew Kiernan would be mortified.

She looked at her sleeping husband and frowned. He wouldn't want her to acknowledge the truth to them. He was a proud man, and if she wrote and asked for money, he would despise it—maybe even come to despise her. He wanted to take care of her himself, and he had promised he would find a way to restore her money.

Oh, God, what am I to do? She prayed and pleaded for answers, but nothing seemed to come clear. They were at God's mercy. God's and the Central Pacific Railroad's.

PART II

June—August
1864

Sixteen

*I*n the weeks that followed their return to Sacramento, Victoria and Kiernan found life to be overwhelming. Victoria had to literally do everything for Kiernan the first week or two, but even as he recovered from his physical wounds, his spirit plummeted and a severe depression set in. If it hadn't been for Li, Victoria would surely have gone mad.

Kiernan suffered from great bouts of pain, sometimes screaming out when the intensity was too much. The doctor hired by the railroad deemed it a normal matter of recuperation, then after dosing Kiernan with medicine, went off to make his other rounds. Victoria hated his seeming indifference. It wasn't long before she begged Mark Hopkins to dismiss the unfeeling man in favor of hiring on Dr. Benson. The only problem with Dr. Benson was that he wasn't a firm believer in the use of laudanum. He thought the medication too habit-forming and feared for Kiernan's mental abilities should he be too long on the drug. Instead, the doctor closely examined Kiernan and, in the wake of doing so, found the wounds of his left arm had festered. For a time he feared he would have to amputate, but after much prayer and round-the-clock attention, Kiernan's health improved.

The comfort Victoria received from her friendship with Li crossed all barriers that could possibly stand between them because of language or culture. Li saw the need in Victoria's life and, with Jia in tow, was often at the apartment from the first moment Victoria woke up until she went to bed that night. Li always seemed to know what to do to offer comfort and hope, and Victoria praised God for having sent this dear woman into her life.

After the crisis with Kiernan's infection, Victoria's routine pretty much set itself, as one day blended into another. She and Li washed bandages and bedding and Kiernan himself before ever attending to anything else. Li took up all of Victoria's mending and many of her household chores, while Victoria worked to knit her husband back together. But it was no easy task. For although Kiernan's body was mending, his heart had hardened. Even Li was surprised by this change in the once gentle man.

Kiernan was surly and outright ugly at times, often refusing to allow the ministrations of his wife or Li. Charlie had come to check Kiernan's condition on several occasions, but Kiernan always remained silent and disinterested. Victoria tried to comfort herself in the fact that hers wasn't the only company Kiernan rejected. She knew it was hard on this once vibrant and well-muscled man to be reduced to a state of bed rest and nursing care. She knew he despised being waited on, but there was nothing else to be done. She could hardly demand that the man get up and come to the table for his meals, not when he could barely remember from one minute to the next what it was that had actually happened to him and why he was injured.

The head wound was taking a long time to heal. Dr. Benson had deemed there was little to be done for Kiernan and that time was the only thing that could help him now. He believed the brain was swollen and, after digging out additional bits of rock and dirt from Kiernan's face, suggested he wear a patch over his wounded eye.

"The light will damage the tissue," he told Victoria as he took his leave that evening. "I will bring you a patch next time I visit. Then we'll remove the rest of the bandages from his face and eye and see exactly what we're dealing with."

"Thank you for coming. I know he's not always easy to work with, but he's just so angry right now."

"Understandably so," Dr. Benson replied. "The recovery will be a long one, and who is to say whether the brain has been permanently affected. We shall hope for the best."

And pray against the worst, Victoria thought as the doctor took his leave. She turned to find Li crocheting, something Victoria had taught her to do. Jia played contentedly at his mother's feet, batting the ball of crochet yarn and laughing at the way it unraveled. Victoria smiled down at the chubby-cheeked boy. His dark-eyed gaze fixed on Victoria for a moment before he got up and toddled over to where she stood. He beamed her a smile, and Victoria couldn't resist picking him up.

Burying her face against his neck, Victoria cherished the feel of the baby in her arms. There was nothing in the world quite so sweet.

"He like you very much," Li said, glancing up. "Maybe more than yarn." She smiled and pointed to the forgotten ball at her feet.

"Well, I think he's the best baby in the world. He comes and plays so quietly. Why, I'll bet Kiernan doesn't even know he's here." Victoria carried him to the rocking chair and sat down to play pat-a-cake with Jia. "Li, you've been so very good to me—and to Kiernan."

Victoria knew she would never have made it through these difficult times without her friend. Surely Xiang was beside himself in her long absences. After all, despite the slowing of business up the line, they were still taking in laundry here in town.

"Li, doesn't your husband resent your time spent here? I mean, what about the washing business and the railroad?"

"Husband gone three week now trying to find more business. He say he go first and find us good place to work. He not know if he find good men or bad. He not want Jia and me to be in bad place."

"Xiang is gone?" Li nodded, then turned her attention back to the shawl she was crocheting. Victoria considered this for a moment. "Are you living in the tent by yourself?" Again Li nodded.

Victoria considered the situation for a moment. "Why don't you come live with me? You and Jia and I can sleep out here in the front room. It's small, but we could help each other that way. You can use the pump downstairs for water and hang the washing on the lines in back of the house. When you need to deliver mending and washing to other people, I could take care of Jia. And when I need to go to the market, you could stay here with Kiernan."

Li nodded. "It would be good."

"Do you know how long Xiang will be gone?"

"Husband no say."

"Well, it's no matter. You can stay here as long as you like. Kiernan won't be able to do much for a while, and in that time maybe you and I can put our heads together and think of a way to bring in some money."

"Put heads together?"

Victoria chuckled at the look on Li's face. "It just means we'll work together." Jia laughed and grabbed hold of Victoria's fingers. Without warning he tried to put them in his mouth. Victoria chuckled and drew the baby's fingers to her own lips. Kissing him playfully, Victoria said, "It'll be nice having a baby in the house."

"There be number two after celebration of Jesus."

Victoria felt as if Li had dealt her a blow. "After Christmas? Another baby?"

Li nodded. "Husband say another son. Plenty strong like number one."

"That's wonderful, Li," Victoria replied, trying to infuse her words with enthusiasm. Victoria ignored the aching in her heart. The longing there for a child was so strong she could hardly speak. She didn't want to make Li feel bad for her happiness, but it was hard to hear this news and not feel overwhelmed.

Deciding it was time to check on Kiernan, Victoria put Jia back down on the floor and went into the kitchen to pour some hot tea for Kiernan to drink.

Tiptoeing into her bedroom, Victoria whispered, "Are you awake?"

"Unfortunately so," came Kiernan's sour reply. He was propped up in the bed, his left arm bound in a sling, the left side of his face bandaged to cover his eye.

"I've brought you some fresh tea."

"I'm not thirsty."

"Kiernan, you know what the doctor said about keeping up your strength. You're supposed to be eating better and drinking plenty of fluids. The tea will make you feel better, you'll see."

"Nothin' will be makin' me feel better except to get back on me feet."

She smiled sympathetically. "That'll come in time, darling." She put the tray down and poured him a cup of tea. Taking it with her to the bed, she sat down beside him, careful not to disturb his body. Smiling at his battered face, she offered the cup. "Won't you please drink this?"

He shook his head ever so slightly. "I told ya, I don't want it. I don't want yarself here, either."

He'd been saying awful things like that ever since the doctor reduced the amount of laudanum Kiernan was to be allowed. Kiernan handled the pain in his own way, which was to counter it with anger. Victoria tried not to let his words affect her. He didn't mean them, of this she was sure. But sometimes they hurt.

"Li's going to stay with us for a while," she went on as if he'd never said anything hurtful at all. "Xiang has gone out on the line to find a suitable place to set up his business and bring his family."

"There are no suitable places for families on the railroad," Kiernan declared bitterly.

Victoria shook her head. "As I recall, Greigsville didn't seem so bad."

Kiernan grimaced. "If yar mother would have kept ya to home in Baltimore, ya'd not be all miserable here with me. Why don't ya leave, Victoria?" He looked at her with grim intensity. "Go on to New York and let yar father care for ya. I don't seem to be able to do the job."

Victoria put the tea on the night table and reached out to touch Kiernan's face. He turned away, but she refused to be discouraged. "You are the man I love and the one I want to spend my life with. Do you know how grateful I am to have you alive and here with me? Can't you see? This will pass. You'll regain your strength, and you'll heal."

"And what are we to be eatin' in the meantime? We have no money."

"We have some," she told him, realizing there wasn't all that much. "I've been helping Li with mending, and since she's coming to stay with me, we might as well take on more laundry, and I can help her with that as well."

"I don't want ya workin' like that," Kiernan protested.

"Well, right now your job is to get well," Victoria ordered with as much force as she dared. "There's nothing that says I shouldn't take on responsibilities for making money while you're laid up. Honestly, Kiernan, you can say what you like, but you aren't going to drive me away." She smiled at his scowl. "Looking like that won't do it either."

"I don't want ya here anymore. Don't ya understand? I want ya to go home where you belong."

Victoria forced herself to remain strong. "I am home, Kiernan. Wherever you are, that's where I belong." She gently stroked his face until he reached up to stop her. He said nothing, but she saw the pain in his expression. Leaning forward, she placed a kiss on his lips. "I love you. Now and forever. For better or worse."

"But it's always worse, never better."

She smiled and shook her head. "You know that's not true. We've had a hard time of it, but it hasn't all been bad. Perhaps we have made mistakes, poor choices, but it doesn't mean we can't hope for better. I've been praying a great deal since your accident, and I firmly believe that God is working to get our attention. There are things we've done and things we've failed to do. Maybe we need to get our house in order, Kiernan."

Still Kiernan said nothing, and Victoria got up to leave. "The tea is right here, well within reach. If you need anything else, just call me." She paused at the door and her heart nearly broke for the sight of him. *Please help him, God. He's so defeated—so wounded, and he's pushed me away so completely.* She tried not to be hurt about it, but it did hurt. She missed her husband and the love they had shared. This stranger in her husband's body was a difficult soul to live with, and she could hardly bear to imagine what she would do if the Kiernan she had loved and married refused to return to her.

Seventeen

$\mathcal{M}$r. Crocker," Victoria said as she happened upon the man coming up her street. She had taken the opportunity of a beautiful summer day to go to the market for what little they could afford.

"Mrs. O'Connor," he said, tipping his hat. "How is our invalid?"

"Better, I think," she said, shifting her empty basket. "I was just on my way to the grocer. Kiernan's starting to eat a little more, so that has to be a good sign."

Charlie nodded. "I know times are hard, Mrs. O'Connor. I've already spoken with Hopkins and Stanford. They agree we need to see this thing through. The CP may be low on funds, but we do not turn our backs on one of our best and finest."

"That's very kind of you to say."

"Well, kind or not," he replied with a grin, "I intend to see you cared for. The Central Pacific can surely do no less."

"I've allowed a friend, a Celestial, to come and stay with me. She and her small son are living with us, and she is helping me with the endless chores. In turn, I'm helping her with her laundry business. It's giving us a little bit of income. Not much, but it's something." She smiled and could see the concern in his eyes. "The worst part is climbing all those stairs," she continued, trying to sound lighthearted, "but the water is plentiful, and Li and I are both young enough to endure the work. You mustn't worry overmuch. I know Kiernan wouldn't want that."

Charlie nodded, then his face lit up and a grin spread from ear to ear. "Say, I have an idea. And it's quite a capital one if I do say so."

Victoria shook her head. "What is it?"

He nodded enthusiastically. "I have a modest property just two blocks away. It's a small house, and in the back is a covered walkway attached to a chicken coop. At least that's what the last owner did with the place. I acquired the property about a month ago in lieu of pay from the Central Pacific. It's mostly on the ground level, and there's a pump right in the kitchen, with another one under the walkway. I was going to advertise to rent the place out, but instead, I think it would be perfect for you and Kiernan, and your little friend too. You could very easily set up a laundry business by converting the chicken coop."

"I couldn't do that," Victoria replied, although the idea sounded wonderful. She could only imagine how much easier their job would be if everything were on one level.

"Nonsense. Consider it part of the railroad's compensation. It will be months, maybe longer before Kiernan will be able to get back to the line."

"Truly?" Victoria's heart sank. "Do you honestly see it taking that long?" Her tone was downcast, for she had tried many times to convince herself that Kiernan would be back on his feet in a matter of weeks.

Charlie smiled sympathetically and took hold of her arm. "Now don't fret, my dear. Come along with me and let me show you the house. You never know, our boy just might surprise the lot of us, and if he does, then I say, 'Three cheers!' But until then, this might well serve as a beneficial solution for both of us."

"But we aren't paying very much in rent where we are," she said, almost embarrassed to discuss financial matters. "I'm sure what we're scraping together now is hardly what you could make from a true renter."

"My dear, the money is hardly the issue. What matters is that we keep Kiernan on the mend and the wolf from the door. Besides, I'll just get the Central Pacific to reimburse me, if and when we ever get our government funding. Ah, here we are now," he said, totally dismissing the subject of money. "What do you think? They tell me it's a Gothic Revival. You can tell because of the steeply pitched gabled roof. And just look at the upstairs window."

Victoria looked to the only window gracing the second floor. It reminded her of a church window with its pointed arch. "I've seen this house when coming to the apothecary." Indeed, she had wondered many times why it sat empty.

"Yes, it's right here in the midst of such workings that everyone will be sure to know of your laundry service," Charlie declared with a sweep of his arm. "You have the apothecary's business to the left. He's a quiet little man who lives above the store with his elderly mother and aunt. Then there's a small furniture store to the right. Both are fairly quiet businesses, and you shouldn't have any trouble with either one. My house used to belong to a doctor and his wife. They kept their bedroom in the upstairs and ran his infirmary out of the downstairs rooms."

She eyed the place with great consideration as they walked around to the rear entrance. The small wood-sided building was narrow in width but long in depth. The back was graced with a canopied walk with long slender posts that went from rock support to the flat roof and attached to another small building about ten feet behind the house.

As if seeing where her gaze had traveled, Charlie said, "We could always close that in to protect you from the elements when passing from one building to the other."

Victoria nodded and allowed Charlie to direct her to the back of the property. "We can go inside, but first look here," he said, quite delighted with himself. "Now just see if this wouldn't make a wonderful place to set up your business."

My business? Victoria thought it sounded quite silly. She was only looking for a way to keep food on the table and see Li and Jia provided for at the same time. She'd never once considered that she herself was truly starting up a business. But once again, Charlie's suggestion had captured her imagination. Why, the chicken coop, as Charlie had called it, was a nice little ten-by-ten-foot building with a pump just outside the door.

Charlie dropped his hold on Victoria's arm and peered into the chicken house. "It'll take some cleaning. The former residents didn't have time to pick up after themselves. They received word that their son had been killed in the war. Their daughter-in-law was left a widow with seven small children. They took the first boat to San Francisco, pausing only long enough to sell their possessions— this house included."

"How awful," Victoria replied. How often had she worried that her mother would write to tell of the death of some loved one in that cursed war. How senseless it seemed, yet from the distance of

California it also seemed quite unreal.

She pushed aside such sad thoughts and smiled. "So the doctor had a liking for chicken, eh?"

Charlie laughed. "He worked extensively with the Chinese and was often paid in goods. At one point he had over one hundred chickens. Sold most of them to the butcher down the way, but he had to have someplace to keep them in the meantime. If you look behind the coop, you'll see a little pen where he kept a pig or two now and then."

She nodded. "It looks wonderful, Mr. Crocker. I just don't know how we could ever convince Kiernan."

"Well, you leave that to me. Come, and we'll make certain that the inside is as fitting to your needs as the outside."

Victoria smiled and allowed the older man to lead the way. She had no doubts the inside would more than meet her expectations. With a sigh of relief, she was beginning to see some light at the end of the same tunnel that had nearly taken her husband's life.

"The Central Pacific can let you have enough fuel to see to your needs, the business included. After all, the railroad took your livelihood; it can just as well help see you cared for in the meantime. I plan to talk to the others, but I'm sure they will have no problem with this. Then, too, we plan to bring over food. The railroad is feeding workers on the line, and there's no reason we can't share a portion of that with you. It won't amount to much, but it should help a little."

"Oh, I don't know what to say," Victoria declared, looking in awe at the front parlor. Why, it was nearly bigger than her entire apartment. There was a wonderfully large stone fireplace against the east wall, and through an arched opening on the west side, she could see a lovely little kitchen. The walls had been papered with a delicate pattern of spring flowers and bold green stripes. It wasn't exactly what she might have chosen, but she wasn't about to protest. Especially given the fact that her present home didn't even have paper on the walls.

Crocker allowed her time to explore, and with each step, Victoria felt her burden grow lighter. God had truly seen her need. They wouldn't be left alone, and she wouldn't have to write to her mother and admit to Kiernan's failings, and they would be given a home fit for a king. She grinned to herself. Maybe not a king, but it suited her just fine.

All in all, there were five good-sized rooms on the first floor. Two were bedrooms, which Crocker told her had once been used for examinations and medical procedures. They were pristine and white with a thick coating of paint on the walls. Victoria easily saw their use as bedrooms. A third room was on the back side and led out to the walkway. It had apparently been used for storage and contained built-in shelves from floor to ceiling. In front of this was the kitchen, with a huge black stove that contained not two burners but four and an oven large enough for her to roast a tom turkey in. If she'd had one.

Upstairs was a large open room with slanted ceilings to match the pitch of the roof. Victoria went to the large arched window and gazed out on the street. Instantly she knew that if they were to move here, she would want this room for their bedroom. Of course, with Kiernan unable to climb stairs, she would probably have to see to him on the first floor. But eventually they could share this room. She felt a silly anticipation at the thought of creating rag rugs for the wood floors and curtains for the windows.

She returned to the first floor and went once again to the kitchen. There Charlie was testing the pump.

"So what do you say?" he inquired as she made one more inspection of the kitchen cupboards.

"It's rather like dying and going to heaven," she breathed, turning to beam him a smile. "If you can talk that cantankerous husband of mine into it, then I would be most gratified to take you up on the offer."

"Consider it a done deal," Charlie replied. "Kiernan will listen to reason—if not, then I'll simply tell him he's not up to fighting the matter." He grinned. "I'm glad I could help. You don't know how I've fretted for both of you."

Victoria lifted her gaze to gratefully meet his eyes. "Your kindness won't be forgotten, Charles Crocker."

———

That afternoon, Victoria stood inside the little chicken coop with Li and Jia at her side. Charlie had dismissed them both while he discussed the matter of the move with Kiernan. Victoria was secretly glad that she didn't have to be in on the announcement. Kiernan would fight against it; she knew that as well as she knew her own name. But she also knew Charlie Crocker was a determined man. He would make her husband see the sense in the matter.

"We do good work here," Li declared. "This plenty good."

"I thought so too," Victoria replied. "I figured we could get some spare lumber and build a counter. Maybe Mr. Crocker could help us." She hated to impose further on Charlie's good nature, but they would need to do certain things if the laundry business was to run efficiently.

"I get cleaned up," Li told Victoria. "This no problem. Jia and I stay right here."

"No, Li, you can have one of the bedrooms in the house. This will strictly be for doing the laundry."

"I have room in house?" Li's eyes grew wide with wonder.

"Absolutely. I only brought you here to see what you thought of the building. I wanted to make sure you thought it would work for the laundry business."

"Oh sure. It work plenty fine. This nice room. I clean up now." She began to gather up pieces of crates and started to hum as she worked.

Victoria smiled at Li's confidence. Leaving Li to consider the coop, Victoria wandered back to the main house and eyed it critically. There was a great deal she could do to make this place into a home. Curtains at the windows, maybe a few pictures on the walls. If Kiernan started to feel better, maybe he could even make them some more furniture. The potential was limitless.

The bedrooms sat just off the back of the parlor. The first was the smallest and would make the perfect place to position Kiernan. It had a window that looked out on the furniture store. It would give him a chance to see what was going on there and maybe even encourage his healing. He loved working with his hands, and maybe if he saw other creations, he would be encouraged to get busy with his own.

The second bedroom was larger and would work nicely for Li and Jia. Later, after Li left to join Xiang, it would make a nice guest room or sewing room. Of course, once Kiernan healed, Crocker might well want them to move on. Victoria frowned at the thought. I'd best not get too attached to this place, she thought. There was just no telling how long they would be able to enjoy the well-kept little house. But it was a pleasant gift and a blessing that she credited God with having provided. Temporary or not, she intended to enjoy the place for as long as she could.

After opening all the windows in order to air the place out, Victoria went back into the kitchen and nearly clapped her hands at the idea of having so much space to work. She would be able to have company sitting in the front room while the work of the kitchen went on out of their sight. But there was room for a table and chairs in the kitchen for more informal gatherings.

Shaking her head, she laughed out loud. "And who were you expecting to have as company?" Her father and mother came to mind, and this naturally led her to thoughts of Brenton, Jordana, and Caitlan. Only then did it dawn on her that she'd not even written to Kiernan's sister in regard to the accident. Caitlan should know what had happened. In fact, it might be the one thing to hasten her to California.

She had often wondered what Kiernan's sister might be like. Would she look like her brother? Would she be kind and gentle, or rambunctious and wild? The very thought of having Caitlan come to live with them filled her with both apprehension and joy. What if they didn't get along? What if Caitlan resented Victoria's relationship with Kiernan? On the other hand, if she cared so much about having a place in her brother's life, then why was she taking so long to get here?

Regardless of the answer to those questions, there would easily be enough room for Caitlan here. Why, even if Li remained with them for a while, Kiernan would heal, and then Caitlan could take his bedroom downstairs. If Jordana and Brenton came with her, as was the plan, then Victoria could just shuffle everyone around in whatever manner necessary. Jordana and Caitlan could share a room, as she knew they already did in Omaha. Brenton could always sleep in the front room. She smiled, working out all the details in her mind. She could very nearly see them sitting down to a meal together, happy, content, blessed. *Oh, God, let it be so*, she prayed, hugging her arms to her body. *Please let it be so.*

143

Eighteen

$\mathscr{K}$iernan stared out the window of his new bedroom. The rope bed had been donated by one of his friends, and in spite of the feather mattress, he found it impossible to get comfortable. Everything hurt and felt swollen or bruised. How could it be that he should still feel so bad after so much time had passed? He tried not to show his discomfort, hoping to keep Victoria from worrying more than she already was, but it was hard. All he wanted was to be healed and back on his feet, and instead, he was living in a borrowed bed.

Of course, most of the furnishings in the house had been donated. Charlie had put the word out to their mutual friends with the railroad, and the donations had rolled in. In fact, the house itself was Charlie's donation, given as a means of support by the Central Pacific. Charlie wouldn't even consider the discussion of rent, and that only made Kiernan feel worse. He had become what he had once feared the most—a charity case.

His wife had to bathe him and help him with meals. She had to work with Li to raise enough money to put food on the table. Charlie and the other Central Pacific board members were doing what they could to see to the other comforts of life.

It would have been better had I simply died, Kiernan lamented, using his good right hand to pound the mattress.

Such thoughts only served to make his head hurt, but in truth, the pain was always with him. Sometimes the pressure was so intense that he worried it would actually rupture something. He didn't tell Victoria. He couldn't cause her further worry. Besides, she was happy with the new house, and as mean-spirited and ill-tempered as he'd been, he couldn't take that away from her.

It was a lovely house, Kiernan had to admit. He would have loved to have furnished Victoria with something this nice all on his own, but that was nothing more than a dream. Scowling, he turned away from the window and reached under the black eye patch to rub his sore eye. It had been nearly a month since the accident, and still his sight had not returned in full. The eye was extremely sensitive to light, and his left arm was still useless. His body hurt, and his mind refused to keep a steady memory of thoughts. He could remember working on the railroad and all the details of his job, but he couldn't remember the accident. Nor could he always remember the weeks just after the accident. Of course, the first two weeks, he'd barely been conscious at all. The doctor had kept him so sedated that he only knew what others told him. And often he forgot about that.

In the last week or so, he had no such excuse. He had been insufferable to live with, and Victoria had borne it all admirably. She never complained or looked hurt when he made harsh, ugly comments. She never even got mad when he demanded she leave California and go home to her parents. This made his recovery even harder. He longed to get up from the bed, to comfort her and promise that everything would be good for them, but he couldn't. He'd lost all hope that it could ever be that way. In fact, he'd decided that if he should manage to fully recover, he would resign from the Central Pacific and take her back east himself. Of course, there was a war going on back there, and that might not allow for the pleasant life of comfort she'd known as a girl, but it would have to be better than what she had known here in California.

A light knocking sounded at his door, and before he could answer, Charlie Crocker opened the door and grinned at him. "Say, you're looking a whole lot better."

Kiernan sighed. He couldn't very well growl at the man to get out. After all, he owned the place. "Good day to ya, Charlie."

Crocker pulled up a chair and tossed his hat to the end of the bed. "So how are you feeling?"

"I've been better," Kiernan replied.

"Oh, that's to be certain," Charlie said with a chuckle. "But you'll recover soon."

"I wouldn't be expectin' so much, Charlie," Kiernan replied with a heavy sigh. "Me body and mind tend to disagree as to who's in charge."

"Well, the doctor seems very positive, and your little wife is quite elated."

" 'Tis the house and not me recovery that has Victoria elated."

"I seriously doubt that," Crocker insisted. "She told me just this morning that you were seeing shadows out of your left eye. That has to be good news."

"Well, I suppose 'tis all how ya look at it. I used to see just fine out of the eye, so shadows now seem bad. Yet a week ago I had no sight whatsoever out of it, so I'm figurin' that to be progress."

"I am as well," Charlie said.

Kiernan frowned. "I'm still not takin' kindly to charity, Charlie. Ya should at least be lettin' me pay ya the same amount of rent as on the other place."

"Nonsense. You're a valuable asset to the Central Pacific, and I want to make sure you come back to us when you are well," Charlie said, artfully changing the subject. "I don't know what we're going to do without you, Kiernan. There aren't enough skilled laborers to keep the line going. We manage to scrounge up a few hundred here and there, and by the time the first payday rolls round, they're gone—back to the hills where their dreams of gold keep calling them. We need to figure out how to keep them on the line."

"I'm sorry, Charlie. I wish I knew what to tell ya." Kiernan looked at his friend, focusing his one good eye on Charlie's intent gaze. "It still doesn't change the fact that ya've placed me on charity."

"I consider it more an act of Christian generosity. On your part, as much as mine. That little Chinese friend of your wife's has no husband to take care of her. Her man's gone off to the railroad camps, and who knows when or if he'll ever return? Your missus tells me that the baby is soon to have a brother or sister. You can't very well be turning them out in the streets, now can you?"

Kiernan shook his head. "I wouldn't suggest that."

"Good. Then you see why it's important to live here. The woman and her child are cared for, as well as the fact that she can keep her laundry business going. Why, even your wife seemed quite excited about the possibilities, and I've already drummed up quite a bit of business for them once they actually get everything up and running."

"I don't like me wife workin' like that," Kiernan replied, feeling his anger creep up on him. "It's me job to be seein' after her needs.

And how can I do that now? I'm tellin' ya, Charlie, I'm nothin' but a blind fool."

"You're only as blind as you want to be, Kiernan," Charlie admonished him in a sterner tone than he had yet used. He got to his feet and took up his hat. "But to my way of thinking, sitting around here feeling sorry for yourself is twice as hard on your wife as having to work at washing clothes."

He didn't wait for Kiernan's response, and it was a good thing. Kiernan sat staring at the door for several minutes after Charlie had gone. How could he go saying something like that? It was hardly fair. Kiernan hadn't asked to be injured.

The afternoon wore on, and with the heat of the day, Kiernan drifted off into a fitful sleep. He found himself back in Baltimore living in the extraordinary opulence he had known after marrying Victoria. They dined every night at seven, and always they wore their very best clothes and entertained other people who wore their very best. James and Carolina Baldwin, Victoria's parents, were well-known and quite respected in the city. People vied for positions at their table—each outdoing the other in order to be able to sit at the right hand of his father-in-law. Kiernan thought it all rather funny. The only time his people had ever fought over a place at the table was in order to be seated closer to the food.

He awoke from the aroma of succulent roast lamb and mint jelly, to the smells of side pork frying. The dream left him feeling more defeated than he'd felt before. It tortured him to remember Victoria pampered and spoiled in her silks and satins, her skin so soft and cared for, her thick black hair piled high on her head and adorned with ribbons and pearls. How could he have taken her from that life? How could he have given her this world in good conscience?

It wasn't fair. He'd tried to be a good man. He'd tried to be a good Christian. Why should his world fall apart when other men, men who cared little or nothing for God, thrived in their evil ways? And it wasn't just small, isolated incidents. He'd seen it over and over again. Con men who swindled and gambled and robbed the innocent of their funds. Despicable characters like Christopher Thorndike who'd tried to entice Victoria to leave her marriage. Word had it that Thorndike made his fortune on the backs of the Chinese. Robbing them blind of their artifacts and possessions, giving them little more than a pittance of their worth. Not to mention that Thorndike's name was very closely associated with the opium dens and

Chinese houses of prostitution—though such a tie was never proven. Yet Thorndike lived in a beautiful mansion and dressed and ate like a king. Where was God's righteousness in that?

Sometimes Kiernan wondered if earthly life wasn't of little concern to God. Of course God would concern himself over His people, but did He truly bother to get in on the little details of the day? Did God really care whether Kiernan O'Connor wore silk waistcoats and dined on poached salmon? After all, if he believed that good came from God's hand, was he not obligated to believe that bad was also passed on that way?

But Kiernan remembered a sermon from not so very long ago. The pastor had spoken of God's desire that all come willingly to the cross. That salvation was a free gift to those who desired it, but it wasn't a gift that had come without cost to the giver.

"We must remember," the man had preached, "that Christ paid with His life for that which costs us nothing. Why do you then raise protests when troubled times come into your life? If God allowed His own Son—a part of himself—to suffer and labor a death that we can only imagine with dread, why do you find it surprising that you too must suffer? Jesus told us there would be trouble—read the Word—it's all there."

Kiernan had read as much of the Bible as his limited skills allowed. It was there. Stories of good men who were persecuted by evil men. Accounts of trials and tribulations that God ultimately had victory over. He thought of Job and the way the devil had heaped trial after trial upon him, and all with God's knowledge. How was that right? Was God not supposed to keep evil from His children? It was almost as if God waited on pins and needles to see if Job would curse Him and die. Yet He had to have known what Job's choice would be. God told Satan that Job was a perfect and upright man, one who feared Him and eschewed evil. And while Kiernan would never pretend that he was perfect and upright, he did fear the Lord and refrained from evil.

Then a thought came to mind—a thought he'd continued to bury since leaving Maryland with Victoria. He wasn't all that good about refraining from evil. He'd forced his wife to live a lie in order to save his pride. He'd kept Victoria from telling her parents that he'd lost her money, and the lie ate at him like nothing he had ever known. The only way he avoided dealing with it was to press it down deep into the darkest recesses of his mind.

His da had once told him, "A man is only as good as his word. If yar known for yar lies, then no man will respect ya."

Kiernan shook his head and closed his eye. He was running from the truth, hiding out a continent away so that he wouldn't lose face with Victoria's parents, yet he'd already lost self-respect. His thoughts tried to go to prayer, but he felt such an overwhelming shame that he avoided even speaking the words.

A verse from the Psalms came to mind. "Search me, O God, and know my heart: try me, and know my thoughts . . ." Oh, it was certain God knew his thoughts. Thoughts of misery and pity and guilt for his actions. ". . . And see if there be any wicked way in me . . ." But could Kiernan really bear the truth? Could he look down deep in his own heart and let God show him the ugly, hidden places? ". . . and lead me in the way everlasting."

Kiernan felt a lump form in his throat. "I'm not worth the effort," he whispered. "I've lied, and in my hardened heart I've been unmerciful to me wife. I've been spiteful and angry, demanding and heartless. Why would yarself be wastin' effort on me?" he questioned God.

"Kiernan?" It was Victoria. Her sweet voice called to him from the opposite side of the door. Timidly she opened it and questioned again. "Kiernan?"

"Aye."

"I heard your voice. Did you call for me?"

He shook his head, not yet ready to confess his dealings with God.

Smiling at him, she came to sit beside him. "I've been thinking about something, and I wondered what you wanted me to do."

He looked at her, frowning at the sight of her. She appeared so tired, and it was all his fault. He'd caused her no end of grief. "What's troublin' yar mind?" He kept his voice low and gentle.

"I suddenly realized the other day that I'd not written to Caitlan to tell her of your accident. I suppose I was just so caught up in what was going on. I'd like to write to her now and let her know of your condition."

Kiernan thought on this for a moment. "I don't want to be worryin' her. I've been doin' little but causin' folk grief." He felt a strange sensation wash over him, but ignoring it, he continued. "The doctor isn't certain of my . . ." His voice trailed off as his thoughts blurred into incoherence. What was happening to him?

He swallowed hard, but even that came by sheer determination.

"Kiernan?" Her voice was calm. Apparently she didn't realize he was struggling.

With all his strength, he looked at her and said, "Write her a letter and tell her I release her from any pledge to come to me."

"But I don't understand. I thought you wanted her here."

"I do," Kiernan said, feeling as though his tongue had suddenly grown too large for his mouth. He began to twitch and then shake all over.

Now Victoria could see there was a problem. "Kiernan!" It was the last word he heard before fading into a world of shadows and endless noise.

———

"A convulsion," the doctor told Victoria calmly. "We see this sometimes in patients who suffer head injuries. It could mean that there's a clot on the brain, or perhaps that the brain is merely trying to right itself, or that your husband overtaxed himself. We really know very little about these sorts of things."

Victoria forced her attention on the doctor rather than her now sleeping husband. When she'd seen Kiernan begin to jerk and twist, his one good eye rolled up in his head, she knew something was dreadfully wrong. She'd screamed for Li and sent her to get the doctor, but then there had been nothing to do but pray.

"Next time it happens—" the doctor began.

"Next time!" Victoria barely stifled a scream. "What do you mean, next time!"

Dr. Benson gently patted her arm. "It's highly possible that until he completely recovers from his injuries, this kind of thing will happen again and again." He looked at her intently. "I'm sorry to say this, but it's also quite possible he might not recover at all. I've seen it before in cases of brain injury and swelling. You can never be sure."

"But he's been doing so well," Victoria said in a strangled tone. "It's been almost a month since the accident."

"Yes, yes, I know. We must have faith that he will survive, but I don't want to get your hopes up only to have them dashed. I said nothing as long as he wasn't suffering from convulsions. But brain seizures are not a good sign in general. We'll simply have to watch and wait."

Victoria bit her lower lip to keep from crying. She wanted to demand that the doctor make things right. She wanted to insist that he knit Kiernan back together and ease her worry. But of course, he could do nothing. He was just a man.

"I've given him something to help him sleep, but should he suffer another episode, send for me straight-away. Oh, and don't forget to put something in his mouth to keep him from swallowing his tongue. More die from this than from the seizure itself."

"Should we stay with him around the clock?" she asked, knowing that she had no intention of leaving her husband's side.

Dr. Benson nodded. "It would probably be a good idea. At least for a couple of days."

Victoria nodded. "Then that's what we'll do. He'll never be alone, I promise you." She looked to where Kiernan lay sleeping and thought of the hideous scene she'd witnessed not even an hour ago. In those horrible moments, her beloved Kiernan had changed from the man she loved to become some sort of creature—writhing and twisting, foaming at the mouth. It was unlike anything she had ever seen, or ever wanted to see again. She had thought the worst was behind them. She had thought he would recover and be well again, and now the doctor was telling her he might even die.

Waiting until Dr. Benson had gone, Victoria sank into the bedside chair and buried her face in her hands. "I simply cannot bear this, Father," she prayed in a hushed whisper between sobs. "I cannot do this alone."

Nineteen

*A*ugust on the plains of Nebraska had heated up in more ways than one. The questionable threat of Indian attacks had rapidly become a reality. In the Platte River area in the western part of the state, rumors held that massacres of white settlers had become a routine event. Territorial citizens began streaming into Omaha for safety, bringing with them their money and other valuables—spreading fear and terror among the occupants of the city, who were afraid they could be the next ones to come under attack.

The threat seemed only marginal, however, until a band of terrified homesteaders appeared in Omaha in the middle of one of the hottest nights of the summer. Without knowing what had happened, Jordana and Brenton showed up at the bank the next morning, only to be told that all business had been suspended for the day.

"There's to be a town meeting at the courthouse," Hezekiah Chittenden told them. "Two o'clock this afternoon, we'll decide what's to be done."

"What's happened?" Jordana asked innocently.

"Indians raided the west bank of the Elkhorn River not far from here. The settlers living there barely escaped with their lives," Hezekiah replied. "They came into town with little more than the clothes on their backs."

"Indians so close?"

"There's been trouble afoot for months, even years. It seems to be heating up, what with survey teams and settlers disturbing the Indians' hunting grounds. I don't know a great deal about it, but I suppose we'll learn at the meeting. Governor Saunders promises there will be action."

"What kind of action?" Jordana asked.

"I couldn't say, but I would imagine it will solidify the governor's desire to form up an army."

Brenton looked away at the mention of this. "Do you suppose it's come to that?" he muttered.

Jordana looked at her employer. "Yes, do you really suppose we need more than the soldiers who are already here? I don't see that we should worry so much that—"

"People are dead, Miss Baldwin," Hezekiah said in an anxious tone that left Jordana little doubt as to his fears. "More will surely die."

"Come on, Jordana. We'll attend the meeting this afternoon with everyone else. Maybe then we'll know what's to be done." Brenton took hold of her arm and moved her off down the street toward home.

"What do you mean by that?" Jordana asked. Her anger at Brenton's bossiness had abated somewhat, but things hadn't been the same between them since Caitlan had moved out.

"I mean, if there's to be a militia raised, if they make it a matter of requirement, then we'll have to move on."

"Because of the promise you made Cousin Nate?"

Brenton eyed her seriously for a moment, then glanced to make certain the street was clear before tugging her along with him. "It's more than that, and you know it. I promised I'd not bear arms against the South." Jordana and Caitlan were among the few he'd actually confessed his situation to. He'd had little choice but to sign the agreement. If he hadn't done so, even their cousin would not have been able to keep Brenton from being imprisoned as a spy, or worse, hanged.

"But this isn't against the South," Jordana protested. "Not that I care to see you in any militia."

"There are those who would argue that point," Brenton replied.

He glanced upward as they passed George Train's latest creation of boredom, the Cozzen's House Hotel. Train was a prominent shipping and railroad magnate who couldn't abide the lack of progress on the Union Pacific. He also had a great disdain for the hotels in Omaha and deemed it necessary to build his own.

Jordana followed her brother's gaze. "Old crazy Train, huh?" She knew everything that was said about the man. He was often in the bank for meetings with Hezekiah. Part of this was due to railroad business, but most of it was due to his pledge to create a chain of towns all along the Union Pacific. They were to be thriving metropolises to rival New York and Boston. He had pledged a great deal of his own money, buying up five thousand lots in Omaha alone. Not to mention building the forty thousand dollar Cozzen's House at a time when many folks were suffering financially because of the war.

Jordana knew Train was considered a bit of an extremist. Many thought him to be quite mad, in fact, and avoided dealing with him, in spite of his wealth and success in business. One could never be sure just where old Train would head off to next, Hezekiah had told her.

"This town is changing more rapidly than anything I've ever known," Brenton finally replied. He drew a deep breath and continued their pace. "Change is inevitable."

"I suppose you mean that for us as well as for Omaha," Jordana replied, not really hoping to bait him but rather to hear how he might clarify his statement.

He nodded. "I think it's quite possible. Still, I can't join the Union army."

"You've mentioned that twice, but as I said, this militia will fight Indians, not the Confederacy."

Brenton shook his head. "I've had it on good authority that many of these so-called Indian attacks are very possibly southern rebels under the guise of natives."

"Oh, really?"

"Yes. Several citizens claim to have seen Confederate guerrillas on the banks of the Missouri just south of town. They say there are caves down there and plenty of places to hide. Some believe an entire armed force is being put together for a raid against Omaha. Some say that the attacks along the Platte have been aided by southern influence."

"I suppose anything is possible." Jordana didn't want Brenton in the army, for his own safety, but she also had a selfish motive. Should he join, he would most certainly send her back to their parents. He might think of her as a child and hover over her annoyingly, but though she'd never admit it to him, this situation was better than the far greater confinement she'd find in her parents' home and in the more civilized New York or Baltimore. She needed to remain independent, to prove that she could take care of herself.

That afternoon Jordana sat quietly beside Brenton in the town grange hall. She had changed from her prim-and-proper blue serge suit to a more casual afternoon gown of goldenrod calico. Caitlan had helped her make the gown, and usually Jordana only wore it for special occasions and church. Jordana figured this was as special as any. After all, it wasn't every day that you sat as audience to the governor of the territory.

"These are troubled times, my fellow citizens," the governor began. "Troubled times indeed. Bloody battles rage to the east of us, tearing this country in two. The war divides loyalties and assets, families and friends, and threatens to engulf every single person on this great soil before its hatred is spent." There were several calls of agreement from the audience before the governor could continue.

"We are witnessing the possible demise of our own future. The Civil War continues to the east, while Indian wars intensify to the west and north. We came to this great frontier knowing there would be a risk—praying we might live in peace, but that is not to be had. Not without a price.

"Just last evening a group of settlers, fleeing for their lives, found refuge here in Omaha. They were attacked by a band of Indians not more than fifteen miles to our west. For all we know, Omaha is next."

The excitement in the crowd intensified. Jordana noted Damon Chittenden several rows ahead of her. She had worked to avoid being alone with him at the bank, but sometimes that had been impossible. He continued to apologize for his behavior during their carriage ride, but there was no longer any appeal for her in his boyish charm and good looks. Instead, a subtle fear had replaced whatever kind thought Jordana might have held for him—fear that he might well impose his will on her, as he had so chillingly declared he'd impose it upon poor Homer Stanley.

Jordana tried to listen to the governor's ramblings. She wondered how much truth there was in the accounts of the attack. All of the settlers in question had escaped unharmed and were praised as they sat in the front row of the meeting hall as the finest examples of the true pioneer spirit. The First Nebraska Cavalry had ridden out at dawn with instructions to reclaim the settlements on the banks of the Elkhorn, but it would be hours before anyone would have the slightest clue as to what was happening out there.

"Therefore," the governor continued, "I am calling for all ablebodied men between the ages of eighteen and forty-five to take up arms immediately and form a militia for the protection of our great town and its people. This militia will drill every Saturday to ensure readiness. We hope this, coupled with our cavalry, will cause the heathen marauders to think twice about attacking.

"We will secure our town from outside attack, making certain that our citizens are safe. You can help by staying close to the protection of our soldiers. If we stand together in strength, we will see the defeat of our enemies. Furthermore, we will see our men put into the fields and form a cooperative with our territory's great forts. We will not be driven from the land as cowards, but rather will fight to the last drop of blood!"

Thunderous applause brought the crowd to its feet. The men of Omaha were ready to meet the demands set upon them. At least, all of them were ready save one. Jordana felt sorry for Brenton. He rose to keep from appearing out of order with the crowd, but he could not bring himself to applaud this announcement.

Nervously, she readjusted the ties on her bonnet and waited for the crowd to disburse. Brenton seemed eager to return home, and Jordana couldn't blame him. There were decisions to be made, and no doubt her own life would be forever changed because of them.

"Mr. Baldwin, Miss Baldwin," Damon Chittenden said, coming to them through the crowd. "What say you of this news? Is it not exciting?"

Jordana stiffened against her brother, hoping that Brenton wouldn't make too much of her reaction. Brenton nodded rather hesitantly.

"I suppose one could say it is that," he replied.

"We won't have to worry about the threat of Indians now." Damon seemed practically lighthearted.

Jordana swallowed a sarcastic retort and instead allowed Brenton to speak. "I suppose we must be ever concerned," Brenton said thoughtfully, "yet I hardly see the necessity of forced service."

Damon nodded. "I know exactly what you're saying, Baldwin. Decent men need not be forced to support their property and loved ones."

Jordana had no desire to see Brenton drawn into the conversation any deeper. She might hold a grudge for his attitude toward her independence, but she'd not force him to endure the likes of Damon Chittenden.

"Brenton, I have a fearsome headache. Do you suppose we could retire to home?"

Brenton looked at her with grave concern. "Of course." He turned to Chittenden. "Please excuse us. It seems my sister has taken ill."

Chittenden eyed her with obvious interest, but Jordana lowered her gaze quickly and clung to Brenton's arm. She knew she could hold her own with Damon, but her mind was overwhelmed with sudden thoughts of his scheming. She now knew him to be ruthless, not merely driven or motivated by success.

———

As the week drew to an end and the dreaded Saturday militia practice loomed over them, Jordana sought to comfort her brother.

"Simply refuse to show up," she suggested. "This town has grown enough that it should take a fair piece of time until someone notices that you aren't there. I mean, there's absolute madness out there. People are coming into town in record numbers, many from the surrounding areas. No one would even notice that you weren't there."

"There will no doubt be some sort of register or count. Besides, what about Matt and Ann, next door? Matt's going to realize I'm not there."

"You could always level with them. He seems like a sensible man. Besides," she shrugged, "we're only here temporarily. Just don't go to the practice, and if anyone questions you, tell them you plan to leave with the survey team on the Union Pacific."

"I can't just avoid it forever," Brenton replied. "I think the only solution is to leave town for good and give up on this idea of working with the UP."

"But I'm not ready to go," Jordana declared.

"I don't see any other way."

"What of Caitlan?" It was a bit heartless of her to pull this trump card, but it was a valid concern.

Brenton frowned and got up from the table. Their early supper had held little interest to either of them. Brenton stewed and fretted over his decision, and Jordana deliberated over hers. Food could hardly compensate for their worries.

"We need to talk to her," Brenton finally stated. "We need to press this issue home and help her to realize that the situation needs to be resolved." He turned and looked at her with such longing in his eyes that Jordana could sense his desperation. "It will have to be you. You'll have to go talk to her. She won't listen to me."

"Nonsense. She adores you."

"No, not anymore. I'm the reason she left," Brenton said miserably. "I'm sure she would find it unpleasant to speak to me on the matter, but if you were to go . . ." He left the rest unsaid, and Jordana sighed in frustration.

"Why don't you just tell her how you feel?"

He looked at her surprised. "I did. That's why she left."

Jordana shook her head. "She left because you spoke dishonorably about her family. You held yourself up as a better caretaker of your loved ones than Kiernan has been of her."

"That's not why she left, Jordana," Brenton replied stiffly.

"No? Then suppose you explain."

He shook his head. "It's over, and that's enough said. What I need now is for you to go tell her of the situation."

A knock sounded on the front door, and Jordana waited to comment until Brenton could go see who it was. Damon Chittenden stood on the other side, looking quite pleased with himself, his flat-crowned hat in one hand, a thick envelope in the other. He was dressed smartly, as usual, in a suit of tan broadcloth. The outfit had been tailored exactly to his medium height and weight, and the black satin-striped silk waistcoat gave an expensive finish to the ensemble.

"Good evening," he said, giving Brenton the slightest bow. "I chanced upon the postman. He had this for you, so I promised to deliver it, since I was coming here anyway."

Brenton took the envelope and motioned Chittenden inside. "That was good of you. What else brings you here tonight?"

"Ah, right to the point, Brenton? Good, let's dispense with the niceties and get right down to business. I suppose that's just as well." He grinned at Jordana, leaving her feeling slightly ill. Her day at the bank had been acceptable only because Damon had been off on business in Council Bluffs. It was just her luck that he would return and deem it necessary to spoil her evening.

"What business is that?" Brenton asked, with a cursory glance at the envelope.

"I'd like to ask for permission to escort your sister to dinner," he replied.

"Well, as you can see for yourself, Chittenden, we've just eaten."

Damon's expression became downcast. He eyed the table as if to confirm Brenton's words, then nodded. "I see."

Jordana took that moment to get to her feet. She began clearing the table, ignoring Damon as she went to work. She murmured a silent prayer of thanks that she and Brenton had decided on such an early meal.

"Then perhaps I might make an even bolder request," Damon continued. "It has long been my intention to speak to you on a much more serious matter."

Jordana felt the nerves in her neck tingle. She turned very slowly to see Brenton eye Damon silently before speaking.

"What serious matter is there between us?"

Damon cleared his throat nervously and smiled. "I'd like to ask for your sister's hand in marriage."

Jordana heard the dish crash to the floor and shatter before she ever realized she had dropped it. How could he just come into her home and make such a nonsensical statement? Marriage indeed!

"I'm afraid, Mr. Chittenden, I am not the right one to speak to on that matter."

Jordana felt a bit of renewed admiration for Brenton. Apparently he respected her feelings after all. But with his next statement, he put her back to brooding.

"Our father is the only one who could issue that kind of permission, and he's in New York City."

"Our father has little to say on the matter either!" Jordana exclaimed. Grabbing up her skirts, she made a great show of stepping over the broken pieces of the dish. "I have told you before, Mr. Chittenden. I'm not of a mind to marry anyone at this time and place. Now, please be so good as to leave our home." Because subtlety hadn't worked, she hoped downright rudeness would finally discourage this man.

Damon's sorrowful expression didn't fool Jordana for one minute. She now knew him to be a master of emotional performance. She put her hands on her hips and narrowed her eyes with challenge.

"But I was hoping—"

"It might be best if you discussed this another time," Brenton quickly interjected with a wilting glance at his sister. He stepped forward to open the door. "Thank you for bringing the post."

Chittenden appeared to consider the situation for a moment before nodding somberly and heading for the door. "Very well. Another time, then."

Jordana waited until he was gone before bending down to pick up the broken crockery. "The nerve of that man! How dare he come here like that and suggest such a thing. And you, standing there all pretty as you please, telling him he needs to talk to our father."

"Well, our father isn't here, now, is he?" Brenton replied, sitting back down at the table to open the envelope.

"What does that have to do with it? You humiliated me."

"I figured that was the best way to handle the man. He could hardly fault us for suggesting such a thing, and it would clearly bring his plans to a grinding halt. But you had to go and open your mouth in protest."

Jordana threw the dish into the trash bin and turned to retrieve the rest of the things from the table. She hadn't considered that it was this and not Brenton's possessive nature that had caused his response. Reluctantly, she had to admit it was an inspired ploy.

"I suppose that makes sense. I'm sorry," she stated briskly. It wasn't that she didn't feel sorry for having jumped to the wrong conclusion, but it irritated her that Brenton's defense should have been so readily acceptable. No one questioned that a woman's father should be the one to oversee her courtship. With a great exhale of breath, Jordana counted herself fortunate that her father was of the mind to have his children marry for love. It also helped to have a progressively minded mother.

She finished with the dishes, not giving Brenton's silence much thought until he spoke to her in a gentle tone she'd not heard in weeks.

"Jordana, come sit with me."

She turned and went to the table hesitantly. "What's the matter?" She looked down at the letter in his hand. Another smaller envelope lay beside the bigger one. "Is it Mother?"

"No," he said softly. "The letter is from Billy Vanderbilt."

"Oh," she said, breathing a sigh of relief. "You frightened me." She had barely taken her seat when the realization began to dawn on her. "G.W.?"

Brenton nodded. "I'm afraid he passed away early in the year. I'm sorry." He reached out and handed her the letter, his large, warm hand closing over hers. "Billy was devastated and apologizes for taking so long to notify us."

Jordana didn't want to look at the letter. She had long lived with the hope that G.W. would heal from his illness. After all, the Vanderbilts had money to spare and had taken him off to the best spa in Europe. The finest physicians in the world were available to see to his needs twenty-four hours a day. How then could he be dead?

She blinked back unbidden tears and looked down at the letter. Her gaze immediately caught the word "dead" and then further down saw her name mentioned.

" 'G.W. bid me to pass along this letter to Jordana,' " she read. " 'Her generosity of spirit and loving nature were present with him, even to the end.' "

"Oh, Brenton!" She brought a trembling hand to her mouth. "He can't be gone. He just can't be."

Brenton reached down for the smaller envelope. "This one is marked for you. There are some other business papers here, so if you want to read this in private, I'll understand."

She nodded and got up from the table. Lighting a second lamp, Jordana took the letter and lamp and retired to her bedroom. She trembled as she placed the lamp on her night table. G.W. was dead. Gone was the laughing young man she had cherished during her days in New York. Her friend was dead.

Slumping onto the bed she tore open the envelope. The writing was hardly the bold and stylistic script of the once vibrant powerhouse of a man. Instead it was a spidery scrawl that belonged to that of a weakened invalid.

Dearest Jordana,

My illness must take me away from you, but I cannot go without dissolving this wall between us. I know I was the one to place this barrier. I built it brick by brick as I brooded over your refusal to marry me. I know now, seeing my own death before me, that you made a wise and fortuitous choice. Perhaps even ordained of God, for how could I leave a grieving widow in her prime? I go to my grave loving you, Jordana Baldwin. I will have that to carry me forward—to still my heart as I meet my Maker. Remember me fondly.

Ever your devoted servant,
G. W. Vanderbilt

Warm tears coursed down her cheeks and dripped onto the single sheet of G.W.'s letter. He had forgiven her refusal of marriage. He had gone to his grave loving her, not hating her for her rejection of him.

Tucking the letter carefully back into the envelope, Jordana curled up on the bed and sobbed softly into her pillow. Life was hard and cruel, and it seemed too much to expect a woman of eighteen to endure.

How could he be gone? Gone for months without her even knowing it.

She cried for his passing and cried for what might have been between them. She wondered silently what his funeral might have been like. Had they buried him in France or returned him to New York?

She had long mourned the dissolution of their friendship, but now she reflected on the days they'd once shared. G.W. had talked to her as an equal. He had respected her ability to reason and think. He had given her special attention, taking her on long walks where they would touch on important issues at hand. He had been a good friend, and now he was gone.

The thought of their friendship caused Jordana to think of Captain O'Brian. He too had offered her friendship. He believed firmly that men and women could be friends. Yet she hadn't seen him in nearly a month.

Well, it's best that way, she decided. I don't need any more friends. It's much too painful to lose them. G.W.'s passing only served to stiffen her resolve. She would be much happier to need no one. She would lean on God and her own abilities, but she would avoid the depths of friendship such as she had experienced with G.W.

Sighing, she thought of Brenton and Caitlan. These were dear friends, and she needed them. How would it be possible for her to gird herself against the risks of giving in such a manner? Perhaps it was a foolish notion, yet she knew that tonight something had hardened within her. A wall had formed that would not easily open up again.

Twenty

$\mathscr{B}$renton shifted nervously in his seat and folded and refolded his hands. He didn't want to appear anxious, but he was. He'd been summoned to attend a meeting of several important people associated with the Union Pacific. Peter Dey had sent a messenger with a formal-looking letter announcing his desire for Brenton Baldwin to be in attendance for a consultation regarding the survey assessments and building of the Union Pacific Railroad.

Now, seated in Dey's small office, with no fewer than ten other men squeezed in around him, Brenton felt rather insignificant. Here he was, not yet twenty-one, and he had been called to a meeting of the most important men in Omaha.

"I can't say that I'm happy about the Hoxie proposal," Dey told them. "I'm not even sure who H. M. Hoxie is and why Mr. Durant believes him capable of constructing the first one hundred miles of this railroad, but nevertheless, his was the only bid received."

Brenton found it surprising that no other construction firm had sought to bid on what would surely become the building project of the century.

"I am further dismayed by the suggestion made by our colleague Colonel Silas Seymour." All heads turned to the man of whom Dey was speaking. The colonel acknowledged everyone with a nod but said nothing, and Dey continued. "I made a valuable survey of the area surrounding Omaha. It need not be compromised with the suggestion by our New York consulting engineer that the grade is too steep. Neither should it be allowed that the Platte River valley is any more of a threat to flooding than any other river, suggesting hundreds of thousands of dollars to be spent on building up levees and flood control."

"My honorable sir," Colonel Seymour said in a low drawl. "I could not in good conscience tell our friend Mr. Durant that your original route was anything but questionable. I see the route as needing much in the way of assistance. I merely suggest we loop to the south and west. True enough it adds nine miles to the length of the railroad, but it would also allow for a more reasonable grade, which would eventually be to our benefit once actual rail travel becomes reality. As for flood control, I have spoken to many regarding this situation and feel confident that this is the most responsible way to proceed."

Dey fumed over the colonel's obvious disregard for his position. Durant was well-known for usurping authority. Even authority he himself had assigned, such as was the case with Peter Dey.

"To bring our attention back to the Hoxie contract, which, I might add, has not yet been ratified or approved," Dey continued, "we must assure the route with the final surveys. Hoxie is working off of my original plans and information provided us by General Grenville Dodge. He has also, no doubt, included consideration for Colonel Seymour's suggestions.

"Hoxie's contract proposes," Dey explained, "that he should build the first one hundred miles for the sum of fifty thousand dollars per mile. He further declares that the cost of all stations, water tanks, machine shops, roundhouses, and any other necessary structures not exceed five hundred thousand dollars. Further, that if the cost of iron rails should increase to more than one hundred thirty dollars per ton, the Union Pacific would agree to pay the excess."

To Brenton, who was unfamiliar with contract issues and railroad management, the plan sounded reasonable. He was amazed that anyone could simply consult a sketchy survey and then decide for themselves that each mile would cost X dollars. He had corresponded with his father by letters and had learned that much of building a railroad was pure conjecture and prayer.

The meeting grew increasingly hostile as the colonel once again joined in the conversation to suggest that Dey's concern was borne more out of injured pride than real concern. This in turn brought Dey to suggest that Seymour and Durant were simply bilking the United States Congress out of unreasonable amounts of money. Colonel Seymour merely smiled and replied that the amount was more than reasonable, given the task at hand.

Brenton listened impatiently as the group continued to argue. He couldn't see what part he might play in the situation, and his patience was growing thin. He despised arguments. Talking calmly and weighing the facts was a much more effective manner of dealing with business. His father had instilled this in his mind from the time he was a youngster, and now that he was a grown man in his own right, Brenton still maintained that it was sound advice. Perhaps it was this that caused him such irritation with Jordana. She had always been reasonable, and for all her daring exploits and ability to bring him around to her will, she had listened to sound counsel. Now she believed herself to have all the answers. She no longer listened or cared about what he might advise.

"Mr. Baldwin, whose father is well-known in railroad circles," Dey continued, immediately drawing Brenton's attention, "has posted an interest in photographing our survey progress, as well as the actual building of the line once we begin to move out across the territory. His proposal has met with Mr. Durant's approval, and I have asked him here today that he might witness our plans for the survey."

Brenton was thrilled. No one had given him any word on the matter since he had expressed his interest.

"Mr. Baldwin, can you be ready to leave within the week?"

Brenton nodded enthusiastically. "I will make myself ready. I have most of the supplies necessary for my photography work. I will need to ready my wagon, which provides my means of transportation as well as my darkroom." He failed to mention that he had no clue as to what he would do with Jordana. Now that Caitlan lived with the Cavendish family, she was no longer a worry to him. At least, not in the matter of whether she'd be safe and well cared for. It didn't stop him from thinking about her on a daily, maybe even an hourly basis.

"Then we shall expect you to be ready to move out with our team at first light on Friday. We will plan to be out for two, possibly three weeks. At that time, we'll return to Omaha and decide where to go from there in regard to your photographs and whether we see them as being of value to this endeavor."

Brenton nodded. His dream was about to come true. He felt an overwhelming gratitude toward God. *Thank you, Father*, he prayed silently. *Thank you for seeing me through this time, and please let me know how to handle the situation at home.*

"You said yourself that transportation out of Omaha is expensive and difficult to come by," Jordana said angrily. "You can't simply sit there and make plans for me. I won't have it."

"You can't stay in this house by yourself. You're barely eighteen."

"Women all over the country are staying in houses by themselves," Jordana curtly replied. "That pesky little war back east has totally interfered with polite society rules."

Brenton shook his head, then took off his glasses and rubbed his eyes. "This is different. Those women stay alone out of necessity. Their husbands or fathers have gone to war, and they have no choice. You have a choice."

"Well, I'm not taking it. If you even try to send me away, Brenton Baldwin, I will cash in my ticket at the first available stop and head out for parts unknown. You'll have no idea where I am or what I'm doing. How would that suit you?"

Jordana suddenly felt almost sorry for her brother in spite of her ire. His expression was one of complete defeat. There seemed to be no working the matter out for him, and Jordana had no viable solution to offer.

"What if you were to stay with another family?" Brenton proposed. He resecured his glasses and looked at her hopefully. "I could arrange for you to stay under the protection of someone like Mr. Chittenden and his wife, or maybe the Cavendish family, although I do not know them well."

"Why not just trust me to be able to handle myself here? What is it you're afraid of—that I'll show you up? That I'll do just fine in your absence and not need you anymore?"

Brenton looked away and sighed. "I'm afraid the ruffians who pour into this town will take advantage of you. I'm afraid you'll find yourself compromised or killed, all because of your foolish pride. Jordana, it's all well and fine that you're grown up and that you have a job of some importance. It's even perfectly acceptable to me that you make more money than I do and have provided us with this house via Mr. Chittenden's generosity. But what is not acceptable is the possibility that in my absence you would be left at the mercy of every roaming bachelor who would choose you for a wife, or worse."

"Oh, you don't have to worry about that," Jordana replied smugly. "I know very well how to say no."

"But what about the ones who refuse to take no for an answer?"

He had her there. She thought back unpleasantly to Zed Wilson's attack and then to Damon's own lustful advances. Sooner or later it was quite possible she'd find herself in a situation that wasn't so easy to deal with.

"I can't just impose myself upon someone," she finally replied.

"Let me talk to Mr. Chittenden. He might well have a solution. After all, he and his wife live in that big house with no one but Damon to concern themselves with. And half the time, as is true of the present, Damon is gone away on business."

Jordana bit at her lower bit and thought of telling Brenton of the ruthless behavior she'd witnessed from Damon in the bank. But despite that, it was just as unseemly for her to live in the home of a suitor as it was to live alone.

She looked at her brother's hopeful face. She did not want to be the one to spoil his dreams. But she could not under any circumstances agree to stay at the Chittendens. Perhaps by confessing about Damon's ardent and lustful advances, she could avoid that. On the other hand, it might also make Brenton decide that she must quit her job at the bank. But the other alternative seemed worse.

"I can't stay with the Chittendens," she finally admitted.

"Jordana, you are being unreasonable."

She shook her head. "No, I'm not. I had thought to save you from worry, but—"

He eyed her with a hint of panic in his eyes. "But what? Has something happened that I should know about?"

She nodded. "I suppose so, but remember, I took care of the problem, and that is the only reason I'm telling you this now. The situation is resolved and in the past, but I will not set myself up for further advances."

"By Damon Chittenden?"

"Yes. Do you remember the day of our fight? The day I went out for that walk and didn't get home until nearly dark?"

"Yes." His voice was steady and even, almost too controlled.

"Damon saw me walking and picked me up for a carriage ride. We drove out to the river, and . . . well . . . he suggested marriage and other romantic notions, and I refused."

"Somehow I get the impression you aren't telling me everything," Brenton replied.

Jordana could hear the strained patience in his voice. "Damon intends to see me as his wife. If you put me in the Chittenden home, you will leave me at his mercy. Perhaps he'd even consider compromising me to force the issue."

"He wouldn't dare!"

"He might," Jordana replied, pressing the matter home. "He's already tried to be more intimate than politeness would allow for. That's why I was so late coming home that night. I jumped out of the carriage and sent him away."

"You walked back alone? All the way from the river?" Brenton was clearly mortified.

"No, silly," Jordana laughed, trying to lighten the impact of her confession. "Captain O'Brian happened along about that time. He and his men were on detail in the area, and he walked back with me."

Brenton's relief was evident. "All right. Your point is understood. Chittenden's residence would not be an acceptable solution."

"And we are not close enough friends with anyone else of influence."

"What about the neighbors? Matt and Ann would have you stay with them in a minute."

"Brenton, the place has three rooms in total. They can't afford to have me there. They simply haven't room enough. Why not just let me stay here and have them check on me from time to time?"

"I suppose that's possible." He appeared to consider this for several minutes, then got up and went for his hat. "I'll go next door this minute and ask them about it."

Jordana smiled triumphantly and leaned back to await Brenton's return. She had won the round, for she was sure that Matt and Ann would have no problem at all accepting responsibility to check in on her.

"As if I needed a keeper," she muttered under her breath.

After nearly half an hour, Brenton returned. His face clearly warned her that things had not gone as they would have liked.

"Matt is going west with the new army. He's sending Ann and the kids down to St. Joseph to stay with Ann's mother. He said someone tried to accost her on the street yesterday. It scared her badly, and she doesn't want to be left alone in the city."

"How awful," Jordana sighed as her own hope plummeted. Before she could speak again, Brenton had made his decision.

"I'm taking you with me. I can't leave you here to face this town alone. You can come along and help me with the pictures. You know some of the procedures, and you can learn the rest."

Jordana opened her mouth to protest, but then realized this might well be the adventure of a lifetime.

"The First Cavalry has returned the settlers to the Elkhorn, and everything seems to be secured here in the eastern half of the state. We won't be going any farther west than Fort Kearney, and therefore we shouldn't be under any great risk. The Indians have been pushed west and north, and Matt assured me that the militia felt confident of their removal."

"I see," Jordana replied, not sure she wanted to show too much enthusiasm. If she appeared too cooperative, Brenton just might change his mind.

"I'll speak to the survey leaders tomorrow and square it away. Captain O'Brian and his men will accompany us as guards, so it's not like he isn't used to bailing you out of trouble."

"The man saves me from a group of bushwhackers, and now suddenly it's a full-time job to save me from harm?" she questioned sarcastically. It was a good thing Brenton didn't know about the incident with Zed Wilson.

"He saved you that day with Damon, as well. You might well have come to harm had you walked back to town alone."

"Thank you for having such confidence in me," Jordana replied snidely. Getting to her feet, she added, "Captain O'Brian will probably resign when he hears that I am to accompany this traveling circus."

"I'm surprised he didn't resign from the army once he found out you were still on this side of the Missouri," Brenton deadpanned.

Jordana stuck out her tongue and made a face. "Well, for your information, Captain O'Brian thinks we could be good friends."

"He and the rest of the single male population of Omaha," Brenton answered matter-of-factly. "But I give O'Brian credit for having enough brains to pursue you for nothing more than friendship. The poor man would die of exhaustion if he had to keep track of you twenty-four hours a day."

Jordana shook her head and rolled her eyes. "Yes, you look to be at death's door yourself."

"I'm sure I do," Brenton replied. "You would weary any man before his time."

―――――――

"This is out of the question!" O'Brian declared.

Governor Saunders, Peter Dey, and Brenton were the only non-uniformed individuals in the room, but they weren't the only source of O'Brian's misery.

"Captain, I understand your misgivings, but it's important that we soothe and calm the nerves of our citizens," his superior began.

"But there are dangers out there that far exceed—"

"Captain, unless you wish to face court-martial for insubordination, I'd suggest you refrain from commenting and allow me to speak."

O'Brian grew rigid, knowing he was totally out of line. "Yes, Colonel."

"Very good. If Miss Baldwin attends this survey team under her brother's protection, she will send a message of confidence to the people of Omaha."

"I agree," Governor Saunders replied. "There has been a general panic in this city since the beginning of August. We would do ourselves a great service to send you off with our utmost confidence. We don't want to keep folks from coming to our great territory just because of a little Indian misunderstanding."

O'Brian wanted to scream that this little "misunderstanding" was responsible for many deaths on both sides of the war. But being a soldier, he remained obediently silent. He would do as they ordered, although God alone would keep them from harm. Nevertheless, as bad as it was to have to worry over Indian attacks, now he'd have yet another problem to contend with.

Jordana Baldwin.

He sighed heavily. The woman positively frightened him more than any thought of Indians or the injury they might cause.

"So you do understand, Captain?" Governor Saunders concluded.

Rich hadn't heard the last few minutes of the governor's winded soliloquy, but regardless, he understood full well. "Yes, sir."

The colonel and the governor exchanged smiles. "Wonderful. Then we're all agreed."

Not by a long shot, Rich thought silently. Not by a long shot.

Twenty-One

$\mathcal{F}$riday morning dawned with a taste of rain in the air. Lacy red-violet clouds decorated the western horizon, while in the east the sun began a steady ascent to start the day. Jordana and Brenton arrived at the assigned point of departure, their unusually enclosed wagon seeming a strange oddity for the traveling caravan of horses and pack mules and covered wagons. The Baldwin wagon looked bulky and not at all suited for enduring rocky prairie paths. Rich had questioned Brenton about this at one point, only to be reminded that the same wagon had seen them through the wilds of Missouri. Rich had acknowledged this with little more than a grunt. He didn't want the Baldwins on this trip. Or perhaps better put, he didn't want Jordana Baldwin on this trip.

Rich eyed the duo as they sat in their wagon awaiting instructions. Jordana had worn a dark blue skirt and long-sleeved calico blouse. Her hair had either been pinned up or tucked up inside the wide-brimmed sunbonnet, while kid gloves covered her hands. She looked very prim and proper sitting up on the wagon seat with her brother. If Rich had not known what a wildcat she could be, he would have thought her poorly suited for the job they were about to face. But he couldn't fault her in that area. Rich knew she was made of strong stuff. She had more spunk and enthusiasm for life than most folks, especially women.

Nevertheless, she *was* a woman, and life on the open prairie was hard on women. Too hard. Rich had seen them suffer and die. Some were left alone too long and suffered prairie madness. Long weeks and even months of howling winds, isolation, and fear of nature

173

and the creatures inhabiting the area left many women unable to cope. He put the thought from his mind. Jordana wasn't the type to go mad from travel or life on the plains. She was strong. Jordana knew her strength, too. She thrived on the adventure and excitement around her, and she had a certain hunger for things that most women would just as soon leave to their men.

"We're ready if you are, Captain," an older man said, drawing his horse up alongside O'Brian's.

Rich looked at his sergeant and nodded. "Very well. Here is the map of locations where the surveyors hope to take measurements." He handed the man a piece of paper and pointed to a heavy black line. "We'll head west to the Platte. After that, we'll move along south of the river. Put a scout out ahead of us. Tell him to keep an eye open for any sign of trouble. I don't care if it's just a hunch—if that man so much as feels the hairs on the back of his neck stand up, I want to know about it."

"Yes, Captain," the older man replied, folding the paper. "I'll make sure he knows what's expected."

The sergeant moved out, instructing a skinny private regarding the area he would be scouting. Rich knew this soldier would be Sergeant Hart's choice. The boy had lived in and around Omaha all his life. He knew this prairie better than anyone. Hart would have been foolish to pick anyone else. The private studied the map for a moment, then saluted and headed his horse out.

The survey team consisted of five Union Pacific men. None of them were well-known to Rich. He had been introduced to the men in rapid-fire succession, with no one dwelling long on any particular man or name. He supposed it was just as well. He would learn enough about each man before their three weeks on the prairie concluded. Besides the men who were traveling mounted, there were two supply wagons and several pack animals for when the surveyors needed to get equipment into places wagons could not go.

Maneuvering his horse alongside the Baldwin wagon, Captain O'Brian touched the brim of his cap. "Morning, Mr. Baldwin. Miss Baldwin."

Brenton greeted him warmly, but Jordana only nodded polite acknowledgment of his greeting, saying nothing. He wondered only for a moment what he'd done to cause her to be so cold and distant, but there wasn't time to worry about it.

"I suppose you have some idea of the job you'll soon be facing," Rich asked.

"I believe we do, Captain," Brenton replied. "We've been working pretty hard on our own for nearly two years."

"Yes, but most of that time has either been in Omaha or east of the Mississippi. Is that not true?"

Brenton nodded. "I suppose you have a good point."

"There is very little, if any, Indian trouble back east. Oh, you get an occasional renegade who causes trouble, but we both know it's never anything all that serious. Out here, however, we are left pretty much to the mercy of the elements and the Indians."

Brenton eyed Jordana for a moment, and Rich wondered if he might change his mind about bringing her on the trip. It wasn't safe or reasonable to have her along, and Baldwin knew this. Rich could read the regret and apprehension in his eyes.

"We'll be just fine, Captain O'Brian," Jordana replied before Brenton could say anything. "You do your job, and we'll do ours."

Rich wondered once more at her cool tone. She had clearly placed a wall between them. "I don't have a problem doing my job, Miss Baldwin. It's just that you doing your job makes my job about ten times harder."

She jutted out her chin, tilting her nose delicately in the air. "That, sir, is your problem."

Later in the day, Rich observed that Jordana had changed her clothes to a full brown skirt and matching jacket. She had apparently wearied of the wagon and was now riding the sorrel gelding that had previously been tied to the back of their wagon. As she rode out away from the others, Rich thought it the perfect opportunity to seek her out and learn what had caused her to treat him with such indifference.

"You need to stay close to the others," Rich warned as he came up beside her.

Jordana acknowledged him with a glance but said nothing.

"Look, I don't know what I've done to irritate you. I only mentioned you remaining in Omaha for your own safety. Forgive me if that seemed less than gallant of me."

She turned to glare at him for a moment. "I am sure you are quite gallant, Captain. I just don't happen to need anyone acting on my behalf. I'm here simply because my brother couldn't bear the idea of leaving me alone in Omaha."

"And he has a good point in his worries," Rich replied. "It's just that bringing you along on this trip is hardly much better."

She shrugged. "I tried to tell him I was fully capable of caring for myself, but he refuses to see me as a grown-up."

Rich chuckled, which he quickly learned was the wrong thing to do. She frowned at him and resumed her stiff posture before replying, "I should have expected that of you."

"Yes, you should have," Rich replied, quite unwilling to show her any pity. She didn't need pity, as he saw it. Maybe a good spanking, but not pity. They were nearly twenty yards off to the right of the rest of the group, and Rich felt confident he could bring up the past without further discrediting her before her brother. "After all," he continued, "I've been there for your encounters with other less-than-honorable men."

"So you walked with me back to Omaha. It's not like I couldn't have done that on my own."

"What about the alley and the attacker you faced?" he asked.

He watched her bite her lower lip, a nervous habit he'd observed of her on more than one occasion. When she did this, she looked very innocent, almost childlike, but that's where any idea of Jordana Baldwin being a child ended. She was a comely woman, and he'd seen men, even his own men, look at her with a clear mind to her beauty and shapely figure.

"I suppose, Captain, that you will be throwing these things in my face for as long as time continues to put us in each other's company."

"It wasn't meant as something to throw in your face, but since you are the one who is intent on proving your independence and ability to take care of yourself, those are situations you must consider."

She nodded. "I realize that. And I have considered them."

"To what conclusion?"

"I believe I shall purchase a gun for my protection."

Rich rolled his eyes heavenward. "God help us all," he said in complete reverence. "Miss Baldwin, do us all a favor, but especially me, since I am the one who generally bears the brunt of your heroic efforts to right yourself of injustice—do not buy a gun."

She looked at him as if he'd spoken in a foreign language, then began to grin. This was soon followed by her laughter.

Rich smiled in spite of himself. It was the first time she'd shown any merriment since they'd left Omaha. "Laugh all you want, Miss Baldwin, but I've been shot before."

"So have I, as you will recall," she said, still smiling.

"I have no desire to face the contents of the blue bottle," he said, matching her good mood, "nor the humiliation of being shot by a woman."

"Well, a young woman has to protect herself."

"Yes, especially when that young woman is you," Rich replied. "Very few other women have a tendency toward knives or clubs."

"But if I had a gun," Jordana stated, appearing to think the matter through quite seriously, "I could protect myself. My father taught me something of shooting when I was young. In fact, I'm a better shot than Brenton. His eyes are weak, you know."

"You are dangerous, Miss Baldwin," Rich said in a low, husky tone. "Most dangerous."

She smiled, appearing to quite like the sound of that. "Then no one should worry overmuch for my safety, for surely such danger will ward off many who might think to tangle with me."

Rich nodded and added, "Or the challenge of beating you out will bring them in droves."

"Are you a God-fearing man, Captain?" she asked out of the clear blue.

Rich wondered at her line of questioning but decided there was no harm in answering. "Yes, as a matter of fact, I am. Why do you ask?"

"Because I am a God-fearing woman. I believe completely in His power to keep me from harm and in His ability to steer me out of dangerous paths."

"And how do you suppose God does this, Miss Baldwin?"

She looked at him oddly for a moment. "What do you mean?"

"Just what I said. How do you suppose God keeps you from harm and steers you out of dangerous paths?"

"Well, by showing me what's best and teaching me what's harmful."

"Like staying out of dark alleys or not taking rides with young men in an unescorted fashion?"

She frowned and turned back to study the landscape of tall prairie grass.

"I merely mention it," he went on, "because it seems to me, in order to be shown or taught, one has to be willing to observe and listen. I would suggest that God does strive to teach you, Miss Baldwin, but if you're unwilling to heed His direction, how do you propose to remain out of harm's way?"

Just then the scout returned, and Rich's attention was taken elsewhere. "Forgive me, but I must go check in with my men." He touched the brim of his cap and gave Jordana a brief smile. He could tell by her expression that his words had found their mark. She didn't respond with a snide or ludicrous comment. She merely considered his words, appearing to realize their importance.

"Oh, and I might add, riding astride rather than sidesaddle isn't exactly the best way to maintain a low profile," Rich added.

Jordana frowned. "Is there any possible hope that I might be left to live my life *my* way, without some man coming along to rebuke me for my choices?"

O'Brian laughed. "Where you are concerned, Miss Baldwin, I would imagine anything is possible."

———

Later, as they set up camp along an ample creek, Sergeant Hart found Rich brooding over Jordana.

"If I didn't know better," Hart drawled, betraying his southern roots, "I'd say your mind is given to thoughts of our young miss."

Rich smiled and motioned Hart to join him. "Now, Wes," he said, letting the formality between them drop, "you know full well that would be completely out of character for me."

Wesley Hart laughed. "Yes, it would be. But I've seen stranger things happen in this world."

"So have I," Rich replied. "I suppose I admire her gumption. She's intelligent and brave. Of course, she's also a little flighty and easily riled."

"You've just described many women. What makes this one so special?"

Rich shook his head. "I'm not sure I know the answer to that question."

"I'm thinkin', Captain, that you've lost your heart to this one, and that's what makes the difference."

Rich looked at Wes and saw the glint of amusement in his eyes. "It would be a disaster if I had," he said firmly, but in his heart he realized how close Wes was to the truth of the matter. "There's no room for a female in my life," he added quickly, before taking himself off to check on the rest of the party. "No room at all."

"Better clear out a corner, Captain," Wes called after him.

Rich shook his head. His relationship to women in the past had proven most harmful—especially to them. He had simply thought to offer this young woman friendship. She seemed so needy of it. But perhaps Miss Baldwin had been right. Men and women couldn't be friends without one or both losing their hearts in the matter.

He stopped just outside the camp and caught sight of her as she cooked over an open fire. She appeared completely at ease, unconcerned with her rugged setting or the lack of comforts. Just then the hem of her skirt touched the edge of the flames and in a flash caught fire. Rich began to run toward her but then stopped as she calmly doused the fire with a nearby bucket of water. She inspected the damage for a moment, pulling her skirt up to reveal shapely legs. She glanced up to catch Rich watching her and quickly dropped the skirt back into place.

She shrugged in a nonchalant manner as if it were quite normal to catch one's dress on fire, then went back to work as if nothing had happened.

She must have one weary guardian angel, Rich thought, turning his attention elsewhere. Then letting out a heavy sigh, he knew he was in for a long and tiresome trip. Make a corner, indeed, he thought, remembering Wes's words. Jordana Baldwin wouldn't need a corner, she'd need an entire room—or in the case of his heart, she was the type of woman who would spread out to fill every conceivable nook and cranny. It would take a stronger man to keep her in line than he knew himself to be.

Twenty-Two

"Can we talk?"

Jordana looked up to find her brother standing nearly ten feet away. She had taken the quiet moments of the early morning to separate herself out from the others to sit on the creek bank and contemplate her existence.

She nodded and waited for Brenton to take a seat beside her. He looked so tired and worn in spite of their night's sleep inside the wagon. The thunderstorm that had kept them awake for part of the night had moved off to the northeast, but already another rain seemed certain.

"What did you want to talk about?" she asked, shifting her gaze back to the creek.

"First I want to apologize."

She started at this and jerked her eyes back to him. "Apologize?"

He pulled his glasses off and rubbed his eyes. "I've been a bear to live with, and I know it better than anyone. I'm sorry."

She smiled. "What has brought about this realization?"

He sighed. "I can't abide the anger between us. I look at you, and I feel a sense of what we've lost. We were so close at one time. We could very nearly read each other's thoughts. Now I can read them all right, but they're all angry and bitter."

She nodded. "True enough, I suppose."

"I didn't set out to make you miserable or to try to run your life. I wanted to be a good man—like our father. I wanted to prove to him that I could be trusted to take a role of responsibility seriously."

"But you've done that and more," Jordana countered.

181

"Not all that successfully. As you've pointed out, your job at the bank provided more for our means than anything I've done."

"That's going to change now that the railroad is paying you for this position, at least in supplies and such. I'm sure once they see what you're capable of, they'll pay even more." Faced with his touching humility, her previous ire began to subside.

"That's not the point. The things I dream of are hardly those that a man could attach much responsibility to. I desire to traipse out across the country, photographing the landscape—seeing what there is to see. I can hardly protect you or anyone else in my life by taking such a road. And I certainly can't offer any stability."

"This isn't really about me, is it?" Jordana suddenly questioned.

"Why do you say that?"

"Because you know full well that I desire nothing more than to explore the country. I don't want to be tied down to any one place for very long."

"What about being tied to one person?" Brenton cocked his brow, and his tone contained a slight tease.

Jordana shrugged. "I don't know. Most men don't take to the idea of a woman traveling around the country, sleeping out under the stars, risking her life by exposure to the elements."

"Most women don't take to the idea of such a life either."

"And you don't think Caitlan would take to that kind of a life? The kind that would see her at your side, helping you photograph the country?"

"When did Caitlan enter the conversation?" Reddening slightly, Brenton shook his head. "I don't see Caitlan wanting someone like me."

"Why do you say that?" Jordana asked more seriously. "You've made similar statements on more than one occasion. Why did you send her away if you desire a life with her?"

"I didn't send her away," he protested. "She went of her own accord."

"She didn't seem that eager to go, if you ask me. Why, every time I talk with her, she sounds even more discouraged than you are."

He looked at her for a moment and shook his head again. "Look, I didn't come out here to talk about Caitlan." He was defensive.

"Maybe you should have."

Brenton fell silent, his eyes focusing on a scraggy stand of trees. "You should come back to camp. I heard Captain O'Brian say rain is coming, and you don't want to get caught out here."

"Captain O'Brian isn't my boss," Jordana reminded him tartly. "Besides, I doubt I would suffer any adverse effects should I get a good dousing of rainwater."

He grinned. "We are pretty dusty, aren't we? Maybe we should have stood outside in last night's downpour."

Jordana smiled and reached out to take his hand. "Brenton, I love you with all my heart."

"But. . . ?"

She laughed. "But I'm growing up, and you have to respect that. I know I'm just a woman, but I'm a woman with the drive and determination to live my life to its fullest and not be bound by convention or unwritten rules of etiquette. Think of our mother. Think of the stories she's told us. She too was desirous for something more. It isn't that I don't value those like Victoria, who long for nothing more than a neat little house and a hearth on which to cook. But, Brenton, that isn't me. Those aren't my desires—at least not yet— maybe never."

"I know. And I know you're very capable. No matter what happens, you always manage to come out fairly unscathed."

Jordana thought of all the problems she'd encountered over the last few months. She thought of her unsavory encounters with Damon Chittenden and shook her head. "It's not necessarily that I've come out unscathed," she replied, "but I do trust God to help me, and I trust Him to keep me safe."

"Always, Jordana?"

"Well, I try. Perhaps there are times I could be more sensible, but even God doesn't expect me to be perfect. Like anyone, I've just lived my life. Maybe I do take some risks, but I just can't believe God wants me to cower by hearth and home when He himself made me as I am. I don't think I am any more foolish than Noah was thought to be when he started building the ark."

"But the ark had a purpose. Do your plans have such a purpose?"

"I don't know. I can't honestly tell you that I know what my plans or purposes are. But I know what they aren't. I know that I'm not ready to marry or settle down to a family and the responsibilities of parenthood." She grew silent for a moment, and when she spoke again, her voice was full of emotion. "I wanted very much to be satisfied in my love for G.W. And, Brenton, I did love him. But I loved him as I love you—like a brother. G.W. respected me, as you used to."

"I still do," he said, squeezing her hand. "I know I haven't shown it, but I do respect you."

"I hope so," she replied with tears in her eyes. "I don't want to lose that. I guess I can't hope for you to understand my feelings, Brenton. I don't understand them myself. I try hard to figure out what I'm supposed to do and where I'm supposed to go, but I'm still very uncertain. That's another reason I don't want you sending me home to Mother and Father. I might not know exactly where I'm going, but I know it's not back there."

"Never?"

She shrugged, smiling sheepishly. "I don't know. . . ."

"Fair enough." Brenton rose to his feet. He reached down and pulled her up. "Walk with me?"

She nodded and looped her arm through his. "So am I forgiven?"

"Forgiven for what? I'm the one who is seeking forgiveness."

Jordana felt the rain-scented breeze hit her face. In the distance a clap of thunder caught their attention. It looked as though they were indeed due for another rain.

"Well?" Brenton asked. "Am I forgiven?"

She laughed. "Of course you're forgiven. Now, what are you going to do about getting Caitlan back?"

He stopped and shook his head. "I'm not going to try to bring her back. Caitlan going to live with the Cavendishes was probably the best and wisest thing that could have happened."

"Why do you say that?" Jordana cast a dubious look at him.

"I love her," he said matter-of-factly. "I can't live under the same roof with her without it giving the appearance of impropriety."

"That's nonsense. I'm there. She and I have always shared a room. There's absolutely nothing inappropriate in what we've done."

"I won't compromise her reputation."

"No one said you would."

Brenton sighed. "You don't understand. When we were living all under one roof, she consumed my thoughts. I thought about her every waking and sleeping moment. It was almost unbearable. She was there, so close—close enough to touch, yet I couldn't touch her."

Jordana suddenly realized the extent of her brother's desire. Why hadn't she seen this before? After all, she'd known all along they loved each other. She often felt the great sense of frustration in their unwillingness to admit their feelings. But never had she thought about the desires and passion that drove men and women to each other's arms. How could she? She herself had never experienced them.

"Oh, Brenton, I'm sorry. I hadn't thought of it that way. Was it terribly hard on you?"

"Worse than anything I've ever known. I can't be leading us into temptation that way. I must find a solution and get her to Kiernan as soon as possible. You see, it was never so much a desire to be rid of you, as a need to put her away from me."

"Why not marry her?"

"Why didn't you marry G.W.?" he countered.

"I told you, I didn't love him like that. I loved him as a brother."

"Maybe Caitlan loves me in that same way."

Jordana's hysterical laughter was clearly not what Brenton had expected. He stared at her with shock and then irritation.

"Oh, please forgive me, Brenton," she said, regaining control, "but Caitlan's love for you has nothing to do with brotherhood. You truly can't see much farther than your nose if you honestly believe her to love you only as a brother."

"Then why did she react the way she did when I kissed her?"

"You kissed her?" Jordana's brow arched in surprise. "She never told me that."

"She was probably too mortified."

"More likely, she was overwhelmed. Look here, brother of mine," Jordana said as thunder once again rumbled in the distance, "Caitlan knows how you feel about God. She's troubled about her own feelings and knows that you could never marry someone who didn't share your faith. But don't give up on her. She was raised to believe."

"Being raised to do something and doing it for yourself are two different things," Brenton replied softly. "She has to come to God on His terms, for herself and not for her family or even for me."

Jordana nodded. "She knows this quite well. I've told it to her over and over. She's afraid to trust. She worries that God won't be all that He promises to be—that He will somehow hurt her as others have, giving big promises, much talk, and then never carrying through. She's wounded from the past and her losses. She's grown up listening to horror stories about the famine and all the subsequent troubles. And not only stories, but, Brenton, she's lived much of the horror herself."

They began walking back toward the wagon, spying Rich as he stood outside his tent deep in discussion with one of the surveyors.

"He's a good man," Brenton commented casually.

"What?" Jordana pulled her focus off Rich, shifting it back on her brother. "What are you talking about?"

"Captain O'Brian. You seem to have a definite interest in him."

She shook her head. "I want no more soldiers in my life."

"G.W.'s death has hurt you very much, hasn't it?"

She felt the tears come once again, and this time she allowed them. "I can't believe that he is gone. It seems so unfair. He was vibrant and young and wonderful. How can he be dead? How can so many of them be dead?"

"You mean the war soldiers?"

"Soldiering is a hard business," she sighed. "Woe to the woman who gives her heart to a soldier. I think I'd make a very poor widow. I think of G.W. and of the fun we shared, and now that he's gone I often reflect on the things we discussed. I wonder at my reaction and replies, and try to second-guess whether I could have somehow made things better by answering differently."

"You might also have made them worse," Brenton replied. "Like you once told me, you have to trust God for the outcome, otherwise life passes by while you sit and contemplate and regret and wonder if you might have done something different."

"But I can't help it," she said, letting go of his arm to pull out her handkerchief. "I worry that somehow I made things worse for G.W. I don't want to have that responsibility in anyone else's life again. I don't want to hurt anyone anymore. G.W. might have gotten better had I returned his love. He might have had something to live for."

"So now God is deciding whether folks live or die based on whether or not *you* fall in love with them?" Brenton put his hands on Jordana's shoulders and forced her to look at him. "Jordana, your love went with G.W. to Europe. He carried it there as surely as he carried his illness. Just because that love wasn't of a matrimonial nature doesn't mean it wasn't every bit as supportive and nurturing. You said yourself that he carried his love for you to the grave. That love should have been enough to set him back on his course and make him well if what you're saying holds weight. But it doesn't, don't you see? People get sick and die, whether or not anyone loves them or needs them. They die whether they've accomplished everything they wanted to do, or nothing at all. The reality is that they pass from this world when God says it's time. Not one minute before, nor one second after. Mourn G.W.'s passing, but never assign yourself more importance in that passing than you are humanly responsible for."

Jordana knew he was right, but it hurt so much. She never wanted to feel that kind of hurt again.

As if reading her mind, Brenton shook his head and said, "You can't go through life shutting yourself off in the hopes of never getting hurt. Love is a precious and wonderful thing, whether it is love for parents and siblings or friends and mates. You will become hard and bitter, Jordana, if you refuse to love or be loved."

Jordana hugged Brenton tightly. "When did you get to be so wise?" She clung to him and sniffed loudly.

"I'm not so wise when it comes to my own problems," he replied, patting her back tenderly. "Maybe one day I can take my own advice and love openly no matter the cost."

Jordana pulled away and nodded. "You must go on loving her," she said with tender admonition. "I feel confident you and Caitlan are destined for each other. You may have a separate road right now, but sooner or later, I see that road joining."

His face held the tiniest hint of a hopeful smile. "I pray you're right, but there's much to be overcome."

"Nothing good ever comes easily," she said, knowing it didn't solve the problem, but also knowing it was the only comfort she had to offer. "I wish it did." She looked away to the coming storm and sighed. Life was full of storms and difficulties.

Brenton squeezed her arm and said, "But good things do come. We have to hold on to that and trust that God is in control, that He sees far more for us than we can see for ourselves."

"The bigger picture?" she asked softly.

Brenton nodded. "A much bigger picture."

Twenty-Three

*I*t had rained all night. Again. Mud splattered everywhere, caking on Rich's boots, his trouser legs, even his coat sleeves. Riding at the front of the procession of wagons and soldiers, he turned slightly in his saddle to briefly assess the group. All seemed in order. The Baldwin wagon was lumbering at the rear, and that fool woman, Jordana, was riding alongside the wagon as if taking a Sunday jaunt. It still both shocked and beguiled him to observe her boldness in riding astride.

Yes, she was quite a woman. A foolish woman. A beautiful woman. An intriguing woman. A dangerous woman . . . for a man like him. But no matter how often he told himself that, he could not get her completely out of his mind.

Rich thought about last night as he had watched her with her brother. He'd glimpsed another side of her then, one that just made her even more intriguing. The two had been talking so earnestly, and there had been such a deep tenderness in her expression toward Brenton. Jordana Baldwin presented to Rich, and probably to the rest of the world, a self-sufficient, slightly tart, very daring character. He thought now that it must surely be a facade meant to mask a tender, vulnerable side. More likely—and this was the intriguing part—she was all those things in one lovely package. She was indeed a rose beset by a good number of thorns.

Rich could have been easily tempted to risk a few scratches to hold that rose and to deserve that same expression she had given her brother. But he was far from ready to take such a risk again.

Rich peered ahead, forcing his attention to matters at hand. All

189

seemed in perfect order, which did not explain the unsettled feeling he'd had since the party had departed Omaha several days ago. Maybe it was only the Baldwin woman. Still, Rich was not a man to become so besotted by a woman's charms that he completely lost his head. He knew better than to attribute the small gnawing in his stomach just to that. And he knew better than to accept words of peace and tranquility without firm proof. The moneymen wanted settlers to think all was safe and secure on the plains so settlement would continue. But too many lives depended on Rich not buying their assurances wholesale. Yet the survey party had gone this long unmolested. Perhaps Rich was just being too much of a doomsayer.

The party paused for a midday meal just south of a small creek. There were only a few cottonwoods along the banks of the stream to shade the group from the sun, which had turned the air hot and muggy despite the dotting of dark clouds still in the sky. Rich ambled around the camp, passing the time of day with his men and the survey team. It was quite natural then for him to pause at the Baldwin wagon. Brenton had taken his camera closer to the creek to take photographs. Jordana was cutting up biscuits left over from breakfast and some beef jerky. Rich had told the group this stop would only be for an hour, so cooking fires were out of the question.

"Are you getting on well, Miss Baldwin?" he asked.

"Yes, quite." She took the cloth she held in her hand and dabbed unconsciously at her neck. "If only we could do something about this heat. How I would love a swim in that creek!"

"I am sorry there isn't time for that now," he said. "And when we move on, we shall veer away from the creek. It will be open, dry prairie for a while then."

He watched her finger a damp strand of hair, tucking it behind her ear. He wondered how one appearing so cool on the surface could be hot and perspiring. He searched in his mind for words that might probe beneath the chilly exterior to the tender heart he knew must be inside. But he could think of nothing. And even if he could, what right had he? They had spoken of being friends, but the sentiment had progressed no further than words, and he felt it was not his place to encourage it more than that.

"Well, there's nothing for it, then, is there? I mean the heat." She shifted her gaze back to her work, then her eyes skittered to him once again. "Would you care to join us, Captain O'Brian? Brenton should be back shortly."

"That is most kind of you, Miss Baldwin, but I have already eaten." He didn't know why he refused. It would not have hurt him to have another meal. He added quickly, "Perhaps another time." He supposed he was just as cautious as she, if indeed her reserve had anything to do with caution. Perhaps she simply disliked him.

"All right, then."

"I best return to my duties." Tipping his hat, he turned and strode away, wondering just what duties he had that were so pressing.

The party continued on after lunch. The heat dried out the earth, quickly turning mud to dust. Rich's prediction about this leg of the journey proved true. Grassy prairie stretched out before them now like an endless sea. Not a tree in sight for mile upon mile.

Rich rode up next to his sergeant. "Wes, I've got this prickly feeling in the back of my neck. But I don't see a blessed thing out there."

"Yeah. It's mighty quiet." Sergeant Hart squinted as if that might change the horizon of unending grass.

"Too quiet."

"I'll keep a sharp look out, Captain."

"Never figured you'd do anything else." Rich grinned, a gesture that did not reach up into his eyes, which were still focusing ahead.

A half hour passed uneventfully—the creak of harness, the snorts of horses, the clouds of dust making a kind of music in the hot air. And it wasn't a soothing music. But for all those sounds, it was just too quiet.

Thwang!

Rich heard the sound, felt the brief rustle of air. The instant it registered in his mind, another followed.

Thwang! Thwang!

"Indians!" someone yelled.

But Rich was already shouting the orders for his men to take defensive positions, that is, circling the survey team, using the wagons for protection from the back. Unless the attackers were simply too many in number, the party's best hope would be to stop and fight it out rather than attempt to outrun the Indians. All his men were armed with good percussion-cap rifles, which should quickly overwhelm the Indians, who he hoped were armed with only bows and arrows or old muskets. He quickly counted about a dozen attackers, who appeared to be Pawnee. Less than half were armed with rifles. How they had managed to keep hidden and get so close, Rich could not tell, but he knew enough about Indians to know they had their ways. They'd probably been following the party for hours, maybe even days.

After seeing that the wagons were positioned to lend maximum cover, Rich was ready to dismount himself and take up a firing position, but before doing so he glanced toward the Baldwin wagon. It had stopped with the others, and Brenton was crouched behind the front wheel, rifle in hand, about to fire. Where was Jordana? The sorrel was not tied to the back of the wagon.

Rich looked frantically around. Curse that girl!

Zing! A sharp pain seared Rich's head, throwing him back in his saddle. He would have been able to hang on too, despite the pain, if only the sudden dizziness from the blow hadn't assailed him. He pitched forward, and the next thing he realized, he had hit the ground and a pair of hands was grasping his arms and dragging him toward the wagon.

"Dear Lord! Are you. . . ?" came Brenton's shaky voice.

Rich blinked and brought a hand to his head. "I . . . I think so." He drew away his hand, finding it covered with blood. "Just grazed, I think. Thanks for getting me—" Suddenly he remembered what he had seen—or not seen—just before he'd been hit. "Jordana! Where's your sister?"

Brenton's head seemed to spin on his neck as he gazed all around. "She's not here! Last I saw she was dismounting."

Rich sat up, and beyond the clouds of dust and gunpowder, he saw the sorrel racing away. What he could not tell was whether it had a rider.

———

Everything happened so quickly, Jordana had no time to be either excited or afraid. She heard the shouts of Rich O'Brian before the chilling whoops of the Indians reached her ears. There were a few moments of chaos as everyone in the party reacted to the captain's orders and their own stunned fear and excitement.

With gunfire all around, both from the Indians and the soldiers, and arrows flying, Jordana was as anxious as anyone to dismount her sorrel and duck for cover behind the wagons. Brenton shouted her name as he reined his team to a stop.

"I'm all right," she assured.

"Let's get to cover!" He grabbed his rifle and leaped over the side of the wagon.

"I'm right behind you."

And she had been. Within seconds she would have been down there safely behind a wheel. Then the sorrel reared suddenly. This was not a battle-hardened cavalry mount. Brenton had rented the animal from a livery in Omaha. The beast had probably never even been hunting before. Snorting with terror, the gelding shot off at a gallop the moment its feet retouched the ground.

Jordana screamed, but who could hear above the riot of battle sounds?

The sudden start of the horse unseated Jordana and would have surely thrown her to either her death or at the least a bad bruising on the ground had her boot not twisted in the stirrup, holding her foot firm. As she hung by the reins to the flank of the sorrel, she saw what had so provoked the animal. An arrow had pierced its right shoulder. But Jordana had no time to feel sorry for the beast, her own life hanging literally by a thread—a leather one gripped fiercely in her hand. As her teeth jarred in her head with the bouncing of the sorrel, Jordana's arms felt as if at any moment they would be wrenched from their sockets.

Struggling with all the strength left in her arms, she finally managed to get her leg over the back of her mount. Two bone-rattling minutes later, she found the strength to pull herself back into the saddle. Exhausted and hardly able to do more than hold the reins, she fell forward, hugging the sorrel's neck. But she did not have the luxury to rest. The horse had to be brought under control. Taking a breath, she was about to do just that when she heard shrill shouts behind her.

Turning in her saddle, she saw the last sight she expected or desired. Two of the Indians were chasing her.

Twenty-Four

*N*ow she dare not stop. She dug her heels into the sorrel's flanks. How would she ever outrun her pursuers? She could already feel her mount tiring, especially as they galloped up a grassy knoll. She wondered how serious its wound was and prayed the animal would not simply drop out from under her.

A rifle blasted behind her, but a quick glance to the rear assured her she was still out of range. Surely the range of an arrow was no more than that of a musket. At any rate, a bobbing target on a galloping horse should do nothing for their aim. But as she crested the rise, she wanted to let out her own war whoop. A stand of trees stretched out about a quarter of a mile away. Either the creek they had left earlier in the day wound around to here, or this was another waterway altogether. Regardless, the trees meant cover—if she could get to them before the Indians got to her.

"Just a little farther," she encouraged the sorrel. *Please, God, help us get there!*

The sun was now setting, and the bright glare was directly in front of Jordana. It was nearly impossible to see. But she hoped it also impaired the Indians' sight as well as she veered toward the trees. It was not easy to slow when she reached the first of them. Of course, the sorrel was more than willing, but Jordana's racing heart made her want to keep on racing as well. At least it was darker within the wood, but the branches and leaves that made it dark also proved to be a hazard to a rider. She had to duck several times as she penetrated more deeply into the thicket. Finally, believing she'd have a better chance on foot of eluding pursuit, she dismounted and tied her horse to a branch hoping she'd be alive to retrieve it later.

In the not-too-far distance, she could hear the gurgling of the creek and, remembering that the water would cover her tracks, headed in that direction. As she went she cocked an ear for sounds of the Indians. Bursts of gunfire in the distance gave her hope that perhaps one of the soldiers had come to her rescue.

A branch snagged at her hair, pulling out the pin holding the mass in place. It tumbled into her eyes. She didn't see the root at her feet and stumbled, flying to the ground on her stomach. Bruised and scratched, and covered with damp leaves and mud, she was not seriously harmed. She jumped up and continued on. She heard no pursuit but knew that Indians had a talent for stealth. They could be within feet of her, and she'd not have a clue. But she made a concerted effort to push such negative thoughts from her mind. Instead, she looked about for a weapon, telling herself that after this, she was never going to travel unarmed again.

A fallen branch proved the best weapon she could find. She grabbed it with trembling fingers and continued on.

The gunfire had died away, and she tried to construe this as a positive sign. But her mind filled instead with all the horror stories she'd heard about Indians. Most she had discounted as tales from folks with wild imaginations. But her own imagination was having a field day now. Scalpings apparently were the least of the dangers. And female captives were likely to have an even more terrifying time of it. She wondered what it would be like to be taken to an Indian camp and forced . . . well, it was best not to wonder at all. She wasn't going to get captured. She wasn't going to end up a "white squaw woman." She was going to get out of here and away from danger. She was going to make it back to camp and to her brother.

"Oh, God, please help me! I sometimes think I am so strong and tough, but I'm not really. I'm just a woman, and even if my heart cries out to be more, you have given me the frail body of a female. I suppose it is so I will depend on you."

She stumbled again, then saw the ebbing light of the setting sun glint off the surface of the water. She was relieved to see the creek, though she didn't know what advantage it would be. But her heart was pounding and her lungs still heaving, so she had to stop for a minute. Her mouth was dry and she was dying for a drink, but she would be too exposed if she stopped at the edge of the water. Ignoring her thirst, she kept to the trees.

But why couldn't she hear anything? Had the Indians given up on her? Brushing back her unruly hair, she strained again to listen. Only then did she hear the soft voice and the sweetest sound she could think of.

"Jordana!"

It was barely a whisper, and the moment the sound reached her ears, a hand grasped her shoulder. It startled her nonetheless, and she gasped.

"Rich . . . I . . . uh . . . mean, Captain O'Brian!" She turned, forgetting the branch in her hand. It clipped him on the shin. "I'm so sorry!"

He grinned, then raised a finger to his lips. "Shush!" he breathed. "I'm getting quite tough, thanks to you, Miss Baldwin. Now, why don't we see if we can get out of here."

"Where are the Indians?"

They spoke in hushed tones.

"I killed one on the edge of the wood. I don't know where the other one is. I managed to circle around to elude him and get to you." He took her arm. "Are you all right?"

"Yes, and thank you for coming after me."

"What else would I do?" And though a little smile played at the corners of his lips, there was an earnestness in his tone.

It was then that she noticed the blood, mostly dried, smeared down the left side of his face. "You've been wounded?"

He gave a self-deprecating shrug. "Just a graze. Let's go."

Keeping to the trees, but with the creek in view at their right, they moved on. Rich had his revolver drawn. Jordana still clung to her branch. They walked for about five minutes, darkness steadily encroaching upon them. But Rich had the step of a man accustomed to the woods and to survival. His feet hardly made a sound, but he was patient with her when she chanced to snap a twig underfoot. Jordana wondered about the kinds of military action this soldier of hers had experienced.

Of hers?

Well, it was getting to be like he was her personal guardian angel. But of course it went no further than that, no matter what Brenton thought. Rich O'Brian was a very nice man, even if he had a few rough edges. He'd saved her life on several occasions at no small risk to his own. She owed him something. Friendship? Well, maybe she could at least be nicer to him. And maybe she could try harder to keep from harming him, accidental though it might be.

Suddenly Jordana was jerked to a stop with a painful wrench to her arm. "Ow—!" But Rich's hand shot to her mouth, preventing further comment.

In the next instant, an Indian leaped as if from nowhere, grabbing Rich and knocking him to the ground. The revolver bounced from Rich's hand, and only then did Jordana see that the Indian had a knife.

The two men grappled on the ground, the knife glinting in the shadows as it hovered lethally between them. Jordana thought about making use of her branch, but she'd done more harm than good with such maneuvers in the past and feared doing so again. Besides, Rich was on top of the Indian now, and she couldn't have done much with the branch anyway. Instead she tried to see where the gun had fallen, but in the growing darkness it was almost impossible to find.

In a moment, the two combatants were on their feet. The Indian still held the knife, and they were facing each other. The Indian made a lunge, the tip of his blade slicing Rich's arm. Undeterred, Rich grabbed the Indian's knife hand, repelling it momentarily.

Suddenly, Rich went down. He must have stumbled over something. It hardly mattered. The Indian intended on taking full advantage of this error.

At that same moment, Jordana spied the gun. She dove for it and took aim, praying it was fully loaded and ready to fire. She fired as the Indian made what would have been a fatal thrust with his knife at the now defenseless Rich. A moment after the explosion of the pistol, the attacker stumbled forward—right on top of Rich.

Jordana screamed, squeezing her eyes shut, fearing she had been no help at all and the knife would still find its mark.

Shaking all over, she forced her eyes open, only to find Rich had rolled away from the falling attacker just in time. Relief swept over her at seeing him safe. Then, in the very next instant, she realized she had just shot a man. The shock of it made her crumble to the ground.

She awoke from her faint to find herself in Rich's arms. It felt very nice, and she just wanted to close her eyes again and snuggle close to his safe and secure body.

"You saved my life, Jordana," he said, forcing her from her sweet solitude.

"I . . . I g-guess we're even," she said with a lopsided smile. She added, "No . . . you are still a couple up on me."

He tenderly brushed a strand of hair from her eyes. "You are a very brave woman." He wore a slight smile, but his tone seemed to vibrate with intensity. "Can you walk?"

That little question jarred her from her shock. Could she walk? As if she were some frail creature! She conveniently forgot she *had* just fainted. Instead, she scooted to her feet, with only a little remaining regret at having to part from Rich O'Brian's strong, warm arms.

"Of course I can walk," she said tartly. But then her gaze strayed to the fallen form of the Indian. A sick feeling fluttered in her stomach, and she swayed on her feet. Rich, having also stood, caught her. "Is . . . is he dead?"

"Yes . . ."

"Oh, dear! How awful! I . . . I . . ." But she didn't know what to say, how to express the horror she felt at having taken a human life. She had been so afraid of the Indians hurting her, she had never imagined her doing the same to them. But he was *dead*, and she had killed him.

Rich put an arm around her. "I'm sorry you were forced to do that. It is never easy to take a life."

"Even for you?"

"It makes me sick every time."

"Oh . . ." She turned to look at him and found him gazing at her.

They both started in embarrassed surprise at the closeness, then jerked their heads away. Rich dropped his arm from around her waist.

"We'd best get back," he said. "Hopefully, my men have fought off the other Indians. I guess it helped that you drew off a couple from the main battle."

"Maybe that was my intention," she said coyly.

He laughed and the sound of his wry humor seemed to break the awkwardness they had suddenly begun to feel. Both of them, Jordana thought, were far more comfortable sparring with each other.

"I think your intention was just to make my life complicated again," Rich said with an amused edge to his voice.

"I am so very sorry! You didn't have to come after me."

"What? And risk one of my men on such a hazardous duty, when I know saving you can be a dangerous business!"

199

With a loud "Harrumph!" Jordana started walking.

"Miss Baldwin, it's the other way." His laughing eyes met hers as she turned.

She fought to restrain a responding smile and keep up her look of haughty affront. But it was a hard battle because Rich's humor was so infectious, and she was so very grateful to him.

After finding their horses, they returned to the wagons where they found the battle had ended. Sergeant Hart reported that their party had sustained only a couple of minor injuries. The attackers retreated after losing some three or four of their number.

"Add two more to that," said Rich. "I killed one, and Miss Baldwin killed another."

"Jordana!" Brenton exclaimed. "Are you quite all right?"

"Yes. It was horrible, but it's over now. And"—she glanced toward Rich and smiled sincerely—"I have Captain O'Brian to thank again for rescuing me."

Brenton said, "Thank you again, Captain. We are once more in your debt."

"Your sister saved my life as well."

"Nevertheless, your superiors will hear of your bravery and of your men's bravery as well."

"Please, Brenton, the last time you wrote my superiors, I got this assignment. If you write again I might end up serving somewhere in the frozen north, where, given my luck, your sister will decide to settle." His gaze skittered to Jordana, and he gave her a roguish grin.

She knew he was just being playful. She liked it so much better that way, and to keep it in that vein, she responded with a click of her tongue and a haughty look.

"The next time an enemy comes at you with a knife, Captain," she countered, "I may just find myself too faint of heart to pull the trigger."

"Speaking of fainting . . ."

"Don't you dare!" she gasped, part warning, part imploring.

He laughed but did not finish his statement, much to her relief, for she'd have been mortified for Brenton and the others to think of her as a swooning female. Then other duties called him away. Jordana watched him briefly before she too turned her energy to helping Brenton.

Yes, she thought, Rich O'Brian might just be a pleasant friend.

Twenty-Five

If Jordana had hoped to find peace at home after the adventures of the trail, she was disappointed. When the survey team returned to Omaha, it was like being tossed into the middle of a fire, or at least a powder keg close to exploding.

Rumors, never completely quelled, were rampant about various threats to the town. It was feared Quantrill's raiders had set their sights on Omaha. After Quantrill's devastating sack of Lawrence, Kansas, in the spring of '63, perhaps the citizens of Omaha had a right to be nervous. The Confederate guerrilla leader—though many considered him more an outlaw than a soldier—along with his four hundred fifty bushwhackers, was an imposing threat.

This, coupled with renewed Indian uprisings along the Platte and Elkhorn Rivers, had spurred on the forming and training of a local militia. Brenton and Jordana were still unpacking from their trip when an acquaintance of Brenton's, along with two strangers, came to their little house.

"We expect you to be there this Saturday when we drill," said Jeff Tanner.

"I've been away on railroad business," Brenton explained, trying to remain cool in spite of Jeff's belligerent tone.

"Well, you're back now. You ain't got no more excuses."

"I'm not giving excuses—"

"Sounds to us like you are," cut in one of the strangers. "Sounds like you are just plain yella."

"That is pure bunk!" But because Brenton did feel a pang of guilt, he felt compelled to add, "I've just returned from fighting Indians

201

out on the plains. I'm doing my part."

"Good, then we'll see you there."

The three men stalked away.

Brenton took off his glasses and rubbed his eyes. Jordana laid a comforting hand on his arm.

"You are only doing what you believe is right," she said.

"Sometimes I no longer know what is right." He sucked in a deep sigh. "I can fight Indians, and fighting Quantrill is only technically fighting the South. I expect there are many honorable southerners who deplore that man's activities."

"Do you think you will join the militia, then?"

"I may. The Indian threat is real enough. I just heard about a settler being murdered right on the outskirts of town."

"Goodness! No one we know, I hope." She had bank dealings with many citizens and settlers in the area.

"A man named Homer Stanley—"

"Stanley?"

"Do you know him?"

Jordana thought back to the conversation between Damon and his visitors she had overheard at the bank. Damon had mentioned that name. Stanley had land Damon wanted. She still felt a chill when she recalled Damon's threatening words and ominous tone: *"I'll take care of it!"*

"Jordana, are you all right?" Brenton broke into her thoughts.

Blinking, she focused on her brother. "Yes . . . I think the Chittendens knew Stanley. He had land Damon wanted to buy."

"Well, he can probably get it for a song now," said Brenton. "No one will want it with the threat of Indian attack so close."

"I suppose that's true." It did seem a good stroke for Damon, and if his hard words in the bank were any gauge, he would probably not grieve much over the death of the settler.

"You are looking kind of pale, Jordana."

"I'm fine." She did, however, find a seat on the parlor divan. "It's just that we left home because of the war—well, not entirely because of it, but it certainly was a factor. Now it seems to have followed us here."

"There can be no getting away from such a catastrophe as civil war." He shook his head morosely. "I should have realized it." Pausing, he plopped down on the divan beside his sister. He lifted questioning, confused eyes to her. "Jordana, you don't think me a coward, do you?"

"Of course not! You are a brave and honorable man, and that is why you feel so caught in the middle. Why, Captain O'Brian told me how bravely you fought those Indians. You have nothing to be ashamed of, Brenton."

"I fired my gun," he corrected wryly. "But it is questionable whether I actually hit anything or anyone, my eyesight is so bad."

"At least you tried. You didn't go running for cover."

"I wanted to!"

"But you didn't, and in my mind that makes you even braver than Captain O'Brian, because you did it despite your fear. The captain simply revels in such activity."

"Well, I don't know if 'revel' is the right word." He cleaned the lens of his glasses on his sleeve as he spoke. "He's very good at what he does, but I doubt he does it for the glory alone, and I am certain he takes no delight in killing."

"I suppose that's true—"

A knock at the door interrupted them. Jordana looked at the door before she even thought to rise. She prayed it wasn't that Jeff Tanner and his friends. They had no right to treat her brother so.

It was Brenton who rose to answer the door. And it was Caitlan who greeted them, but it wasn't her usual cheery greeting.

"Brenton, Jordana!" Her lip trembled, and her red eyes indicated she'd been crying.

"What is it, Caitlan?" asked Brenton with concern.

She held up a fist, which Jordana saw was clutching a piece of paper. Jordana now rose and hurried to her friend and put an arm around her, taking the paper as she did so.

" 'Tis me brother . . ." New tears spilled from Caitlan's eyes. "Kiernan has been in an accident!"

"Dear Lord, no!" breathed Brenton and Jordana almost in unison.

"He was in an explosion . . . it's . . . serious." Caitlan's tears now grew into trembling sobs. "Just like our brother . . . just like what killed . . . Red. . . ." She suddenly seemed to turn into a rag doll. As her knees weakened and she pitched forward, it was not Jordana but rather Brenton who caught her.

Jordana watched her brother's arms wrap around Caitlan, his hand smoothing her hair, his voice murmuring words of comfort.

Jordana's own eyes were filling as she thought of dear Kiernan hurt and possibly dead. She had been so young when she last saw him, but her memories were only fond ones of the big, gentle Irishman who had won her sister's heart. And suddenly, with an awful pang in her own heart, Jordana thought of Victoria and how devastating this must be to her.

It was some time before the three friends had assuaged one another's tears. They had taken seats. Caitlan and Brenton, still with his arm around her, had settled on the divan. Jordana was sitting in a chair adjacent to that. And it was she who made the first attempt to buoy them up in their grief.

"We must have faith that Kiernan is all right," Jordana said. "It has taken some time for this letter to reach us. He's probably much better by now."

"Or—" Caitlan began but could not finish the other possibility.

"Well, we just have to think positively, that's all. Caitlan, I know you don't want to believe in God, but I believe that we are all in His hands and we can trust Him for the best."

"But ya can't deny God takes folks sometimes, too," countered Caitlan.

Brenton took Caitlan's hand gently in his. "That's true," he said quietly, "and if that's the case, then He will give us the strength and courage to bear it."

"I never got to see him," Caitlan said, fresh tears rising to and overflowing her eyes.

"That's my fault alone," said Brenton. "I should not have wasted time in getting you to California."

"No, Brenton," said Caitlan, obviously finding some strength in comforting him, for her tears had abated a bit. "We all agreed to do what we did. 'Tis no one's fault. It's just that . . . oh, I so wanted to see him again."

"And you will!" Jordana said, as if she were announcing a given fact. "We can still get to California. And I feel certain we will find Kiernan there to greet us."

"But the money—" Caitlan protested.

"This is no time to worry about money," put in Brenton firmly. Jordana's words seemed to have brought him to a sudden resolve. "I'll hear not a word about charity either! We *must* go to California. It is your duty, Caitlan, to get there any way you can. You have to do it for Kiernan. And even if . . . well, even if the worst has happened, Victoria will need us."

A small smile bent Caitlan's lips. "Yar right, of course! I can't be lettin' me pride get in the way of doing what I can for me brother." She dashed a hand across her damp eyes. "I'll be worryin' about how to pay the money back later." When Brenton opened his mouth to protest, she shook her head. "Later, Brenton. But even that aside, how will we be findin' the money for such a trip? Ya said yar own self that a seat on the stage could be as much as two hundred dollars."

"I'll wire my parents," said Brenton without hesitation. "If they have heard about Kiernan, they are probably frantic with worry and will be relieved to send us on our way, since we are closer and can get there much faster than they."

"Thank you, Brenton," Caitlan said humbly. "I don't know what I'd be doin' had ya not been here for me." She looked up at Jordana, "And yarself too, Jordana. I've never had good friends, and if I were of a mind to, I know I would be thankin' God for ya both right now."

Jordana and Brenton smiled, but both seemed to sense this was not the time to press the issue. Jordana just knew Caitlan's words were the most precious she'd heard in a long time, and as she'd always believed, Caitlan was slowly being drawn back to God. It might be that Kiernan's accident would be the thing to finally bring Caitlan fully into the fold of God. But Jordana hoped it would not be at the expense of Kiernan's life.

Her thoughts were arrested by Brenton's voice.

" . . . Damon Chittenden or his father might help there, don't you think, Jordana?"

"What?" Whatever it was, she didn't like that Damon might be involved.

"I said," Brenton repeated, "that our biggest problem will be finding stage passage. And I wondered if the Chittendens might be able to pull some strings for us."

"In what way?" Jordana hedged.

"They have some influence in this town. Could they wrangle us stage tickets?"

"Well . . . uh . . . I don't know." Her sudden hesitancy brought questioning looks from her companions. She was ashamed of her attitude, especially if it would keep them from California, but how could she do as Brenton wanted? She knew she had to be honest about it. "Brenton, the last thing I want is to be indebted to Damon Chittenden for anything. He'll want me to marry him as payment."

"Even he couldn't be so crass," said Brenton.

Jordana was no longer sure of that. "Perhaps I can ask his father."

"I will inquire of some of my railroad acquaintances, too," offered Brenton.

Jordana nodded, then glanced at Caitlan's hopeful, tear-streaked face. She would do it for friendship's sake. The worst Damon could do was say no.

Twenty-Six

The next day, Damon approached Jordana at the bank. "My father tells me you have asked him about securing seats on a stage bound for California."

"Yes, I asked him this morning," Jordana replied coolly.

"What's in California?"

"I believe I told you my sister and her husband are there." Jordana paused, wondering how much she wanted to tell him but could think of no reason not to tell him what she had told his father. He probably knew it all anyway. "My brother-in-law was injured in an explosion, and we—that is my brother, Caitlan, and I—need to go to them."

"I see." He thoughtfully tapped his lip with his finger. "I told my father I would take care of the matter."

Jordana's heart sank. It seemed he had found a way to foil her attempt to avoid his involvement. "That's not necessary, Mr. Chittenden."

"Ah, but it is. . . ."

His eyes were so cold. Jordana had never noticed before, or had never let herself notice. She wondered now if he was capable of murder.

"At any rate," Damon went on, "my father is a very busy man and was happy to unburden himself of his task. Also my connections are far better than his. I should have no problem acquiring stage passage for you."

"At what cost, Mr. Chittenden?" she forced herself to bluntly ask.

207

"The usual price is two hundred—"

"That's not what I meant. I don't think you are a man to act simply for charity's sake."

"Oh, I am cut to the quick!" he exclaimed mockingly. Then he smiled, a rather benign smile she found difficult to read. "Jordana, there is but one thing I want from you."

"My brother was wrong—you *are* crass enough to expect me to marry you for tickets!"

"I appreciate that at least your brother sees me in a good light. How can I get you to do the same?" Another smile twitched his lips. "I would never trade a woman's favors for gain. However, I must tell you my friends who are in a position to make stage passage would probably be far more inclined to do so for my *fiancée* than for a mere bank employee."

Fury swelled up within Jordana. "No matter how you couch it, Mr. Chittenden, you are a crass, self-serving scoundrel! I wouldn't take tickets from you now no matter what!"

He laughed icily. "Jordana, you approached my father and me believing we had the power to obtain passage for you, and you were right in your thinking. But do understand that we also have the right to *block* your getting passage—from anyone else. All I need to do is drop a word to my friends, and neither you nor anyone associated with you Baldwins would be able to find even a broken-down mule to carry you to California."

"You can't do this!"

"Try me!" he sneered.

Jordana spun around and left the bank, not caring if she lost her job for leaving in the middle of the day. She no longer wanted the job anyway if it meant spending even a minute more in Damon's presence. He acted so superior, so all-fired powerful. He was barely twenty-one years old! She'd just like to see him pull those strings he tried to brag about. A broken-down mule indeed! Brenton had connections, too. And Caitlan's employer, Mrs. Cavandish, was also from an important family in town, and she had taken a liking to Caitlan.

Jordana now wondered why she had bothered to approach the Chittendens at all. She would find her own way.

But three days later it appeared as if Damon had indeed made good on his threat. Brenton had a good lead that was so firmly shut down the next day that Jordana had to wonder about the validity of what Damon had said and her low estimation of it. Stage seats were suddenly as scarce in Omaha as ice in summer.

Jordana had returned to work, the immediate need for finances overtaking her distaste for Damon. Hezekiah Chittenden avoided Jordana, which made her think he was as much under his son's thumb as everyone else. But he didn't upbraid her for her departure from work the other day, and when contact was unavoidable, he was civil, if not his usual warm self. Damon, on the other hand, did not avoid her at all. He seemed to go out of his way to be near her and to make sure she saw his gloating expression.

Jordana hated to admit it, but he might just win out. Caitlan continued to be beside herself with worry, and Jordana knew her friend would be comforted by nothing else but the sight of her brother, alive, if not well. More than once in those terrible days, Jordana asked herself just how much she was willing to sacrifice for stage passage. When her parents wired the money necessary for the trip and expressed their grateful encouragement of the plans, Jordana knew she must do *something*.

Perhaps she didn't have to agree to marriage. There might be another way to get to Damon. Since her discovery of those discrepancies in the ledgers some time ago, Jordana had been subtly investigating, redoubling her efforts in the last few days. She still had not come up with anything specific, but she was almost certain that something crooked was going on. And she was just as certain that the elder Chittenden was unaware of the inconsistencies in the bank's books. She had approached him about some of her discoveries, and he had responded with genuine surprise, but he had assured her there must be merely an error.

But Jordana had gone over the items too many times for that to be the case. She had also mentioned to Hezekiah—casually, of course—about Damon's several meetings with the man from the Union Pacific, whom Jordana had learned was named Albert Scofield, and Clayton. Hezekiah had little reaction to the name of Scofield, but he did rankle at the mention of Clayton, whom he said was a scoundrel and one of his longtime rivals. He had no idea what Clayton had to do with his son or the bank, but he also seemed disinclined to dwell on the matter.

If Damon was up to no good—and she was almost certain he was—then perhaps she had a small trump card to play against her would-be suitor. Of course, the idea of taking such an action was at best distasteful to Jordana, but she saw little other choice. Had she seriously believed Damon was even vaguely involved in Stanley's demise, she would never have considered using such means to get to Damon. But she had convinced herself that, although Damon was a lot of nasty things, he was not a killer.

So, taking up the second ledger, she knocked on Damon's office door.

"Come in," he said.

She chided herself when her hand trembled a bit as she grasped the door latch. She was being absolutely foolish. There was nothing to worry about. Damon was a romantic fool and a hard-edged businessman, but that was all. He wasn't going to bite her head off. He hadn't thus far even with her numerous rebuffs, so why should he now?

"Mr. Chittenden, do you have a moment?" Jordana's throat was dry despite the bravado of her inner encouragements.

"Always, for you, Jordana." He smiled. It was the nice smile she remembered from before. His friendliness disarmed her. What had she been thinking? Perhaps she had the man all wrong.

"Listen, Damon, I—"

"Ah, so you have decided to be familiar after all! I am pleased." This time his smile was just a tad oily.

"I wasn't thinking . . ." But she guessed she was probably thinking just fine and had spoken in this manner, albeit unconsciously, to wheedle her way onto his good side. "Mr. . . . uh . . . Chittenden, I still have some questions about this ledger." She held out the book in question.

Damon's expression noticeably fell. "And here I thought you had finally come to your senses about my marriage proposal." His tone was dead serious.

"I haven't changed my mind about that."

"You should, Jordana . . . you really should." Each word was even and well studied, his look as sharp as a dagger. This was no request by an eager suitor. It was a warning.

Jordana swallowed and continued to tell herself she was overreacting. "Do you wish to discuss this ledger?" she asked with a resolve she did not feel.

"Why should I?"

"Because if you don't make an attempt to satisfactorily explain it to me, I might be forced to take it to someone who can."

"Do I detect a threat?" He smiled. "Will you show it to my father, then?"

"I have taken it to your father, and he is ignorant of it all and wishes to remain so. I think he refuses to believe ill of his son. I, on the other hand, have no such compunction. Your father may not be interested in this matter, but I'll wager I can find men who are. Have you heard of Peter Dey? Or Colonel Silas Seymour? Or perhaps a Mr. Durant?" Jordana hoped she was wearing her best poker face. These men were on the UP board, but they hardly knew her from Adam. Even Brenton would be hard pressed to get an interview with them over this matter. No doubt they would think her nothing more than a silly woman should she attempt to approach them. She was gratified to see that Damon, at least, was taking her seriously. His expression fluttered slightly at the mention of these UP officials, who would surely consider Damon's schemes, whatever they were specifically, to be opposed to their own.

"What are you getting at?" His voice rose slightly.

"I believe you are doing something, if not outright illegal, then certainly underhanded. You are going to bring this bank to ruin, and though I don't give a fig about you, it pains me to see your father ruined as well, because he has been kind to me—"

"I have been kind to you also, Jordana," Damon cut in, not sharply, but with a soft tone that so contrasted with previous moods it made Jordana jittery. She wondered more and more about a man whose moods and expressions were so mercurial. "I have loved you," he added with emphasis.

"I am sorry about that, Damon," she said earnestly. And she truly was, for she believed he did love her. She didn't understand it, nor did she understand the sudden fear that realization caused in her.

"You don't have to be sorry." He rose from his desk and walked to where she stood. He placed his hands, feeling heavy and hot, on her shoulders. "You also ought not to fight this any longer. You will marry me, Jordana. Of that I am certain. I will not take no for an answer."

"I . . . I don't see how—"

"Shush . . . I said don't fight it." He laid a finger against her lips. "I'll be patient, you know. Very . . . very patient."

She knew then she had to get out of Omaha any way she possibly could. She had to get away from this man. He wasn't safe. But it also wasn't safe to soundly reject him. She must be subtle.

"Damon . . . you know, I must get to California. I must go comfort my sister. I can't think of anything else until I see for myself that her husband is well."

"You'll forget about that ledger? You'll forget about Homer Stanley?"

She blinked. She had said nothing about Stanley, had she?

"H-Homer Stanley. . . ?" she stammered. For one rare moment in her life, speech was nearly impossible. His eyes were boring into hers . . . his hands felt like hot irons on her shoulders, his voice as slippery as ice. "I don't know what you mean."

"I told you once before, I get what I want. Nothing stands in my way." He was so close to her, his hot breath made her eyes tear up.

"Yes, you did. But I have to get to California, Damon. I have to . . . first."

"First?"

"Before I can think of anything else. . . ."

"You give me your word?"

"Why shouldn't I?"

He grimaced. "That's not a very direct answer."

She tried to smile and sound coy. "Why, Damon, if you can't believe me, who can you believe?" She prayed he wanted her enough to accept her vague response. She would not be able to tell him an outright lie.

"I will think about it," he said just as vaguely.

And he dropped his hands from her shoulders and returned to his seat. She left the office not quite sure what she had agreed to, hoping she hadn't sold her soul to the devil.

But when she returned to her desk from an errand later in the day, she found an envelope containing three tickets for passage on the westbound stage.

The celebration at home was short-lived when she confided to Brenton about the scene in Damon's office. Brenton was ready to challenge the man to a duel. At the very least he was going to report him to the police. Jordana agreed this must be done, especially if Damon had anything to do with the death of Homer Stanley. However, she felt traitorous in doing so. She hadn't actually given her word to Damon about anything, but she had let him believe she had. Brenton assured her that she had merely acted in self-defense. Even if Damon were innocent of their suspicions, he hadn't acted honorably in preventing them from getting tickets, so Jordana was justified in her actions.

The irony was, after all that soul-searching, when Brenton spoke to the sheriff, the man all but laughed in his face. The Chittendens were one of Omaha's finest families. Surely Jordana's accusations were all in her imagination. The man even intimated that Jordana might be attempting to discredit Damon because he had rejected her! The sheriff did say he would look into the matter, leaving the distinct impression that he would do it as soon as he saw a Nebraska pig fly through the sky.

Jordana could not have been more ready when, two days after her confrontation with Damon, she and Brenton and Caitlan boarded the stage and jerked away from the Omaha depot.

PART III

September — October 1864

Twenty-Seven

*E*ven Kiernan's spirits had lifted briefly from his morose mood that first day he had been able to get up and walk. He had taken it slowly at first, but now, almost four months since his accident, he was getting around quite well. His left arm was weak, but he was using it and religiously exercising it so it would return to full capacity. Only his eye continued to evade improvement, still seeing only shadows, and it was so sensitive to light he continued to wear the patch. The doctor hinted it might be a permanent fixture. Victoria told him it made him look rakish and mysterious.

"I look like a silly pirate," he had countered. "And there's nothin' rakish about a redheaded pirate!"

"That's your opinion." She bent down as he sat on the sofa in the front room of their borrowed house and kissed him passionately. "I rather like it."

"Victoria, me love, I don't deserve a woman like you."

She opened her mouth, and he knew she was about to give him her usual lecture when he made such statements, telling him what a good and fine man he was, how handsome, how loving, how he was the best husband a woman could want . . . and so on, and so on. He wanted to believe her. And most of the time he at least acted as if her words encouraged him. But today he was feeling especially useless. He had tried to do too much, helping Victoria and Li in the laundry, but after an hour, he had been exhausted and had flopped down on the sofa like an old man at the end of his years.

Nevertheless, Victoria was forced to save her lecture for another time as a visitor knocked on the front door. It was Charlie Crocker.

217

Kiernan appreciated that the man paid regular visits and attempted to keep Kiernan up-to-date on the happenings with the railroad. The man was trying to make Kiernan feel useful, but the visits only made him feel restless and more helpless than ever—not that he would ever tell his friend that. No matter what the visits made him feel like, he didn't want them to stop, because they were his only outlet in an existence that had become excruciatingly dull.

"Seems I've come with my usual tales of woe," Crocker said with a wry grin.

"Makes us even, then," Kiernan said. His own grin was far less sincere.

"So what problems are there now?" asked Victoria.

"Progress continues to be at a standstill." Crocker sighed. "We are beset by lawsuits, and everyone imaginable is challenging our funding. Kiernan, you chose a good time to be laid up. I wonder if I could have kept you on anyway."

"I'm glad I could accommodate," said Kiernan dryly.

"What work I do have, I am hard pressed to find laborers, much less pay them. I fear when the funding is finally established, I won't have anyone left to do the work. It's the same old story, I'm afraid."

"The call of the goldfields," Victoria put it wistfully.

Kiernan knew how glad she was those fields no longer called her husband.

"I should be able to work soon"—Kiernan stopped when Victoria shot him a surprised glance, then he went on quickly—"if ya can use a one-eyed pirate. Why, I'd even be takin' a cut in pay just to have somethin' worthwhile to do."

"I was merely jesting about what I said about you working, Kiernan," said Crocker. "There will always be a place for you, no matter how many eyes you have. Half blind and with an arm tied behind your back, you can still do the job better than many men I've encountered."

"Thank ya kindly, Charlie." Kiernan hated to admit it, but having a male colleague offer such approbation went further to encourage him than any of Victoria's lectures.

"But you would still need a crew."

"If you are this concerned," said Kiernan, "then it must mean ya'll be moving forward soon."

"I keep hoping. The war can't last forever. The South is practically beaten. Sherman has taken Atlanta and demonstrated the

Union Army's determination to bring a decisive conclusion to the war. It is only a matter of time now, and when the war ends, as you well know, it will mean full steam ahead, quite literally, for the transcontinental railroad. It could happen in a matter of months, and I want to be ready."

"As do I, Charlie," Kiernan said with as much enthusiasm as he'd felt in weeks.

Victoria cleared her throat daintily, then interjected, "I believe you may be overlooking an important labor pool in the state. Li tells me there are Chinese arriving daily to this country and all in dire need of work."

"Of course, it is not the first time I've been approached with that idea," Crocker responded. "But I think it would cause as many problems as it would solve."

"I know for a fact," added Kiernan, "that the Irish I've worked with on the line despise the Chinese and would refuse to work with them."

"But most of those Irishmen hate any who are different from them," countered Victoria, "and they hate some of their own people as well. Not all Irish are as tolerant as you, dear Kiernan."

"'Tis true enough. But one thing the Irish have that many of the Chinese don't is sheer size and brute strength."

"Yes," agreed Crocker. "I simply have my doubts that such small-statured men have the stamina and strength for the job. The rails alone weigh fifty pounds a yard, and then there's the tons of rock that have to be moved on a daily basis. And I have seen many a brawny Irishman weary at driving spikes."

"But Kiernan has complained to no end about the laziness of many of the men on his crew. He's said they have even gone so far as to post guards along the line to warn the others that he is coming to inspect so that they can make a show of working." She glanced at Kiernan as if for approval, and he had to nod because her words were true enough. "I have gotten to know many Celestials through Li, and I find them to be serious, hardworking people."

"I won't argue there," said Crocker. "Perhaps it would be no worse with the Chinese, perhaps even better. And no doubt they would work for less pay as well. But there is still the question of stamina."

"And ya are forgetting the cultural differences," added Kiernan. "I have me doubts about supervisin' people whose needs I know so little about. And that's not even to mention the language problem. Even the ones who speak some English are mighty difficult to understand."

Victoria gave him a wily smile, and Kiernan knew what she was thinking. How many times had he been criticized for his thick accent, especially in those first years after coming to America? And he supposedly already spoke English! But he hadn't liked the criticism, and often felt it was simply an excuse for employers not to hire him. He didn't want to be like that. America was quickly becoming a nation of many nationalities, and that should not stand in a man's way toward success.

He cocked an eyebrow at his wife. "And I'm supposin' ya have an answer to that?"

"I'm sure there must be some Chinese competent in the English language who could act as interpreters. Li's husband, for example, learned his English from missionaries in his country and is quite good. He could act as Kiernan's assistant and liaison to the Chinese crew."

Crocker rubbed his chin, then grinned at Kiernan. "The little woman here has quite a head on her shoulders, doesn't she? And she makes a good case."

"She does that indeed." Kiernan grinned proudly, then added playfully, "I know it well, since I am hard pressed to ever win an argument wi' her."

Laughing, Crocker said, "Well, I shall give this conversation some serious thought. Perhaps we have found a way to solve at least one of our railroad problems."

After Crocker departed, Kiernan and Victoria continued to visit. Kiernan was pleased at his wife's buoyant spirits. She chatted about the laundry and about all she was learning from Li. Kiernan refrained from his usual speech about hating her to be working as a common washerwoman. Victoria also went on about little Jia's antics, and again Kiernan made himself not think about the emptiness he sometimes felt at not having children of his own. He'd felt this more since the accident than ever before, because it had occurred to him that had he died, he would have had no part of him to live on.

Victoria's laughter broke discordantly into his thoughts. He smiled, though just for form, because he had no idea what she had said that was so amusing. Well, at least she was finally happy, and he must try to put on a show of the same himself. He must not think about all the ways he was letting her down. Or how he was also letting Charlie down. He needed to keep thinking how daily he was getting better.

But for some reason, it was just not enough.

Twenty-Eight

$\mathcal{S}$unday morning brought a warm September day to Sacramento. Humming a little Irish tune that was one of Kiernan's favorites, Victoria prepared a breakfast of potatoes, side pork, and a half dozen precious eggs someone had given her in payment for their laundry bill.

Kiernan came into the kitchen as Victoria dumped the chopped potatoes into the lard. Grease spattered loudly.

"Music to me hungry ears!" Kiernan remarked as he poured a cup of coffee and sat at the kitchen table.

"It is fortunate I married an Irishman for all the potatoes we eat." It was a glib comment, but she saw immediately it was ill spoken. Any amusement that might have crept into Kiernan's usually dour expression faded. "Goodness, Kiernan, you needn't be so sensitive!" She tried to chuckle lightly. "I feel truly blessed to have what we have and . . . well, you don't need to feel bad." She laid her hand on his shoulder, which tensed beneath her touch.

"And from what charitable hand did ya get those eggs?" he asked snidely.

"They are payment . . . for services rendered."

"Oh, I see, ya worked for them yarself, eh?"

"Sometimes, Kiernan, I don't even care to talk to you." She returned to the stove to stir the potatoes. "To be perfectly honest, I think it is time you stop all this confounded self-pity and begin to count your own blessings."

"And if I had some to be countin', maybe I would!"

"You are impossible."

223

She busied herself once more with meal preparations. She felt as if she had come up against a solid wall in knowing how to deal with her husband. Sometimes he seemed congenial, even cheerful, but mostly he was sullen and temperamental. She had begun to think that even his congenial moments were merely an act for her sake. She didn't know how to get through to him, how to make him realize she loved him for who he was and thought no less of him now that he had hit a difficult time. She believed firmly in "for better or worse." But she could not get Kiernan to believe her. She felt as if her words of encouragement—lectures, he sometimes called them—fell on ears as deaf as his eye was blind.

"I'm sorry, Victoria, me love," he said contritely, turning in his chair to gaze at her. "Yar one blessin' I must never forget to be countin'."

But she had heard his contriteness once too often. Perhaps he meant it to some extent when he said it, but it wasn't good enough.

"Stop it, Kiernan!" she burst out. "You are only saying you are sorry because that's what you think I want to hear. I guess it's noble that you want to please me, but I know you are just play-acting."

"Ya lecture me when I'm glum, ya lecture me when I go tryin' to make up for it! I'll not be winnin' no matter what I do!" he exclaimed with frustration.

"I just want you to—" But sudden tears sprang to her eyes. She tried to dash them away with the back of her hand but to no avail. "I want you to be the way you were . . ." she murmured softly.

"I'm damaged. I'll never—"

"That's not what I mean, and you know it!" She realized suddenly her tears were both from sorrow and anger. "I'm talking about your heart, not your body, you thickheaded Irishman! Do you think I am so shallow, a blind eye bothers me? Then, after all these years, you don't know me at all."

"It bothers me . . ." he breathed, as if he were afraid to admit it.

"Oh, my darling!" She went to him and wrapped her arms around his neck. "I don't believe you are that shallow either. There is so much more to you. Of all the things I love about you, your body is quite low on the list. Please . . . please, Kiernan, can't you see that?"

He was silent for a long time as she held him, then he nodded his head. "I will try," he said. But she couldn't tell if it was sincere or more play-acting. Then he added with a grin that was so much like his old self, she truly did want to believe him, "So I'm thick-headed, am I?"

"I'm sorry. That was a mean thing to say."

"But true, I'm supposin'."

They had a fairly pleasant breakfast after that, and when Li and Jia left the table, Victoria attempted to broach another tender subject.

"Kiernan, I was wondering . . . if maybe you were feeling up to coming with me to church today." She fiddled with her spoon in the silence that followed her question. But she thought it was a fair question. Since his accident Kiernan had stopped attending church, using his health as his excuse. For a time it was quite a valid one indeed. But Victoria had deemed him well enough for the outing a couple of weeks ago. Still he made excuses.

Finally, Kiernan answered, "I'm afraid I'd fall asleep during the sermon." He made an attempt to lightly wave off the topic.

"What's new about that?" she said cuttingly. The fact was, Kiernan had always been attentive in church, but she just needed to vent her frustration over yet another of his excuses.

"That's not fair, Victoria!"

"I'll tell you what isn't fair," she retorted. "It isn't bad enough you blame yourself for all your woes, but you blame God as well! When you know better. And now you are turning your back on the only thing that might possibly help you."

"I am not blamin' God!"

"Well, it certainly looks that way when you refuse to attend church. And I've seen you when Reverend Carlton comes to visit, how you drum your fingers on the table while he's praying and how you nod and smile benignly at his words, refusing to let anything sink in. Well, that does it!" She shoved back her chair and jumped to her feet. "If you want to continue sitting about sulking and feeling sorry for yourself, then be my guest. But I will no longer be drawn down with you. I am going to church today, with or without you!"

She strode from the kitchen and marched to their room, where she finished dressing. Her hands trembled as she combed her hair and pinned it up. And she kept expecting, hoping really, that Kiernan might come into the room, truly contrite and ready to give up his anger and whatever else was so distressing him.

But Kiernan did not appear in the doorway, and when Victoria left, he was sitting in the parlor, seemingly absorbed in a book. When she said good-bye, he made no response.

––––––––

Kiernan never hated himself more than when he let his wife leave without a word. He knew her actions were from concern and love. Yet he didn't want to believe that he blamed God for all his misfortunes. He'd been through other difficulties in the past and had not turned from his faith. Why would Victoria think he was now? Just because he didn't feel up to attending church?

Sometimes he had tried to be angry at God, but it didn't last long because it always came back to his own fault in the matter. God had not kept him from miscounting the dynamite charges. That had been his own stupidity. But Kiernan's anger, whether directed at himself or elsewhere, had been building since long before his accident. It might not have affected his faith, or at least his church attendance, but it had been steadily gnawing away at him for years. Steadily beating him down.

A man could only take so much.

It had all really begun that day he had found out about the loss of Victoria's inheritance. Nothing seemed to have gone right after that. And he surely couldn't blame God for his poor financial judgment. Yet he now thought of something Victoria had said that morning.

"Do you think I am so shallow, a blind eye bothers me? . . . I don't believe you are that shallow either."

No, and he also wasn't shallow enough to believe this had anything to do with money. It went far deeper than that. And as that realization hit him, it made him audibly gasp. This was really about the lies and deceptions that financial loss had led him into. It was about his rotten pride. And not only had he put himself on that path, but he had forced Victoria along it also. He had all but forced her to lie to her parents, the people she loved most in the world next to him. He had forced a wedge between her and her parents.

Because of his pride.

He thought of the Scripture "Pride goeth before a fall." And he knew now he had definitely fallen. And taken the woman he loved with him. Because of him they had suffered want and poverty; because of him Victoria was forced to labor at a lowly job now and take charity from others. Because of him she was apart from her dear family. And who knew? Maybe it was also because of him, because of the poor diet and hard work that Victoria was unable to conceive a child.

And for a brief moment, Kiernan began to think his accident, directed solely at him, was his punishment for all the calamity he had brought to their lives. But as quickly as the idea came, it brought an ironic smile to his lips. Just as God was not to blame for his misfortunes, so was God not punishing him with more misfortune. That was not what a God of love did. But like any caring parent, God the Father would very likely use misfortune to get a man's attention. And God would help a man to use misfortune to become a better man and to grow and learn to be more mature.

When Kiernan asked himself how he could use his accident thus, several responses came to him. First was the matter of feeling sorry for himself, not only for his physical infirmities but also for all his past failures. He had to stop that before he destroyed both himself and Victoria. He had to keep focused on all the positive aspects of what had happened. He was alive after a mishap that should have killed him. He had healed remarkably well and would soon be back to normal with but one eye that wasn't functioning properly.

It was harder to find the good in losing Victoria's money. Pride and guilt were simply too strong in him. Pride mostly. He remembered something he'd heard once, that pride was the sworn enemy to contentment. How very true it was. And one prideful act seemed to lead to another and another, feeding on each other, building on each other until a man had nothing left to him but pride—and not the good kind of pride at that. This was a very empty, very shallow thing.

And Kiernan desired to be more than that. But how? How could he change all that had happened? He could never restore the money to Victoria. He had been trying to do just that all these years with absolutely no success. But he already knew the money itself wasn't the problem. It was . . .

Kiernan leaned forward in his chair, taut with excitement. *It wasn't the money—it was the lies.* It might not be the answer to all his problems, but he knew suddenly where he could at least heal one of his largest inner wounds. He had to be honest. He had to confess what he'd done.

As he thought of the word "confess" another Scripture came to his mind. He couldn't recall it exactly, but it had something to do with confession. What was it?

He jumped up and went to the small shelf of books and found his Bible. Victoria had given it to him years ago when she had taught him to read. He was sorry that he still could not read well enough to grasp all the book contained. He browsed through the pages wishing he'd had time to learn to read as well as Victoria. She'd be able to find the verse easily.

The thought of Victoria made him recall why he remembered that verse. It was in Victoria's favorite book, First John. He found the book quickly near the end of the Bible, and the verse was in the very first chapter.

"If we confess our sins, he is faithful and just to forgive us our sins, and to cleanse us from all unrighteousness."

He knew now that's what he needed. Cleansing.

Standing there by the bookshelf, the Bible still in his hands, he closed his eyes and prayed for the first time in months.

"Father in heaven, I don't know why ya haven't given up on me long ago. I've been lettin' such filth grow inside me, such shame. My pride is all those things, and now I'm confessin' it to ya, that it has kept me from being content in yarself and in the wonderful life ya have given me. Forgive me, Father. And help me to clean it from my soul. My pride is worthless after all, because I am nothin' in and of meself. It is only yarself who makes me the man I am and desire to be. Thank ya for that, God. Thank ya for not givin' up on me."

When he lifted his head from his prayer, he knew there was one more thing he had to do to complete the cleansing. He went to Victoria's writing table, sat down, and took paper, pen, and ink from a drawer. If reading was difficult for him, writing was more so, but what he must do now must be in his own hand, illegible as it might be.

An hour later, Victoria returned home. Kiernan greeted her with a smile that, though not broad, was warm and sincere.

"Kiernan, what is it?" There was concern mixed with anticipation in her tone. She obviously knew something had changed.

"While ya were at church," he replied, "it was me who did some soul-searchin'." He took her hand and led her to the sofa, where they sat side by side. "I ask ya to forgive me, Victoria, for all I've put ya through these many years." She started to protest, but he shook his head. "No, I'm not goin' to start whinin' and blamin' meself.

But I do know I've been too proud for me own good, and for yars. I've made too much of me own strength, forgettin' I am nothin' without God. With His help I plan to mend that now."

"Oh, Kiernan," she smiled through her tears. "Of course I forgive you, though in truth I never held anything against you—well, hardly anything!" she giggled tearfully.

"How I love ya, Victoria! And I don't care what ya say, I don't deserve you, but I know now I hardly deserve any of God's good gifts. No one does." He held out the paper he had been holding. "This is something I should have done long ago. Read it if ya can past all my scribblin's and misspellin's."

Victoria took the paper. The words were brief and to the point, for Kiernan didn't have the ability to do more. But it was enough. She read aloud through her tears:

Dear Father and Mother Baldwin,

I am writing this to confess that I have lied to you all these years regarding Victoria's inheritance. Through poor judgment I lost it all in the bank crisis in 1857. If that was not bad enough, I was too ashamed to tell you, and I asked Victoria to keep the matter from you also. I know I do not deserve your forgiveness, but I ask for it anyway. You are two people I respect most in the world, and the loss of your love and trust is as bad as losing a fortune.

Yours, most humbly,
Kiernan O'Connor

Victoria refolded the paper. "Kiernan, you know they will never hold this against you."

"Knowing them, I am sure they won't, but it had to be said."

She nodded. "Yes . . ."

"I am so sorry I made you lie about it."

"Well, it is behind us now," she assured.

"It will be as soon as that letter is mailed."

Twenty-Nine

$\mathcal{V}$ictoria was elbow-deep in soapsuds when Li came to the laundry shed with mail, actually a telegram delivered to the house a few minutes before. Taking dripping hands from the water, Victoria dried them on a towel. But she didn't take the missive immediately. She just stared at it.

"What wrong, Victoria? You always like to get letters," said Li.

"But people only send telegrams to deliver good or bad news—usually bad." Victoria reached out her hand. "Well, here goes. . . ." she said, taking the paper and opening it. She scanned it quickly, then let out a "Whoop!"

Li frowned. "That mean good or bad?"

"Good!" exclaimed Victoria. "It's from my brother, sent from Utah. He, my sister, and Kiernan's sister are en route to California. They'll be here in a couple of weeks. Oh, Li, I can't believe it! Only now do I realize just how much I missed them. And Kiernan will simply be beside himself to know he will soon finally see his sister."

There was indeed a grand celebration when Kiernan saw the telegram. And they immediately began preparations, Kiernan wondering if he could wait two weeks, Victoria wondering if that would be enough time to get everything ready. She was thankful they were in the larger house where they had room to accommodate everyone, but the fact that there were not enough beds and covers did pose a problem. But when word circulated among their friends about the upcoming reunion, it seemed many were thrilled to help out. A woman at church who ran a boardinghouse said she had two beds in her attic they could borrow. Others loaned quilts and blankets.

Then Charlie Crocker got into the act. He just happened to have a quarter section of pork lying around if Victoria had the time to preserve the meat. Of course she had the time.

The most amazing thing was that Kiernan did not raise his usual protests about "charity." He seemed able to discern that the giving brought the givers such joy, it would be foolish to protest.

But into the joyful chaos of those days, there did come one sad note. Xiang arrived in Sacramento with the announcement that things were going well in Newcastle, and he felt it was a good time for Li and their son to join him. Victoria had known this time must come eventually, but she had let herself forget it as her dependence on Li's friendship had grown.

She put on a brave front for Li when the day of her departure came. But she simply could not keep back the tears when she gave Jia a hug and the child's arms reached around her neck in a tight embrace.

The tears came in full order after Li and Xiang and their son disappeared down the road. Victoria threw her arms around her husband and wept unashamedly.

"What will I do without them?" she cried. "Every time I make a friend, I end up losing them."

"I know 'tisn't easy, me love," he cooed. "But thanks be to God, He's sendin' someone in short order to fill the emptiness."

"Yes . . . that is fortuitous, isn't it?" she sniffed and dabbed her eyes with a handkerchief.

"Ya'll be so busy when our kin arrives ya won't know what to do with yarself."

"But what about when they leave. . . ."

"Now, don't go thinkin' negative. And no matter what, I'll always be here for ya—I'm one friend who won't go away."

Sniffing again, she smiled. "Thank you, Kiernan! I guess I should look at it as God never takes but that He doesn't give something else in return."

"There ya go!"

"How long do you think they will stay—Brenton, Jordan, and Caitlan, I mean?"

"It's hard telling. But I'll warrant there is enough here in California to keep a trio of adventurers like them occupied for a good long time."

They were almost there. Jordana had begun to wonder if their excruciating journey would ever come to an end. She had traveled by many different modes in the two years since leaving her childhood home, but even compared to attacks by Indians and bushwhackers, travel by stage was the worst.

The three lady passengers, Jordana, Caitlan, and a portly matron named Mrs. Burleson, were crammed on one side. Jordana supposed she had it better than the four men taking the opposite seat, except that Mrs. Burleson easily took the space of two men. And the woman had the most annoying habit of not only snoring in her sleep, but she also flopped over heavily on Jordana when she slept, which was often. When Mrs. Burleson was awake, she talked incessantly, so that if Jordana couldn't sleep when the woman slept—a near impossibility given the noise and discomfort—she was unlikely to do so when the woman woke.

The discomfort of the stage itself was another matter. Jordana couldn't believe she had nearly sold her soul for these seats. The first thing the driver told them upon boarding was that if the team of horses ran away, the passengers should stay with the coach as they were more likely to get injured if they jumped off the coach. He didn't warn them about overturns, probably because that was such a common occurrence it hardly warranted mentioning. Also, probably for the same reason, he said nothing about the dust and bumps.

Jordana glanced over at Caitlan, whose gaze was fixed out the window. She had been sitting this way for the last fifteen minutes. Jordana didn't want to tell her that "a watched pot never boils." Not when Sacramento had to be around the next bend. Like her two companions, Caitlan's anxiety had to be mixed with anticipation and fear. None of them yet knew what they would find in Sacramento. If Kiernan had died, it would surely be great grief and sorrow. But Jordana made herself believe only the best. She just could not believe God had brought them this far only to mourn a dead brother.

"Do you see anything yet?" Jordana asked her sister-in-law.

"Only dust and rocks and trees. But it can't be too far ahead. The driver said we'd get there well before sundown."

"That should be soon, then."

Jordana glanced at Brenton, who had also drawn the middle seat that day and so had no window to occupy his time. But he was looking at Caitlan and did not notice Jordana, who smiled to herself at the sight. She imagined that the trip in such close quarters must have been difficult for both him and Caitlan, but they had been reserved with each other to the point of being aloof. Even Mrs. Burleson had commented to Jordana about the situation.

"Either those two love each other a great deal, or they are sworn enemies—but I'll wager my dessert at the next stop that it is the former!" And Mrs. Burleson would only risk her dessert on a sure thing.

Jordana didn't know how she was going to get those two ninnies together. Maybe Victoria would have some ideas.

Perhaps Jordana's efforts would be better spent in working out her own "love" problems. She wondered if she would ever be able to heal so completely from her hurt over G.W. as to find true love. But did she want that really? She wanted adventure and independence, too. Could she have it all?

Certainly not with Damon. How could she have been attracted to him in the first place? She was all but certain now that he might very well be a bit "touched in the head." Not so much because of his questionable business activities, but more because of his practically obsessive attitude toward her. Most normal men would have taken the hint long ago and would have moved on to greener pastures. Not Damon. Sometimes she thought he was actually encouraged by her rebuffs.

Rich O'Brian would certainly not behave so.

Hmm . . . why would she think of Captain O'Brian? Perhaps because of all the men she had encountered since coming west, he was the only one who didn't get all mushy around her. She appreciated that. She liked a man she didn't feel she could *handle*. He definitely had his own mind, and that made him pleasantly unpredictable. He didn't treat her like something between a goddess and an imbecile. But he did treat her with respect—she could tell that even when he was teasing her and browbeating her about her behavior. G.W. had been a lot like that. She had felt on an equal footing with him, and she felt the same way with the captain, even if he was constantly rescuing her from one disaster after another.

Yet, despite that sense of equality, she felt a great respect for Rich. He was smart and levelheaded and strong . . . so very strong. Not to mention tall and good-looking. Closing her eyes, she felt a little tingle course through her as she began to visualize his handsome visage.

"There it is!" Caitlan broke into Jordana's disconcerting thoughts.

Jordana leaned forward to glimpse out the window and could see buildings up ahead and the definite beginnings of a town. She grasped Caitlan's arm and smiled reassuringly. No matter what greeted them in Sacramento, they would be together, to love and support one another.

In another ten minutes, the stage rumbled to a stop at the Sacramento terminus of the Central Overland Stage Company. The wheels had barely stopped when Caitlan opened the door latch and jumped out. Jordana followed quickly just as the driver was about to put a step in place. He gave both young ladies a disapproving look for not waiting to be properly escorted in a more seemly fashion from the coach.

Quickly forgetting him, Jordana began to look wildly about for familiar faces. For a moment she despaired, and Caitlan came up beside her with a look on her face Jordana was certain mirrored her own. What if their telegram hadn't arrived? What if Victoria was too wrought with grief to meet them? What if . . . all manner of outlandish scenarios raced through Jordana's mind.

Then she saw Victoria step from the station building.

"Victoria!" she cried and ran like a child into her sister's arms.

It took a full minute before she remembered poor Caitlan standing there alone, not knowing a soul and no doubt feeling forlorn. Jordana reluctantly broke from her embrace and tugged Victoria to where Caitlan had now been joined by Brenton.

"Oh, Brenton! Look at you!" exclaimed Victoria. "You are taller than Papa now. And"—she turned a smiling face toward Caitlan—"you must be Caitlan." She threw her arms around her sister-in-law and kissed her cheek. "I don't care if we have never met. You are my sister, and I love you already."

Caitlan could not speak because of her tears, which flooded even more when a tall redheaded figure appeared close to Victoria.

"Me baby sis! Look at ya!" he said, holding out his arms.

"K-Kiernan!" Caitlan managed. " 'Tis really yarself?"

"None other."

"Oh my!" And she accepted the invitation of those open arms

and wrapped her own around the brother she had not seen for so many years.

After everyone else had been properly greeted, the party turned their attention to the pile of luggage on the sidewalk.

"Good thing I have borrowed Charlie Crocker's wagon!" Kiernan said.

"Brenton had to pay extra for all his photographic equipment," commented Jordana. "But he couldn't leave it behind. There are sure to be many new and exciting things for him to capture here in California."

"I'm doubtin' ya've seen anything like it," said Kiernan proudly.

And in that single comment Jordana realized this was truly Kiernan and Victoria's home. She wondered vaguely if she would ever find a place to call home—her very own home.

————

Caitlan's bewildered sense of being lost had disappeared the moment she had set eyes on her brother at the station. Though she knew she could not be closer to anyone than she was to Brenton and Jordana, there was still something about her own blood. Perhaps it was the Irish in her, but seeing Kiernan had made Caitlan feel *connected* as never before. Perhaps it was seeing the face of her dead father again in Kiernan's green eyes and in the shape of his nose and the rise of his forehead, and the red hair that had definitely come from their mother, and their ma's full, expressive lips. It was so sweetly comforting when he put his arms around her, for it was briefly like having her parents back again.

But something else had occurred to Caitlan when that mop of red hair had materialized in the crowd at the station. Perhaps Brenton and Jordana were right after all with their talk of faith. During the stage trip Caitlan had all but convinced herself that her brother would be dead. That she had come thousands of miles, all the way from Ireland, only to have her quest end in sorrow. Something inside her made her fear believing that good could happen to her. Yet, since coming to America, only good had been happening, at least when one looked at the broad picture. She had found Brenton—ah, especially, Brenton—and Jordana, her dearest friend. She had been kept safe through countless dangerous adventures. And now, the best thing of all—she was at last with her brother and he, and his wife, had accepted her, literally, with open arms.

Could it be that God had answered prayers she had not even uttered? Could it be that He really did know and care about a poor Irish girl who had never given God His due?

Could it be. . . ?

"You must eat something, Caitlan," came Victoria's voice into Caitlan's wandering thoughts. "I've heard how that stage food is, and we need to put meat on your bones."

"I'm sorry . . . guess I was daydreamin' a bit. . . ." Caitlan took the plate of biscuits and snatched one off before passing the plate to Jordana.

They were all seated at the table in the O'Connor kitchen, where a delicious warmth radiated from a fire in the stove and an even better warmth came from the people surrounding Caitlan.

"You must be tired," said Victoria.

"Not really," said Caitlan. "I'm just . . . overwhelmed. Everything is so much more wonderful than I could have imagined." She reached over toward Kiernan, who was seated at her other side at the head of the table, and took his hand. "We were so afraid for ya, Kiernan, that ya might be—" She shook her head as if knowing such thoughts were not for this joyous gathering. "But ya are here, and so are we—finally! And 'tis almost as good as getting a chance to know our da."

Kiernan's eyes were glistening with moisture, and his fingers tightened around Caitlan's hand. "I'm only a big brother, but I'll take care of ya just like a da, if ya'd like." He smiled and added, "But how would ya be knowin' that I look so much like our da? Ya were no more than a babe when he died. In fact, it's been so long, I can scarcely remember."

"I had their wedding photograph to remind me," Caitlan said softly. "And I talked to our sisters. They told me stories about Da. Believe me, Kiernan, ya are more like our da than any of the boys. Except for that patch, if ya don't mind me saying. Da never had something so dashing and distinguishing on him."

"Dashing!" Kiernan laughed with disbelief.

"See, I told you," put in Victoria. "I've been trying to tell him how attractive it is."

"I think he looks like a pirate," teased Jordana. "A very nice pirate, though."

"Women!" chuckled Kiernan. "And what do you think, Brenton?"

Caitlan lifted her eyes, taking this opportunity to freely gaze at this man she could love only in secret. Her heart fluttered and she felt heat rise in her cheeks.

"Well . . ." Brenton swallowed as he considered a thoughtful answer. "It does give you an air of authority. I'd say you will have a much easier time managing your crews now."

Everyone laughed at this, and Brenton looked bemused as if unaware that he had made a joke. How Caitlan did love this serious, unassuming young man. Then his eyes momentarily strayed to hers. Their gazes met, and she hated herself for thinking just then of that shared kiss back in Omaha. The memory, and the fact that she chose just then to think about it, made flaming heat surge into her face. She jerked her eyes quickly away from his, hoping no one had noticed.

"Are you quite all right?" Jordana asked, and there was something in her voice that seemed to say she knew quite well what was happening and wasn't going to let Caitlan off easily.

"Sure'n I'm fine," Caitlan lied. "I was just thinkin' how sorry I am I didn't get here sooner. I hope ya'll forgive me that, Kiernan?" She thought it was a good dodge, even if it opened up another can of worms.

"I never gave it a thought," said Kiernan. "I believe ya came at just the time God wanted ya to. And I am too happy to see ya to be questionin' anything else."

Caitlan wondered if she should explain the reasons for her tardiness. But that only made her glance once more at Brenton, who, thankfully, was occupied elsewhere at the moment. At any rate, explanations weren't really necessary. Besides, Brenton would be returning east soon enough to continue his work with the Union Pacific, so why torture herself? She just had to be thankful that she had her brother now and would somehow make a life for herself in his new home.

Thirty

The next morning Jordana, full of excitement, awoke before dawn. Unable to return to sleep and worried that her restlessness would wake Caitlan, who shared the bed with her in the spare bedroom upstairs, she carefully slipped from beneath the covers. After dressing quietly and wrapping a shawl around her shoulders against the early morning chill, she made her way downstairs.

A lamp burned in the kitchen, and she followed the light and was greeted by Victoria and a warm fire in the stove.

"You are an early riser also," smiled Victoria.

"This morning I am. There are so many new and exciting things to look forward to, I just couldn't sleep another minute."

"Let me pour you a cup of tea. I've just poured myself one." Victoria took a cup from the cupboard and filled it from a china teapot and brought it, with her own cup, to the table. She sat opposite Jordana. "So what is the first thing you want to do while you are here?"

"Goodness! I don't even know what there is to see and do. A real gold mine! Yes, I'd like to see one of those for certain. Then, do you suppose we could go to San Francisco sometime? And I have heard there are huge trees not far from here called redwoods that are so huge around a coach could drive through one if it was of a mind. And I'd like to see—"

"Wait a minute," laughed Victoria. "That's enough to keep you busy for a good long time."

"I guess I am a bit overenthusiastic." Jordana sipped her tea thoughtfully, then looked up at her sister. "I want to see it all, Victoria. Not only California, but the whole country. No—the whole

239

world! Imagine seeing the wonders of the Orient or the dark jungles of Africa. Or, if I want to be more civilized, London and Paris. There is simply no end to what is out there. And then, after I see everything, I'll write books about it all." Jordana paused, surprised at her own words. She had never really considered writing but now realized it would be perfect for her. Her enthusiasm continued to build. "I always wondered how I would use my travels constructively, and writing is the perfect way. Wouldn't it be a great encouragement to other women who would like to travel? Not only to hear about exotic places from a woman's point of view, but also to know that a woman can do such things."

"But you haven't done them yet," Victoria remarked.

Jordana tried to ignore the fact that her sister's tone was rather droll. "I will. I just know it."

"Well, Jordana, I hate to be the one to burst the bubble of your little fantasy, but adventure isn't all romance and glory as you seem to think. There's a lot of reality that goes with adventure, and not all of it is pretty."

"I always envied you for your bold journey all the way to California." Jordana looked at Victoria as if for the first time. She realized this was no longer the big sister who had set out eight years ago, full of youthful zest and grand anticipation.

The person who stared back at Jordana was a twenty-seven-year-old matron, with sad eyes and a drawn, almost reproving expression. She nearly reminded Jordana of her Aunt Virginia, despite the fact that they were not related by blood. It was just a glimpse, a brief flicker of familiarity that in another moment was gone, but the hint of it was bad enough. Virginia had suffered a hard life from a disastrous marriage and too much drink. She looked ten years older than her actual years.

"Has it really been so hard?" Jordana asked her sister plaintively.

"I'm happy," Victoria answered quickly, defensively. "But happiness hasn't been dished out to me on a silver platter. I've lived in mining camps, in filth and squalor, around men who could make a woman feel dirty just by the way they looked at you. I've gone hungry and cold. I've—oh, never mind, you would probably just think it's part of the adventure."

"I'm sorry it was so hard. But—" Jordana stopped. She wondered about Victoria's money and how she could have been hungry, but she didn't say anything because she suddenly felt as if her sister were a stranger.

"And, Jordana, speaking of men, how are you going to find a suitable husband traipsing all over the world? You won't run into a lot of gentlemen in the places you want to explore."

"Why, Victoria!" Jordana could not keep from exclaiming. "You do sound like Aunt Virginia!"

"Well, it is something you *should* think about. You could ruin your reputation doing the things you speak of—"

"If I do decide to marry, it will be to a man who looks at me for the person I am and doesn't judge me for silly societal standards that say nothing of the character and quality of the person but only gauge the exterior." Jordana set her cup down a little too hard in its saucer. It made a *clank* sound.

"Silly standards? Oh, Jordana." Victoria shook her head and took on an annoying maternal appearance. "The notions you have are silly and just not practical for the world we live in. I know Mama has some of the same feelings, but at least she was able to adjust them to the practical, real-life world."

"Men don't have to do that! If a man goes exploring, he's a hero."

"That's just—"

"No! I don't give a fig about society! If someone doesn't make the attempt to change it, then we will continue in ways that even you must see are repressive and unfair." Jordana could hardly believe she was having such a discussion with her sister. She'd never imagined finding such disapproval in her own family.

"I'm sorry we disagree," Victoria said softly.

Jordana could tell she was no doubt thinking the same thing. "Well, disagreement is a healthy thing." But Jordana only half believed it.

"I suppose so."

They concentrated on their tea, but the tension remained. Then Victoria refilled their cups, which Jordana took as a good sign that their "words" hadn't spoiled things so badly that Victoria no longer wanted to be around her sister. Jordana searched in her mind for a neutral topic to discuss.

But Victoria spoke first. "I may not agree with your dreams, Jordana, but you deserve to have them come true. At least one Baldwin woman should."

"What do you mean?" Jordana asked, her eyes searching her sister's, finding great sadness there.

"For all the adventure you think I had, all I ever wanted was a home and family of my own. . . ." She sighed, gazing at her fingers as they hugged her cup.

"But you have a wonderful home here, and Kiernan is a wonderful man, too."

"The home is on loan from Mr. Crocker while Kiernan recuperates from his accident. We have never had our own home, though this is the best we have had, and I am thankful for it. As for Kiernan . . . yes, he is the finest husband a woman could have. I could not love him more, and I believe he loves me with his life. Yet I know I have let him down too, and it will always be a small wedge between us."

"Let him down. . . ?"

Victoria's brow arched, then she reddened a bit with embarrassment. "I thought you knew. I guess Mama didn't tell you, but surely I thought you had guessed . . . it's not something I care to discuss—" She stopped, her cheeks flaming.

"I truly don't know what you are talking about, but now you must tell me." She took her sister's hand for encouragement. "I know I can't help you solve your problems but . . ."

"It has been so long since I have had a friend to talk to," Victoria confided. "Li has been wonderful, but we have so many cultural differences we don't always understand each other, and not just because of our different languages."

"I remember when we were little," Jordana said, "how I wanted to be your friend."

"But I could not have my little sister tagging along! What would my friends think?"

Jordana chuckled. "I went to Mama once in tears, feeling so left out. She told me someday I would catch up to you, and then Mama was certain you'd want me to be your friend. Well, we may not have a lot in common, but I think I have 'caught up,' in a way. And I still want to be your friend."

"Thank you so much, Jordana dear!" Victoria stared into her cup for a moment, then seemed to come to a resolve. "Have you ever wondered why I have no children?"

"I suppose I simply thought you and Kiernan were just too busy exploring and such—" Jordana gave a sheepish shake of her head. "Pretty naïve of me, huh?"

Victoria nodded. "We want children desperately. I just have not been able to conceive."

"Oh, Victoria! I am so sorry."

"I don't know why I wanted to tell you. Like I said, I don't talk about it much."

"I'm glad you said something, even though there is little I can do about it. I will pray for you if you'd like."

"Please do. Perhaps a new voice might do some good." Victoria smiled and added, "Now for a more cheerful topic. Tell me about Caitlan and Brenton."

"So, you noticed—"

Before more could be said, Kiernan came into the kitchen. The two women fell silent.

"Now, don't stop yar talking because of me," he said, sounding in a chipper mood.

"You wouldn't be interested in girl talk," said Victoria.

"Ya just never know now, do ya, what an Irishman might be interested in—especially if it involves two of me three most favorite girls in the world."

"Well, it involves all three," said Jordana. Now that there was an opening, she didn't see any reason why she shouldn't enlist her sister's and brother-in-law's help in the sticky issue of Brenton and Caitlan.

"Hmm, now that sounds mysterious." Kiernan headed to a cupboard and took down a cup.

"Let me get that, Kiernan," said Victoria.

"Stay where ya are. I can help meself for a change!" He poured his tea and sat at the table. "Now, can ya clear up this mystery, Jordana?"

"Well, it's only a mystery to Brenton and Caitlan—at least it appears that way."

Kiernan smiled. "I did notice some peculiar exchanges last night. Those two tried so hard *not* to look at each other, they may as well have kissed passionately all evening."

"Kiernan!" Victoria gasped as if scandalized. Then she giggled. "So is it true, then? Is there something between them?"

Jordana rolled her eyes. "They love each other, but the two ninnies are just too thickheaded to admit it."

"And why not?" Kiernan scratched his head, obviously unable to fathom the logic of it.

"Well, your sister seems to have the idea she isn't good enough for him. Believe me, I have been working on her for two years trying to change her low opinion of herself. No matter how much I try to drum into her that she is just as good as anyone, she continually tries to act as maid and servant to us. It drives me batty, to be sure." Jordana smiled, then added, just in case anyone should get the wrong idea, "She is my best friend. I love her dearly, but she can be exasperating."

"Nothing like you Baldwins," Kiernan said with dry humor.

Jordana laughed. "You speak from experience, I see."

Kiernan glanced at his wife, then grinned. "An experience I wouldn't change for naught. But surely Brenton might have a wee part in this romantic misunderstandin'."

"He doesn't think *he* is good enough for her!" Jordana tittered, then more earnestly added, "But there is more to it on his part, and I am afraid I see his problem. You see, Caitlan has turned her back on God. I think down deep she still believes, or wants to believe, but she had seen so much evil wrought in Ireland in the name of God that she now questions Him."

"Yes, I sensed that in a few small things that were said last night," said Kiernan. "And I understand and respect Brenton's hesitation in marryin' someone who doesn't share his faith."

"I believe she is close."

"Close only counts in horseshoes."

After a short pause, Jordana asked, "Kiernan, would you approve of the match if all other things worked out?"

"I would indeed! I can think of no finer husband for me sister. Brenton has grown into a responsible, serious young man—of course, he was always that way. But I'd be proud to have him for me brother-in-law, that is, if he wasn't already me brother-in-law . . . but that would just give me one less in-law to deal with, eh?"

They all laughed at this, then Jordana leaned forward and inquired, "Well then, how are we going to make this happen? It is a sure thing those two are going to need some help."

Kiernan rubbed his chin, and there was a conspiratorial glint in his good eye. "Jordana, you handle Brenton—that's always been your forte anyway. And I will handle that sister of mine, settin' her straight on a few matters, as a big brother should."

They all but shook hands, then as the two in question appeared, nothing more was said, but Jordana's mind was working on the problem, and she could tell Kiernan was thinking about it, too.

Thirty-One

$\mathcal{V}$ictoria just couldn't understand how Caitlan was desperate for something to do. But after three excruciating days of being waited on and served, Caitlan was nearly beside herself with frustration. Perhaps it just spoke more than anything of her *commonness*, but Caitlan couldn't help it. She needed to work. And she could not bear for others to wait on her. Kiernan had mentioned how that very attitude had nearly driven him crazy during his recovery from his accident, but that he had finally gotten over it. He said God had to make him practically dependent to finally shake his pride from him.

Well, Caitlan wasn't there yet and didn't know if she ever could be. Thus, she had nagged Victoria constantly about working in the laundry until Victoria finally broke down and put her to work.

"You are my guest, and it simply mortifies me to make you work, but . . ." Victoria had tried to protest.

"But if I don't do something," Caitlan said only half jokingly, "ya'll have a crazy guest on yar hands, and ya don't want that, now do ya?"

And there was plenty of work to be done. With the departure of Victoria's assistant, Li, the piles of laundry were . . . well, piling up. There would have been no way Victoria could have filled her orders without help. Even Jordana had begun pitching in. However, on this particular day, Brenton and Jordana had gone with Charlie Crocker to tour a gold mine and take photographs. Caitlan hadn't been interested—that is, in seeing a mine. She would have loved nothing more than to take up her old job of assisting Brenton in his work, as she had done in their travels before reaching Omaha. But things

247

had become so awkward between them that it seemed they had even lost the friendship they had once shared. She was miserable about this, and it made another reason why she was more than happy to throw herself into the work in the laundry.

Kiernan wandered into the laundry shed late that morning as Caitlan was taking a bushel of clean things out to hang on the clothesline.

"Can we talk a bit as ya work?" he asked casually.

"Sure'n."

He reached for the basket. "Let me carry that for ya."

"And with ya just gettin' your strength back?" She held tight to the basket. "I don't think so."

"And do ya think I'll get me strength back by just sittin' around?" He gave a firmer tug to the basket until she released it. "Yar a stubborn lass, to be sure."

"It comes through the blood, I'm thinkin'." She grinned good-naturedly.

"Ah, it does me good to see ya smile. I don't remember ya bein' as serious as ya are now."

"I was a carefree three-year-old when ya left Ireland." Reaching the clothesline, she plucked a shirt from the basket. "A lot has happened since then."

"And sorry I am about all that, Caitlan." He offered her such an earnest look, it made her heart nearly break.

"'Tis not your fault."

"And 'tis not God's fault either."

She bristled slightly at this remark. She had almost forgotten that Kiernan had become quite a man of faith since coming to America. She had often wondered about this, coming as he had from the same background as she. She had told herself that she would ask him about it, but now that she was face-to-face with him, and now that the opportunity had presented itself, she found herself reluctant. It had been easy to brush off Jordana's and Brenton's comments about God because they had come from an entirely different life. But how could she argue with her brother? He had known the same poverty and hardships as she. He had witnessed the same violence and injustice, all in the name of religion, as she. He had watched their parents die because of these things . . . just the same as she.

"Why don't ya put down that basket?" she said a bit too sharply.

"So now 'tis the basket yar mad at?"

"I'm not mad at anyone or anything." She jammed a clothespin into the shirt as if she were thrusting a knife.

"Ouch! And now the shirt must suffer, too!"

"Stop making fun of me!" she retorted and turned eyes filled with flaming anger at him.

He blinked contritely. "Forgive me, sis. 'Twas wrong o' me. It's just that . . . I don't know how else to reach ya."

"Why do ya feel as if ya have to reach me a'tall?" she asked, but there was more challenge than questioning in her tone.

"Because yar sad, and yar hurting . . . and I love ya, and it pains me to see you in such a place."

Shrugging, she grabbed another shirt from the basket. "I'm happy enough. These last two years with Jordana and Brenton have been the best of me life."

"But ya still carry the past with ya."

"And don't ya, Kiernan?" She could not help the accusatory tone of the question. "Sometimes I think ya've forgotten yar past completely. But it still goes on in Ireland. Our people still suffer."

"Yar wrong there," said Kiernan with gentle firmness. "I'll never forget. If I let it, it could crush me with bitterness, even hatred. But the weight of all that could kill me for certain. As it will you, Caitlan. If ya don't find a way to unload that burden, it will smother you. 'Tis already robbed the joy from ya."

"And I'm supposin' ya'll now say God is the way. . . ?" She wanted to inject mockery into her tone but couldn't, not after knowing of the good and pure relationship Jordana and Brenton had with God. It both drew and frightened her.

"I think ya see it for yarself."

"It scares me, Kiernan," she said with a sigh, the admission almost as freeing as everyone said submission to God would be.

"Why, sis?"

"What if . . . ?" She licked her lips nervously and nearly dropped the shirt in her hand. "What if I go reachin' out to God and find Him to be just as . . . well, as elusive as everythin' else? Why would God have anythin' to do with a poor Irish girl?"

"I can't believe ya'd be sayin' such a thing after spending two years with Brenton and Jordana." He set down the basket, took her hand, led her to a little grassy place in the yard, and bid her to sit.

It was a warm October day, and their spot was under a sprawling apple tree, which lent a nice bit of shade. Caitlan sat reluctantly, not wanting to give up the protection and distraction her work offered. She realized now that work was more than a means to salve her pride. It was a way to avoid things, too. The truth, for instance.

"Haven't ya learned anything from them?" Kiernan persisted. "Or is yar Irish head too thick to see God for who He really is? True, the Catholics and Protestants in our country are always fightin', but if ya take the time to study God's Word, ya'd see quick enough none of that has anything to do with God, not really. God is much bigger than Catholics and Protestants—bigger even than rich Americans or poor Irish. I'm rememberin' a verse in the Bible that says something to that effect. That there's not Jew or Greek, slave or free, even male or female in Christ. He sees past all that, right to *individuals*. And even then, He sees only into a person's *heart*. It does not matter to God that yar a poor Irish washerwoman. He sees *yarself*, Caitlan, and that is all."

"And what if He's not likin' what He sees?"

Kiernan chuckled, not in a demeaning way but with just enough irony for her to see how ridiculous her question was. Yet for some reason she could not fathom, resistance was strong in her. As was fear.

Kiernan responded tenderly. "I can't imagine that, sis. But if on the off chance that He was less than pleased with ya, there's a simple enough way to fix that. Ya see, God isn't looking for ways to keep people away from hisself. Just the opposite is true. And He's made it easy—easy enough even for me addlepated sister!" He grinned and winked at her. "If He's had room for the likes of me, sis, He'll have room for ya."

"It's easy enough to say such things, but acceptin' them is much harder." She plucked a blade of grass and gazed at the bright green surface. There were no answers there, and even in her brother's eyes she could not find the one elusive thing that would take her beyond her inner sense that no matter what she did, she would not be good enough, for God or for . . . anything. "I just couldn't be standin' it if I reached out to God, and He . . . well, I learned there just wasn't room for me."

"And 'tis the same way yar feeling about Brenton, isn't it?"

She winced. That was the last thing she wanted to hear. And she wanted to fight it. "I'm not thinkin' that to be any of yar business!" she lashed out, knowing even as the words were spoken how wrong they were.

"Well, I have to disagree wi' ya there," Kiernan countered calmly. "With both Da and Red gone, I'm thinkin' I'm now the head of the family, which means it is very much me business." He scratched his chin, a slightly malicious gleam touching his eyes. "In fact, if Da were alive, I'm certain he'd be arranging a match for ya—seems yar well past marrying age. Perhaps I should follow tradition in this matter—"

"Ya wouldn't dare!"

"And give me one good reason why I shouldn't?" he taunted.

"Well . . . because . . . y-ya just couldn't . . . I'd die. . . . Oh, Kiernan, ya wouldn't . . . ?" she sputtered. She simply did not know her brother well enough to judge how serious he was.

Only the easy smile that now slipped across his lips made her realize he had been teasing her. "Yar safe for now, sis, but I think ya better be honest with Brenton about how ya feel . . . or I may just have to interfere meself."

"Even if I was honest . . ." she hedged, "there is still our differing ideas about faith."

"Then ya better straighten that out first."

"I'm not going to take on faith just to snag a man, nor would Brenton want me if I did."

Kiernan rolled his eyes. "Of course not! But ya know well enough yar gonna end up puttin' yar faith in God, so ya may as well do it now before ya lose the man ya love."

"Oh, dear me . . ." She brought a trembling hand to her throat. "I can only say, I will think about what ya've said."

"'Tis all I ask, sis."

After Kiernan left, that was *all* she could think of.

Thirty-Two

Jordana was enjoying herself immensely in Sacramento, seeing the sights, helping Brenton with his photography. Even working in the laundry was a nice diversion. But thinking of both Brenton and the laundry made her immediately think of Caitlan. She was truly beginning to think that the only people on earth who didn't know her brother and Caitlan were destined to be together were the would-be lovers themselves.

It was most frustrating.

As a diversion, Jordana suggested an afternoon of shopping to the other females in the house. Perhaps in this setting, with both Victoria and Jordana working on her, Caitlan would come around in her stubbornness. But Victoria begged off that morning, saying she felt ill. Just an upset stomach, nothing to worry about, but enough to keep her inside that day. So it was just Caitlan and Jordana.

They had a nice time exploring the shops in downtown Sacramento, but only if it was kept to window-shopping. The moment Jordana suggested Caitlan actually purchase a ready-made gown of an emerald green that was particularly stunning with Caitlan's eyes, the girl balked.

"And would ya be lookin' at the price of it?" Caitlan flipped up the tag, which read an astonishing $9.98. "That's more'n what Mrs. Cavendish paid me for a week's work. I couldn't justify such an extravagance knowin' me own people could well be starvin' back home."

"I feel as bad as you about poverty, Caitlan," Jordana replied evenly, "but you being miserable isn't going to help anyone."

"I'm not miserable, but I would be if I spent $9.98 on a dress!"

"I think you are just afraid of being more than a lowly, poor Irish girl. I think you just hide behind that, but for the life of me, I can't understand why."

"Well, 'tis none of yar business," Caitlan replied hotly. "Even if it were true, but it isn't."

"The world isn't going to collapse if Caitlan O'Connor buys a new dress!"

"All right then, what about this one—?" Caitlan plucked a dress from the rack. It was a dowdy gray, with a horrid pink ribbon at the collar. "'Tis two dollars!"

"Arggg!" groaned Jordana. "Is it *that* much? I could get you one for free from my granny." She sighed as another wave of frustration assailed her. "Is that really how you see yourself, Caitlan? Dowdy, dull, washed out, faded, lackluster—"

"That's cruel even for yarself, Jordana!" Caitlan shoved the gray dress back into its place.

"Well, I don't mean to be cruel, and you know me better than to think it! What I am trying to say is that you are none of those things. You are beautiful, Caitlan—inside and outside. Why else do you think Brenton loves you?"

"Now, don't ya bring him into this."

"But he's a big part of it all, isn't he?"

"I don't want to talk about it." Caitlan spoke with such uncharacteristic firmness that Jordana dropped the subject.

Instead she suggested that since it was late, why didn't they stop someplace for a bit of refreshment before heading home. They were near the Tea Room, and Jordana led the way inside.

"Oh, Jordana," Caitlan said, looking about the lavish place in awe, "can we afford—?"

"Caitlan," Jordana broke in, "if you say one word about the expense, I'll scream. Now, sit down and enjoy this."

They were escorted to a table, and Caitlan obediently sat down but obviously wasn't enjoying herself. They sipped tea and ate fancy cakes and tried to make casual conversation, but it was all very stilted. Jordana could hardly bear it because it had never been this way with Caitlan before. Her anger and frustration mounted.

"Caitlan," she finally said in a tight voice, "why can't you just enjoy yourself?"

"I'm sorry," Caitlan replied snidely, "I wasn't brought up in the lap of luxury where a dollar for a pot of tea and a few cakes is nothing but spare change."

"Well, just spare me your tales of woe—I'm sick of them!"

"Are ya now!" Caitlan pushed back her chair. "Then, I'm thinkin' ya must also be sick of me. I'll be on me way."

"Don't be ridiculous!" Jordana said as Caitlan turned and strode from the Tea Room.

Stubbornly, Jordana stayed where she was, just watching her friend walk out. She was not going to run after her and apologize. It was well past time for someone to let that hardheaded girl know just how silly she was acting. Eventually Caitlan would thank Jordana for her truthfulness.

Jordana deliberately finished her tea, and two more cakes, then paid her bill and exited the Tea Room. She half expected to see her friend standing outside waiting. She imagined they would both apologize and embrace and all would be back to normal. But still, normal was not exactly good for Caitlan. If matters remained as they were, Caitlan would never give herself credit for the wonderful woman she was, and then she and Brenton would never get together.

Yet Jordana realized that she herself had probably not handled the situation in the most tactful manner. She had let her frustration get the better of her good sense and in the process had spoken hurtful, if well-meaning, words. Well, she supposed she would apologize and then find a better way to express herself.

But Caitlan was nowhere to be seen. Jordana glanced in a couple of nearby shops but could not find her. It was only a few blocks to Kiernan and Victoria's home, and it was likely Caitlan had walked quickly and taken a side street, for her to have disappeared so fast. Perhaps it was for the best, and they both could use a time for cooling off before facing each other again.

Jordana decided to use the time to stretch her legs and do some thinking while seeing more of the town. It would be dark in an hour, but even if she walked a bit she could still be home before sundown. She turned off the main street to a side street where one of the shopkeepers had mentioned a fine milliner was located. She could use a new bonnet—and maybe she would buy one for Caitlan, too.

But she must have heard wrong, because there were no milliners on this street. A store owner suggested another possibility and gave her directions. She followed these until she was hopelessly lost. And the sun was sinking quickly.

The shopkeepers were starting to put Closed signs in their windows and to take in outdoor displays. She knew she could take care of herself and wasn't worried about the gathering darkness. Only vaguely did she think of Rich O'Brian's many admonitions to her about using good sense. She laughed them off even now . . . until a small chill prickled the hairs on the back of her neck.

She wasn't afraid but had the strangest sensation that someone was following her. Of all the silly notions!

She kept walking and soon had something real to be nervous about. She had no idea at all about how to get back to her sister's house. She paused and asked a passerby, but he had never heard of the street and gave her a disapproving look. And before long, it was fully dark, and even people with disapproving looks were growing fewer on the streets.

And that pesky feeling on the nape of her neck returned. She remembered, as if for the first time, that this was a big city, but it was also as rough and uncivilized as any western town. She thought of robbers and vagrants, drunks and gunmen. But she also thought that she was being foolish, letting her imagination get the best of her. If a shop were still open, perhaps she would duck inside, but, alas! The few shops on the street were closed. The remainder of the buildings were dwellings—and she certainly wasn't going to annoy some strangers in their own home with her questions.

She walked a little farther, and, in the quiet of this back street, she distinctly heard the *clack* of heels that were not her own. And, to her horror, when she stopped, feigning interest in a shop window, the heavy *clack* stopped also.

Dear Lord, have I done it again? Put myself in harm's way through my carelessness?

She was trembling now and no longer could deny even to herself that she wasn't afraid. But what could she do? If a criminal was after her, she certainly couldn't outrun him. Invading a stranger's home was looking better and better.

Still, it went against Jordana's plucky nature to simply turn tail and run. First, she should find out if there was really any danger. She must turn and see if anyone was actually following her.

She stopped walking. But turning was never more difficult. Her heart was thudding louder than those clanking footsteps, which, by the way, had ceased again. Then, just as she had mustered the courage to turn, the clanking began again, this time faster. Whoever it was intended on making their move now that it was apparent she had discovered their presence.

She spun around just as a large, hot hand grabbed her shoulder.

"P-please . . . I have a little money. Take it!" she cried.

"You are safe now, Jordana."

The voice was familiar, but identification evaded her, and in the darkness she could not immediately make out the features of her . . . assailant? Rescuer?

He knew her name. He said she was safe. She blinked her eyes desperately, and finally her vision cleared.

"You!" she said.

"Yes, I'm here for you. . . ."

"But—"

His hand, the one that wasn't grasping her shoulder, reached around her, hooking her head in an armlock while the hand clamped over her mouth. She struggled but couldn't get free. When the cloth appeared in her face the next instant, she was confused, wondering what was happening. She did not wonder for long. In fact, she did not do anything for long. Breathing in a sickly sweet odor, Jordana felt her knees go limp. She tried to scream, but nothing came from her lips.

The darkness pressed in upon her, and she felt as if she were slipping into it as one slips into death.

Thirty-Three

Caitlan did not wait outside the Tea Room. Perhaps she should have; perhaps she had been too hasty in her anger. It was just so much easier to vent her confusion and fear upon her friend. Especially when Jordana had said some tactless things.

Instead, she hurried away, all but running down the street. She was barely able to keep her feet from flying. She wanted to run—far away from this place where she so obviously did not fit in. Not only from the fancy tea place, but from Jordana, Brenton, Victoria, and even Kiernan. The Baldwins had tried to be kind to her; Jordana had even professed her friendship. But a person like Caitlan would never fit in with people like them. They were practically nobility—American nobility. And she was the child of a poor crofter. The twain would never meet in Ireland, and she had deceived herself into believing it would be different in America.

The worst of it all was that now that she had finally found her brother, she didn't even fit in with him. But with Kiernan it wasn't social station that separated them; it was this confusing matter of faith.

And suddenly Caitlan felt more alone than she ever had in her life.

Pausing at a cross street to wait for passing traffic, Caitlan decided to turn onto this street, so that if Jordana did decide to come after her, she would not find her. Caitlan couldn't face her friend now. Her friend? Oh, how she wanted to believe it! But how could they be friends when so much divided them? They couldn't even go shopping without disagreeing. And this certainly wasn't the first time Caitlan had balked at what she perceived as Jordana's extravagance—it was just the first time it had escalated so heatedly. Caitlan must blame herself for that. Her growing tension and confusion had made her impatient.

She'd been afraid that the discussion would turn to God as it had with Kiernan. She knew Jordana had been keeping back her Christian sermons for a long time, trying to let Caitlan make up her own mind. But it had been plain to see that words, or sermons, or whatever were rising close to the surface in Jordana, and she wouldn't be able to hold her tongue much longer.

And God, like everything else, was also a barrier between Caitlan and Jordana, as He was with Kiernan and . . . oh, and especially with Brenton.

Caitlan was walking so fast that she was panting and her heart was racing. She made herself slow down. She didn't want to be taken for a fugitive or some such thing. She'd had a friend in Ireland who had that very thing happen. He had been running down a street in Belfast trying to catch an acquaintance he'd seen ahead of him. The police stopped him and hauled him into the tollbooth. They held him for a week with no charges against him simply because he had *looked* guilty.

These things happened. But Brenton and Jordana would never be able to understand. It wasn't their fault. They had simply been raised in a different society. Nonetheless, it was still a wedge. Between her and them, and between her and God. Because how could a just and loving God allow such injustice to happen?

Or was such questioning merely an excuse to avoid what was really troubling her, what she had confessed to Kiernan? That maybe she wouldn't be good enough for God.

Everyone kept telling her differently. If only she could believe it!

Caitlan had been so deep in thought, she had paid little attention to her surroundings. Only when she happened to nearly bump a passing woman and her child did Caitlan give her head a shake and take note of where she was. The cross street she had turned onto had taken her slightly out of the way from Kiernan's house, but she had realized that when she turned. She had but to go another block to reach the main street again, and from there it was a short distance home.

When she looked up, however, and saw a pretty stone church on the corner, she knew she was going to take yet another detour.

It had been years since she had been in a church, probably since her ma's funeral. Brenton and Jordana went regularly, but they had not insisted she accompany them, though she knew they had wanted her to and would have welcomed her.

Oh, Caitlan, ya foolish girl! If yar alone now, 'tis only because of yarself.

She turned toward the church and mounted the steps to the large oak double doors, which were closed. It was a silly notion to go to a church now. It would probably be locked anyway, since it wasn't Sunday. But perhaps it was time. If she didn't do something, she *would* be alone, for she would lose the only people she cared about and who cared about her. And she would lose the man she loved, not that she had ever had him in the first place.

Yes, she would go into this church. Oh, she didn't plan to make any commitments, but the least she could do was try to have a bit of a talk with God. Straighten out a few matters. Maybe they would come to an understanding. Maybe they wouldn't. But at least she would have tried.

With a trembling hand she grasped the great brass latch and gave a little yank on the door. It opened. She was both relieved and fearful. Ignoring her fear, she stepped inside, into a small vestibule. It was dark and gave Caitlan a chill. Obviously no one cared to waste lamp oil on an empty church. She felt like an intruder. Perhaps she was committing a crime by going in uninvited. But the doors had been unlocked. This encouraged her, and she walked through the vestibule, through an open arched doorway that led into the sanctuary.

It wasn't as dark in here because there were several stained-glass windows catching the afternoon light. One wall of windows in particular was lit up to the point of being glaring. This wall faced the west and was absorbing the light of the setting sun. It was really quite beautiful with fragmented and fractured beams of multicolored light dancing over the pews on that side of the sanctuary.

Caitlan took a seat opposite this so she could watch the pretty light display. But after a few minutes she knew she was merely avoiding her real purpose for venturing into this place. She inhaled a deep breath. But even with that to steady her, it wasn't an easy thing to open a dialog with the Creator of the universe.

"Why is it that I must be left out? All me friends have this special thing, but I cannot seem to grasp it. Is it possible that all of them are wrong and I am right?''

She smiled.

It did not seem possible. Jordana might be mistaken; she was, after all, somewhat given to flights of fancy. Kiernan could be wrong, too. Caitlan really didn't know him very well.

And Brenton . . .

No, Brenton could not be wrong. And it wasn't just because she loved him. She had simply never known a person who was steadier, more levelheaded. If Brenton believed something, then there could be little question of its validity. She would stake her life on it.

Yet, if she believed Brenton was right about the existence of God, the love of God and all the rest, then why was she fighting it so?

And it came back to her own sense of inadequacy. If she couldn't believe Brenton could love her as she loved him, how could she believe it about an invisible God? She thought suddenly of the beautiful green dress Jordana had wanted her to buy. And she realized Jordana had truly believed it suited Caitlan. Imagine that! Jordana saw her as someone who could actually wear a $9.98 dress, of fashionable cut and fine Irish lace.

Was it possible that God could see her in that way also?

But what if she invested in the dress and put it on and realized it was ridiculous on her? After all, you couldn't make a silk purse from a sow's ear.

"I'm so afraid . . ." she murmured.

And suddenly she jumped up and fled that church. And she ran the rest of the way home, not caring if the police arrested her. At the moment, arrest was the least of her problems.

Victoria cornered Brenton in the parlor. Not that he had been avoiding her. But they hadn't really had a good visit since his arrival. He supposed he had been keeping a bit aloof from everyone. He felt lonely and out of sorts and could hardly figure out his own feelings, much less explain them to others. He hoped to work it out for himself, but it seemed he was just sinking deeper and deeper into a pit of disillusionment.

"Brenton, do you have a moment to talk?"

He was seated on the sofa reading a book he'd found on the small shelf. Dickens' *A Tale of Two Cities*. He'd read it before, so he was merely reading it now for diversion.

"Of course, Victoria." He closed the covers of the book. "Have a seat."

She sat in the wing chair facing the sofa. "I should have brought tea. We haven't really had a chance to visit—just you and me."

"I'm sorry if I have appeared to ignore you. I didn't intend to. I suppose I just feel . . ." He paused, then shook his head. He did not want to get into that. "What did you want to talk about, Victoria?"

"Well, some of my lady friends—they're not close friends really. I know them through church. We meet monthly for a small sewing circle and do some charitable work. Anyway, I happened to mention to them the last time I was at church about your photography, and they were quite interested in seeing your pictures."

Brenton practically sighed with relief. He'd feared a more personal request. "I'd love to do that."

"I thought I could have a luncheon here, and you could give a small lecture along with the showing. I know it would be fascinating."

He gave a self-deprecating shrug, but in reality he did think his work was fascinating, and there was no reason others would not think so, too.

"You just let me know when, and I will prepare something," he said.

"Wonderful." She paused, glanced at her hands in her lap, then added, "Tell me a bit about this dream of yours, to photograph the country."

"You don't want to wait until my lecture?"

"It might help you organize your thoughts to talk about it ahead of time."

He wondered vaguely if she had some ulterior motive in her interest, then chided himself for his suspicion and launched into a brief sharing of his dreams and hopes for his profession. Then he made the mistake of mentioning how Caitlan had assisted him.

"She is becoming quite a proficient photographer in her own right," he said proudly.

"I expect it's because she has had a good teacher," suggested Victoria.

"She learns quickly."

"But . . ." Victoria paused hesitantly.

"What is it, Victoria?"

"Well . . . I only wish she were easier to get to know. Sometimes I wonder if she . . ." She glanced away as if she had said too much, then took a breath and continued. "Well, she seems a bit standoffish."

"Oh, I can't believe that," Brenton said defensively. "I think it only appears that way because she is shy. I've never seen her treat anyone with anything but kindness. You must be mistaken."

"Perhaps . . ."

"Give her a chance, Victoria. She probably acts withdrawn because she doesn't feel that she's good enough. She just won't believe in herself and can't seem to see what a sweet, loving, generous woman she is." Brenton exhaled a ragged sigh. Sometimes that separated them worse than her lack of faith. "She has so many wonderful qualities. Everyone can see them but her."

"That's very interesting, Brenton." She paused, then arched a brow in a most peculiar way. "Can I ask you something else?" He nodded, and she went on. "How long have you been in love with her?"

"Well, I—" He stopped suddenly as the full import of the question struck him. "Wh-whatever do you mean?" But he knew it was too late for denials. "Almost from the first minute I saw her," he added quietly, reverently.

Victoria moved to the sofa beside him and took his hands in hers. "Oh, Brenton!" she smiled. "That is so sweet."

"Were you just baiting me before, with all that 'standoffish' business?" he asked matter-of-factly, but he already knew the answer. What he didn't know was why.

"I confess." Victoria grinned. "I guess there's a bit of a conspiracy among those who love you both, to . . . well, nudge the two of you together."

"All the nudging in the world won't do a bit of good if she doesn't love me back, and Victoria—" Did he dare tell her everything? He'd always looked up to his big sister. Maybe she would know what to do about the fool he had been. "We used to be friends, we got along so well, then I did . . . I was such an idiot! I kissed her!"

"You kissed her?" The corners of Victoria's mouth were twitching as if she could barely contain her amusement.

He hated being laughed at, especially when she did not understand. "Victoria, immediately after I took advantage of her, she moved away and went to live with her employer. I'm sure she despises me now. I was so crass. I ruined everything!"

A giggle now escaped Victoria's lips.

Brenton gaped at her, incredulous that she could be so unfeeling as he poured out his heart to her.

"I'm sorry," she said, trying to be serious. "But my dear brother, you have so much to learn about women."

"What does that mean?"

"I don't know what Caitlan thought about that kiss, but there is not a single person who sees the two of you together, even now when you are both trying so hard to avoid each other, that can't see Caitlan is very much in love with you."

"Are you still making fun of me?" He took off his glasses and rubbed the bridge of his nose. This was too much for him to fathom. She loved him? How could it be?

"Brenton, have you ever thought that perhaps she moved out because she feared her feelings for you—her feelings of love?"

"Well . . . I know I feared my feelings for her. And it was getting very difficult to live under the same roof."

"There you go!"

"Do you think it is truly possible—that she loves me? I don't dare believe it." His head was spinning.

"Believe it, Brenton. And then you should decide what you will do about it."

Now his stomach began flip-flopping in sync to his spinning head. "D-do about it?"

"Uh-huh." She gave him a superior big-sister nod.

"Would Kiernan even consider me a suitable match for his sister?"

Victoria burst out laughing now, no longer able to contain herself. "Well, he found at least one Baldwin suitable to wed an O'Connor. What's one more?"

But before he could respond, the front door opened, and in a moment, Caitlan herself walked past the parlor door.

Thirty-Four

When Caitlan glanced into the parlor and saw Brenton and Victoria, she wished she had just walked past without looking. But of course when she saw them, and they saw her, she couldn't very well pretend she hadn't.

"Hello," she said from the door.

They both returned the greeting. Brenton avoided her eyes.

Victoria smiled, then looked over Caitlan's shoulder. "Where is Jordana?"

Caitlan would have welcomed any question but that. "Oh . . . um . . . she wanted to do a bit more shopping. . . ." she lied. How could she admit, especially to Brenton, that the two of them had argued and she had walked out on Jordana?

"I hope she won't be too much longer," said Victoria. "It's getting dark out."

Brenton chuckled. "She'll probably stay out after dark just to emphasize how independent she is."

"Well, this isn't Baltimore, or even New York City," Victoria cautioned. "There are many rough characters hereabouts."

"They are everywhere, but I'll admit a good share have drifted west. But in our travels we have encountered more than our share. Jordana has learned something about taking care of herself."

"'Tis how you truly feel, Brenton?" Caitlan responded with such surprise, she forgot she had wanted to avoid him. "You have fretted over Jordana more than anyone."

"That's true. Maybe I've relaxed a bit now that I am no longer the only one responsible for her." He paused and slipped on his

267

glasses, which he had been holding in his hands. "That is careless of me. I am sorry."

"I didn't mean—"

"I do appreciate your saying something, for I have only now realized what I've been doing. I will remedy that by continuing to assume my responsibility."

"Jordana won't like to hear that, I am sure," Caitlan said wryly.

"Well, at any rate," Victoria said, rising, "I must see to dinner. Brenton, I have enjoyed our visit."

"Thank you, Victoria."

Victoria exited the parlor.

Caitlan said, "Let me be puttin' away me coat, Victoria, then I'll come and help ya."

"You must be tired from your outing. You are welcome to sit with Brenton and pass the time. I'll call you if I need you."

"Goodness! I wouldn't hear of just sittin' around while ya work." Caitlan was already halfway to the stairs. "I'll be back down in a minute."

Victoria shrugged with a peculiar look on her face.

An hour later, while Caitlan was helping Victoria in the kitchen by peeling potatoes, Brenton opened the door and poked his head in.

"Has Jordana come home yet?" he asked. "I thought perhaps she might have come in the back door."

"No, she hasn't," answered Victoria.

"She should have been home by now," said Caitlan.

"That's what I'm thinking," agreed Brenton, coming all the way into the kitchen. "She has been known to take some foolish risks, but I think even she understands the dangers of being out alone after dark."

At that moment the front door opened, then closed. Relieved looks invaded each of their expressions. But it was Kiernan who made an appearance.

"Oh, it's only you," said Brenton.

"Now, how's a man supposed to take such a greetin'?" Kiernan said, feigning affront.

"He didn't mean anything, Kiernan," said Victoria. "We hoped you might be Jordana. She hasn't come home yet from shopping, and Caitlan has been home herself for over an hour."

"Were ya together then, sis?"

"Aye . . . but . . ." Caitlan's lip began to tremble. Her concern over Jordana's absence had been mounting in the last hour. At first she had tried to shrug it off as just Jordana being . . . well, Jordana. Then she began to worry in earnest and knew she should say something but had been reluctant to admit they had had a fight. She kept hoping Jordana would come in. She had been about to say something when Brenton had come. Now she could not contain her growing fear and sense of guilt. Maybe Jordana had done something foolish because of their argument.

"What's wrong, Caitlan?" Brenton asked in that gentle way of his.

And that was enough to bring to a head all of Caitlan's fears and worries. "We had a fight and I walked out on her. If anything's happened to her . . . oh, I shall never forgive meself!"

"You had a fight?" said several voices, all incredulous.

" 'Tis me own fault. I was impatient and mean tempered." Caitlan put down her paring knife and the potato she was holding. "I've got to find her." She spun around to leave, but Kiernan caught her arm.

"Hold on there! I'll not be losin' another sister."

"But—"

"Now, let's not go off half-cocked," said Brenton evenly. "No doubt she came home and just slipped past us. Caitlan, you go upstairs and look. Perhaps she went to her room and, being tired from shopping, lay down and fell asleep. Kiernan, you look around out front, and I will look out back."

"And I will finish dinner," said Victoria, "because when Jordana does come home, it's a sure bet she'll be hungry."

But the search around the house proved unsuccessful.

Caitlan now was crying in earnest. " 'Tis me fault."

"It's not true, Caitlan," said Brenton.

"She wouldn't have been left alone if I hadn't up and walked out on her." Sniffing, she began to wipe her hand across her eyes.

"Here." Brenton handed her his handkerchief.

She hesitated a moment. How could he still be so kind to her after what she had done—not only leaving Jordana but treating him so coolly after that sweet kiss in Omaha?

"Go on . . ." he said tenderly, "take it."

"H-how can you, B-Brenton, when I-I'm so terrible—" But her words caught as sobs clogged her throat. She didn't know if she fell into Brenton's arms or if he had reached out for her, but all at once, that's exactly where she found herself. It was nothing romantic, of course. She was blubbering like a ninny, and he was only comforting her as if she were a child. He even lifted his handkerchief up to her nose.

"Blow," he said like a father instructing a child. "And no more of this talk about you being terrible and at fault. I won't hear of it."

"B-but—"

"Hush, Caitlan," he admonished softly. "We have to concern ourselves with Jordana and nothing else."

She nodded, realizing how self-centered she was being. She took the handkerchief, blew her nose, and wiped the tears from her eyes.

"You'll be all right, then?" he asked.

She nodded, much calmer now, and moved from Brenton's comforting embrace. How she hated to do it, but he had only intended to support her while she was upset. Nothing more. "What shall we do?" she asked. "Go back into town and look for her?"

Brenton glanced at Kiernan. "It's a big town for two of us to cover."

"We'll enlist the help of Charlie Crocker," said Kiernan. "He'll have horses we can use. And we can send word to others of our friends."

Caitlan marveled at how easily her brother suggested seeking help from someone outside the family. But then this was an emergency, and so it would have been selfish to think of pride now.

Within another hour, several search parties were combing the city. Caitlan was nearly undone when she realized there was no way she could convince either her brother or Brenton to let her join them. But it would have only heaped more worry upon them. Besides, someone needed to stay home in case Jordana did show up. However, that possibility was looking more and more remote. She should have been home by now if something hadn't happened.

Victoria and Caitlan tried to busy themselves with preparing a meal. They were far from hungry, but as Victoria had already suggested, Jordana would be when she was found. Also, there would be the men to feed. When the meal was prepared as far as it could go, and there was no further distraction to be had here, the two women began pacing, practically bumping into each other. Finally, Victoria sat at the table. Caitlan then thought of another distraction. She fixed a pot of tea. The two were silent as Caitlan worked because they were too worried for casual chatting, and anything more serious only would have made them worry more.

When Caitlan finished the tea and turned to carry it to the table, she paused. Victoria's head was bowed, her eyes closed, her lips moving silently. She was praying.

Stricken with a new sense of aloneness, Caitlan set down the pot and quietly left the kitchen, going to the one place she believed she belonged—the laundry room. She glanced around the rough shed with its several washtubs and scrub boards and stacks of dirty clothes. Was this really her destiny? And worse, was it really where she belonged? A voice inside cried out, "No!"

It was only in her own mind that she was fit for nothing more than dirty laundry and servants' work. Those who knew her best kept telling her differently. They loved her; they cared about her. They would not lie to her.

That could only mean she was lying to herself, then. Her fears alone kept her, or at least her spirit, locked in a rough shed. They kept her from reaching out to those who cared, and especially kept her from seeking God.

And now she needed God desperately. How she envied Victoria's ability to sit and quietly talk to her God, receiving comfort and, Caitlan knew, hope. She wanted those things, and she knew she could have them. She had but to take the risk. What was the worst that could happen if she did just that? Could she be any more alone, or hopeless? By not doing so, she was very close to losing what good there was left in her life—her friends and family.

"Ya have nothing to lose, Caitlan, girl," she told herself out loud. "Just like when ya came to America. 'Twas a risk, but look what happened. Ya found wonderful friends. True, ya also found confusion and all, but ya have to admit that only came from yar own stupidity."

She thought of her failed attempt to talk to God just a few hours ago in the church. In a way it was more fitting that it should be here where she felt comfortable. She thought of the idea of meeting someone "on their own ground." She thought that's just what God would do, at least the God Brenton and Jordana followed.

She took a deep breath. This time she was going to do it.

"God . . ." She glanced around, then remembered Victoria with her head bowed and her eyes closed. Assuming this stance, she went on. "Ya know I've never been one for prayin' and churchin'. I hope ya don't hold that against me—no, I'm not supposin' ya would. I hope ya also don't mind me finally coming to ya when I've got such a terrible need. I promise I won't be the kind that comes only when things are bad. If I take this step, I'll do it through thick and thin. Leastways, I'll try me best." She paused almost as if waiting for that resounding rejection she had feared for so long. Only silence met her ears. "Well, then, Jordana does say I won't be hearin' any real voice. That's all right. If it is good enough for me friends, it will be good enough for me.

"Anyway, God, I have a need so great—" A sob escaped her lips. She hadn't expected to cry, but the thought of her need, of her friend being in danger, suddenly overwhelmed her again. "Please, God, keep Jordana safe. She is one of the best people I know, and I don't know what I'd do without her. Take care of her, as I know she believes ya will.

"I guess I can't be blamin' ya for bad things if I don't credit ya with good, too. I don't understand it, but I do know ya have brought so much good my way—and Jordana is one of the best things."

Before Caitlan realized it, she had crumbled to her knees, her head resting in her hands, and uncontrollable sobs shook her body. And it all began to tumble from her heart—her fears, her hopes, her feelings of inadequacy, her need . . . her great need.

That's how Victoria found her. She knelt down beside her, wrapped an arm around her, and held her tight.

"It's all right, Caitlan," she cooed.

Caitlan nodded through her tears. "I know that now. I . . . I think I have made me peace with God. I know He will watch out for Jordana."

"Yes . . . He will!" Victoria's voice shook with her own tears.

And Caitlan held tightly to that hope.

Thirty-Five

*I*t was dark, so very dark. Jordana at first wondered if she was blind. She wanted to rub her eyes, but that's when she realized her hands were bound. She writhed around on the cold, hard floor, finding that at least the rest of her body was functioning, and as her eyes adjusted she realized they also were working. But what had happened? Why did she have this horrible headache? Why was she—?

Panic seized her as she remembered what had happened. Someone had accosted her on the street, and then, after breathing some terrible substance, she had fallen unconscious.

Someone. . . ?

Suddenly a door opened and a beam of dull light sliced momentarily through the room before the newcomer closed the door, shutting out the light as well. But another light remained, from a lantern. It swung back and forth, dimly illuminating the floor and the feet of the visitor. It glared painfully, however, right in Jordana's eyes. She squeezed her eyes shut, and when she opened them again, the light was sitting on a rough table, and the beams it cast were a bit more normal. She could now see the visitor, though his face was still in shadows.

Damon Chittenden.

Before she could speak, he turned back to the door and locked it. It was such an ominous, final act, it made her stomach clench. She quickly took in her surroundings. It was a storage room, probably for a maid. Brooms, dustpans, buckets, cleansers, and similar items filled shelves and were leaning against the walls. There was also an acrid odor stinging her nose—lye, furniture polish, and such.

Then he turned around. His eyes, caught in the flickering flame of the lamp, had a gleam in them that did not match the apologetic smile twisting his lips.

"I hope you have not been too uncomfortable, Jordana," he said in a tone that sounded so polite, so normal. But Jordana knew now that Damon Chittenden was not a normal man. "I've brought some food for you."

"I'm not hungry," she said, then added, "What do you want, Damon?" She wanted to be strong and calm, but her voice quavered. She was afraid she had finally gotten into a fix from which there might be no escape.

"I've told you many times what I want." He sat in a chair by the table. The light now cast eerie shadows about his face, and he looked ethereal, almost demonic.

She made herself shake such images from her mind. She could get out of this. She *would* get out of this. "I thought we had an understanding."

"Understanding. . . ? No one understands."

"P-please, Damon, what are you going to do?"

Ignoring her question, he went on, "Marrying you would have pleased my father. It would have been the only thing I have ever done to achieve that. Do you know what it is like having a dead hero for a brother, or even a living brother whose success your father is always holding up before you? I could never come close to them, no matter how I tried."

"I'm sorry about that." In a way, Jordana truly was, but she had to remind herself that this man might very well have been involved in murder, and now he certainly was guilty of kidnapping. He was probably quite insane.

"You will change all that for me," Damon went on in a low, intense voice. "Father adores you. But I adore you, too, Jordana. All will change once you become my wife."

"But, Damon, surely you want a wife who loves you," Jordana said gently. "You deserve that, and I am certain you would have no trouble finding one. You are handsome and . . . well, sweet." It was hard to make that last part sound convincing, but she hoped his own vaulted self-image would buy it.

"It is you I want."

"But—"

"I'll have you, Jordana. Arguing will not help. And I am sure once we have been together, you will find me to be a good mate. You really have no choice at any rate. I'll have you tonight, or you will not see the dawn. Do you understand? I don't like forcing you, and I truly wouldn't, except I know once I do, you will find me a desirable lover."

"You couldn't, Damon. You are not capable—"

"Of murder?" He laughed, a sharp, evil bark. "I have already committed murder."

"D-did you kill Homer Stanley?"

"Not with my own hands. I paid a gang of thugs to do it and make it look like an Indian attack. But there was another man a few years back. He stood in my way also. I strangled him with my own hands." The fact that he seemed to be bragging sent a chill down Jordana's spine. "No one ever suspected me. It too was made to look like Indians had done it."

Jordana knew then that reasoning with this deranged man would be futile. Her only hope seemed to be to give the impression of yielding to his demands. Maybe then he would untie her hands, and she could fight him. Of course the chances of surviving such an unequally matched battle were minuscule, yet what other choice did she have? Besides, she'd sooner die than do what he appeared to have in mind.

"What will we do about my brother?" she asked, trying to buy time and also make it appear that she wasn't changing her tune too quickly. "He may not give his consent."

"Oh, he will once I have spent the night with you and tarnished your reputation." He smiled. "But he will see how much I love you and how I can offer a secure future for you."

She thought about mentioning her parents, but that seemed too argumentative. Instead she said sweetly, "You know, Damon, it is hard for a girl to think clearly about such things when her hands are tied. I know you must mean well, but it is difficult to believe it trussed up like this. It is not exactly the way I have dreamed of receiving a marriage proposal."

"What do you mean?" His eyes narrowed, and Jordana feared she had changed her tack too quickly.

She held up her hands. "Won't you untie me so that I can accept your proposal properly?"

"You will accept?"

"As you said, I have little choice. But I do see that you mean well—" She thought she should seek a stage career after this performance! "You have always been kind and genteel with me. In fact, my refusals have had less to do with you than with my own desire for independence."

"I will never try to dominate you, Jordana, my love!" It seemed an incongruous statement, considering her present position, but she bit back a snide rebuttal.

"That's all I want to know," she murmured.

"It is true, then?"

"Need I say more?"

He rose now and came toward her, lifting the flap of his jacket and removing a knife from a sheath on his belt. Jordana noted that he was also wearing a pistol. Her heart sank as she realized anew how unlikely escape was.

He dropped to his knees and lifted the knife to her hands. "Jordana, I love you so. . . ."

The tenderness of his words cut through her as surely as his knife would do if she tried to escape. How wonderful it would be to have a man feel thus toward her to whom she could also return the sentiment. If she could ever find such a man, it would almost be worth considering sacrificing her independence for him. Unfortunately, Damon was not that man. Still, despite what he had done to her, and was planning to do to her, it pained her to so deceive him. He truly did love her. He was to be pitied. Instead, she might be forced to kill him to save her own life—not that she had a prayer of doing so.

Nonetheless, she sent a quick but fervent plea to God.

Then Damon's knife sliced through the ropes binding her wrists, and her hands fell free. It took all her restraint not to run away from him that instant. But if she had any hope at all of escape, she would have to use cunning. He sheathed the knife, then wrapped his arms around her, caressing her hair and face with kisses. All the while, Jordana was thinking about how she could lift the knife or even the gun from his belt.

"I want you so badly!" he mumbled into her hair.

With trembling fingers, she reached up and tugged at his jacket.

"You do want me also, don't you?" he breathed as he slipped the jacket off the rest of the way. He loosened his tie and collar.

She pressed close to him. "Ouch!" she said, then giggled. "You best remove that gun before someone is hurt."

She could tell he was too besotted with her now to think clearly. He fumbled with the buckle of the holster, undid it, then tossed it aside, along with the knife. He pressed toward her with more ardor. She pretended to move into a more comfortable position. He could not see her hand slither down to the floor toward the holster. She stretched her fingers, but they were an inch shy of her target. She wiggled again.

"What is wrong, my love?" he said, an unsettling edge to his voice.

"I . . . I've never done this before. I don't know what to do."

"Follow my lead."

He pressed her back, but she managed to twist her shoulder far enough around so that she could now reach the gun. Her fingers wrapped around the butt, and she slipped it from the holster.

"What—?" he murmured.

Then he saw what she had been up to. He responded so quickly, striking the gun from her hand, that she realized just how strong and agile he was. The gun tumbled to the floor. For one brief moment he was distracted as he twisted to gather up the pistol. Jordana knew she'd have no other chance.

She swung away from him and jumped up. But her moment of freedom was short-lived as his hand raised, now wielding the gun.

"Stop!" he cried.

She dove for the door. She only made it halfway, as far as the table, before the weapon exploded. The shot missed, and she wasn't certain if he had intended to miss or not. But surely his next shot would find its target. Desperate, she looked around for some weapon of her own, anything! The light of the lamp caught her eye. As he raised his hand to fire again, Jordana grasped the lantern handle and flung the lamp at her adversary. It grazed his head before crashing to the floor.

Damon's second shot went wild. Jordana sprang toward the door. Thankful the bolt did not require a key, she turned it, then grasped the latch. As she flung open the door she saw, out of the corner of her eye, flames licking along the floor and up a wall. Then, to her horror, she saw Damon raise his arm again, but this time it didn't hold a weapon. It was, instead, encased in flame. Licks of flame were also spreading along the floor, engulfing Damon's weapons. She didn't waste another minute with these observations.

She bolted out the door and started running.

Thirty-Six

Jordana was nowhere to be found. Search parties had combed the streets of Sacramento for two hours without success. Brenton had resorted to knocking on doors to see if any residents had seen or heard anything. He was growing more and more disillusioned. If she had not been found by now . . . well, it simply did not bode well. However, he did hold some hope that if her . . . body had not been found, then it was a good sign.

At least he told himself this as he was turned away by yet another resident who knew nothing about his sister.

Suddenly a sharp blast cut through the still night air. It almost sounded like a gunshot. He wondered if one of the other searchers was trying to signal the others. But they had not prearranged any such signals. Brenton now thought that would have been a good idea. Yet firing shots in a busy city, even at night, was also risky.

Then another shot echoed.

It couldn't have been more than a couple of blocks away. Brenton turned in that direction. It was probably nothing, but it warranted an investigation. He was turning a corner when a figure hurtled toward him. He had only a moment before it slammed into him to note that it was a female.

Then *thud!* He was nearly knocked off his feet with the force of the collision. He stumbled back several steps, and only the brick wall of a building kept him on his feet.

"Oh, goodness!" the woman panted. "I'm so—Brenton! Thank God."

"Jordana!"

279

Brenton threw his arms around his sister, and she did the same around him, only her arms were shaking and she was gasping in great gulps of air.

"I'm . . . so . . . happy . . . to . . . see . . . you!" she sputtered between gulps.

"We've been looking everywhere for you. What happened?"

But before she could answer, he saw another person racing down the walkway toward them.

"You little vixen!" yelled this person. "You won't get away from me!"

"No, please!" Jordana cried.

Brenton had no idea what exactly was going on, but he knew immediately this man meant to harm his sister. In one swift motion, Brenton shoved Jordana behind him as he stepped into the man's path.

"You can't keep her from me!" shouted the man, and Brenton recognized the voice first, then the face.

"Chittenden! What on earth—?"

Damon skidded to a stop two feet from Brenton. He was panting, and oddly enough, an acrid smell of smoke and charred cloth rose from his body. One of his shirt sleeves was quite damaged.

"Don't get in my way, Baldwin!" Damon warned.

"What do you want with my sister?"

"He kidnapped me!" Jordana answered.

But Damon had apparently had enough of talk. He dove toward Brenton, who, unable to avoid the attack because of his close proximity to Jordana, took it full force, and was slammed up against the wall. Evidently Jordana had stepped out of harm's way.

"Get help!" Brenton gasped to her.

Damon was about to forget Brenton in light of this new threat, but of course Brenton could not let that happen. He had to give Jordana time to get away. With Damon momentarily distracted, Brenton took his advantage and aimed a solid blow at the man's jaw. Damon staggered back, and Brenton followed this advantage with another blow to his ribs. As Damon doubled over, Brenton noted that Jordana had hurried away. Other members of the search party were nearby, and she was sure to run into them soon.

However, he momentarily lost his focus and did not see Damon recover from Brenton's blows. He charged at Brenton, hitting him with enough force to shake Brenton's teeth, and also knocking off his glasses. Brenton lunged for the spectacles as they fell, but he missed, and they hit the ground. The next sound he heard was a scrape as Damon's boot kicked the spectacles far out of reach. Did Damon know how worthless Brenton's sight was without the spectacles?

In the next instant Damon's calculated removal of the spectacles was all too clear. A blow smashed into Brenton's nose before he saw it coming. Blood spurted down his face, and he felt as if his head had been detached from his body. Black spots, the only clear things his blurry vision could discern, appeared before his eyes. But he must not pass out. He had to keep Damon occupied until help arrived.

Swallowing back nausea, he took another swing. Damon made the mistake of grabbing Brenton's fist to deflect the blow. Despite his impaired vision, this physical contact aided him in finding his target. He struck with his free fist and clipped Damon on the chin. But the young banker shook this off easily and sent a fist hard into Brenton's stomach. Apparently any injury Damon may have suffered to his arm from the fire was negligible, considering the strength of the blow, which knocked the wind out of Brenton.

This would certainly have finished the battle, but at that moment, the sound of several pounding boots reached Brenton's ringing ears. He prayed it wasn't his imagination. He was doubled over and half blind, so he could not be certain that help had arrived until he heard Jordana's voice.

"That's him! Don't let him get away!" she was yelling. Then Brenton felt arms around him. "Brenton," she said. "Are you all right?"

"Did they get him?" he panted.

"Yes!"

Brenton looked up, and in the blur of several figures surrounding him, one was obviously being held by two others. Damon was struggling mightily, screaming and cursing.

"How could you do this to me . . . to us?" he cried.

Jordana just silently shook her head and seemed to grip her brother tighter. Brenton lifted his hand and gently patted hers.

"It's over now," Brenton said.

"It was so horrible!"

He heard the tears in her voice rather than saw them spilling from her eyes. He didn't often catch his sister crying. He knew this had been an ordeal, and he feared Damon had done more to her than merely hold her captive.

"Jordana, you are all right, aren't you? He didn't . . . well, hurt you?"

"I'm fine. He didn't harm me. But . . . I'll tell you about it later. Can we just go home?"

One of the men in the search party informed them that they were taking Damon off to jail and offered Brenton and Jordana a horse to use to get home. He also said he would see that word was sent to the other parties to call off the search. Thanking him, Brenton retrieved his spectacles which were a bit bent but still serviceable. He then returned his attention to his sister.

Jordana was shaking and Brenton was sore and bruised, but, helping each other, they managed to mount and soon enough were riding up to the house that had become their temporary home. Never before were they happier to see a house.

Jordana smiled as she watched Caitlan fuss over Brenton. She did not begrudge him the extra attention at all. He was as much a hero in her eyes as in Caitlan's, not to mention everyone else's in the family. He had never been in a fight in his life, yet he had fended off Damon's brute force bravely, even without his spectacles.

They now sat around the kitchen table with tea and a hot but slightly overcooked supper. Jordana wasn't hungry. She was still in shock over what had happened. It was hard to believe that Damon Chittenden had been so deranged and that she had somehow managed to be placed at the center of his insane delusions. She feared that somehow her rebuffs had sent him over the edge. Perhaps she could have been gentler back in Omaha. But then she shuddered at the thought that she *could* have given in to his pressure months ago. Many girls would have. He had seemed like fair husband material.

She thanked God for directing her away from him and for keeping any other unsuspecting women from falling prey to his charms.

"So, Jordana," Brenton broke into her thoughts, "have you had enough of adventure for one lifetime?"

She laughed, and it was almost a completely sincere gesture. "For now at least," she said. Then she looked around the table, amusement for a moment fading in her eyes. "I hope you don't think me selfish. I truly don't wish to be. But . . . ." She let her words trail away.

She didn't quite know how to put what was on her heart.

"But you deserve to have your dreams just like anyone else," Brenton finished for her, his tone full of deep sincerity. As when they were young, he still seemed to know best what was in her heart.

She smiled.

Later, when she and Caitlan were in their room undressing for bed, she told her friend a bit more detail about her ordeal.

"I'm so sorry I left you," Caitlan said. "It would never have happened—"

"Pshaw!" Jordana waved her hand carelessly in the air. "Then both of us would have been kidnapped." She paused, then grinned. "On second thought, I don't think Damon would have had a chance against both of us. But, Caitlan, you mustn't blame yourself. I won't hear it!"

A small, sheepish smile bent Caitlan's lips. "I know God was with ya, Jordana. Ya see, when ya were missing I was terribly afraid, and . . . well, I prayed for ya." Her smile broadened. "Then that wee prayer turned into so much more, and before I knew it I was makin' me peace with God."

"Oh, Caitlan!" Jordana flung her arms around her friend. "I knew it was only a matter of time."

"Seems everyone did but meself."

"It was almost worth getting kidnapped, then," Jordana beamed. "But then, God does have a way of turning bad things to good." As she spoke, the joy of her friend's newfound faith helped Jordana let go of some of the horrors of her ordeal that day.

Jordana returned to the dressing table and picked up her hairbrush. "You know, Caitlan . . ." she said casually, "with all that has happened to you, there is very little now standing in the way of you and Brenton getting together."

Caitlan's cheeks immediately reddened. "I'd truly like to believe such a thing were possible."

"All things are possible with God," Jordana replied. "And don't forget, He has brought us this far, hasn't He?"

Thirty-Seven

$\mathcal{B}$renton wandered out to the laundry shed, though he realized his action wasn't as aimless as he hoped it appeared. He knew Caitlan would be there.

He paused at the open door before making his presence known. Caitlan was working at the washbasin, her back to him. She was humming a jaunty tune and scrubbing a shirt against a board. She had tried to put her hair up in a chignon on top of her head, but wayward curls had slipped from their bonds and were falling like licks of flame against her face. She raised her wet, sudsy hand to shove one from her eyes. The small, insignificant gesture made Brenton's heart clench. How he enjoyed watching her every movement!

Could it be possible that there might finally be a chance for them to be together? He had spoken to Jordana after breakfast, and she had revealed to him that last night, after her rescue, Caitlan had shared that she had given her heart to God. Brenton had thrilled at the news, but he still feared that might not be the only barrier between them, despite Jordana's assurances that Caitlan was not about to reject him.

Finally, feeling a bit guilty for observing her unannounced, Brenton, making a fair amount of noise, stepped into the shed.

She turned sharply, obviously startled. The shirt was still in her hand, and a stream of water flew across the small room, splashing his coat.

"Oh, I'm sorry, Brenton!"

"It's nothing." He smiled reassuringly. "I hope you don't mind my bothering you out here."

285

"And why should I? I'm only working." She dropped the shirt back into the tub, then dried her hands on her apron. "Did ya want something?"

"Do you like doing this kind of work, Caitlan?" he asked, ignoring her question because he wasn't quite ready to forge ahead with what was truly on his mind.

"I like to work. Well, I like to keep me hands busy." She glanced at her hands. They were mottled and a bit shriveled from the water. "I'm supposin' there's some things I enjoy doing more than others. Why did ya ask that, Brenton?"

"I don't know. You were humming and seemed content. Are you, Caitlan?"

She shrugged. "I'm here with me brother at last. Why shouldn't I be?"

"Yes, of course . . ." Shuffling from foot to foot, Brenton tried not to look directly into her eyes, though he wanted to. He wanted to know if she truly was content or if she was just saying it to brush him off. He knew he was being ridiculous. It was time he was direct with her. "Did you like working with me, Caitlan? At my photography?"

"Oh yes!" she said without hesitation. "Unlike this"—she nodded toward the washtub—"yar work was the kind that both kept me hands and me mind busy. It made me feel useful in a way I had never felt before. If I wash a shirt or clean a house, it just gets dirty again, but what ya were doing, Brenton, was somethin' that is going to last forever. I know cleanin' is necessary, but having a part in preserving a way of life, and in passing it on to the future . . . it made me feel important. Not in a vain way, I don't think, but more like I could touch others, even people I did not know. It makes me tremble just to think of it!"

"You are important, Caitlan." He now ventured to lift his eyes and found hers, wide and green, staring at him in wonder.

"Yar kind to say so," she replied with a self-deprecating shrug.

"I'm not being kind. I'm being truthful. With or without the photography, you are important. And you have touched *my* life, Caitlan. I know it isn't much—"

"I have?" she broke in, her tone soft and unbelieving.

"Of course you have." His tone was edged with the tiniest bit of impatience. "Do you think I could have fallen in love with you otherwise?" He gasped when he realized the words were out.

"What?" she said incredulously.

"Why else do you think I kissed you that day in Omaha?"

"That kiss . . ." she murmured.

He could not read her tone. Dreamy? Regretful? "Yes, that confounded kiss! I don't blame you for despising me afterward."

"I could never despise you, Brenton."

"But—"

"I was afraid afterward, yes," she said hurriedly. "But mostly I let meself think ya were just caught up in the moment, tryin' to comfort me and all. I could not see how one such as yarself could mean the kiss in any other way."

"What does that mean?" He was suddenly defensive. "Do you think I am not a man that could feel love and passion for a woman?"

"No, 'tis not that at all!" She was truly distressed. "I only meant that I thought it impossible for a man such as yarself to feel love for a girl of my station."

"Confound your station!" he burst out harshly. "I am sick to death of hearing that. You are in America now, and such ideas are ridiculous. Look at your brother! That alone should show you that Baldwins, at least, don't give a fig for such things. Not that Jordana and I haven't preached to you about this over and over."

"I'm supposin' I'm a mite thick."

"A mite?"

"Quite a lot, then."

"You have the thickest, hardest head I have ever seen—you make Jordana seem like a lump of clay! Let me see if I can get this through that thick, beautiful skull of yours. To me, Caitlan, you are a noble woman of highest quality. I see you as a princess, and you make me feel like a prince, a man of value and worth. If I could but worship at your feet I'd be content."

She merely stared at him.

After a long, silent minute, he spoke up again. "Say something, Caitlan." Even rejection would be better at this point than simply not knowing what she was thinking.

Her lips moved and her mouth opened, but still no words came out. He wanted to shake her. Or embrace her. But he just stood, staring, his arms dangling uselessly at his sides.

She lifted her hand to brush an errant curl from her eyes. She licked her lips and opened her mouth again. "I . . . I don't know w-what to say."

"You don't?" All his world suddenly seemed to crash in.

" 'Tis true, as yarself and Jordana have always said. God does give good and wonderful gifts. And I have not even asked Him yet. I don't know if I would have had the nerve to ask Him for you."

"Would you have? I mean, if you had the nerve?"

"Do ya know that I made me heart right with God yesterday?" When he nodded, she went on. "He is helping me to see that I am good enough."

"And?"

"You truly see me as a princess?"

"I do."

She smiled. "And I have always seen you as a king, the finest, noblest man I know. I feared loving ya, Brenton. Not only yar rejection, but worse, that you might return me love and I'd drag ya down to my level."

"That would be impossible, since we are on the same level . . . well, you are a little higher than me, but I won't quibble—" He stopped suddenly and blinked. "Did you say you loved me?"

"And now who has the thick head?" Her lips curved in the prettiest grin he had ever seen. "I love you, Brenton! I truly do."

"Oh, my. . . !"

Now, instead of crumbling, his world turned bright and clear and crisp. And he looked with wonder at the woman who had made it so and who was so much a part of that world. And in two quick strides he shortened what was left of the distance between them and gathered her into his arms. He kissed her with the tenderness a princess deserved, though fired by the deep passion in his heart. And she responded as he never thought possible. Their worlds became one, and Brenton knew, in the core of their beings, they would never be separated again, not by ill-perceived stations nor by differing faith. In that single embrace they each gave to the other what they both so needed, what they could only give to one another—a deep sense of their self-worth, their value to each other and to God.

"Ah-hem!" intruded a deep voice.

Brenton and Caitlan broke apart. Brenton found himself staring at Kiernan, who was standing in the doorway, arms folded across his chest, an inscrutable look on his face.

"Hmm, what is this, then?" said Kiernan.

"I . . . I . . ." Brenton momentarily forgot he was a king. He stared at his brother-in-law's brawny figure, feeling small and weak. This was not helped by the trembling in his knees.

"Brenton Baldwin," Kiernan said, "if yar of a mind to take such liberties with me sister, I'll have to be insistin' that ya marry her."

Brenton gaped, not knowing what to think or say. Then Kiernan's lips parted, and a huge grin appeared.

"Well, if you insist," Brenton replied lightly, suddenly relaxing. "I'll take my punishment like a man, then."

"Hold on a minute!" Caitlan gave Brenton a gentle shove. "I'll not be any man's punishment." Her green eyes were dancing with amusement. "And I don't think I'd be wantin' a marriage proposal with me brother's invisible shotgun pointed at me either. A princess, ya know, is deservin' of a proper proposal."

Brenton dropped quickly to his knees before her. "Indeed you are!"

"But wait—" she smiled sheepishly. "I'm not meanin' to be choosy—I really won't let all this princess business go to me head. But don't ya think there is someone else who should witness this, that is, if we are going to have an audience anyway?"

Brenton grinned. "Yes, you are right. Jordana would never let us hear the end of it if Kiernan had witnessed this and not her." He grabbed Caitlan's hand. "Come along, then."

They raced into the house. Victoria, making bread in the kitchen, looked up, perplexed.

"Where's Jordana?" Brenton asked.

"In the parlor, I believe. Dusting."

"You best come, too."

Victoria was still looking bemused but followed the little party into the parlor where Jordana was indeed, with rag in hand, dusting. She looked up, and her brow immediately arched in question.

"Stay right there, Jordana," Brenton ordered. "Don't talk, just listen."

She opened her mouth, but when he shook his head she clamped it shut and obeyed.

Brenton took Caitlan's hand, then dropped to one knee before her.

"Caitlan O'Connor," he breathed aloud, now all amusement had dimmed, replaced by sheer awe and sincerity, "you have won my heart, and in doing so, I find that with you I am a complete person. You bring light and life to me, and for that and for many other reasons, which I hope to have the rest of our lives together to tell you,

I love you! And I ask—no, I beg, for your hand in marriage!"

Tears brimmed Caitlan's eyes, making them sparkle like green pools. "I would be most honored to accept your wonderful proposal!"

Behind him, Brenton heard a small "Whoop!" and a giggle from Jordana. "Now, you must kiss her," she said.

"He's kissed her already," Kiernan offered.

But Brenton needed no further encouragement in this matter. He was on his feet in an instant with his arms around the woman he loved. Kissing her, he lifted her off her feet and whirled her around.

Then the room burst into joyous laughter and congratulations. Still holding Caitlan close, Brenton knew he had just been given the finest gift in the world. He had found a prize worth more than diamonds or gold. He had found love.

PART IV

November 1864

—

January 1865

Thirty-Eight

A wonderful gift came in time for Brenton's twenty-first birthday in November. A telegram arrived from his parents. They were departing for California posthaste and, traveling by ship, planned to arrive in San Francisco the seventh of January.

"Well, then," Jordana said as she and the family enjoyed a small birthday party for Brenton, "we need to start making plans. To begin with, we can now set a date for the wedding."

Brenton and Caitlan exchanged looks. Jordana thought it too sweet—as if they had been thinking of anything else! But it had presented a difficult conundrum. Brenton wanted his parents present at his wedding, but when he sent them a telegram telling them of his happy news, he hadn't expected them to make the arduous journey, thousands of miles, to be present. He had suggested that he and Caitlan travel east, though not very enthusiastically. That very likely would leave out Kiernan and Victoria. It also would mean another long and awkward period of time in close quarters with Caitlan, a strain he was not willing to endure.

Thus, they had put off setting a date.

Jordana thought they should just get married. Their parents would not blame him for doing so in their absence. But Brenton had dragged his feet over the matter.

Caitlan smiled after the telegram from New York was read. "I was praying about this very thing! I did not want to be marryin' without yar parents being here. It didn't seem right."

"And it seems God answered your prayer," said Brenton.

"Aye, it does at that! Can ya imagine that? He heard me for certain, and He answered." She chuckled. "I hope it never stops feeling this grand!"

"He will be there even if it does," assured Brenton.

"I know. . . ." And her smile grew. "I truly know!"

Now the wedding plans could begin in earnest. January tenth, the first Saturday after the arrival of their parents, was set as the date. Money was tight for the group. Brenton had his inheritance to look forward to, but nothing could be counted on from that until he spoke to his parents. They had said nothing of it in the telegram. However, his skills as a photographer were quite novel this far west, and he was keeping quite busy taking portraits and doing other assignments. He was making enough to cover living expenses and a few extras.

Kiernan, of course, was still unemployed, though his doctor said that he could resume light duties. He still had to wear his eye patch, but all his other injuries had healed well. Unfortunately, the railroad was having its own financial crisis at the moment, and work had slowed to a standstill.

The only one in the household with any money to spare and with a steady income was Victoria. The laundry business was booming, and because there was no rent to pay, she was building a nice little nest egg. For the time being, Brenton allowed her to pay for wedding expenses, promising to repay her as soon as he received his money. Victoria declared she hardly cared if he ever repaid her, because she was having too much fun to worry over it.

Caitlan had begun to voice her old concerns about taking charity, until Kiernan took her aside and had a very long talk with her. Jordana would never find out just what he had said, but whatever it was, it had worked wonders because Caitlan did not make another protest about money.

Like everyone else, Jordana was caught up in the plans for the upcoming nuptials. Only a couple of shadows seemed to interfere with the happy time. One was Damon Chittenden. Jordana, much to Brenton's chagrin, had refused to press charges against him. She said he needed help more than imprisonment. The police officer in charge of the case kept trying to convince her otherwise. He warned that because Chittenden seemed normal on the exterior, he was very likely going to be released rather than even committed to an asylum. As Damon appeared unrepentant for what he had done, Jordana rightly feared that if he were released, she would continue to be in danger from him.

She struggled over this dilemma for several days until she came to a solution. She went to Damon and proposed that she would not press charges for the kidnapping if he would have himself committed to an asylum. There was very little difference between prisons and asylums, but at least in the latter he could get help and hope for a shorter confinement. Damon, with not many options open to him, agreed to the proposal.

Brenton and Kiernan were distressed about this, but Jordana reminded them that soon enough his crimes in Omaha would catch up to him—and in fact a wire had already been sent to the sheriff in Omaha to look more closely into the Stanley death and also into the death of a Tom Ludlow, the man Damon had bragged about killing to Jordana. It did not appear as if Damon Chittenden would be bothering anyone again for a good long time.

One other thing troubled Jordana during this time, but she could not quite identify if. Every now and then she would find herself filled with melancholy. She put on an excellent front, and no one noticed, but she knew all was not quite right inside herself. She wished she knew what it was. Or did she? Perhaps it was best ignored because she feared it might have to do with her selfishness, seeing everyone's lives work out in wonderful ways while her own remained uncertain, unsettled.

One day just before Christmas Brenton came home with a gift for Caitlan, who was learning to accept gifts graciously. She opened this package and found the most beautiful ivory silk fabric and a matching length of incredible Irish lace.

"'Tis what I was admiring at the store the other day," she exclaimed.

"I thought it might do for a wedding dress," said Brenton.

She flung her arms around Brenton joyfully. Caitlan had been dragging her feet about a choice for her dress, and with only three weeks until the big day, time was running short. Not wanting to complain about the expense, she had simply avoided the issue.

Victoria and Caitlan immediately put their heads together about making the dress. Jordana offered a few remarks about style, but as sewing was definitely not her forte, she was quiet the rest of the time, finally taking herself out to the laundry room to see to the clothes that had been hung to dry earlier.

The Christmas Eve service at Kiernan and Victoria's church was very nice, but afterward Jordana still felt . . . well, perhaps restless was the best way to describe her emotions. She threw herself into the holiday festivities with the others and did enjoy herself. She loved these people more than any others in the world, besides her parents. And they loved her. But despite the sense of joy and support she felt in their presence, that small cloud of sadness would not disappear.

New Year's Day, 1865, came at last, and Jordana let herself truly believe that her parents were actually coming. A week later, Kiernan and Brenton borrowed one of Charlie Crocker's carriages and drove to San Francisco to pick up the Baldwins. Because it was several hours' drive, they would spend the night in the city before returning to Sacramento. The women at home were in varying states of excitement. Victoria was nearly beside herself with anticipation, but she was a bit nervous also. She had confided to Jordana about the money she and Kiernan had lost and how Kiernan had written the Baldwins about it, but there had been no response. She had no idea what to expect from her parents.

Caitlan was so nervous she could neither eat nor sleep. Of course she had met Brenton's parents that one time in Omaha, but they had been there only a short time, and Caitlan had stayed in the background as much as possible. No amount of encouragement from Victoria and Jordana would allay her fears. And really, neither one of them had ever had the experience of meeting their future in-laws, so they could not offer much in the way of personal advice. They tried to tell her how James and Carolina were the gentlest, kindest, most accepting people on earth. Caitlan knew that from the previous meeting, but this time it was different. Now she was presuming to become part of their family by taking their oldest son.

Jordana was the only one who wasn't nervous at the prospect of the reunion. She longed to see her mother, to talk to her. Maybe her mother might have some insight about this uncharacteristic melancholy Jordana was experiencing.

———

Shortly before noon the following day, Victoria announced that the carriage was pulling up in front of the house. Jordana raced down the stairs from her room, followed a bit more timidly by Caitlan. When they reached the bottom, Jordana took her friend's hand.

"They will simply be delighted with you," she smiled encouragingly.

"Do ya truly think?"

Jordana just shook her head and rolled her eyes. Caitlan would enchant her parents, she knew very well. She *looked* enchanting for openers. Jordana had finally persuaded Caitlan to buy the green dress they had seen the day of their fight. She convinced the frugal girl that it would serve many uses, first to impress her future in-laws, then as a going-away dress for her honeymoon.

"And where would I be goin'?" Caitlan had returned lightly.

In fact no honeymoon had been planned beyond a brief stay in a nice hotel in town.

Nevertheless, Caitlan sparkled in the gown of green poplin, edged with scallops trimmed with black piping that ran along the straight sleeves, and down the bodice and the front of the skirt. Jet black buttons followed the line of the scallops, and black lace encircled the neckline. Her hair was piled upon her head in a fetching array of ringlets, which Victoria had spent hours fixing. They had laughed that if it took this long to get ready to meet the parents, they'd best get started now to dress her for the wedding.

The three young women arranged themselves in the entryway as elegantly as their excitement would allow. Jordana wanted to open the door and run out to meet them, but Victoria's admonition had prevailed that they needed to do all they could to assure their mother that her adventurous daughters were still ladies.

The door opened and Kiernan appeared, then quickly stepped aside for his guests. Jordana's heart simply leaped when her mother stepped inside, and no amount of effort could keep her from racing into her mother's arms.

"Oh, Mama!" Tears sprang to Jordana's eyes. "I was trying to be a lady, but . . . I'm just so glad to see you."

Carolina laughed and kissed Jordana. "As am I, my dear!"

Then Carolina opened her arms for Victoria, who was only a breath away from doing the same thing. It had been far too many years, and both women burst into tears. Thus it was longer than expected before attention was finally drawn to Caitlan. Jordana had stepped back next to her friend and was holding her hand. But by the time Victoria and Carolina had recovered a bit from their emotional reunion, James and Brenton had stepped inside, followed by the younger children—Nicholas, now thirteen, and Amelia, who was eleven.

As Brenton moved quickly to stand next to his fiancée, Jordana embraced her younger brother and sister, exclaiming at how they had grown.

"Mama and Papa, you remember Caitlan," Brenton said, drawing Caitlan to the front. His eyes were aglow with pride and love.

"Of course we do," said Carolina with a gracious smile.

Caitlan gave a dainty curtsey. "I am most honored to meet you again, Mrs. Baldwin . . . and Mr. Baldwin."

There was a brief moment of tense formality. Then James grinned and spoke. "You will be my daughter in a few days, young lady," he said, "so I hope I will be allowed the honor of hugging you."

"'Twould be my honor, sir."

Then James gathered her up, kissed her cheek, and exclaimed at how lovely she looked. Caitlan's cheeks pinked in a most becoming way, and her eyes glowed. But before she could recover from this, Carolina also held out her arms.

"This family may not see each other very often, but when we do we are an emotional and expressive lot." Carolina embraced Caitlan. "Welcome to our family, Caitlan. We are proud to have yet another O'Connor enrich our Baldwin bloodlines."

"I can't believe you're finally here," Jordana said to her family. "Nicholas, what did you think of Russia?"

"It wasn't half so grand as England," he replied. "I want to study architecture in London when Papa says I am old enough."

"And I want to live in Paris and wear beautiful gowns," said Amelia, her dark eyes sparkling. "The ladies there dress so beautifully."

Jordana laughed. "Well, it seems you both have your lives quite planned out."

The happy group moved to the parlor to await the luncheon Victoria and Caitlan had prepared. For the rest of the afternoon the little house fairly buzzed with animated conversation, interspersed with frequent hugs and much laughter. Jordana wanted this joyous reunion to never end. And as that thought occurred to her in the course of the afternoon, her melancholy tugged at her again. She suddenly realized it would end, and life would never be the same.

Thirty-Nine

After supper Jordana wandered out to the front porch of the house. It was a chilly January evening, and she wrapped her wool shawl tightly about her. The sky was clear and dotted with an array of faraway stars. A breeze blew from the north, brushing her upturned face with an icy hand.

She didn't know why she had felt the need to come out here where it was not very comfortable. Why had she wanted a break from the warm togetherness of her family? Her family was everything to her. And having them all together for the first time in years was simply the best thing she could imagine happening. But all the reminiscing over old times had left a knot in Jordana's stomach. Being reminded of their growing-up years in Greigsville and Baltimore had made her sad instead of happy. It was because she would never be able to go back to that happy time. It had never bothered her before. She had always been one to look ahead to new vistas, new adventures.

Why was now any different?

"What a lovely night!" came Carolina's voice from the doorway. "Do you mind some company?"

"Please, Mama, do join me." Jordana made room on the wicker bench where she was sitting.

Carolina sat and placed an arm around her daughter. "You're shivering."

"It's a cold night."

"There'll be snowstorms in New York now. It amazes me that here in Sacramento in January it's as mild as a fall afternoon back home."

"They say it is even warmer south of here."

"Are you truly interested in discussing the weather, Jordana?" sighed Carolina.

Jordana shook her head. "I can think of far more important things I want to talk with you about, Mama."

"What is it, dear?"

"Oh, but I don't want to burden you on your first day here."

"Nonsense! I have come here specifically to share my children's joy and their burdens. I haven't much time, so I want to get an early start." She gave Jordana's shoulders a squeeze. "So. . . ?"

"Everything is so wonderful, Mama. We finally made it to California and found Kiernan alive, and Caitlan gave her life to God, and she and Brenton are about to be married. And . . . I don't know. All is perfect. But why am I feeling so sad at times? Am I jealous that they have found love and their futures are laid out before them? I could have found love too. I've had men propose—" Her brow arched. "Well, one has died and the other has turned out to be insane. But I could find love—"

"If you wanted it?" prompted Carolina.

"Yes, but I don't think that's what is bothering me. I am happy for Brenton and Caitlan, and I don't think I envy them. But we had such grand times together. Now . . . what will happen now?" The tears she had feared might surprise her during the afternoon finally made an appearance. She dashed at her eyes with her hand. "They are both my best friends, Mama. What am I going to do?" And the tears came harder, too fast for her to wipe them away.

Carolina handed her a handkerchief. "Are you resenting them just a little bit, Jordana?"

Sniffing, Jordana nodded. "Brenton has always been there for me. You know how close we have been, and now he will marry and transfer his allegiance to Caitlan. Oh, I love Caitlan. But she is taking away my brother!" Now Jordana was bawling as the full impact of her feelings was finally expressed. She had always known that one day she and Brenton would find marriage partners and their relationship would change. Selfishly, she had always thought she would marry first and thus her pain would not be as great. But now she felt as if she were being abandoned.

"Isn't this the silliest thing you ever heard?" Jordana sobbed. "I'm insufferable!"

"There, there . . ." cooed Carolina. "You are neither insufferable nor selfish. Some changes are just harder to take than others."

"But how am I going to get over the way I feel? I should be so happy now."

"Tell me something, Jordana. Besides how you are feeling about Brenton, are you worried about your own future?"

She looked at her mother and smiled through her tears. "I don't think I'm worried, just uncertain. There are so many things I want to do, but I suppose . . . well, maybe I am worried that I won't be able to do them because I am a woman. I'm worried and a little angry, too."

"I understand. . . ." murmured Carolina.

Jordana knew indeed they were more than mere words, for her mother had experienced the same things at one time, the same dreams and hunger for adventure as Jordana now knew.

"I guess besides missing what Brenton and I had before, I am also going to miss his presence, which gave me the freedom to do many things that would have been forbidden me had I been alone." Pausing, she shook her head. "That really does sound selfish, but . . . it is true. Do you know, Mama, that we were attacked by Indians while traveling on the prairie with a survey party? How many single women could have gone on such a trip? It was frightening and thrilling all at once. My horse spooked during the attack and took me on a wild run."

"What an ordeal!" Carolina exclaimed.

"Captain O'Brian had to rescue me," Jordana went on, "and he got in a fight with one of the Indians and I had to shoot the Indian to save Rich. Oh, Mama, it was horrible."

"It makes me appreciate more than ever that you are safe and sound," Carolina remarked earnestly, then added, "Captain O'Brian? Rich?" Carolina arched her brow inquisitively.

Heat flared up Jordana's cheeks. "Mama!"

"This was just some old army officer, then, of no particular consequence?" The irony in Carolina's tone was hard to discount.

"Not old," Jordana admitted. "Young, in fact, and rather handsome. But I have no interest whatsoever in him. He is an arrogant, insufferable sort. Just because he has rescued me on several occasions, he thinks he can boss me around."

"Lord save the man who thinks that!" laughed Carolina.

Jordana tried to look quite affronted, and it almost worked, until a small smile intruded upon her lips. Then a grin followed. "I suppose I might be a *bit* insufferable myself at times."

"But this Captain O'Brian does seem to keep on rescuing you, it appears."

"Well, I rescued *him* last time."

"Good, that should keep him in his place," quipped Carolina.

"He's really not all bad." Jordana smiled as she thought of some of those encounters with Rich O'Brian. He did have a way about him.

Mother and daughter fell silent for a few moments, then Carolina said, "We ought to be getting inside before we catch our deaths. But before we go, I was thinking about something you said earlier about being alone."

"Yes, Mama...?"

"I have a feeling that even though Brenton is getting married, he will still miss you as much as you will miss him. Of course, it may not be as intense because he'll have Caitlan, but..." Carolina tapped her finger against her lips thoughtfully. "I gather from talking to Brenton this afternoon that he still holds to his dream of photographing the country."

"It is his and Caitlan's dream."

"Yes, and they both look forward to traveling all over fulfilling that dream. Not at all unlike the three of you have already been doing."

"But, Mama..." Jordana said warily, "there is one difference—they will be married now."

Carolina tittered lightly. "Married, Jordana, not fallen off the face of the earth. It may well be they would welcome your company on these adventures."

"I couldn't! I'd feel out of place."

"You were and are both Brenton's and Caitlan's best friend. I don't think it will be so easy for them to part from you. Of course they will want a time of adjustment alone, but I should think they would welcome the company of their best friend. You don't have to be tied to their hips, yet neither do you have to be cut off from them completely. It is something to think about, and to talk to them about."

"I wouldn't want them to pity me."

"Jordana, you are the last person anyone would pity. Just give it some thought. Who knows what God has in store for you?"

"He hasn't let me down yet."

"And He won't, Jordana. Whatever His plan for you, I am certain it will be something that will keep you sufficiently stimulated."

Jordana smiled. She hoped that wasn't expecting too much of God, but then she remembered He had promised, "Delight thyself also in the Lord, and he shall give thee the desires of thine heart."

Forty

*J*ordana had not been the only one out of sorts that evening. Kiernan had been both anticipating and dreading the arrival of his in-laws. After hearing of their intent to visit California, he hadn't expected a written response to his letter of confession. In a way, he would rather have had it in writing than face-to-face. He comforted himself with the fact that they had been not only cordial with him thus far, but actually very warm.

Now that they were here he hoped the matter would be settled very soon. It was excruciating to wait and wonder. But he didn't know how to broach the subject and wasn't certain if he should do it or let them choose the place and time. It made Kiernan most uncomfortable.

Especially as the evening progressed, and James, after his wife and Jordana had returned from some mother-daughter tête-à-tête on the porch, made a special presentation to his son.

"Brenton, as you know, you have reached your majority, and because your mother and I have been wise in our investments, we find ourselves able to provide each of our children with a monetary inheritance." Pausing, he took an envelope from his coat pocket. "I'd like to present yours to you now." He handed the envelope to his son.

Brenton opened it, his eyes wide. "This is far more than I expected," he breathed, leaning over to show the check to his fiancée, whose eyes sprang open even wider than Brenton's.

"It was invested wisely over the years and has nearly doubled," said James.

305

Kiernan cringed at this statement, though it was in no way directed at him and was spoken in the most matter-of-fact manner. Nevertheless, he wanted to crawl under the threadbare carpet beneath his feet. This feeling wasn't helped when the conversation turned, quite naturally, to the railroad, and all he had to report were failures and roadblocks.

Victoria, bless her heart, was quick to sing her husband's praises. "Before his accident, Kiernan was Charles Crocker's right-hand man. And Mr. Crocker intends to take Kiernan back on as soon as work begins again. He will probably be one of the main supervisors when the construction moves east."

"I've heard the Supreme Court has upheld the government's pledge to honor the Central Pacific's contracts. So it shouldn't be long now," said Carolina.

"It won't be soon enough for me," said Kiernan, beginning to feel some of the angst he had felt during his recovery from his accident.

The conversation continued, but Kiernan was distracted. He poked at the fire in the hearth, then, seizing on the excuse of needing more wood, escaped from the parlor and made his way to the kitchen and out the back door to the woodpile. He was gathering up an armload when James stepped outside.

"Can I give you a hand?" James asked.

"I've got it, sir, but thank you."

"Would you mind a word before you get the wood?"

Kiernan let the wood slide back to the pile. "Of course not." He licked his lips, suddenly nervous as he sensed the moment of truth had finally come. "Would ya be wantin' to go into the kitchen?" His accent was thicker than ever.

They returned to the kitchen and took seats at the table. The minute they were seated Kiernan jumped up again. "The coffee's warm. Would ya be wantin' a cup?"

"Yes, thank you."

Kiernan poured two cups, but he knew the distraction would not last.

"You know, Kiernan," James said casually after Kiernan resumed his seat, "now that the court has ruled in favor of the CP, bonds will be released for sale. I plan to purchase several."

"Ay . . . well, 'twill be a good investment."

"You might think to do the same," suggested James.

Kiernan blinked, then his healthy eye squinted with confusion. Suddenly he began to wonder if his letter had ever arrived in Baltimore. With the war on and communications so unreliable, it was a good possibility. His stomach knotted at the prospect of having to go over the matter afresh.

"Sir, did ya by any chance receive a letter from me. . . ?"

"I did," said James. Then he reached into his coat pocket and withdrew yet another envelope. "And I have something for you."

Kiernan took the envelope, his hands actually trembling. Now, what was he going to do? No doubt out of sympathy, James was giving him money. How could he accept it? Yet, how could he refuse it? Especially since Victoria would be the one to suffer most. Had she not already suffered enough from his pride? He thought, too, of all his recent lectures to Caitlan about pride. Yet it made it no easier now to accept charity—he could think of no other word for it—from his father-in-law.

"Go ahead, Kiernan," prompted James, "open it."

Kiernan did so and found a check inside—a sizable check! But he couldn't smile; he couldn't feel joy. He could feel only the depths of his inadequacy.

"'Tis difficult for me to take this, sir," Kiernan finally rasped through a constricted throat.

"It is your money, Kiernan."

"Sir? I'm not understandin'."

"Kiernan, your mother-in-law and I were, understandably I think, upset when we received your letter," said James. "But it was not because you had lost Victoria's dowry—"

Kiernan thought it decent how James referred to Victoria's inheritance as a dowry, somehow making it seem as if it were in fact as much Kiernan's money as Victoria's.

James went on, "What upset us was that you felt you could not tell us, and that because of that, you were forced to suffer—as I am sure you must have, in a new land with no money to live on besides what could be earned by the sweat of your brow."

"We did suffer, sir, I will admit. Victoria especially, and thus I would be understandin' yar disapproval of me. 'Twas so wrong of me. I clung to what I perceived of as pride, but only when I wrote ya that letter did I finally realize it was the wrong kind of pride. I am sorry for that now. But I still don't feel right acceptin' this check from ya. I will for Victoria's sake, but—"

"Let me finish before you say anything else," interjected James. "First, you are a good man, Kiernan, a fine man. I am not merely blowing air when I say I am proud to have you as part of our family. You are not perfect, but who is?" A peculiar look crossed James' face, then he continued. "We have all made mistakes in our lives. Perhaps because of my own mistakes, I was able to perceive in the beginning when you married Victoria that you had some maturing to do. Oh, I had no doubts that you would make a good husband to my daughter, but I did have my doubts about your understanding of finances. Thus, Kiernan, I practiced a little deception of my own. I did not turn over to you the whole of Victoria's inheritance. The check you now hold is the balance plus interest of that inheritance."

Kiernan gaped at James' astounding revelation, unable to conjure up a verbal response. It was best that he did not, for his immediate response was that James had treated him rather like a child, not trusting him even enough to share his misgivings with Kiernan. Yet, Kiernan's good sense quickly prevailed. For one thing, he had proven James' treatment to be exactly proper because Kiernan *had* behaved like a child. Moreover, he was certain that if James had shared these things with him years ago when he first married Victoria, he would have been unable to hear them.

"Will you forgive me?" James was saying. "What I did was wrong—"

"My actions proved ya were not wrong, sir," Kiernan said quickly. "And I know ya only had mine and especially Victoria's best interests in mind. I was a prideful, cocky boy back then. I can honestly say that life has seasoned me considerably, perhaps even matured me."

"I see that too, son."

As James spoke the word "son," Kiernan's chest tightened with pride and love for this man who, indeed, was the closest person he had to a father.

"Let us agree to be open and honest with each other from now on," James added.

"Agreed, sir. And if yar not mindin', I would ask that ya act as my financial advisor in the future."

"Happily, Kiernan! And my first bit of advice would be for you to invest in Central Pacific stock."

The two men rose, and before they returned to the gathering in the parlor, they embraced warmly as father and son.

   In the parlor, Kiernan caught Victoria's eye several times, smiling broadly each time. He couldn't wait to get her alone and tell her about how God had blessed them yet again!

Forty-One

*T*here was a lovely church ceremony on the tenth of January. Brenton was handsome in his dove gray cutaway coat over black pinstripe trousers. But Caitlan was stunning in the ivory silk-and-lace gown she and Victoria had copied from a photo in the latest *Godey's Lady's Book*. On her cinnamon red curls, which fell in ringlets around her shoulders, she wore a tulle elbow-length veil. She carried a bouquet of white roses.

Besides family, there were about two dozen guests, mostly close friends of Kiernan and Victoria and also a few who had made the acquaintance of the bride and groom during their stay in California. Before going to the church that morning, photographs were taken by Jordana—of course, Brenton had set everything up so his sister had only to make the final exposure.

The entire group left the church immediately after the ceremony for a luncheon at the O'Connor home. Then, amid tears and laughter, the newlyweds departed on their honeymoon. Much to their surprise, James and Carolina had presented to them the gift of a week's stay in one of the best hotels in San Francisco.

Jordana bid her brother and new sister farewell, crying only a little. She hadn't yet spoken to them about future plans—there would be time enough for that later—but she felt far more positive since speaking to her mother.

The house seemed especially quiet that evening after the departure of the newlyweds and all the guests. Yet, with just the family seated in the parlor, there was a wonderful sense of warmth and companionship. Everyone was relaxed and comfortable. Amelia had

311

fallen asleep against her father's shoulder, and Nicholas was quietly snuggled up next to Jordana on the sofa. The last three days had been a whirlwind with the arrival of James and Carolina, followed so quickly by the wedding festivities.

Jordana sighed contentedly, wondering what she had been fretting about before. She might actually enjoy a few adventureless months.

After a while, the menfolk decided to go out for some fresh air, leaving mother and daughters alone in the parlor. Within moments the conversation began, as they seemingly all at once realized it was just the females now and they could open up and share with one another on an entirely different level. And, though they had not been together for years, it was as if all that time and distance had not separated them. They were as they once had been, chatting easily about the day's events, and just as easily about feelings and futures and problems.

"I thought I'd die when the minister showed up late," said Victoria. "I'm certain I told him the wedding was to be at eleven, but . . ." She shrugged to complete her thought.

"It wouldn't be a proper wedding if there weren't some mishap," said Carolina.

"It is hard to believe, after all those two ninnies went through, that they are finally married." Jordana smiled. "Brenton . . . married! Never thought he'd rise above his shyness to even meet a girl, much less marry one."

"It took a special girl," said Carolina.

"Yes, and Caitlan is that. They are perfect for each other."

"Shall I fix us some tea?" asked Victoria.

"You have been working so hard all day," said Carolina. "Just sit and relax now. And, if you feel up to it, I'd love to hear about what your life is like here in California."

"There's really not much of any import to tell." Victoria sighed. "I have to confess it has been better lately since Kiernan has been forced to stay home for a while. I feel so bad it took a terrible accident to bring that about, but . . . it was hard to have him gone so much. I was pleased that he finally had a good job—he is indispensable to Mr. Crocker. And I know he will be going back soon, and I will have to get along without him again. I do dread that time, though."

"It is not an easy adjustment," said Carolina. And all knew Carolina did not speak emptily, because she had experienced that same loneliness in the early part of her marriage when she had been often separated from her husband due to his work.

"At least you had children, Mama, to keep you busy, so that you didn't have to feel the loneliness so very intensely." Victoria's eyes were so sad, Jordana could feel her sister's emptiness. "I keep telling myself that with the way our life has been, so unsettled and all, it would have been hard on children. So I can see how our childlessness was God's providence. Yet . . ." Victoria paused as her voice caught on her emotion. "Never mind. I don't want to spoil a lovely day."

Carolina rose and went to her daughter and put an arm around her. "Speak your heart, Victoria. Maybe it will help."

"Oh, Mama! I ache so to have a baby of my own. Sometimes my arms just ache with their emptiness. I try to be content with what God has wrought, but it isn't always easy."

"No, it's not." Carolina paused, then added, "Have you thought about adopting? It worked out wonderfully for me." She smiled, giving her adopted daughter a gentle squeeze. "There are so many lost and abandoned children out there whose little bodies, I am sure, are also aching to be held by loving arms such as yours, Victoria."

"Yes, I have thought about adopting, Mama," Victoria replied. "But I think it would be important to Kiernan to have a child of his own blood."

"You think?" Carolina asked. "Haven't you talked to him about this?"

"I supposed I haven't." Victoria rubbed her chin. "Maybe I should. . . ."

As Jordana listened to her mother and sister, her previous melancholy began to slip over her again. This time, though, it was more because she felt for the first time that she had so little in common with these women she loved. She did not long for home and family. Her arms did not ache to hold a child. What she really ached for was to return to the wilds of the prairie. How she had loved those times when she and Brenton and Caitlan had traveled in his wagon, and even when she had traveled with the survey party . . . never knowing what the next day would bring, a new adventure around each turn of the road, or simply one's eyes beholding a strange wonder, something that perhaps no human had yet to see.

Once on the trail she and her companions had met a grizzled old mountainman. He had been wearing stained and worn buckskin, with a pack and a musket strapped to his back. He'd told them how, after fighting in the Mexican war, he'd traveled west to the goldfields, then, heading back to the prairie, he'd ended up living with the Sioux Indians for a few years. Then he'd tried his hand at trapping, and when Jordana met him, he was off to explore the Wyoming Territory.

She knew it was foolish to think of herself in buckskin and such, especially when she did like to wear the latest styles and have a new hat occasionally and stay in fancy hotels. But she envied that mountainman, too. Was it terrible to want it all?

"Jordana, you do have a faraway look in your eyes," Carolina broke into her thoughts.

Jordana flashed a smile, tinged with the slightest bit of guilt. "I guess my mind wandered."

"Yes, I forgot how domestic talk bores you," quipped Carolina. Then she added more earnestly, "Do you care to share what you were thinking?"

"Oh, the usual . . . wondering where my future will take me."

"Jordana, I have been meaning to talk to you about that," said Victoria. "I want you to know you are welcome to remain here with me for as long as you like."

"That's kind of you, Victoria, but I don't want to become an imposition—"

"Don't even think that!" came Victoria's emphatic, almost desperate, reply. "How I would love your company, especially after Kiernan returns to work."

"Well . . ."

"Now, don't you worry," Victoria assured with a smile. "I will not stand in your way of adventure—within reason, of course! I think you will find California a place that could hold even your interest for some time."

"In that case, I will give it serious thought."

Jordana reminded herself that again God was providing for her, and the beauty of it was that He was doing it in a way He knew would be palatable to her. God, she was certain, did not wish to stifle that sense of adventure that very likely had come from Him in the first place.

Just then, she heard a knock on the front door. Victoria rose to answer it, returning in a few moments with a perplexed look on her face.

"Jordana, there is a man to see you," she said. "He says he is a friend of yours from Omaha."

Jordana's heart gave a surprising leap as she immediately thought of Captain O'Brian. But what would he be doing all the way out here? And why on earth was her heart suddenly pounding so?

"He is waiting in the entryway," Victoria was saying. "Feel free to receive him in here."

Jordana rose on ridiculously unsteady legs and went to the entryway. But it was not the tall, broad-shouldered man in the dark blue uniform who greeted her. Rather, her visitor was short, stocky, and a bit rotund. It was Hezekiah Chittenden.

"Mr. Chittenden!" She almost wanted to embrace the kindly man, but since she had never taken such liberties in the past, she restrained herself now.

"Jordana, I do hope you don't mind my seeking you out like this."

"Of course not. Would you care to join my mother and sisters in the parlor?"

"Well . . . uh . . ."

At his hesitancy, she decided this was not a social call. He most likely had grim matters to discuss.

"If you would like to visit alone, I have only the kitchen to offer," she said. "Would that be suitable?"

"Yes, thank you so much."

They went into the kitchen and took seats at the table. Jordana thought about offering tea but knew instinctively that would not be appropriate. She prepared herself for an unpleasant encounter. After all, he might well see her as responsible for his son's difficulties.

He allayed her fears immediately. "Jordana, I must tell you how sorry I am for all the distress my son's actions surely have caused you. I hope you can find it in your heart to forgive me."

"But you did nothing, Mr. Chittenden."

"He is my son." The man sighed. "And perhaps my doing nothing contributed as much to his problems as anything. There were signs of his unstable mind before all this transpired with you, but I chose to ignore them. I could not accept that he was not completely normal."

"Well, sir, I hold nothing against you."

The poor man nearly sagged with relief. "Thank you, my dear."

"Tell me, Mr. Chittenden, do you know yet what will become of Damon?"

"I have come to escort him back to Omaha. Of course an officer of the law will be along as well, but I thought perhaps my presence might make the journey easier for him. A preliminary investigation was made in Omaha, and there were sufficient findings to make a formal arrest. There will be a trial, of course, for the Stanley . . . ah . . . death. Perhaps for the other one as well."

"I am so sorry."

"You were kind not to press charges, my dear. However, my son will answer for his deeds. I have also discovered some irregularities with his accounts at the bank."

"Yes, I know." Jordana wondered what he would think of her now. "I tried to tell you, but I had no real proof and feared no one would believe me anyway."

"I have to agree with you about that. At one time I would have easily discounted a woman's opinions." He smiled apologetically. "Until I met you. You have taught me to judge people on their merits, not their gender. I hold you in great esteem, Jordana, and if you ever return to Omaha and wish to work, your job at the bank will always be there for you."

Jordana grinned. "I take that as high praise!"

Chittenden rose. "I don't want to keep you from your family. I appreciate seeing you." He held out his hand.

Jordana took the hand, then, on impulse, did what was on her heart to do. She put her arms around the round little man and kissed his cheek. He beamed at the gesture, and when she let go, he bowed respectfully, kissing her hand.

As she walked him to the door, he stopped with a small gasp. "Dear me! I nearly forgot. I have something for you." He reached inside his coat and withdrew an envelope. Handing it to her she saw it was addressed to "Miss Jordana Baldwin." "A friend of yours asked me to deliver this to you, a nice young man, a soldier."

After Chittenden departed, Jordana took the letter and returned to the kitchen. Gazing at the envelope, she wondered why Captain O'Brian would be writing her. She ignored the little flutter in her stomach as she opened the envelope and removed the missive.

Dear Miss Baldwin,

I heard about young Chittenden. I am relieved to know you are all right, but didn't that foolish man realize what a dangerous risk he was taking tangling with you? Had he asked me, I could have warned him. Nevertheless, I find I rather miss the bit of excitement you brought to my staid life as a dull soldier. Perhaps you would consider taking me on as a pen pal. That way you could at least keep me posted on all the victims you are abusing in my absence.

Jordana tittered softly. Yes, he was insufferable, but dearly so, she realized. And oddly, holding his letter in her hand, she didn't feel as lonely or frustrated. In a strange way, he was a connection to the life she desired, the dreams she hoped for.

Rising, she went to a drawer in the sideboard where she knew Victoria kept writing things. She took out paper, pen, and ink, sat at the table and, with growing anticipation and an inexplicable happiness, set the pen to the paper.

Dear Captain O'Brian . . .